Reincarnation

REINCARNATION

CHRONICLES FROM THE
LONG APOCALYPSE

BOOK TWO

BENJAMIN WILKINS

WILSON
BOULEVARD
PRESS
WILSON

Copyright © 2018 by Benjamin Wilkins

First Edition

Printed in the United States of America

ISBN 978-0-9979086-2-6

Jacket design by
Benjamin Wilkins

Wilson Boulevard Press
Sedona, Arizona

www.wilsonblvdpress.com

To Mark

For always leaving the door open
And the light on
As I've sprung
and fallen
Like the seasons

Author's Note

This is the second book in this series. You're going to want to read book one first, and maybe even the short story "The Shibuya Incident" before you continue on with this. I want you to love this book, and failing to read this series in order will certainly negatively impact your experience.

Hopefully that's obvious. But maybe it's not. I know there are lots of serial novels that are episodic to the point you can just jump right in with any of the books in any kind of willy-nilly order you want without really missing a thing—spy novels and detective stories seem particular prone to this style of writing. And let me be clear that I am not saying there is anything wrong with telling stories like that. Hell, for all I know, I would have been better off if I *had* actually written this series that way. But I didn't. That ship sailed, was attacked by pirates, was looted, and then sunk. And while I will admit a stand-alone novel in the Long Apocalypse universe is an intriguing idea—and maybe once I complete the story of this series, I'll even write one or two or ten of them—for now Book Two assumes you've read Book One, *Transcendence*.

But hey, don't worry; if you haven't read Book One yet, you can get a digital copy of it for **FREE** just for signing up to hear about when I have new books coming out. Just go here:

BookHip.com/PBBCPK

Okay, then... With that, I welcome you back for the second installment of Chronicles from the Long Apocalypse. Grab a beer. Maybe some chips. Empty your bladder...

The world's been ending for a while now, but like I told you before, we've still got a long way to go.

Prologue

ARMAGEDDON. The word grew in Jennifer Kessler's subconscious like one of those animal-shaped sponge toys, vacuum-packed into a gel pill capsule and dropped into a warm bath. The gel containing it broke down molecule by molecule until the pressure from the growing warm-water-infused sponge was strong enough for it to break free. The squishy mass slowly took its dreadful form.

Armageddon, it seemed, was coming in the shape of a girl.

For Jen, who was trapped deep down in the bottom of her consciousness, witnessing this bizarre birth was a frightening familiar experience—very similar to the one when the berserker inside her took control. Only Armageddon wasn't kind enough to force her into a fugue state to spare her from experiencing the horror it wrought. Instead, she gripped Jen by the shoulders and slapped her across the face every time she tried to turn her mind away.

The saucer-eyed little girl was playing with what could only be good in one hand and evil in the other. Even in Jen's dream, the difference between the two was blurry at best. But the game was crystal clear. This was the last battle, in the last war, for the eternal soul of mankind, and it had appropriately been reduced to a nonsense conversation between dolls.

Jen's sleeping mind spit out images of blood and fire, of monsters and men. Of death. Of redemption. Betrayal. All swirling around this little baby she somehow knew but had never met. Her brain attempted desperately to connect the dots between the fragments of her memories, her imagination, and the existence of the baby into a narrative that made sense, but it failed.

She wanted to protect the baby.

She wanted to destroy it.

But she could do neither, for though it was her dream, she wasn't actually in it. It wasn't her eyes that saw this girl. It wasn't her mind that knew she was Armageddon. It wasn't her skin that felt the searing lick of the flames she played in. It wasn't her ears that rang with the screams and laughter of the tormented. Jennifer was the little girl. Jennifer was the flames. She was the screaming. The tears. The blood. Lost in this dank, forgotten corner of her mind, she was the dream, not the dreamer. Nonetheless, the experience felt as tangible as any of the horrors she had participated in over the last few years, more real than most of them in fact.

She woke choking on a scream that never made it out of her mouth. She wondered for a half beat of her heart if this was how the monster that slept within her dreamed, and instinctively she knew the answer was yes. The demon inside her didn't have nightmares. It was the nightmare.

But the nightmare is over now, she thought to herself with a half smile. The nasty grip of her spindly-fingered subconscious was slipping so quickly away that even just a few seconds after waking up, Jennifer had forgotten all about what had woken her.

Enjoying the morning sun's brilliance as it bounced off the snow, Jen basked in the first moment of peace she'd felt in days. But the moment was short-lived. The nightmare wasn't over at all. In fact, compared to what was coming, it hadn't even begun. It didn't take long for her to sense it out there, like a pregnant pause, hanging in the air around her, demanding an answer to a question she couldn't even imagine.

Very few folks would ever know what was about to happen on this little farm in a forgotten corner of what used to be Iowa. Even fewer would believe that the consequences of the events about to unfold would end up being the source of mankind's ultimate salvation—or demise, depending on which side you fell on. Truth is, folks have never been any good at telling the difference between things that matter and things that don't—which is probably a big part of why the world ended in the first place.

Not that Jennifer Kessler really cared about the future at that moment. Or the past for that matter. She was just grateful to be alive.

And hungry.

Extremely hungry.

Her stomach let out a growl that shook her body so hard it actually hurt. She had never experienced hunger like this. She could actually feel her body breaking down tissue and cannibalizing itself. Her appreciation of the sunset reflecting off the snow (in July no less) was quickly swallowed by the ferocity of her starvation. She'd thought a moment ago that she'd like to meditate before she headed up to meet her hosts. But she knew promptly that would have to wait. She needed to find something to eat. Now. Before she did anything else, or she wouldn't be able to do anything else. Maybe ever again.

Groaning, she moved stiffly off the bed and out of her room in search of food.

*   *   *   *   *

"That's not good," Tiny said as he pulled his considerable girth up straight and quickly redirected all of the JLP drones to the same coordinates as the one which had the video feed he'd been looking at.

Silhouetted by the lowering sun and steadily rolling over the tracks Jennifer Kessler and her little sister Bobby-Leigh had left in the snow, a fair number of men and several trucks had appeared on the horizon. The girls had dragged their surrogate father, Brennachecke, on a sled straight from Vedic City (aka Blood City) to their uncle's abandoned farm—which Tiny and rest of Anoona's crew had since claimed for themselves. Their trek had left an easy trail to follow through the snow. They'd expected the Man-in-Charge of the blood pirates to seek out the girls and the old soldier for revenge. They had been confident they could handle more than a few of the bastards when that time came. But, now that the hour was upon them, it wasn't just the dozen or so they'd expected. As Tiny gathered the video feeds from his drones, it looked like all of the blood pirates who had ever occupied Vedic City were descending upon them.

"Fuck. Me," Tiny whispered as his computer quickly matched faces to his database of the current Jefferson County residents. A few seconds later, the computer had compiled information on most of the men and women approaching. The *army* was almost a thousand strong.

Tiny's eyes bounced between the video feeds of the drones and the feed of the surgery being performed downstairs. He wasn't sure if the old soldier, Brennachecke, could survive an interruption in the operation to remove the arrow from his chest or not, but he was sure that if he didn't stop it and get everybody battle ready in the next five minutes, nobody on the farm was going to survive the night, because these motherfuckers obviously weren't coming for tea and finger sandwiches.

"Girls, turn the TV off," Tiny said as pushed away from his desk and tossed them augmented reality glasses. "Put these on." He then broadcast the situation over the farm's network and waited. Bobby-Leigh and Mari didn't argue with him. As the drone footage flashed across their lenses it was all Mari could do to keep breathing. Bobby-Leigh was more emotionally desensitized to being at the receiving end of the universe's cruel jokes, but the hopelessness of what was developing still trickled into her heart. Thirty seconds passed, and nobody responded. Then a minute. Tiny was about to repeat his alert, when finally the silence in his earpiece was broken. Not surprisingly, it was their leader Anoona who was the first to respond.

"Rodney, as soon as the perimeter is breached, start painting targets. Hamm, how much time do you need to stabilize Brennachecke enough to leave him?"

"At least twenty minutes," Hamm said.

"Estimated perimeter breach is in eleven," Tiny said.

"Well…you'll just have to hold them the fuck off without me for a bit then, won't you?" Hamm snapped curtly.

"I've already started painting. No need to wait for the breach to set them up," Rodney broadcasted over the network from the steeple-like *kalash* that Anoona's crew had converted into a sniper crow's nest. He'd mounted his .300 Win Mag sniper rifle to its tripod and started laser painting the incoming blood pirates with the weapon's tracking point precision guidance system as soon as the drone footage had flashed across the digital lenses of his glasses. With a flip of a switch, the scope's video feed split from Rodney's glasses and was mirrored on one of Tiny's monitors. The gun would automatically take out the painted targets once they were in range, or at least that was what it was supposed to do. They'd never actually had the opportunity to test it out.

"How many can you preset?" Rachel said to Tiny as she exited the basement to the house's main level with her girlfriend Sarah only two steps behind her, as they headed for the bedroom that had been converted into an armory.

"The gun can only store ninety-nine targets in its memory at once," Rodney answered from them above.

"Tiny, can't you boost that?" Anoona said, again over the network.

"That *is* me boosting it. Out of the box it can only do seventeen," Tiny answered.

"Why the hell are there so many?" a voice said.

Tiny had to look at his bank of monitors to identify the source. It was the librarian, Maddie. One of Eric's crew. All things considered, the fat man was surprised that he wasn't more resentful of her or the rest of Brennachecke

Junior's people. Arguably, they had been the ones that had brought this last-stand-at-the-Alamo bullshit on them. Well, not exactly, he thought, as he looked over at Bobby-Leigh. He didn't have the heart to blame the twelve-year-old for anything, which meant the only person he *could* blame for what was about to happen was her berserker sister Jennifer.

"You better go wake your fucking sister up," he said, making no attempt to hide his building hatred. "She should at least have to watch us all die with her own eyes—since, just about any way you slice it, this bullshit is on her."

"I'm up!" Jennifer's voice came from the basement stairway a second before she rounded the top of the stairs, a box of Little Debbie snacks in her hand. Tiny blushed, his anger snuffed out by an embarrassment he didn't quite understand. Even in the middle of the apocalypse and facing certain death, the fat man had a hard time not desperately wanting the pretty teen to like him. That was until he noticed that she has eating his last box of Star Crunches. A box he'd been painfully saving for a special occasion. *I should have just eaten them when I had the chance,* he thought. Now he was going to die, and the stupid redhead had beaten him to their sweet crunchy goodness.

"Should I go?" she asked in a small, apologetic voice that made it clear if anybody said yes, she would march out to the oncoming army of blood pirates and put up the best fight she could. Alone.

Nobody said yes, not even Tiny. At least not out loud. But truth be told, more than just the fat man thought it. Nobody said no either, not even her sister Bobby-Leigh, a fact that threatened to collapse Jen's whole universe in that way only the self-centered fragile ego of teenagers can be so irrationally collapsed. The fact that her sister was busy counting in her head just how many people she thought could adequately use a weapon against what was coming for them and hadn't even heard a word her sister had said was completely beside the point.

This was the calm before the storm.

But nobody was calm.

*   *   *   *   *

Seven minutes later, Rodney's .300 Win Mag suddenly moved on its automated tripod and let off a shot. Then another and another, as the automated weapon discovered its targets were within range and opened fire.

"Perimeter breach," Tiny said flatly.

The live drone footage would be fed to them throughout the battle. In theory, it would reveal enemy positions and allow for better strategic moves on their part, but in practice, it was probably just as distracting as it was useful. Worse, being able to see the immensity of the forces they were up against was, to say the least, disheartening.

On Tiny's monitor and relayed to everyone's glasses, the Man-in-Charge of the blood pirate horde laughed in eerie silence as a man to the left of him was shot through the neck and fell to the ground in a fountain of jugular blood.

Everybody could see the footage, but only Tiny's blood drained out of his face as he intuitively knew something was off. He frowned as he confirmed what he was afraid of. The dead man had not been the painted target. The gun had missed.

"Fuck-tastic," he said to himself. But since he was miked and broadcasting continuously like everybody else, his muttering didn't remain self-contained.

"Now what?" Anoona chimed in from the tractor-trailer she and the rest of Brennachecke's people were getting into position on in preparation for ambushing the incoming bastards. Except for Eric, Ace, and Matt, Tiny couldn't remember the names of a single one of the new kids on the block, but he didn't care enough at the moment to bother looking them up. They had bigger fish to fry.

"The TPPG missed."

"English, Tiny!" Hamm said so loud Tiny heard him both in his earpiece and with his actual ears from downstairs where he, Eric, and Jen were tending to Brennachecke. The effect of which was a weird echo that only made the surreal experience of being sure he was about to die all that much worse.

"The gun that is not supposed to miss. It just missed."

"Rodney's gun?"

Tiny bit back a scream or a laugh—he honestly wasn't sure at this point which. *What other gun could he possibly be talking about?*

"Yep."

There was a long silence, then Rodney said, "If it misses again, I'll go manual. We can do this."

"Okay, well…it just missed again—and again. *But* it's still hitting a solid eighty-three percent with a three point eight rate of fire—which is a hell of a lot faster than you or anybody else could do. So I'd say just keep painting new targets and let it do its thing."

"Copy that," were the last words Rodney would ever say.

* * * * *

Bobby-Leigh and Mari were hiding in the small electrician shack that sat between the two longest solar panel rows behind the house. They could hear the gunfire being traded between the sides, and while they couldn't see much of anything out the single small window, they were receiving the live drone footage, so they had a pretty good idea of what the situation was.

They were fucked.

But that wasn't new information. It had been Anoona's idea to put the girls there, and at the time, Bobby-Leigh hadn't argued with her. The African woman with almost no hair had a way of speaking that made arguing with her difficult. It was the same with Brennachecke, or at least it had been. She was usually comforted by that almost godlike tone of conviction the two group leaders had, but now its magic over her had worn off, and she was regretting being separated from her sister. This was the first time since Walmart that she'd not known exactly where Jen was. She found it utterly unnerving. Her big sister was still weak and worn-down by the one-two berserker combo punch of killing her boyfriend and the ordeal in Vedic City. Bobby-Leigh was pretty sure she wouldn't be able to really protect herself on her own.

But it was too late to move. Mari was already starting to sob, and if Bobby-Leigh left the ten-year-old alone, she was sure the little girl would be discovered.

"It's going to be okay," she told her. Though one glance at the drone footage broadcasting to their glasses made it ridiculously obvious she was lying. So much so that Bobby-Leigh suddenly burst out laughing only a few seconds after the words had left her mouth. And once she started laughing, she couldn't stop. Over the last few days, she and Jen had survived so much that it just seemed impossible that this could really be the end. And yet, here they were, outnumbered by at least fifty to one. So surely this was in fact going to be her last day on Earth.

"Who the fuck is laughing? Knock that shit off!" Anoona's voice blasted over the network.

But Bobby-Leigh couldn't help herself.

It wasn't until Mari grabbed her hand and squeezed it so hard it hurt that Bobby-Leigh got her shit together. The little girl was squealing that she could see them coming for them, not from the drone feed, but through the window itself. In the same way as a toddler, Bobby-Leigh had known the stove was hot, but she didn't really understand just how hot it was until she touched it and burned the crap out of her hand. She'd known they were fucked from the drone footage that overlaid her field of vision whenever she looked for it, but now that she actually could see blood pirates outside the window, she finally got just how fucked they were. It silenced her like a noose. She wiped the tears of laughter from her eyes and forced herself to forget about her sister.

"There's so many of them…" Mari whispered as men by the dozens rounded the house and positioned themselves in firing positions. From the *kalash* a steady *tat-tat-tat* of sniper fire dropped any of them who were not adequately covered, but even as they bled out, staining the white snow crimson with their blood, more just showed up and replaced them.

* * * * *

Ka-boom!

The explosion sent a horrible wave of feedback through the network, as if Rodney's spirit had managed to escape the RPG that had taken out the kalash and incinerated his corporal form, only to get tangled in the wireless broadcast itself as he was hurtled screaming to earth—or hell. At the moment, there wasn't much of a distinction between the two.

Jen ripped her glasses off and threw them to the ground like they had bitten her. Even on the ground, the god-awful nails-on-chalkboard sound of feedback coming out of the built-in earpieces made her wince. And yet, a second later when it was gone, she felt no sense of relief. One from their side was dead. Maybe more than one. She'd slept through the introductions, so she didn't know who, but the loss was nonetheless poignant. She was weak, yes, and hungry in a way that felt just as dangerous as any of the gunshots echoing all around her, but she was not helpless. The berserker inside her that had threatened the lives of everybody she'd loved for as long as she could remember was locked away tight. There was no doubt in her mind that if she berserked out again before she had a chance to fully recover, she would die, which was probably for the best. Because another episode, if by some miracle she were to survive it, would also probably leave her body freakishly bulked up. And she desperately didn't want to be a freak. Plus, there was the fact that inevitably the berserker would murder people she cared about, which would also suck.

Chiding herself for being so shallow, especially while people were dying around her, but unable to change how she felt, she met Hamm's eyes and then Eric's.

Hamm clearly was itching to take a pound of flesh or two from the assholes who had just killed one of his friends.

Eric on the other hand looked extremely conflicted about what he should be doing. Jen felt sorry for him. But suddenly the truth that everything the dude had suffered in the last few days and was about to suffer over the next few hours was ultimately going to be her fault hit her, and that pity shape-shifted into shame.

"I've got Brennachecke," she said, nodding to the old soldier who was still unconscious on their makeshift operating table.

Eric looked at her, the anger in his eyes as violent as a slap across the face. "The fuck she does. I'm not leaving my father," Eric said, deliberately speaking to Hamm and not to her.

Jen smiled at him nervously, not sure how to respond. She thought about her sister. *How the fuck did I agree to be separated from her in all this?* But she knew the answer. The house would undoubtedly be penetrated soon, if it didn't just burn down on top of them. Bobby-Leigh at least had a chance hiding in the electrician's shack with that Anoona woman's little daughter. There simply wasn't enough room in it for Jen too. Plus, she was in no condition to make a run for it, if it came to that, which it most likely would. She and Brennachecke were in the same boat as far as fleeing for their lives was concerned—and that boat was utterly landlocked and nowhere near so much as a puddle. There would be no escaping. The room might as well have had *Thermopylae* written above it.

"I'm so sorry I brought this on you all," Jen said, as Hamm slapped thirty-round drum magazines into the five AA-12 Atchisson assault shotguns one after another like he was working on an assembly line. He slung one gun over his shoulder and picked up a second one, leaving one shotgun for each of them along with extra drums of shells.

"Don't," Hamm told Jen as he turned to shut the door on his way out. "You never need to apologize for the evil others do."

"Even if you're the reason they're doing it?"

Hamm smiled at her, and in that moment, his smile felt like the kindest thing anybody had ever done for her in her entire life.

"Honey, this isn't about you or him or us. No matter what it seems like, this is just how the world is now. Some days you're the good guys, and some days you're the bad. Being able to die with a white hat on—it's a gift."

"You're fucking crazy, dude," she said, but what she wanted to say was *thank you*.

"See you soon," Hamm said with a wink.

But Jen was pretty sure that she wouldn't—at least not alive. As the door clicked shut, she looked at Eric as if to say, *Well, it's you and me for better or worse, dude.* But the second her eyes met his, she couldn't stop her thoughts from jumping immediately to his brother. The boy she loved. The boy she'd thrashed to death in a berserker fit less than a week ago. The grief came flooding into her so hard her knees threatened to buckle.

"Eric, I—" she started to say, but the young man cut her off.

"Don't," he said, echoing Hamm, yet somehow—with nothing but the tone of his voice—he made it clear that he did not share the man's opinion that she didn't have anything to apologize for. His one word—the only word in fact that he'd actually spoken to her since she'd reunited him with his father—spoke volumes.

As far as Eric was concerned, she most certainly did have something to apologize for. But there were no words she could say that could mitigate her role in his brother's death—or in the hell that was now descending upon them. It didn't matter that the human minds of berserkers were locked away in the trunk when the monsters were behind the wheel. It didn't matter that the same monster that had torn his brother Jimmy to pieces had also been the one who had saved his father's life in Vedic City.

She had a mountain of shit to be sorry about. But Eric would never accept an apology from her. Not for any of this. To even hear her say that she was sorry and to not then immediately put a bullet into her face would be an act of forgiveness on his part. There would be no forgiveness. Not from him. As far as he was concerned, just being a participant in some things, regardless of whether you could reasonably be held at fault for them, was enough to be categorically unforgiveable.

Don't.

Jen understood his meaning maybe even better than he did. She fought against tears but lost. She knew the goddamn waterworks were only going to piss Eric off more. She knew he'd think she was just trying to manipulate him into some kind of feeling of sympathy. Just like his younger brother—and his father for that matter—Eric was as easy to read as a child's picture book.

He had no pity for her.

Not now, and probably not ever.

Don't.

Eric snatched one of the assault shotguns violently out of her hand and positioned himself at the door, his back to her. She turned away from him. Her wet eyes drifted to Eric's unconscious father. At least the old man had forgiven her, not that it mattered anymore.

Why couldn't you have just let us go, dude? she thought as she wiped her eyes, grabbed her stupid glasses from the floor, and took a position just behind Eric.

Jimmy is on me. I know that, she thought as hard as she could at the back of Eric's head, *but it's not my fault your dad was compelled to hunt us down. And it's not my fault he sent your ass here.* She was trying to match his anger, but it didn't work. She wasn't angry, especially not with either of the men in the room. She was heartbroken.

Guilt-ridden.

Exhausted.

Hungry.

Sad.

Stop crying, dude, she told herself. *You can fucking cry later.* But the tears would not go away. She was just too exhausted on every level to control anything beyond the other threat to her life and the lives of everybody else within arm's reach—the demon that slumbered deep within her.

*   *   *   *   *

Rachel and Sarah had the fire under control before Hamm had even rounded the stairs and made it to the main floor. The house was still solid. Rodney, however, was not. The explosion from the rocket-propelled grenade had ripped him apart so much that except for a leg that still twitched against the wall, what had once been Hamm's best friend was now simply unidentifiable.

The grief that exploded in Hamm's heart was so intense that for a second he just stood there paralyzed by it. He felt a sob coming and forced it back. He felt tears coming and squeezed his eyes shut to block them out. When he finally opened them again and took a breath, a terrifyingly dark smile had slowly crept across his lips.

You crazy motherfucker, he thought. Rodney must have seen the RPG coming because he'd managed to protect the gun by taking the explosive in the back. Hamm pulled it, automated tripod and all, from the rubble.

"Can we target without his glass?" he asked Tiny.

"What?"

"He protected the fucking gun, Tiny. Can you target remotely or not?"

Tiny was dangerously close to going into shock. He'd never been this close to the action before. He'd seen his fair share of death, sure. Anybody alive these days had, but it'd almost always been on a screen. And even then, he'd—his mind was spinning. What was the question again?

"What?"

Hamm marched up to him and slapped him hard.

"Can you target remotely?" Sarah yelled.

Tiny's face stung, but his head had cleared.

"Yes," he said with a nod, tears slipping down his cheeks.

Without a word between them, Rachel, Sarah, and Hamm raced to set the automated gun up at the large arched picture window in what had originally been the dining room of the house.

After pulling a pistol from her belt, Rachel put a bullet through the tempered glass, and the three of them quickly knocked out the shattered remnants. The gun had started firing again before they'd finished.

"We should have gotten more than one of those fucking guns," Rachel said to nobody in particular.

"Agreed," Anoona said over the network, reminding everybody that they were all still on an open channel—a fact that had slipped even Tiny's mind for a beat in the heat of the moment.

*   *   *   *   *

Knowing that they were undermanned, but that they had vastly superior technology, Anoona had told everybody that the plan was to draw the blood pirates in as much as possible before revealing where she and the bulk of their side would be lying in wait. But there was another reason she hadn't just opened fire on the incoming horde. Anoona had never taken another human being's life. The closest she'd come was directing those in her group to kill in self-defense. Murder was just a part of life in the apocalypse. It was as necessary to survival as food or air, and yet she'd still never been able to personally put a man—or woman—down. It was utterly ridiculous. She knew it. She felt it. She wished desperately that she could force her stupid fingers to just squeeze the fucking trigger, but her muscles simply refused to obey her brain when the moment came. Hamm had loved her all the more for it, but a fuck lot of good that was going to do them now.

The blood pirates had rounded the house, and now that the automated gun was out of the tower, they were able to gather in force behind it. Rachel and Sarah were deliberately focusing on the west side of the property, so that once the pirates rounded the building and made it to the east side, they'd be lulled into a false sense of calm. The plan seemed to be working. They'd stopped taking potshots and were now restlessly awaiting instructions from the Man-in-Charge, who for the life of Anoona's crew, they could not seem to take down.

"Tiny, give me an update," Anoona whispered.

"Three hundred and change dead on the west side. They seem to have abandoned the direct frontal assault for the most part, and the majority of them are now moving to flank the house and try from the east. You should see about two hundred or so in front of you at this point. There's a solid hundred hunkered down just out of range of the gun still on the west side. Their berserkers are with that group. I've got most of those targeted though, so when they do finally advance, the gun should take most of them out."

It was all information that she could more or less see for herself from the drone feeds, but it reassured her to hear Tiny tell it just the same.

"I don't have eyes on the M-I-C," she said.

"He's with the group flanking to the south. ETA maybe twelve minutes."

"Can you tag him for us, so we all can ID him when he arrives?"

"Done."

"That's who we take out first, then it's the fish in the barrel in front of us, and from that point, we make it up as we go along."

"Copy that," Hamm said over the network. His confirmation of the plan was echoed by most of the others. It was a good plan, Anoona thought. But she was much less confident that the bullets in her gun would do anything but sit in their magazine.

What the hell is wrong with me?

*　*　*　*　*

Bobby-Leigh watched and waited, holding Mari in her arms and softly rocking her to keep her quiet. Men were less than twenty feet from their little shack. Men who were getting bored standing around. Men who thought they'd gotten past the defenses and were now confident in their belief that the danger was behind them.

"This is fucking stupid," she heard one complain.

"Why don't we just go in and get them again?" another said.

"He don't want any of us to kill her," a third one said. "He wants to do that himself."

"My feet are fucking cold, man."

"At least the snow stopped."

In her visor, Bobby-Leigh suddenly saw a convoy of vehicles and men appear to the south. She recognized the man in the lead truck, but even if she'd never seen him before, her visor had him glowing ominously in red.

"Here we go," someone said quietly over the network. It sounded like Ace, but because his words were whispered, it was hard to be sure.

Bobby-Leigh took a deep breath and held it. Instinctively, she took Mari's glasses off and put them in her pocket, silencing her protest with a finger. The kid had already seen too much.

*　*　*　*　*

Anoona lined up her shot and drew in a deep breath. She felt the resistance of the trigger with her finger and exhaling long and slow applied ever increasing pressure.

Nothing happened.

She pulled harder and still the trigger didn't move.

Shit, she thought when she realized it wasn't her aversion to killing that was locking up with the firing mechanism of the gun. It was the safety. By the time she had flicked it off and retrained her aim on the M-I-C, the others had already started shooting.

The first shot took the right side off the Man-in-Charge's face. It was a kill shot. Still, no less than twenty other bullets landed in his already dead body before he fell from the truck onto the snow.

* * * * *

The moment was a disappointing one for Bobby-Leigh. In fact, it almost seemed unfair to snuff the man out like that. She preferred to deal out death looking a man in the eye. But it was what it was. As her side opened fire on the completely unsuspecting men waiting to at best kill her and her sister, but probably do much worse, her pity was quickly blown away.

Chaos followed.

Then panic.

It took almost ten minutes for the blood pirates to regroup, and by the time they did, more were dead than alive behind the house. Alas, the defenders of the Kessler Farm were still outnumbered, and once their ambush position was identified, making it up as they went along proved much more difficult than any of them expected.

Ace and Matt didn't even make it down from the top of the trailer. Bobby-Leigh watched them fall on the drone feed and instinctively looked out the little window to see if she could see them with her own eyes. What she saw instead was a gnarly kid not much older than her sister, running straight for the little electrician's shack she and Mari were hiding in. He was obviously looking for a hiding place of his own. Their eyes met a split second before he got to the door. Without thinking about what she was doing, Bobby-Leigh flipped the latch and using her whole little body as a battering ram, shoved the door open as hard as she could.

The wooden planks hit the teenager in the face so hard both he and door broke from the impact. The kid dropped like a rock and lay screaming in the snow. The door swung wide hard and fast, then was ripped off its hinges and also lay in the snow, but silently.

Bobby-Leigh and Mari were exposed.

The pirate horde took notice.

It takes a particularly awful kind of man to target unarmed little girls in the middle of a firefight, and it was exactly those kinds of men that had survived the ambush. Hard. Evil men. Men that Mari and Bobby-Leigh would be lucky to be killed by because killing was not the first thing that crossed these men's minds when they saw little girls.

Bobby-Leigh knew their kind instantly when she saw them. They were Walmart Men. They were Cage Men. If Bobby-Leigh hadn't lost her secret little bear-claw blade in the ordeal in Vedic City, they would be Dead Men. But she was unarmed, and she had Mari with her, so fighting was out of the question.

"Run!" she screamed at the little girl.

But Mari didn't move. Bobby-Leigh grabbed her hand and yanked her along past the rows and rows of solar panels and into the woods behind them, a half dozen of Blood City's finest in hot pursuit behind them.

* * * * *

Anoona's gun still had not fired. Not once. Not even as she had watched the six men race after her daughter and Jennifer's little sister through the scope. Folks don't think about grand designs and divine plans when they came face-to-face with their worst fears. Anoona was no different, she didn't wonder why of all the people to be in a position to take out the men now stalking the little girls, it just happened to be her – the one person who was powerless to stop them. That questions was sown behind her back and left to sprout in the calm dead of night with the rest of her nightmares.

Anoona tried one last time to squeeze the trigger. Her hands shook, but the gun did not release a round.

Standing up and wiping her eyes, somehow knowing she had failed her child in a fundamental way that would change the very person she was in the days to come, Anoona did the next best thing to putting bullets in skulls.

"Tiny! Get a drone on my daughter! Now!"

"Copy that," Tiny's voice spat back as a drone broke away from the cluster monitoring the firefight to follow the girls.

"Send me the feed!"

"No, Anoona," Hamm said softly. "I'll get them. Tiny, patch it to me."

And then out of nowhere, Hamm was next to her, smiling a smile that sent the truth straight to her heart without a word. They needed her commanding their little force. And the girls needed somebody who could pull the fucking trigger.

His hand touched her shoulder, then her cheek. His eyes twinkled with a confidence she would never see again.

She kissed him.

Trusted him.

"Patch the feed to Hamm," she said, not thinking for a second that her words had just killed him.

* * * * *

The house was breached from the basement. In another time, Allen Kessler had built the foundation of the home now under attack so that the basement windows could be a full forty-eight inches high and the large wells they looked out on could be shallow enough to let in sufficient light to make the basement not feel like a basement. It was a beautifully effective design, but now it wasn't just light those windows were letting in. Tiny was simply not as skilled at painting targets for the TPPG as Rodney was, partially because he'd never done it before, but mostly because he was extremely distracted trying to keep the drones in optimal positioning for battle intelligence. With Rodney gone, Sarah and Rachel couldn't even adequately cover the main floor between them, forget about the window wells below, especially as quickly as the chaos on the east lawn was devolving against them. There were just too many pirates to hold them off forever.

It was the window well in the southwest bedroom that was hit first. A tractor-trailer carrying four berserkers slipped through the trees and smashed to a stop into the corner of the house.

The blood pirates' method of controlling the demon possessed was as crude as it was effective. Each berserker was sedated and chained to the trailer. Each wore a black box on their head that completely blocked out the sights and sounds of the world around them. Octopus arms of hoses carried oxygen to them from a central tank in the middle of the trailer. The pikers—four in all—jumped out of the cab of the truck and set about removing the black boxes from each monster. And these berserkers were monsters. Literal hulks, weighing nearly five hundred pounds apiece without an ounce of fat on them, their size and power the result of years of forced development. They'd been forced to go berserk so often back to back that each of them was covered in scars from where their skin had split open unable to keep up with the growth. Under the black boxes, the berserks all wore adapted horse blinders as a method of directing their utterly unpredictable destruction. Even with blinders, the pikers had learned not to bother removing the chains.

The four men grabbed poles outfitted with hypodermic loads and speared each monster in turn with a mix of amphetamine and adrenaline that was concocted specifically to simultaneously wake them up and set them off. The whole protocol took them less than ninety seconds. Breaking out of their chains took the weaponized berserkers less than thirty. Well-timed flash-bang grenades shot through the window drew the monsters into the house with their noise and light, and kept them from beating on each other as they smashed their way inside. The pikers followed a safe distance behind them.

* * * * *

Everybody in the house had felt the tractor-trailer's collision with the wall. The two minutes of silence while the pikers did their work outside had felt like decades. Sarah and Rachel looked at each other and then at Tiny. None of them were going to go downstairs to investigate. They all knew to do so would be strategic suicide. There was only one way up to the main floor from the basement, and it was better to pick off folks as they came up than to go down and face the unknown. Eric, his dad, and Jen were on their own.

*   *   *   *   *

For the entire two minutes of silence before the flash-bangs heralded in the end of the world, Jennifer Kessler looked at Brennachecke lying helpless in the bed. An IV of whatever the fuck they put in IVs was hanging over his head. Blood-soaked bandages were wrapped around his chest. She'd already saved his life once, or at least had tried to, and yet, it didn't matter. The scales of the universe just refused to balance. It may have been the old soldier's wording bouncing around in her head, but it felt like she owned that point of view now too.

When the fuck did I take that on?

Sometime in Vedic City, she guessed. Not that it mattered anymore. She'd murdered his youngest son. Contrary to what he'd told her less than twenty-four hours ago, she was positive now that saving his life did not in fact balance shit. Only death can balance death. Given time, the universe hadn't ever really needed Brennachecke's help in righting the scales. She had killed herself the second she'd killed her boyfriend Jimmy. It all suddenly made perfect sense to her. And she was surprisingly okay with it.

She was wrong of course.

The universe's equation was way too complicated to be shifted by a single act. In fact, the entire battle she was about to sacrifice herself to had been set in motion hundreds, if not thousands of years ago, long before any of the folks involved had even been born. Jen, just like the rest of mankind, would play her part in the grander scheme of existence without ever knowing what her part actually was or why it was significant.

Jennifer Kessler would forever think she was making a choice to step alone into that hallway—combat shotgun gripped tight in her hands—to fight to the death against whatever was coming for them. She'd have sworn she was acting of her own free will. And yet, in that moment, considering all the moments that had gotten her there, was there really anything else she actually could have chosen to do? Free will was just the head of the incestuous ouroboros of fate.

"Protect your dad," she said as she pushed Eric out of the way and opened the door, no longer able to stand the eerie silence that had followed the house shaking crash.

Flash-bang!

The light and sound of the nonlethal stun grenades were nondestructive. But the berserkers who chased after them certainly made up for that. Not that Jen could see or hear them after the blinding flash and ear-shattering bang. But that didn't really matter. The hallway was narrow enough and her adversaries large enough to make simply opening fire in the right direction effective, which is exactly what the redheaded teen did.

Bam! Bam! She inched forward a half step. *Bam!*

Her eyes recovered enough to see basic shapes, but the ringing in her ears still overpowered all other noises. Afterimages made aiming with any kind of precision difficult, so she didn't bother.

Bam!

The lead berserker took more buckshot to the chest, but he kept coming unfazed. Jen shifted her focus to his knees as best she could without being able to see straight.

Bam!

She missed.

He was almost on her. In her mind, she grabbed the mental focus ring that governed how deeply she experienced any given moment. This was how she kept her lizard brain calm enough to keep it from triggering a berserker response, but at the moment, a berserker response might just be the only effective response she had at her disposal. She readied herself to open her mind up with a mental twist so that she could tag the demon inside her to enter the ring. This was the nuclear option. But if she was going to die, she thought, thinking of Hamm's final words to her, it was for damn sure going to be with a white hat on. She'd exhaust every means of defense she had access to first, obviously. But even it didn't earn her a white hat, if she was going to die, she'd just as soon not have to experience it. She knew the demon would grant her that final wish.

Before she handed over the reins to her very real inner demon and set off her suicide bomb of rage, she took one last shot.

Bam!

The enormous berserker crumbled to the ground as his right knee was eviscerated by the shotgun blast. The monster may not feel pain or fear in his altered state, but he couldn't very well lead the charge with the lower half of his leg hanging on to the upper part by only a thin line of red snotlike viscera. Jen started to smile, but her vision had cleared enough to see that there were at least three equally giant berserkers smashing their way toward her behind the one she'd clipped. One berserker coming at her would have been enough to wipe the smile off her face. Three was just—

Before she could finish her thought, the next monster up crushed the head of the one she'd knocked down with a violently powerful stomp. She brought the shotgun up, intending to take him out at the knee too, but this one was faster, and the shot went wild as she stumbled back to stay out of the demon's reach.

The hell with aiming, she thought and just started pulling the trigger as fast as she could. The second berserker looked like it wasn't going to be stopped before he got his hands on her, and maybe it wouldn't have been. But it was slowed down enough for the one behind to catch him. Weakened by Jen's shotgun blasts, the monster was torn apart and tossed out of the way like yesterday's news.

Two down.

Two to go.

This time she did smile, and the smug grin stuck to her face like armor. A maniacal laugh exploded from her lips as she stepped forward toward death incarnate and rained buckshot into the monsters. Her sight was almost back to normal now. She could actually aim as she moved, and after three successive blasts to the head, the third berserker dropped.

And then there was one, she thought. *Except that wasn't actually true, was it?*

There was somebody else there behind them. Somebody with a rifle. And a big one at that.

Jen didn't think berserkers like these could have wrapped what little remained of their minds around the mechanics of pulling a trigger. The only use they'd have for a gun would be to bash in a head or two. So it was somebody else shooting. Not bullets. The barrel was too fat for that.

Pop!

As if to answer the question she'd hardly had time to even ask, a tiny flash of muzzle fire sparked in the cloud of dust well behind the carnage she'd stacked up between herself and the last berserker. For a split second, Jen actually saw the small black canister silhouetted as it exited the barrel, but before she could react, the flash-bang had whizzed past the berserker and—

Smack!

The grenade struck her hard in the head. Jen heard herself grunt just as the thing went off. The blinding light and ear-ringing sound that exploded out of it knocked her grip off the mental focus ring she used to keep the berserker locked away inside her. She dropped the shotgun, and an instant later Jennifer Kessler was gone.

*   *   *   *   *

The snow was going to make hiding next to impossible, Bobby-Leigh realized quickly, as she dragged Mari through the white ground cover leaving tracks so obvious a blind piece of patio furniture could have followed them. At least they were in the trees now, she told herself, but their cover wasn't very comforting as long as their tracks were so obvious.

Fucking snow.

In fucking July.

"Why are we stopping?" Mari asked in a heart-wrenchingly shaky voice. The little girl was obviously doing her best to be brave but still pretty much totally failing at it. She'd stopped crying though. Bobby-Leigh was actually kind of proud of her for the effort.

"We have to do something about our tracks."

Realization hit Mari's ten-year-old brain like a Mack truck. The tears came back, but they were silent ones. Bobby-Leigh smiled at her. It was a genuine smile. The kind of smile only a big sister can give you. One that somehow said *Get your shit together and stop being a little baby*, while simultaneously saying, *You're doing great and I'm proud as shit of you right now*. Mari, an only child, had never experienced anything like it.

"Get that branch," Bobby-Leigh commanded, pointing to a cedar bough already half broken off by the weight of the unexpected July snow. Mari tried to break it free but couldn't. Even with Bobby-Leigh's help it still took the girls almost a minute to get it loose.

It was minute they did not have.

"We ain't goin' hurt ya girls!" an ugly voice called out to them.

Bobby-Leigh couldn't see the man yet, but he could probably see her.

"Well, we might hurt you little," another voice called.

Bobby-Leigh snatched the cedar bough from Mari as their pursuers cackled behind them.

"Watch what I do," she ordered, and then she walked backward as fast as she could swishing the branch over her footprints. It didn't make them disappear, but it did make them significantly less recognizable as what they were. Bobby-Leigh moved under a tree and continued to try to hide her tracks with the branch.

Bingo.

"Okay," she said. "Try to stay under the trees where the snow is shallow as much as you can. Use the branch like I just showed you. Once you've gone for a mile or so, then stop and find a place to hide."

She pulled the little girl's glasses from her pocket and handed them to her. She put them on like a robot. "Keep those on. We'll use them to find you once it's safe."

Mari just stared at her. Bobby-Leigh held out the cedar limb, but this time Mari just stood there.

"Mari," the older and wiser of the two girls said. "It'll be okay, but you have to do what I tell you, right the fuck now."

"What are you going to do?"

"I'm going to lead them away from you."

"Please don't leave me!" Mari cried in panic.

"I'm not leaving you, kid," Bobby-Leigh soothed. "Okay. I am. But just so I can get these assholes away from you. You got to do this, Mari. Otherwise they are going to catch us and...we don't want that to happen."

Again, she tried to hand the younger girl the branch.

Again, Mari just stood there.

"Come out, come out wherever you are!" a third voice called out from somewhere behind them.

How many followed us into the woods? Bobby-Leigh wondered.

"You got this, girl! Go!"

Mari finally took the branch. But it was another ten seconds before she started to move away like Bobby-Leigh had shown her. Still, when she did, she did a pretty decent job of hiding her tracks.

"Try to stay under the trees!" Bobby-Leigh called out to her and then reversed course and headed back the way they'd come. If she could have seen the sheer terror in the little girl's eyes when Mari looked up at minute later and realized she was now alone, Bobby-Leigh would not have been able to go.

* * * * *

Anoona was watching her side slowly flank the remaining pirates on the east side of the house, when suddenly the drone feeds cut out.

"Tiny!"

"I know. I know. Power supplies are toast. At critical levels, they're programmed to auto return to their charging stations so they don't fall out of the sky. There's nothing I can do about it."

"Didn't you fucking do the programing?" somebody said.

Anoona didn't recognize the voice. So it must have been one of Eric's crew.

"It can't be overridden remotely, and even if it could, you'd only get another three maybe five minutes before the drone was lost. It's not worth losing drones for that."

"Says you."

"And me," Anoona chimed in. She flicked her eyes to see which one of the assholes with Eric was giving Tiny shit. Her display showed it was Rodger Halburn, but she couldn't place which one he was.

"We'll finish this old school. What's the score?" Anoona asked Tiny through the comms.

"We're still outnumbered at least nine to one. They seem to be regrouping to the southwest. My guess is they're going to try to follow the guys in who breached the basement and take the house."

The snow behind the house was so trampled and blood soaked it had become a muddy gore-colored slushy without so much as an inch of white in sight.

Bodies were everywhere.

"So are we still taking these guys out, or are we retreating to defend the house?"

"Yes," Anoona said with a coy smile that could be heard in her voice. "Take these assholes down and then rendezvous at the north side of the house."

The eruption of gunfire was almost instantaneous. It lasted two minutes and then abruptly stopped. Rodger, Cooperman, and JP suddenly appeared in a full retreat heading straight for Anoona.

"Berserkers!" was the last word Rodger ever said, as another set of four weaponized berserkers exploded from the trees hot on their trail.

The giants were faster than the men.

Anoona lined up her gunsight and, fully expecting not to be able to pull the trigger, was shocked when the gun leaped in hand and a bullet tore through a berserker's shoulder just as it grabbed Rodger.

She had time to wonder what it was about herself that allowed her to murder men possessed by monsters, but not men who were monsters themselves. But then the wounded berserker not only refused to release Rodger, it proceeded to beat the berserker next to him with the man's clearly now dead body.

Anoona stopped caring about the hows and whys.

Switching her gun from semiauto to full, she stepped from her blind and opened fire just like Hamm had taught her.

Eventually she brought the four monsters down, but only after Cooperman and JP had been torn to pieces along with her remaining forces. Even when she could pull the trigger, it seemed she still couldn't save anybody. The grief and frustration were overwhelming.

"Tiny! What's happening with Hamm?" she sobbed.

"They're in the woods. Hamm. The girls. And six or seven bad guys. They're all still alive, but without the drones, that's about all I can tell you."

Still alive.

Anoona clung to those words like a lifeline and forced herself to move.

"I'm coming to you," she said, forcing herself to pull her shit together, at least for a little while longer.

"Copy that. Stay out of the basement," Tiny replied.

*　*　*　*　*

It dawned on Bobby-Leigh that on the list of stupid fucking things to do, she was currently doing what had to be in the top five. She had no weapon and yet was running as fast as she could straight toward a bunch of assholes who not only had weapons, but all of whom had far darker thoughts than murder on their minds when it came to what they wanted to do to her.

She picked up her pace.

It only took a minute to reach them, and it only took a second to get their attention, but it took no time at all for them to follow her as she sprinted west diverging from Mari and her original trail into a new one back toward the house in the opposite direction of where Mari was headed. When Bobby-Leigh finally stopped and turned to face them though, there were only four of them.

"Where're your friends?" she called out to them defiantly.

"Oh, them other boys ain't had chocolate in so long, they ain't about to be distracted by a little vanilla, even if it does come in such a hot little wrapper."

Bobby-Leigh recognized the man's voice from earlier. The man was balding, with stringy, long hair and a patchy beard. His eyes were piercingly blue, but nothing else about him was even remotely attractive. The man on his left was short and chubby. He looked like a middle school softball coach pedophile in a PSA about sexual assault. The man on his right was young, maybe twenty years old, and unlike his cohorts, he was extremely well groomed. He smiled at her, and to her horror, it wasn't a monstrous smile at all. She decided she'd take his ass out first. But then the last man spoke and she changed her mind instantly.

"You look just like my daughter," that last man said with his little rat mouth and his huge black saucer eyes.

The charmer would have to get in line. Incest-Is-Best was going to die first. If only she could figure out how.

*   *   *   *   *

The snow was trampled where Hamm was standing. The girls had clearly split up here. Their pursuers as well, but the tracks didn't make any sense. And then Hamm realized that Bobby-Leigh must have doubled back before splitting off in an effort to give Mari a chance.

"Smart girl," he said to himself, quietly feeling extremely guilty that he had no intention of trying to save the Goth-Lolita decked-out twelve-year-old—at least not until Mari was safe. Forced to choose between his daughter and a brave little stranger, the man was capable of making only one choice. Had he been able to choose something else, he'd have lived.

He came upon the two men tracking his daughter just as they were pulling her from her hiding place under a snow-covered tree by her ankles, but in his haste to save his own flesh and blood, he'd missed one very important fact about the men he was trying to stop.

"Daddy!" Mari screamed when she twisted around to face her fate in the eye and saw him.

Hamm smiled at her. It was a powerful smile. The kind of smile that only fathers can give to their children. A smile that promised it was going to be okay, even when there was no way it could be. Hope could be hung on it. Pain could be mollified by it. Terror could be erased by it. And yet, like so much of what fathers pass on to their children, it was a lie. Hamm raised the combat shotgun and prepared to fire on the two men without a word.

But Mari's cry hadn't been a shout for help. It'd been a warning. As the cold steel of the hunting knife sliced through his back piercing his lung, Hamm discovered the very important thing he'd missed: there were not two men chasing his little girl.

There were three.

He felt the gun being ripped from his hands.

He felt his lung fill with blood.

He felt the cold against his head as he lay in the snow. But he didn't feel any pain until the man who had so slyly taken his life stepped forward and pulled the pants off his girl while the other two held her down in the snow.

She didn't scream.

She didn't resist.

She didn't cry.

He was pulled deeper and deeper into the ever-increasing eternity of darkness. Time slowed. Sound lengthened, and what would last only a minute or two for the men raping his daughter became an infinity to her father. He was killed as much by a broken heart at his failure to protect her, as he was from the gapping knife wound in his back. Even Death himself pitied the man, though not enough to leave him be.

* * * * *

When the door to the makeshift operating theater where Eric anxiously stood guard over his father came crashing in, the boy was ready for it. The piker who had knocked the door in, however, was not and found his face torn through the back of his head by the pellets of the boy's shotgun before he even saw Eric in the room. The piker behind the dead man, however, did have time to see Eric, and more importantly, he had time to fire his stun grenade into the room before the boy filled him with lead too.

Flash-bang!

Eric felt the tug of bullets entering his body even though he couldn't see or hear where they were coming from. Stepping forward and pulling the trigger as fast as he could, he stood between his father and the men intent on killing them both until he felt the dry click of the gun trying to fire without any more ammunition. He was still pulling the trigger as his vision cleared and the click of the gun at last found its way through the ringing in his ears.

Nausea suddenly grabbed him and tossed him to his knees.

Faintness followed.

He blinked.

"Eric…" his father groaned behind him.

The boy wanted to stand up and go to that voice, but as he turned, he felt the world slip away from him. Brennachecke Senior watched in horror as the last of his progeny fell to the floor and closed his eyes. Without a thought for the pain in his chest or the risks to his health moving after surgery would undoubtedly have, the old man dropped ungracefully off the bed and pulled his son to him.

Eric's eyes opened once more and met his father's before he died.

Alone in the bullet-riddled room with the corpse of his eldest son in his arms, his chest and shoulder burning with pain, and not a clue in the world as to what was happening, the old soldier, for the first time since he was a small child, allowed himself to cry.

*   *   *   *   *

Even in the backwoods of snow-covered postapocalyptic Iowa, confidence was still a remarkably effective deterrent when it came to rape. Maybe because rape is as much about power as it is about sex. Maybe because confidence was in such short supply these days that it spooked the men inclined to hurt women. Maybe it was because that particular subset of assholes had been feeding on the all-you-can-rape buffet for so many years now that they'd just gotten lazy. Whatever the reason, as Bobby-Leigh stood there sizing up the four pedophiles trying to decide on the best strategy for killing them, she was not afraid. Even without a weapon. Even without a plan. Bobby-Leigh knew she had the advantage. She had something they wanted, and there was power in that. Not much, but enough to work with. Her adversaries hung back, increasingly unsure of what to make of the little girl who refused to cower before them.

Bobby-Leigh locked eyes with the rat-faced fucker who had said that she reminded him of his daughter. The man whom she intended to take out first—as soon as she got her hands on a weapon. She smiled at him seductively while she looked him up and down, her finger slowly drifting up to her mouth and sensually pulling on her bottom lip as she did.

Suddenly, the twinkle in her eyes flashed so bright Rat-Face himself couldn't help but smile with her. The man had a small six-shot .38 Ruger revolver in an ankle holster sticking just barely out of his left half-laced combat boot. Bobby-Leigh could miss twice and still kill them all if she could get her hands on it.

"I can do things that would make your little girl's head spin," she said to the still grinning Rat-Face. Slowly kneeling in the snow with her legs open, she suggestively pulled her skirt up an inch higher on her thighs. But the moron just stood there. So she beckoned with her finger for him to come to her and find out what she meant.

In her head, she visualized her attack. She'd slowly run her hand up his nasty leg like she was going for his dick, and then instead, she'd pull his gun from his boot and shoot the fucking thing off. Then she'd pop the other three in the head before anybody knew what the hell had happened. It was going to be beautiful, she thought, as Rat-Face stepped forward answering her siren call.

CRACK!

The Charmer suddenly stepped forward and kicked her in the side of the head. She didn't see it coming. She'd been so focused on Rat-Face she'd completely lost track of the other three.

Stars exploded painfully behind her eyes as she went sprawling across the snow. Her ears were ringing, but she was not dazed by the blow. Quite the opposite actually—her focus became razor-sharp. *This isn't a game, so why the fuck am I playing around with them?* Softball Coach grabbed her arm and twisted it up painfully behind her back as he pulled her to her feet. The charmer smiled viciously and stepped up to her, pulling out an old Wild West revolver, the make and model of which Bobby-Leigh was unfamiliar with, and jabbing it under her chin.

Bobby-Leigh waited.

Silently.

Quietly.

Patiently.

The opening would come.

The charmer pulled the hammer back and looked away from her to the fat asshole holding her. Then the man turned his head to look at Rat-Face behind him.

"If anybody's head is going to spin around here, it's going to be hers," the Charmer said with a smile.

And there it was. The moment Bobby-Leigh was waiting for.

Using her free hand, she reached behind her back and grabbed Softball Coach's hand, pinning her other arm behind her. In a quick move, she pushed the man's hand down with all her might and held it fast, so he couldn't break her arm as she twisted and dropped her full weight to the ground. The man's grip became a hinge, and she used it to swing between his legs.

Caught completely off guard, Softball Coach stumbled forward into the barrel of the gun that a split second ago had been under Bobby-Leigh's chin.

BANG!

The muzzle flash singed her hair as the bullet passed over her skull and landed in the chest of Softball Coach. The man's grip on her arm slipped, and she rolled completely between his legs to freedom.

One down.

Bobby-Leigh quickly launched herself up and into Softball Coach's back, driving him as best she could into the Charmer. It was a clumsy, awkward move, but she hoped it would send the man's six-shooter to the ground so she could snatch it up and drop the motherfucker.

It did not.

The Charmer was quicker than she'd expected. This was the second time she'd underestimated him, and she knew immediately she'd be dead if she did it a third. He sidestepped the flailing body of his cohort, the gun still firmly in his hand.

Incest-Is-Best took a step back in shock.

Bobby-Leigh had lost track of Patchy Beard, but she didn't have time to panic about it. She needed a fucking weapon, and the only one she had a chance of reaching was the one that looked like it had come from a John Wayne movie.

Knees. Nuts. Neck. Her uncle Allen had made her and her sister repeat it so many times it might as well have been a new mantra for the Transcendental Meditation technique he also taught them.

Without missing a beat and before Softball Coach had hit the ground, she drove a blue Doc Marten into the Charmer's kneecap and brought the edge of her small hand, flat and knifelike, up into his scrotum as hard she could.

The gun waved wildly but was not released.

She couldn't get to his neck.

But she could get to the gun.

Grabbing the barrel and twisting it as she moved, Bobby-Leigh once again kicked up her feet and dropped to the ground using her full weight as leverage.

The gun went off again. This time the bullet landed harmlessly in the snow, but the weapon itself came loose from the Charmer's hand.

Bobby-Leigh was now armed.

BANG! BANG!

The Charmer's head broke open like a watermelon dropped off a roof as both of her shots at close range landed.

Incest-Is-Best turned and ran.

Bobby-Leigh leveled the long barrel at him and shot him in the back. He dropped without a word.

She felt, more than she heard, Patchy Beard coming up on her from behind, and without a thought, for the third time in less than ten seconds, she threw her feet out from under her and dropped heavily onto the snow, turning and firing blindly as she did so.

BANG! BANG!

Click!

She was out.

Patchy Beard smiled, unscathed—for now—an almost comically large survival knife in his hand.

"Overcompensate much," Bobby-Leigh said with a grunt as the man dropped on top of her. But the man didn't hear her and wouldn't have cared about anything she'd said even if he had. She was a little surprised that Patchy Beard still obviously intended to fuck her against her will after she'd just killed his three friends, but she knew she really shouldn't be. Bobby-Leigh locked her arms as she held him momentarily at bay by the shoulders.

Then, exactly like she'd been taught, she waited for the opening.

Patchy Beard's huge knife came up fast. Clearly, he intended to use it as a threat to force her submission. But as he moved, Bobby-Leigh ended up supporting his full weight for a pivotal split second.

And just like that, the opening she was waiting for appeared. If she'd had time to smile, she would have. But she didn't.

At exactly the right moment, she twisted her hips and pivoted to her side. Patchy Beard came crashing down, pinning his knife arm under his own weight just long enough for Bobby-Leigh to escape from underneath and get on top. She didn't weigh much, but with his arm awkwardly pinned below, it was enough to hold him down for the second she needed.

A second later, she had control of the small sword of a knife.

In the second that followed, she drove the ridiculously long blade through the back of the man's neck, twisted it, and left him for dead.

*   *   *   *   *

"Hamm!" Anoona shouted over the network as she watched Tiny's screens for any sign of what was happening in the woods.

"He's not responding," Tiny said softly.

"What about the girls? Girls!"

"Nothing from them either. The gear all seems to still be operational, but none of them have moved in almost thirty minutes."

"Can you turn on the cameras?"

"Not from here."

"Well, what the fuck good are you then?" Anoona screamed.

"I'm sorry, boss lady," Tiny said quietly.

"Anoona," Rachel said, touching her shoulder. "We can't do anything for them until we deal with…them."

She pointed to Tiny's screen that showed the blood pirates slowly advancing on them from the house-mounted surveillance cameras on the southwest side.

Anoona took three deep breaths and shut a door in her heart on her grief. She nodded at Rachel and her girlfriend. *Was it really just the four of them left? Could they even run the farm with so few crew?*

Fuck.

"What's the score?" she asked tonelessly.

"We've still got about a hundred and fifty approaching. Slowly. But that's good news. It should have been more like three fifty, but the guys are starting to desert.

"Still. One fifty? Somebody must have taken over command."

Anoona looked up at the charred hole in the ceiling where the kalash had been before it was taken off by an RPG. She looked at the gun mounted on the tripod and pointing out the dining room window. The gun that was currently completely idle. She looked at the monitors.

"Well, first thing we need to do is get the TPPG somewhere it can actually do something."

"There isn't anywhere that has line of sight on this level," Sarah said.

"I know. That's why we're going to move the gun to the basement."

"I've got no eyes in the basement, Anoona. It was definitely breached. Anything could be down there," Tiny said.

"We were thinking it might be better—tactically— to pick them off as they came up," Rachel explained.

Anoona shook her head, "No."

Nobody argued with her, even though everybody wanted to. Anoona felt it, but it didn't matter. Even though this was hardly a military unit, especially now that Rodney and most likely Hamm were both dead, orders were orders. She was in charge. But at the same time, she didn't see how an explanation of her thinking would hurt things.

"If we have a hundred plus assholes come up those stairs, the four of us will simply not be able to kill them fast enough to stop them. Our only chance is to deter them enough to get them to abandon their mission before they get here. And the only way to do that is to take advantage of the one piece of superior tech we still have: the TPPG."

Especially since I can't seem to force myself to even pull the fucking trigger to save my own daughter, and Tiny is about as useful with a weapon as a goldfish, she added in her mind.

The ladies nodded.

"We need eyes back up down there, Tiny. So as soon as we get the gun in position, you let us know what we need to do to fix those cameras."

Tiny nodded.

As Rachel and Sarah checked their weapons, Anoona walked over and picked up the TPPG. Leaning the bulk of its weight against her shoulder, she carried the weapon toward the women waiting for her at door, and down into the unknown they went.

*   *   *   *   *

Bobby-Leigh found Mari mostly naked, bleeding, and more than half-dead from exposure, to say nothing of the assault in the snow. She was huddled in a ball about twenty feet away from Hamm's body. There was no question what had happened to either of them. But the men who'd done it were gone. Bobby-Leigh's first instinct was to hunt them down and kill them all, but as she got closer to the utterly broken little girl, she knew that Anoona's daughter was going to die if she didn't get her home right now.

For a fleeting second, she wondered if maybe she should just put the girl out of her misery herself. She was almost dead already. Maybe that would be a mercy. It was such as cold thought that it stung her heart just to have it pass through her head, but she found herself looking at the long-barreled pistol in her hand just the same.

With a heavy sigh, she slipped the gun into the waistband of her skirt. Even if she wanted to do, mercy killing was not something she was capable of. This fact had already been proven. She'd failed to put her own sister down after all. So there was no way she was going to be able to put a bullet into Mari's head. Even if it had been the kindest thing she could have done for the girl—which it probably was.

By the time she'd gotten Mari back to the house and into her mother's arms, the blood pirates had been turned away. Bodies were everywhere. Jen had survived but was in a coma. Brennachecke was awake and would live, even though without his sons he didn't really want to. The only other folks alive were Tiny, Anoona, and the two lesbians, or so Bobby-Leigh thought at the time. It would still be months before anybody discovered that deep inside Mari's defiled body, a baby was growing.

Part One:

Shots Fired

"*Sometimes the person you'd take a bullet for is the person behind the trigger...*"

> —Taylor Swift and/or Tupac
> (Likely misquoting Fall Out Boy, "Missing You")

"*Without the shedding of the blood there is no forgiveness.*"

> —Hebrews 9:22

"*Here's your ticket, pack your bag*
Time for jumpin' overboard
The transportation is here
Close enough, but not too far,
Maybe you know where you are
Fightin' fire with fire"

> —Talking Heads, "Burning Down the House"

Chapter One
Don't Mess with Texas

FOR THE OLD MAINE State Prison guard called Black Jesus by the men in his custody, but Captain Waters to his face, the trip to Texas had been an eye-opener for sure. But it had been an exercise in some kind of bizarre existential surrealism for his final two wards, the wife-murdering father of two, Emmett Kessler, and his berserker cellmate, Wiley DuPont, who had been dubbed simply "Beast" back before the world had ended and the prison they'd come from had burned to the ground.

Intellectually, the convicts had known for a while now that the society that had locked them away was long gone—or at least Emmett had known it. Frankly, it was hard to tell how much information Beast's ruined mind allowed him to assimilate, and harder still to talk to him about it. But the monster of a man certainly seemed more confused now that they were out of their concrete cells and in the wild than he had when he'd first entered the correctional system over a decade ago. Both Black Jesus and Emmett were pretty confident that at least some of the chaos they saw around them was sinking in.

Over the weeks that had turned to months on the road, Emmett had faithfully honored his agreement to stay in the custody of Black Jesus until his time was served. A trust had built between the convicted and the guard. A trust that had allowed the two men to become friends—at least so far as it was possible, all things considered.

They'd originally intended this journey south to be a road trip in the van they'd appropriated from the dead men who'd attempted to take the prison that fateful day in July. Considering it had inexplicably started snowing not thirty minutes after they'd left town, all three of them were happy to be in a vehicle and not on foot. When they had realized the van's navigation system was still receiving location data from orbiting GPS satellites, it had seemed like a sign the universe was supporting their travel plans. However, in the entirety of mankind's short history on this planet, when it comes to the universe's signs and signals, folks have never been able to interpret them with any kind of reliable accuracy. This was not the exception. So, in Waldoboro, not even an hour into their travels, when they had attempted to engage on the auto-drive system, they had gotten the first of many nasty surprises.

They'd failed to look closely enough at the map before they'd hit the switch. If they had zoomed out even just a little, they'd have seen that the van's navigation system thought they were hundreds of miles north, up in Canada. And with the map data and the GPS coordinates being received from space being so far off from one another, the van had immediately driven off the road and into the Medomak River.

Without operational ground stations to constantly keep the clocks on the GPS satellites and the clocks in the devices receiving their signals on the ground in synch, the whole system had been rendered totally useless. Plus, the van's internal sensors couldn't tell the difference between pavement and water—at least not until it was too late. So it turned out the universe was not so supportive of their journey after all. Or maybe this was just a cautionary tale in the dangers of anthropomorphism in general. Whatever it was metaphysically, practically, it had cost them their wheels on day one.

"Well…that sucked," Emmett had said, breaking the awkward silence after the crash.

Black Jesus had looked at him and rubbed his mouth, obviously trying to assess what the best course of action was at this point. He had looked back over his shoulder to the nestlike pile of prison blankets where Beast still slept. They'd used a Pharmajet tranquilizer to knock Wiley out for the trip—it was so far the only thing Emmett could reliably say they'd done right. It was the reason they were all still alive, because if Beast had berserked out on them in the middle of all this, it certainly would have been the end of them.

Not sure what to do, but certain the van was lost, Emmett had opened his door and jumped into the two feet of water that flowed around the van. The river had been warmer than he'd expected, but still by all accounts cold.

"We need to get DuPont out of the van," Captain Waters had said. "Without waking him up—so I am going to need you to dose him again…"

Seven hours later, the two men had managed to maneuver the unconscious hulk from the van and unload all the gear into a nearby barn. They'd stayed in that barn overnight. In the morning after a long discussion over the risks verse the potential advantages, Black Jesus and Emmett had introduced Wiley to a horse.

"A horsey is of coursey a famous little horsey-dorsey-do," Beast had said as he gently patted the creature on the nose.

"Can you by any chance ride, Wiley?" Emmett had asked, not sure what kind of answer he'd get and scared shitless of what would happen if it turned out the big man with the ever-ticking time bomb inside him tried to saddle up and could not control the animal beneath him.

"Doodley-do!" Wiley had said with a toothless grin and then suddenly kicked his leg up and over, squaring himself on the saddle before either of the other two men could stop him.

Beast could not only ride, it was immediately apparent that he was the best on horseback of the three of them.

Entering Brunswick through the woods instead of via the highway the next day had revealed to the three of them what could happen to folks with enough moxie to travel through town in a vehicle alone. As it turned out, regardless of the firepower and provisions they'd had to leave behind to go from motor vehicle to horseback, their accident with the van had been a blessing in disguise.

"Captain, I think we've got some Highwaymen about five hundred yards up," Emmett had said as they were crossing the Sagadahoc county line bridge. *Highwaymen.* he'd been annoyed when Black Jesus had chuckled at the terminology, but it'd since proven to be a more than accurate choice of wording. Approaching through the trees, they had been able to observe the dozen or so men in secret long enough to determine they were, without a doubt, both hostile and dangerous.

From that point forward, Black Jesus had decided it'd be best to travel as far away from population centers as possible and to stay off the roads.

Emmett had been in no position to argue.

Navigating via paper maps stolen from long out of service gas stations through recurrent snowstorms—which Black Jesus steadfastly refused to accept were now the norm for summer—they had progressed slowly.

A hundred miles and a few weeks later going the long way around Portland, they'd came upon the aftermath of a Highwaymen attack. By then, Emmett's mind had finally started to let go of the world he knew and accept the new reality of the one he was in now.

A thirty-seven-foot Coachmen Mirada motor home had been knocked on its side and lit on fire. The owners of the motor home had clearly been well armed and had put up a solid fight. Bodies were everywhere to prove it, but it was equally obvious the highwaymen had prevailed—if for no other reason than whatever had knocked the RV on its side was now nowhere to be seen. For the rest of the afternoon, Emmett and Black Jesus had debated whether the RV crew had set the vehicle on fire themselves to keep their attackers from getting anything once it had become clear they were going to lose the fight, or if the Highwaymen had torched it during—or maybe more likely after—the attack.

Emmett had begun to accept that folks these days were vindictive enough to destroy what they had out of spite like that, but at the time, it had still shocked him to see it with his own eyes. However, by the time they'd finally crossed the Sabine River and moved from what was once Louisiana into Texas some eight months later, they'd seen the aftermath of so much carnage, cruelty, and violence, he'd grown quite embarrassed at ever being so naive.

*   *   *   *   *

The tiny Texas towns of Burkeville and Wiergate were utterly abandoned, which shouldn't have been a surprise to anybody—they'd looked more or less like alternative locations for the *Texas Chainsaw Massacre* film franchise even before the world fell apart. But as they came up on Jasper, it suddenly became clear that Texas was not going to be like any of the other states they'd crossed through.

"You hear that?" Emmett said.

Captain Waters nodded.

There was a *buzz* in the air.

The sound seemed to be coming from high above them, and unlike the natural sounds they'd grown accustomed to in their trek across the country, this sound was mechanical.

Both men shielded their eyes from the sun and looked up trying to place the source of the buzz. An occasional glint of light above them, like glass catching the sun, was the closest they could get to identifying it.

"I think it's a drone," Black Jesus said.

"There's two of them," Emmett said, as a second glint popped in the blue sky.

"Seven in heaventy-heaven," Wiley said in his nursery rhyming singsong way.

"Two," Emmett corrected, thankful it wasn't snowing today. Without the sun's light to reflect, the drones would been invisible.

"One, two, didiley-do—"

"That's right—"

"Three, four, farty whore. Five, six, seven, heaventy-heaven."

Emmett turned his attention from the sky to correct Beast again, and suddenly saw that Wiley wasn't talking about the drones overhead at all.

"Captain."

Black Jesus turned his gaze to Emmett and immediately saw what DuPont was counting as well. His horse snorted loudly under him as if she was giving him a reprimand for being distracted by the drones.

There were seven men watching them. All seven wore crisp, black uniforms. All of them wore glasses. They looked to be in their mid-twenties and were all extremely fit, clean, and attractive. Each wore a sidearm and held Heckler & Koch MP5 assault rifle in their hands. Three black luxury SUVs waited patiently off in the distance behind them.

"Welcome to Jasper, friends," one of them said. "Can I ask where you're coming from?"

It was a simple enough question delivered without any indication of ill intent, and yet Emmett felt the hairs on the back of his neck stiffen. A quick glance to Black Jesus confirmed he was not the only one hearing warning bells. Even Wiley seemed uncomfortable—and an uncomfortable berserker was nothing short of a death sentence waiting to be carried out. Black Jesus had exhausted all the Pharmajet injections from the prison long ago, so if Wiley was triggered into a berserker rage, all they'd be able to do was duck, cover, and wait the storm of out.

Considering how huge Wiley was, and the fact that his friendly smile down on them was completely toothless, it seemed frankly impossible that these men hadn't immediately sized him up for what he was. And yet they didn't seem the least bit concerned. If he had to put his finger on what was triggering the alarm bells deep in his subconscious, Emmett would have guessed it was that fact. Men who acted without fear or caution toward the destructive power Wiley held inside—a power so destructive that it had already crushed the world as they'd known it—simply could not be trusted.

"What difference does it make," Emmett asked, mirroring Wiley's smile, as he read the name tag on the uniform of the man who had spoken, "Mr. Sinclair?"

"Well, friends. Y'all ain't in the Registry. Now depending on where you're coming from, that may not be a problem. But I'm afraid I'm obliged to ask you. So—and I mean this as politely as I possibly can—where the fuck are you coming from?"

"I see. Well, let me respond with an equal level of decorum then, gentlemen. I'd be a little more concerned about what Mr. DuPont here will do if he gets upset, if I were you, than our route to get to wherever the fuck this is," Emmett said with a nod to Wiley. Unfortunately, Wiley, for his part, just grinned happily back at him, which didn't exactly add much zing to Emmett's threat.

"Friendly-bendly, dindly-dong?" Wiley asked, hopeful.

"Yes, DuPont. Friends. It's all okay," Captain Waters said calmly to the giant.

"All okie-dookily-do!"

Sinclair smiled in a way that seemed almost nostalgic. Then he turned to the man on his left and said, "You recall how much I hate repeating myself, Mr. Smalls?"

"Oh, yes, sir. A whole lot, sir," the man to Sinclair's left—the name on his uniform confirming his surname—answered.

The other five men on the welcome wagon said nothing. Sinclair seemed to hope that his rhetorical question would be enough to avoid asking Black Jesus where they'd come from again or escalating the confrontation. But when Emmett looked at Black Jesus for a sign of how he wanted to handle this, he found he couldn't read the old prison guard at all.

"You know what I hate, Mr. Smalls?" Emmett said, his hand dropping to the handgun holstered on his hip.

Black Jesus waited on his horse a second, almost daring Sinclair with his eyes to take the bait and answer. Then, as soon as the man opened his mouth to do so, he must have decided that avoiding an escalation was in everybody's best interest—and besides, Black Jesus already knew a long list of the things that Emmett hated and probably had very little interest in hearing another one.

"Stand down, Kessler," Black Jesus said, sliding off his saddle and extending his hand to Sinclair. "We're from Maine. Heading to Austin. Friends. My name's Bill."

"See?" Sinclair said, leaving Captain Waters hanging. "Was that hard?"

"No, sir. It was not," Smalls answered unnecessarily.

"It'll be just one second there, gentlemen," the man to Sinclair's left said—his name apparently McKinney.

"Shake the boy's hand, Roberts," Sinclair said to the man to McKinney's right in a tone that suggested there was something funny about the order, even though nobody was smiling—except for Beast. Sinclair's eyes flicked around behind the lenses of his glasses like he was reading something only he could see.

The man Roberts did not shake Black Jesus's hand like he was told, and the old prison guard ended up awkwardly putting his arm down as Sinclair spoke up again.

"There you are, boyo. Oh, my goodness, son! You're an officer! Well now, Captain William Paul Waters of Maine State Prison, welcome to the Republic of Austin."

Black Jesus smiled at the men and gave them all a knowing nod that Emmett knew to be the Captain's go-to response when he thought he was encountering something racist.

Emmett for his part was too distracted by how completely unfazed the Captain was after Sinclair had identified him with only the knowledge of what state they'd come from—and in a matter of seconds no less—to analyze the situation for malicious racial intent. What Sinclair had just done seemed almost like magic to him. He was dumbfounded.

"Am I correct in assuming your travel companions were inmates at the facility? We don't have much in the way of out-of-state incarceration records in the Registry yet, but I've got matches in the high seventies for their faces and links to their trial transcripts. Guess you decided bygones are bygones, huh, boyo? I don't blame you none—"

"No, sir. That's not correct," Black Jesus said matter-of-factly. "Mr. Kessler and Mr. DuPont are still serving their sentences out under my care. Our facility was compromised, that's all."

Sinclair looked at Emmett, who honestly didn't know what to say at this point, so he just sat on his horse and nodded like an idiot while thinking as loudly as he could, *Why the fuck would you tell these assholes that?*

"Okay, then," Sinclair said incredulously. "Honestly, I'm not sure what to make of that. What about you, Smalls?"

"No, sir."

"Roberts?"

"So," Roberts said slowly, "the old man and the berserker are your prisoners then, even though they're not in restraints, and they're carrying weapons?"

"Kessler and DuPont. That's correct."

"Okay," Roberts said in a tone that made it sound more like *Bullshit*.

"I have to say, boy. This is a first for us," Sinclair said. "Um, could you instruct your prisoners to dismount please?"

"Get down," Captain Waters commanded.

"Down-dittily-do!" Wiley said and jumped from his saddle with a surprisingly nimble move.

Emmett fought very hard against the urge to say something sarcastic and undermining. Black Jesus hadn't made him feel like he was subject to his authority since—well, since the day they'd left the prison still smoking behind them. Yes, he'd agreed to this arrangement. Hell, it had been his idea, but this was the first time in almost nine months that he'd felt it. He'd come to see the man as a friend. It stung him to think that maybe he wasn't. But, stung or not, he managed to get off his horse without saying a word.

"Take the horses," Sinclair told Roberts.

Roberts looked at his boss like he was crazy.

"Well, we can't just leave them here," Sinclair said, not really clarifying anything. "Captain, you ride with me. Your"—Sinclair made a quotation gesture with his fingers—"*prisoners* can ride with Smalls and McKinney. The rest of you go and prep one of the bays at Goodman."

Waters looked at Emmett with an infuriating calm smile and walked toward the SUVs in the distance with Sinclair. Emmett's eyes almost burst from his head, as he willed his thoughts to somehow find their way into the Captain's consciousness. *What the fuck're you doing? You're going with them? You're—*

But it was useless.

"I think we're going to need your weapons, friends."

Fucking useless.

Smalls and McKinney quickly disarmed Emmett and suddenly slapped handcuffs on both him and Beast before either one of them realized what was happening. Emmett half expected Wiley to berserk out on them, but he didn't. He just smiled his big toothless grin and said, "Friend-dittity-do."

Fuck.

"Seriously, the fuck am I supposed to do with these horses?" Roberts asked Smalls and the others, but he got only laughter for an answer.

Emmett's nag, which he had taken to calling Maggie for no particular reason, let out a frightened whinny as the man who had ridden, fed, and groomed her for months was driven away by strangers.

"Oh, calm down, horse," Roberts said. "I ain't going to fucking hurt ya."

* * * * *

"Hey, Smalls!" Emmett yelled at the Zac Efron wannabe on the other side of the bars as the man was leaving him locked away, alone. "You ever heard of a man named Julius Weiss? A doctor, fertility doctor. I heard he's in Austin now."

Emmett was in a small holding cell in the Jasper County Sheriff's Building—which bleak as it was, was not nearly as soul-crushingly hopeless architecturally as Maine State Prison had been. In the back of his mind, he wondered about why he'd been separated from Wiley, but it was an afterthought next to this chance to find out more about Dr. Weiss without making Black Jesus suspicious.

Smalls turned, his eyes flicking behind his glasses as he opened his mouth to say something, which took a second longer to get out than it should have. "Why, Kessler? He do something to your wife besides deliver your little girls before you blew her brains out in the snow?"

Emmett was forcing himself to adjust to how fast these people could get their hands on information as quickly as they could. But, try as he might, it was just impossible to keep up with. It was like they were all plugged directly into the information superhighway and nobody cared about privacy anymore.

"Oh, wait a minute now," Smalls continued. "He is in Austin. Fuck me, Kessler, he's the director of public health and welfare for the Republic. You know what that means, right? It means you ain't never going to get to talk to him. That's what that means. If you get lucky, you might get a look at him this evening at the service for your man DuPont, but I can pretty much promise you that is as close to him as you'll ever get."

"Director of public health and welfare?" Emmett echoed in disbelief, so wrapped up in the first part of what Smalls had said that he'd barely even registered the second part. "That's rich. How's that even possible? The man is over a hundred years old." He'd muttered it under his breath, but Smalls had heard him just fine.

"So? That shit don't matter no more. I'm eighty-three myself."

"Look…can you just do me a favor and pretend like I came here from somewhere else—like somewhere faraway, dude—and I have no idea what the fuck is going on?"

Smalls smiled. "What do you want? A history lesson?"

"Yes! God, yes. That's exactly—"

"Well, too fucking bad, son. I ain't got time to be explaining the Lord's plan to you. Suffice it to say, things may could be a little more advanced around here than where y'all are coming from."

"Okay, fine. Then just tell me where DuPont is. Or Captain Waters for that matter?"

Smalls did not tell him either. Instead he just left the holding area with a chuckle, leaving Emmett alone to flinch as the huge metal door that separated the holding cells from the rest of the sheriff's station shut.

CLANG!

* * * * *

Sinclair sat behind his desk in the large county sheriff captain's office and smiled up at Waters until the old black man sat down in the chair across the wooden desk. It was a startlingly normal-looking office. Cheap institutional furniture. Grayish, beige walls. Framed important-looking documents looking down on them from their places on the wall above several vintage pistols in display cases. There was a flag in the corner, but it wasn't a Texas flag or one for the United States. It was white with a large blue ichthus, or Jesus fish, in the center and a red cross in the upper left corner where the stars would be in the US flag. Sinclair had the same flag on the shoulder of his uniform. Waters guessed it was the flag for the Republic of Austin.

The drive into town from the river where they had been picked up had been a short one, but after all the destruction they'd witnessed coming to Texas, it had been exhilarating to be in a place that was completely intact. People lived here. Worked here. It was dirty and run-down, but functioning. It was amazing to him how much he'd missed just feeling that society had rules. That there was some kind of order.

As the driverless electric SUV hummed along the snow-covered streets toward their destination. Captain Waters hadn't said much. But Sinclair had babbled on about the crazy weather and any number of other things of zero importance. Waters was too taken in by his surrounding to give the man's trivial ramblings much consideration beyond growing more and more annoyed with how often the man used words like boy and son in reference to Waters himself. And it was only in the very back of his mind that he noticed every inhabitant of Jasper, Texas appeared to be white.

Sinclair hadn't seemed to mind the one-sidedness of the conversation during the drive. Waters guessed he was the kind of cat who liked to hear himself talk.

But that didn't mean the man didn't have questions. Now seated across from one another in this place that seem to have dodged the bullet that had blown the brains out of the rest of the world, captain to captain, those questions came.

"So, my big question here, boy, is this: how did those two end up traveling with you the three thousand odd miles from northern Maine to eastern Texas as your prisoners. I mean, Lord have mercy, you gave that Kessler feller weapons for the love of all that is blessed and holy, and yet not only did the man not murder you in your sleep, or just plain run out on you in the middle of the night—I mean, my Lord, son—he actually allowed himself to be put *back* into a cell just a few minutes ago with no significant resistance. In the whole history of the world, there is no record of anything like that ever happening, ever."

Black Jesus told himself that if this cat called him *son* or *boy* one more time he'd be totally justified in putting a bullet in his head. This was a new world after all, right? He could choose not to tolerate the usual barrage of unconscious belittling that came from whites—even those who would be mortally offended to be called out on their racist mannerisms—which at this point, was the kind of man he believed Sinclair to be. He'd never actually pull his gun on the man, much less pull the trigger, at least not over this shit—especially considering how many questions he had of his own at the moment. Sinclair was his best source of information. But it was a nice fantasy all the same.

"Tell you what, Mr. Sinclair, I'll trade you one for one, answers for answers if you've got the time. There is a lot I'd be interested in knowing too."

Sinclair smiled. "Deal, son. You answer mine first though. Why you think that Kessler feller stayed with you instead of leaving your black ass in a ditch somewheres?"

Captain Waters explained how the prison had been attacked and how Emmett had risked his own life to help him get Wiley out. He explained how they'd made a deal to travel together to find and confront the fertility doctor Emmett believed was responsible for the whole apocalypse in exchange for honoring the social contract between prisoner and guard. He explained that the alternative would have been one of them murdering the other in cold blood and that neither of them had that in them.

"Well, he did murder his wife in cold blood," Sinclair said.

"I don't believe he did."

"That's what they locked him up for."

"Yep."

"So what then? You believe he's innocent. Actually, that would explain—"

"No. I have no doubt that he murdered his wife. It just wasn't in cold blood."

"You, son, are a heck of stickler for details, ain't ya? So he's got what? A little less than a year left on his original sentence?"

"Where are you getting all this information from?" Waters asked instead of answering. It was his turn.

"Tit for tat, yeah, yeah… Okay then, let's start at the beginning, yes? When the shit was hitting the fan, a company here in Austin saw the writing on the wall, so to speak—Lone Star Dynamics, they was called then—they started consolidating the public record—just to preserve it through the chaos and what have you, you know what I'm saying?"

Waters nodded.

"Now mind you there was a lot of stuff that wasn't supposed to be included, because of you know, legacy privacy laws and that old rag, the constitution, and what have yahs, but a crew of—eh, hackers I supposed you'd be right to call them—a little crew of these fellas in the company saw the end of the United States looming up against us all on the horizon and what have yah—and well, they just started breaking in and adding social media, criminal justice, financial, medical—any and all the data you could have on anybody and anything—they made sure to include it in the mix. At the time it was totally illegal, sure, but the laws done changed a bit now, if you know what I'm saying? Anywho, LSD—Lone Star Dynamics, not the drug."

He laughed at his own joke in a way that was as endearing as it was obvious this was not the first time he'd used that particular pun.

"LSD then made all that data—and I mean all of it. The good. The bad. And the ugly, as public as a weather report on one of them old iPhones. But they wasn't done yet. They created this intelligent query engine thing to catalog and index the whole mess on top of it. So nowadays, in theory at least, if there was ever a record of something happening, or somebody sayin' something, or doing something, or commenting on something, or—well, just about anything I guess, it's all now linked, cross-referenced, indexed, and available to anybody who wants to know it. You got your facial recognition, your voice recognition, good Lord save us, I heard they even got identifying data on heartbeats now."

Sinclair paused to give Black Jesus a chance to mentally catch up.

"Now mind you, the farther from the Republic a feller gets, the more gaps are in the data links, so it ain't perfect yet by any means, but even with them faults, it's still one hell of a resource. The whole things got some long technical name, but nobody uses it. We all just call it the *Registry*. Anywho, to make a long story short, I had your whole life's story the second them drones had a look at you and you told me you'd come from Maine."

Black Jesus didn't know how to respond, so he just joked, "Yeah, insurance companies must love it."

"Actually, there ain't no insurance companies in the Republic of Austin."

"What's that now?" Black Jesus asked, not sure if this was another joke or not.

"People don't need insurance here." Sinclair paused and smiled, then attempted to change the subject. "So... why horses?"

Black Jesus sighed. *Who were these people? How could they know so much information, but be so ignorant to the state of world?*

"Well, *son*," Captain Waters said. "The roads most places are dangerous as a motherfucker. Being on horseback meant we could travel off them. Plus, animals never ran out of gas or needed to charge batteries. And they gave us extra sets of eyes and ears along the way. Honestly, I can't tell you how many times the choice to travel on horseback probably saved our hides, or at least allowed us to avoid one kind of nasty business or another."

Captain Waters smiled and took his turn to ask a question before Sinclair could get a follow-up question of his own out. "So why don't cats here need insurance?"

"Oh, well, you know. All citizens of the Republic have been blessed by God, so we don't get sick. We don't get old. We don't—Lord have mercy, for the most part—we don't even die. So I guess that kind of changes things, you know what I'm saying? Insurance just ain't necessary in *our* world."

"How's that now?" It was clear the man was being sincere with what he was saying, even though he had to be joking.

"Have you taken our Lord Jesus Christ into your heart, Captain?" Sinclair asked.

Captain Waters smiled as big as he could and—still not sure if he was being led on or not—answered with a perfectly straight face.

"Absolutely!"

*   *   *   *   *

Emmett didn't know how long he'd been in the holding tank before Black Jesus walked through the outer doors and nodded to him from the other side of the bars, but it had felt like a lot longer than a nod hello was appropriate for.

"For God's sake, Captain—" he began, but Black Jesus cut him off.

"This is not a good place to be taking the Lord's name in vain."

"The fuck you talking about, dude? Where is Wiley? Who are these guys? How do they know everything?"

Captain Waters told him about the Registry.

"So much for privacy and peace of mind."

"The glasses that everybody is wearing—"

"Yeah, yeah. It's how folks interface with the thing. I figured that much out on my own."

"Oh, they're way more than that. They're recording everything with those things, audio and video, and they've got some kind of supercomputer cross-referencing and indexing it all. They don't have any laws because you simply can't get away with anything."

"What about crimes of passion? Husband's killing their wives in fits of drunken rage and what have you? No all-seeing eye is going to stop that kind of shit."

"That's where it gets a little weird."

"It's been a little weird, dude."

"You think so, eh? Well, you better hold on to your proverbial hat then my friend because *citizens of the Republic of Austin don't get sick and for the most part don't die*—those are the exact words Captain Sinclair said—because God has saved them all, again his words."

Emmett's head shook as he was trying to wrap it around what he was hearing. Black Jesus gave him a moment, and then another, but it didn't matter. Emmett's mental capacity to process information had been pushed way too far into the red for any of this conversation to be properly assimilated. Black Jesus was surprised smoke wasn't pouring out of his ears and his hair hadn't caught fire.

"And Wiley?" Emmett asked, relieving the pressure in his head by changing the subject.

"There're no berserkers in Texas."

"What the fuck does that mean? Come on, Captain. I'm fucking dying here with your cryptic bullshit, dude. Are they going to fucking execute him? Send him back to Louisiana?"

Black Jesus shook his head. He'd had an hour or two to process what Sinclair had said, but as the words started to come out his mouth, he realized he didn't have nearly the handle on the issue as he thought he'd had.

"They're going to exorcise him."

*   *   *   *   *

When Smalls had taken Emmett away and left Wiley alone with the too-perfect-to-be-natural looking McKinney, sitting on the plush leather seats of the electric SUV, he hadn't been afraid. When the vehicle drove off without anybody behind the wheel again, he had only smiled his big toothless grin and marveled like a child at the magic of the enchanted land he'd stumbled into. Wiley DuPont had been conditioned—half on purpose and half just from being sheltered by his guardians in the wild—to trust first and ask questions later. Black Jesus and Emmett had gone out of their way to protect the man from the monster that slumbered inside him—more cynical folks might say that they were just protecting themselves once the Pharmajet was all gone with their efforts at painting the destruction, danger, and death they traveled through in as warm and fuzzy a light as possible. But cynicism just makes you an asshole and a coward.

McKinney brought DuPont through the gates and into the yard of the Glen Ray Goodman Transfer Facility—Jasper's claim to prison fame—without a single word to the big brain-damaged man. But Wiley didn't mind. It was hard for him to follow even the simplest of conversations for more than a minute or two, and he'd just as soon not be bothered to try.

"Doodily-do," he commented simply now and again, as the familiarity of the prison setting warmed his heart.

"Doodily-doodily-do. Home come back to you."

McKinney smiled in spite of himself as he opened the outer door to the block and led Wiley to a dormitory that had been retrofitted a long time ago to be able to handle a berserker inmate population. The other equally perfect men from the bridge had already arrived and were setting up chairs for the crowd that was sure to come.

"It's been a long time since we've had one of these. I bet by the time it starts it'll be standing room only," McKinney said to one of the men setting up chairs as he walked DuPont up onto a small stage and sat him on a simple, yet unmistakably throne-like chair.

A young woman wearing a thick red cassock under a simple, but pristine white surplice appeared from behind a curtain at the back of the stage and nodded a hello to McKinney. She was more beautiful than any woman Wiley DuPont could remember ever seeing. Carrying a tray with a large silver bowl, a pitcher, and a thick white cloth folded neatly in a square on it, she approached him, slowly exuding kindness and empathy. The soft smile that danced on her lips was enough to subdue him completely.

"May I wash your feet, sir?"

Wiley could only smile his toothless grin in response. She laughed kindly back at him understanding that his permission had been granted and knelt at his feet. Meticulously, the woman slowly removed his boots and socks. There were no sexual undertones to her actions, but it had been so long since Wiley DuPont had felt a kind touch from another human being that even if he'd been in full control of his faculties, the man couldn't have helped his heart rate, to say nothing of other parts of his body, from rising.

"I think he likes you," McKinney said.

The woman looked up at the perfect face of the man who'd brought Wiley in and gave him an entirely different kind of smile. Then she turned her attention back to the task at hand.

Suddenly another woman—as perfect, or maybe even more perfect than the one washing his feet—stepped into Wiley's field of vision. She too wore a red cassock and white surplice like she was an altar boy or something. She too smiled at him kindly. She too carried something in her hands: a simple golden chalice filled with a dark red liquid.

But she did not offer it to Wiley.

At least not yet.

*   *   *   *   *

A sea of young, beautiful, entirely white, and mostly male faces surrounded Black Jesus and Emmett as they stood with the crowd that had filled the ceremony chamber in the Goodman Transfer Facility to capacity and then some. McKinney had been right. It was standing room only.

Suddenly, the buzz of conversation stopped, and everybody's attention turned to watch three men enter the chamber and mount the short set of stairs to the stage. One man was dressed in a white cassock with a blue silk sash and golden cloaklike cope. The Jesus fish and cross from the flag Captain Waters had seen in Sinclair's office adorned the ospreys in the front and the hood hanging off the back. A gold-banded white bishop's mitre sat atop the man's head. The two men with him wore significantly less adorned blue chasuble sleeveless robes over white cassocks—like everybody else, they looked like they were in their mid-twenties and were textbook examples of perfect health. All three wore the glasses that linked everything and everyone to the Registry just like the rest of the crowd. The bishop—if in fact that was what the man was—looked oddly familiar to Emmett, but for the life of him, he could not place the man's face.

"That's an awful lot of white folks in robes," Emmett observed, hoping Black Jesus would let him in on his thoughts.

"It is that."

"That doesn't make you nervous."

Black Jesus smiled cryptically.

"Makes me nervous and I'm about as white as they come."

"You're nervous because you don't believe in God, Kessler."

"That's not true," Emmett said quickly, louder than he needed to. "But, even if it was, this is definitely not the right place to discuss it."

"Fair enough."

In the silence that followed the two men watched as the bishop—who still hadn't said a single word—knelt and kissed Wiley's feet.

"What the fuck're they doing to Wiley, Captain?"

"Relax. Sinclair assured me that the—"

"Exorcism?"

The bishop stood and grinned at Wiley, then turned his radiant smile on the crowd, patiently waiting for them to grow silent.

"That whatever they're doing will not hurt him."

"Well, you've known the guy like six hours, so obviously you can trust anything he says," Emmett said sarcastically.

"It doesn't seem like cats here do much lying. With everything being recorded in their Registry, I think they generally either speak the truth or shut up."

"Mostly they just shut up," a raspy voice whispered from behind them.

Emmett turned and saw an old woman with several brutal scars across her face looking up at him through the lenses of the standard issue glasses everybody else wore.

"But just because they're not lying, doesn't mean they're telling you the truth," she continued. "Are you actually interested in that—the truth?"

Black Jesus looked at her and then back at Wiley seated on the huge chair in the center of the stage.

"We're interested."

The woman nodded, and then without a word, turned and disappeared into the crowd.

"Think we're supposed to follow her, Captain?" Emmett asked.

"Follow who?" Sinclair's voice suddenly whispered in his ear.

In the undulating mass of the crowd, Emmett could see several of Sinclair's black-clad and armed henchmen attempting to pursue the old lady, but coming up empty. He couldn't help but smile.

"You tell me," Black Jesus said. "You're the one plugged in to the whatever you called it."

Sinclair smiled but said nothing.

"There before the grace of God, go I," the bishop said at last, his voice booming. "Have mercy upon this, your humble servant, Lord, according to Thy loving kindness; according to the multitude of Thy tender mercies, blot out his transgressions. Wash him from his wickedness and cleanse him from his sin. For your humble servant acknowledges his transgressions. His sins are ever before him. He has done evil in Thy sight, and Thou art justified to speakest Thy judgment against him."

"Let's get closer," Black Jesus said, discreetly passing the handgun that had been taken from Emmett earlier that day back to him.

Once they were far enough away from Sinclair to not risk being overheard, Emmett whispered, "I thought you said you trusted these guys."

"I never said that. I just said that I don't believe Wiley is in any danger."

"Yeah, right. That's why you got me released from my cell and just handed me a gun."

Black Jesus said nothing, but continued to move slowly closer and closer to the stage. Emmett followed.

"Behold, this man who hath been shaped by iniquity, conceived by his mother in sin. Behold, the truth! Though it be hidden. Thou shalt know it and by that allow this your humble servant to know wisdom," the bishop continued.

Though the closer Emmett got, the less he believed the young man could really be a bishop.

"Purge him with Thy blessing, and he shall be clean; wash him, and he shall be whiter than snow. Create in him a clean heart, O Lord, and renew within him a right spirit. Cast him not away from Thy presence. Take not Thy Holy Spirit from him. Restore unto him the joy of Thy salvation and uphold him with Thy free spirit."

Black Jesus looked at Emmett and said, "This is Psalm 51—more or less."

"Is that going to be on the test later?"

Emmett couldn't help himself. The sarcasm was a defense mechanism. It just popped out of his mouth like a belch after a good meal—only he'd be hard-pressed to tell anybody what was good about the bullshit he was currently trying to swallow.

"He will teach transgressors Thy ways, and sinners shall be converted unto Thee by his hand," the bishop continued. "Deliver him from blood guilt, O Lord of salvation, and his tongue shall sing aloud of righteousness. Open his lips, that his mouth may accept the blood of your only son and henceforth show Thy praise. For Thou desirest no longer his sacrifice, though he would gladly continue to give it. Thy Kingdom hath come. On Earth as it is in heaven. Take account, O Lord, of this broken spirit; this broken and contrite heart. Thou wilt not despise him further, that he may do good in Thy grace unto Thou republic; may Thou be pleased with the sacrifices of righteous men."

The woman with the chalice stepped forward and handed it over to the bishop who then held it up high for the crowd to see. A number of voices shouted out,

"There before the grace of God," and a number of others responded with, "Amen." But Wiley simply smiled like a child watching his favorite television show through it all. The bishop then handed him the golden cup.

Emmett popped the safety off his weapon and opened the slide until he confirmed a bullet had already been chambered.

"Wiley DuPont," the bishop's voice boomed.

"Doodily-do!"

"The Lord hath called His disciples together and gave unto them power and authority over all demons. To cure all diseases. He sent them to preach the kingdom of God and to heal the sick."

Black Jesus put his hand on Emmett's gun and shook his head.

"Oh, come on, we have no idea what's in that cup. Tell me you're not going to let him actually drink it."

"Sinclair said the ritual wouldn't hurt him."

"Then why am I even here, Captain?" Emmett could see Black Jesus calculating and suddenly realized why the Captain was not putting a stop to this crazy shit.

"Oh, fuck me."

He sighed and lowered his head, as the potential carnage that could—would—come if Wiley berserked out in this packed of a space hit him like a sucker punch to the gut. Black Jesus hadn't given him the gun to protect Wiley from the congregation; he'd given him the gun to protect the congregation from Wiley.

The two men with the bishop positioned themselves on either side of Wiley and started chanting in unison: "I release you! I release you from the demon carried within your flesh. I release you from martyrdom in this great transition between Earth and heaven. I release you into the loving arms of our Savior, Jesus Christ. You are free. You are free. You are free. May the Lord heal you and keep you. You are free."

"Drink my son."

Wiley obeyed.

Emmett half expected a demon to come erupting from his friend's mouth like in some second-rate horror movie. He remained committed to his theory that Dr. Weiss was responsible for the whole apocalypse. Because it was a fact the man had been a Nazi mad scientist. It was a fact that the doctor had performed extensive experiments on female prisoners at both Sachsenhausen and Auschwitz. A fact that he'd then found his way into the newly developing science that would eventually become modern in vitro fertilization. And it was more than likely—though admittedly, not a proven fact—the man had been instrumental in humanity's sidestepping the natural processes that protected the genetic integrity of the species—which in Emmett's theory is what had ended up planting the berserker gene in generations upon generations of hard to conceive children. But *more than likely* wasn't quite the same thing as *fact*, was it? No matter how bad he wanted it to be.

Yet, Watching Wiley drink the blood of Christ, Emmett felt compelled to admit—even if just to himself—that the possibility did exist he'd been wrong about everything. Fact was, there had never been a commonly accepted scientific explanation for the berserker phenomenon. Fact was, there were at least a hundred other fairly convincing scientific takes on the origins of this long apocalypse. There was no consensus between the top scientific minds of the world. That was a fact, too, and yet, there was near complete consensus in all the religious explanations. The only real bone of contention there was whose God was punishing man. Maybe all of this had just been the End of Days after all. Maybe he shouldn't have spent his whole life turning his nose up at Bible thumpers claiming to have found Jesus. Maybe he should have been looking for salvation himself.

Emmett watched Wiley hand back the goblet and smile up at the familiar-looking young man dressed like a bishop. He held his breath and waited. In that long second of silence, Emmett felt himself teetering on the brink of the deep black abyss of his faith and wondering for the first time in his life what might be looking back at him from its depths.

Nothing happened.

His breath had turned so hot and stale in his lungs, Emmett was tangibly relieved to finally let it escape through his clenched teeth.

"You like your man's little show there, convict. Told you, you wasn't gonna get to talk to him." It was Smalls. How long had he been there?

"What the hell are you talking about, Smalls?"

"Weiss, boy. You're like ten feet from him."

Suddenly it hit Emmett why the bishop looked so familiar. In his research on Weiss he'd come across a professional portrait of him just before his graduation from Heidelberg University in 1929. The man in that picture and the man now taking the chalice from Wiley were nearly identical. "He's a bishop? I thought you said he was the director of health or some shit."

"All the cabinet members of the Republic are bishops, you moron."

Emmett felt dangerously close to giving into the urge to shoot Smalls in the dick. Black Jesus must have sensed something was up because he stepped between them. Emmett turned his back on them both. His gun was heavy in his hand.

"We thank you, Lord, that you have fed us with the holy mysteries of the Blood of your Son our Savior Jesus Christ," Weiss continued. "By taking of His Blood, we circulate as his agents in this world. Help us to be the distributors of your blessings, the agents of your providence, the instruments of your grace, and the ambassadors of your love to all the people we meet. All this we pray in the most holy and precious name of Jesus Christ, because He is alive, and He reigns with you in the unity of the Holy Spirit. You are one God, now and forever, Amen."

I could kill him right now, Emmett thought, *but Wiley would probably freak out and—a whole lot of other people would probably die.* The question was: if he didn't do it now, would he ever get another chance?

"Be free!" Weiss's two assistants chanted in unison. "Be free from that demon carried within your flesh. Be free from martyrdom in this great transition between Earth and heaven. Throw yourself into the loving arms of our Savior, Jesus Christ. You are free. May the Lord heal you and keep you. You are free."

Cries of "Praise be to the Lord!" shot out from the crowd, but Emmett didn't hear them. Would he get another chance? Could he live with the blood on his hands, if Wiley lost it in the middle of Emmett's assassination attempt? The answer to both those questions was probably no.

As Emmett was going back and forth in his mind, Weiss and his assistants started to walk off the stage.

BAM!

Emmett heard the shot before he realized it had come from the gun in his hand. He heard the shot before he realized Black Jesus had grabbed his arm at the last second and foiled his aim. He heard the shot a second before he felt the butt of a gun crack his skull and drop him into the dark.

* * * * *

Emmett fell to the ground.

Chaos erupted as the crowd pushed and shoved for the single exit. There were screams. There was blood. And for the first time in a very long time, Wiley DuPont was afraid.

Captain Waters was screaming something at him, but he couldn't make it out. Everything was completely out of control. A chair was thrown and hit Beast in the side of the head. Pain exploded across his temple. He grabbed the chair and threw it away with a monstrous roar, but as the sound of his ferocity hit his own ears, Wiley DuPont suddenly stopped yelling and began to sob.

He knew what was coming. He looked at Black Jesus—an immovable rock in the sea of men dashing around him. Wiley loved him. He loved him like a father. Loved him like a brother. Loved him like a friend. His scrambled brain circuitry couldn't delineate the emotion. It was simply there. Pure and whole.

Black Jesus raised his weapon and aimed. Wiley had never been more grateful for anything in his life than he was for the bullet he knew would keep him for hurting anybody else.

But the man he loved didn't pull the trigger and save him.

"Shooty-shoot! Shooty-snooty-shoot!"

He screamed in anguish as he stared down the barrel of Captain Waters's gun, willing it to save him from himself. The stampeding crowd rose like a tide and washed over the stage. Bodies smashed into Wiley like debris caught in the path of a tsunami. He felt the adrenaline dump into his system.

And still Black Jesus did not put him down.

Tears raining from his eyes, Wiley waited for the black to come and Beast to take over. But it didn't.

The demon inside him was gone.

Chapter Two
Farming Sucks

MARI MOANED SOFTLY. Her mother looked at her across the dining table and clinched her teeth hoping to god this time she would be able to keep her toxic thoughts from pouring out of her mouth.

Why the hell her daughter insisted on keeping her rapist's baby was not something she'd ever understand. She could have—should have—just forced the little girl to abort the thing. But Anoona couldn't handle the thought of her baby's little body being violated again. And Mari had been crystal clear—and frustratingly consistent—in her instance that the little girl fetus growing inside her was not a curse. She'd threatened to die before she gave it up at least a hundred times now. The discussion—if you could really call it that—was so ridiculously beyond anything Anoona was prepared for as a parent that she was almost positive at times she could smell her brain frying inside her skull when she thought about it—it was a sickly sweet marshmallowy kind of stink.

Mari had always been an amazingly stubborn kid. She'd shit all over herself for almost a year on a regular basic because Anoona and Hamm had refused to let her poop in a diaper once they'd started potty training. She'd hold it for days, and then when she couldn't keep it in anymore, the little angel would march right up to her mother, look her square in the eye, and open the floodgates of excrement. She claimed the toilet scared her, but she'd pee in the damn thing without so much of a second thought without even being asked. Hell, she'd sit on the potty for hours as long as there was no poop coming out of her butt. But the minute Anoona asked her to sit when the dirty duce was calling—to just try it—the tantrums that inevitably ensued were so epic that Mari would be shaking and hyperventilating uncontrollably before she finally calmed down—hours later with her bowels still full. And yet, Anoona would gladly trade that full year—maybe even longer—of shit tantrums, if her daughter would just consent to aborting the abomination growing inside her.

The little mother-to-be didn't seem to care where the thing had come from. And if she did, she clearly didn't care about how fucking horrible a person the father had been. The child inside her and the rape that put it there appeared to be completely unconnected in her mind. Anoona guessed this was because it had taken them so long to realize that she was pregnant. A fact that only added to her rage.

She blamed herself for that too—along with everything else that had happened that day and after. For the record though, none of the other survivors did—and the dead, well, they were dead so they kept their opinions to themselves. But even if they weren't, nobody in their right mind would have faulted her for missing the subtle signs of her daughter's pregnancy in all the chaos and grief.

Mari had just started menstruating only a few months before the blood pirates had shown up and all hell had broken loose. The little girl's soreness, cramps, fatigue, bizarre appetite—it all seemed perfectly reasonable after what had happened to her out in the woods. Until about the twelfth week, when it all had suddenly clicked in in the mind of Maddie Love—the fucking librarian. Her little ten-year-old girl was fourteen weeks along and clearly showing before Anoona herself was willing to accept the truth. Mari must have known for a while though. That much was clear from the moment they'd sat her down and spoken to her about it.

Though it shamed her deeply, Anoona simply didn't know how not to be angry about the whole thing. For months and months now, she just could not let it go. And she hated herself for it—maybe not as much as she hated the father of what would be her granddaughter, but it was a close race between the two.

She'd had the motherfuckers in her sights! That was the worst part of it. Had them dead to rights, but hadn't been able to pull the trigger. And it wasn't just that the bastards had caught up with and violated her daughter. Hamm had died too—he was dead because she'd sent him to do something she should have be capable of doing herself. *What kind of world do you think you live in, huh?* she asked herself. *Nobody gets to have clean hands here! You better learn how to kill more than just berserkers,* she told herself, *or you might as well just figure out how to kill yourself.*

And yet, she had the sinking feeling that when push came to shove, both killing somebody else and killing herself would remain out of her control—her fingers would be simply paralyzed on the trigger while everything she loved, worked for, and held dear was burned alive right before her eyes.

"You going to throw up again?" Bobby-Leigh asked Mari.

"No," Mari said. "Just heartburn."

"Well, enjoy it, kid. You chose this," Anoona heard herself say and was instantly mortified.

Mari said nothing in response, but she met her mom's eyes. Anoona could see the sting there—the hurt sat right next to that goddamn raw defiant strength always goading her, always cataloging her failures as a parent, as a human being.

Brennachecke's mouth tightened, as if he was biting on words of his own—words Anoona was sure she deserved, but was grateful not to have to hear. She wondered if he'd always been so reserved or if that was just part of his grief. *Just part of his grief! What the hell is wrong with you?* she screamed at herself inside her head. Why couldn't she stop these repulsive thoughts? Why couldn't she—

Bobby-Leigh subtly rolled her eyes, establishing, yet again, that she was on her daughter's side in all this—as if everybody didn't already know that.

Mari smiled back in acknowledgment of the support, mostly just with her eyes, but her mom saw it just the same. Anoona's train of thought derailed. She felt more words coming. Cruel words. Words she was embarrassed to even think, much less say. But this time—thank God—she was able to kept that bile down.

An awkward and tense silence filled the dining room.

Mari's defiant eyes remained locked on her mother's, as if daring her to release whatever curse she was holding back behind those clenched teeth. Tiny shot a sideways glance at Maddie, but Anoona couldn't read it. The lesbians, Rachel and Sarah, just kept their eyes on their food. Brennachecke gave Bobby-Leigh a look admonishing her for fanning the flames between the mother and daughter. Anoona could see the old soldier's opinion carried a lot of weight with the utterly inappropriately dressed girl, but instead of being grateful that at least somebody was actively trying to keep the peace, Anoona found herself cursing Jennifer Kessler for not waking up from her coma and drawing the attention away from how shittily she was handling all this.

But Jennifer didn't wake up.

Desperate to just retreat before she did any more damage to her relationship with her daughter, Anoona abruptly stood up, grabbed her nearly full plate, marched off to the kitchen, and dropped it into the sink.

A second later, everybody heard her bedroom door slam. A minute after that, everybody at the table heard Anoona start to sob and then strangle it back. It wasn't until they were all sure this wasn't the day she finally lost it that anybody dared to say a word.

* * * * *

"Are we ever going to fix that window?" Tiny asked, breaking the silence and with it the tension. As if they didn't know exactly what window he was referring to, everybody turned their heads and stared for a second at the boarded-up picture window overlooking the setting sun at the far end of the table—everybody except Bobby-Leigh, who had other things on her mind.

The window—broken out so Rodney's automated targeting rifle could be positioned to fire from it after the RPG had blown him and the sniper's nest they'd set up in the steeplelike *kalash* at the center of the *Sthapatya Veda* house to hell—was the last thing on the property that needed repair since the battle with the blood pirates had left them in tatters. They had a replacement standing by. They'd had it for almost three months. They'd probably be able to do it in half a day or less—especially if the snow let up.

And yet, they didn't.

It was as if it was somehow wrong for the house to fully recover before they had—not that any of them could have articulated the reason for the procrastination that clearly. As far as they were concerned, they weren't even procrastinating. Things just kept coming up.

"May I be excused?" Bobby-Leigh asked Brennachecke. It was an old habit from long ago, back before she'd survived being snatched at Walmart, back before she'd transitioned into her Goth-Lolita persona, back before her sister had killed the man's youngest son. It was a habit from the simpler days of the apocalypse. The good old days, when the death of Uncle Allen—whose dining room table they were all seated at—felt like it was the only death they'd have to mourn. Brennachecke's group had always eaten together from the first day they'd taken Bobby-Leigh and Jennifer in after their uncle had been murdered over a Diet Coke and a case of

Twinkies. It wasn't coat and tie or anything, but it was formal nonetheless, a testament to the old soldier's deathlike grip on the manners that held together our humanity. She couldn't give him back his sons, but she could at least pay homage to that.

"Of course," Brennachecke said.

Bobby-Leigh took her plate to the sink, but instead of putting the uneaten food into the compost bin, she added Anoona's uneaten meal to her own, plus anything else that she could get her hands on that wouldn't be missed.

And then, making sure nobody saw the plate, she slipped downstairs and into the room she shared with her still comatose berserker sister. She set the plate of food inside the top drawer of her dresser. She checked Jen's vitals on the monitor they'd salvaged from Jefferson County Hospital after the blood pirate attack. She checked the IV drip. The catheter. She rolled Jen's limp body over and wiped her down. She massaged and exercised the young woman's legs and arms. She rolled her on her left side for half an hour and then rolled her onto her right. Finally, after massaging her back, she fluffed the pillows that made sure her sister's head was elevated and gently laid her body back down. Bobby-Leigh spoke to Jen the whole time she was working with her. She used her name a lot. She did everything she was supposed to do before she went to sleep. Including getting into the twin bed next to her sister's and turning off the light on the nightstand between them.

But under her covers in the dark, with the soft *beep-beep* of her sister's machines trying to lull her to sleep, Bobby-Leigh was still fully dressed. Still fully awake. Patiently, she waited for the house to tuck in for the night, because before she could go to sleep herself, Bobby-Leigh had her secret to feed.

And she didn't want to get caught.

*   *   *   *   *

It was fucking snowing again—which wasn't exactly abnormal for the end of February in Iowa, except, of course, that this year winter had started in July and had lasted almost nine months straight so far. It just seemed only fair to Bobby-Leigh that if the ice and snow was going to show up two seasons earlier, it could have at least had the courtesy to go away earlier as well. But the insolence of postapocalyptic Mother Nature was the least of her problems at the moment.

Snow meant no moon, and it meant that she'd be leaving tracks. So, on top of the added risk of having to use a headlamp, she'd also be exposed longer because she'd have to drag that damn branch behind her to keep her secret a secret. In a nutshell, she was much more likely to get caught when she did this in these kinds of conditions. Being caught would be bad. Probably. Bobby-Leigh was positive that nobody would like what she was doing, but exactly what Anoona and Brennachecke would do if—when—they discovered her secret was a hard thing to predict.

Bobby-Leigh wrapped the rabbit-fur cloak Rachel and Sarah had made for her tighter against the wind and looked back over her shoulder to make sure all the lights in the house were still off.

They were.

Taking a deep breath, she grabbed the branch she had stowed away under the first row of the solar array and began her slow process of covering her tracks as she moved through the rows of panel-mounting frames toward where she was keeping her secret.

Technically she supposed, Anoona was in charge, so maybe it didn't matter what Brennachecke thought about it at all. Yet, ever since she'd brought Mari half-naked, violated, and freezing in from the woods, the African lady had not been the same. It seemed to Bobby-Leigh that she did not really want to be in charge anymore, but just didn't know how to give up the role. As far as the soon to be thirteen-year-old (not that anybody would remember that her birthday was in a month as long as her sister, who was probably the only one who actually knew anyway, was in a coma) could tell, losing so many of her friends—especially losing Mari's dad—had fucked the poor lady's whole world right up the ass. So maybe it didn't actually matter what Anoona would think if her little secret was discovered. Maybe it would be Brennachecke's call after all.

Who the fuck knew?

Either way, they'd probably just kill him, Bobby-Leigh guessed. If Jen would just wake the fuck up, then maybe she'd have one person on her side, but the rest of them—they're going to have a hard time seeing that her little secret was just as much a victim as anybody else in all this. She didn't really blame them for seeing the world that way. If Jennifer had been a normal girl—as opposed to a berserker—and Bobby-Leigh hadn't spent half her life learning firsthand that there was a very real human being entangled in the same flesh as the monster—she probably would have just murdered the poor bastard when she'd found him wandering—starving, freezing, and confused—through the solar array a few days after the war or battle or whatever the fuck you wanted to call it.

It was scary to think that her sister could one day be as fucked up as this guy was. Of course, she'd have to wake up first, and then probably berserk out a hundred more times, but as she pulled aside the stick and blanket woven door to the nest she and her secret had built and the monster inside smiled his ridiculous toothless grin up at her like a giant puppy, she knew this was what was waiting for Jen somewhere down her path. Maybe she'd be better off if she didn't wake up. That particular thought twisted Bobby-Leigh up inside every time she had it. And she had it a lot.

"Bah-Leh," the berserker said.

"Hey, Bobo," she responded with a smile of her own. She turned on the battery-powered lantern hanging from the ceiling of the woven branch dome. "You can turn on the light, as long as the door is shut, dude. Nobody'll see it."

"Bah-Leh!"

She'd named her little—well, not so little really—secret after their dog who had been torn apart by her sister a few years after they'd started living out here with Uncle Allen. That had been Jen's first time berserking out—and just about the worst birthday present the universe could have ever bestowed upon her.

Bobo had been just about as stupid and loyal an animal as dogs came. Her sister and the little guy had been inseparable even when they'd lived in Maine. Even when Mom had still been alive. So much so that Bobby-Leigh used to be jealous of them. Since Jen blacked out when the demon inside her came out, nobody really knows exactly what happened that day, but Bobby-Leigh remembered like yesterday the aftermath. Her sister stumbling up the steps—stupid birthday party hat still somehow on her head—covered in blood—too much blood for the little pug to have been the only victim—holding the dead dog in her arms and sobbing so hard her whole body was shaking and her entire face was smeared with blood-soaked snot.

Bobby-Leigh had screamed in terror at the sight. Neither girl had understood what was happening yet, but the thought of Uncle Allen finding out about whatever it was terrified them both even more than the questions they had. Bobby-Leigh had helped to clean Jen up. They'd buried the dog in the woods—not too far from where this new Bobo was hiding out—and told Uncle Allen it had run away. As far as Bobby-Leigh knew, her uncle had never known that Jen was a berserker.

"Foo? Foo? Ee?" the giant asked eagerly, gesturing with his hands.

Bobby-Leigh took the leftovers from the bag under her cloak and handed it to him. He very slowly, meticulously—almost daintily—started to eat. He'd eaten his food this way now for almost nine months, but for some reason, it still surprised her. The man's size just made it seem like he should snatch the food and devour it—inhale it—like the pug he was named after. It was impossible to know who Bobo had been before the blood pirates had gotten their hands on him, but the little girl was quite certain that if she'd known the man before the berserking-out-induced brain damage had locked his mind away, she'd have liked him just as much as a real person as she did as a pet. She'd had a soft spot for people who still bothered to be polite for as long as she could remember.

She spent about an hour with Bobo. Then, once she

was satisfied he was okay, she said her goodbyes and began her trek home. As she rounded the last of the mounting frames of the solar array, she stowed away the branch she'd been vigilantly dragging behind her to cover her tracks. She looked up at the house to confirm the coast was still clear and froze.

It was not.

There was a light on in the basement.

A single light.

Coming from her room.

Fuck fucking motherfuck!

* * * * *

Brennachecke was sitting on the chair next to Jen's bed when Bobby-Leigh came in. The little girl was so wrapped up in trying to come up with a viable excuse for why she was sneaking out at night that it wasn't until Jen actually spoke that she realized her sister had come out of her coma.

"Hey…" Jen said weakly, turning her head in Bobby-Leigh's direction.

The little girl stood there for a second as her brain switched gears.

Maybe my secret is still safe, she thought and immediately flushed with shame.

Maybe you should be focusing on the fact that your sister is awake!

"Hey" was all Bobby-Leigh got out of her mouth before the lump in her throat silenced her. She was still standing in the doorway half mesmerized like a rabbit caught by headlights about to be run over.

Brennachecke stood up and smiled cryptically.

"I'm guessing you can catch your sister up now that you're back, yeah?"

Bobby-Leigh nodded, still trying to figure out if she was busted or not. She walked into the room and took the seat the old soldier had just vacated.

"Is she okay?" Bobby-Leigh asked.

"I'm fine, dude."

Bobby-Leigh registered the near empty peanut butter jar on the nightstand and suddenly wondered how long her sister had been awake. She'd been gone for only a couple of hours checking on Bobo. At least she thought it had been only a couple of hours.

What time was it? she wanted to ask.

"How long have you been awake?" she asked instead.

It was Brennachecke who answered, and his answer neatly answered a number of the other questions bouncing around the girl's head like the balls in the old Atari game, Breakout. "She woke up about ten minutes after you stepped out for your nightly adventure," he said as he shut the door.

Ten minutes after—

He knew what time she'd left.

Nightly adventure—

He knew that she left most nights. The answers just raised more questions though. Did he know where she went? Or just that she left? Did he come in here and sit with Jen each night while she was gone? In the dark? Bobby-Leigh fought the urge to call him back in and find out how much he actually knew. Then suddenly, she realized that no matter how much he was aware of, her surrogate father had thus far kept it to himself. Her secret was safe. At least for now.

"Are you going to tell me your secret?" Jen asked.

"Brennachecke didn't already do that?"

"I don't think he knows it."

Bobby-Leigh looked her sister in the eye. For somebody who had been sleeping for almost nine months, she still looked tired. But it was Bobby-Leigh who was exhausted.

"I'm sorry I wasn't here when you woke up…"

Jen gave a weak shrug—it wasn't a big deal to her apparently.

"Is it a boy?"

"No!" Bobby-Leigh said incredulously, but then she thought about it. "Well, maybe technically, but not how you mean."

Jen waited. Bobby-Leigh smiled at her and then, using her sister's bed as support, laid her head down. Jen's hand patted her on the head. A second later, Bobby-Leigh felt her pigtails being pulled out. The little girl didn't realize it until then, but nobody had really touched her the whole time Jen was in the coma.

"God, I missed you," the little sister said.

Jen smiled. Bobby-Leigh took a deep breath that might have been a yawn in disguise.

"After the…fight, or whatever you want to call it, with those blood pirate assholes, things were really fucked up around here, you know? There were so many bodies. Everybody was just… I don't know."

Jen nodded.

"Mari was…"

Just from the way Jen's hand moved on her head, Bobby-Leigh somehow knew she didn't have to finish the sentence. Her sister knew the words she couldn't bring herself to say. Something about being so understood drove tears to the little girl's eyes, but she refused to let those tears out. And just in case, she kept her head down and her eyes aimed at the foot of Jen's bed.

"It's not your fault."

Bobby-Leigh knew that, but it was still nice to hear. "She's pregnant now, because of it and all. But she won't let her mom kill the baby."

Jen smiled. "Do you think she should?"

"It's not my baby."

"No…"

"Mari doesn't think that just because the father was bad, it means her little girl will be bad like him."

"But Anoona does?"

"I don' t know. I think maybe for Anoona it's more about constantly being reminded of what happened to her kid, than it is about any kind of fear that the baby will turn out to be some kind of bad seed."

"Yeah, I can see that." Jen smiled and nodded.

Bobby-Leigh couldn't see her sister's head or mouth, but she knew she'd done both just the same.

"Doesn't really matter anymore," Bobby-Leigh said through another yawn.

"Well, it might matter a little bit."

"I guess."

"What happened to Mari doesn't have anything to do with your secret, though, does it?"

"No. It's just that everything was so tense and…sad here, I needed to…I don't know…"

"A break."

"Yeah. I started walking in the woods to—"

"Clear your head."

"Yeah. That's when I found him."

"One of the blood pirate's berserkers?" It wasn't really a question. Jen was reading her mind the way only sisters can.

"He wasn't doing very good. Those guys really fucked him up, you know? He's like covered in scars—can't even really talk."

"Yeah."

"He's not dangerous…"

"I trust your judgment."

"Yeah, but you're probably the only one."

"I doubt that."

Bobby-Leigh rolled her head over so she could see her sister's face. "I named him Bobo."

Jen's eyebrows lifted—sister telepathy aside, she didn't see that one coming apparently.

"He's kind of more like a dog than a person."

Bobby-Leigh could see by the shadow that crossed behind her sister's eyes that Jen did not like the way she'd said that, but the little girl could not for the life of her understand why. It was true.

A long second or two ticked off in the silence that followed. If she closed her eyes now, Bobby-Leigh was pretty sure she'd be asleep before she could open them again. *What time is it?* she wondered for the second time.

"What does Hamm think about Mari wanting to keep the baby?"

"Hamm's dead, Jen."

The older girl exhaled hard, and Bobby-Leigh realized just how little her big sister actually knew. Even though it felt like cannonballs were hanging off her eyelids, the least she could do was catch Jen up before the sleep whisked her away into oblivion.

"So is Eric, Ace, JP, Rodger, Matt—only Maddie and Brennachecke, and well…us, made it from our…side. Anoona lost both Hamm and Rodney, but Tiny, Rachel and Sarah survived. Plus, her daughter obviously."

Jen blinked at the tears that started to well up in her eyes, but just like her little sister, she refused to allow them to escape. Bobby-Leigh smiled sleepily in condolence before she continued.

"The snow's been falling—off and on, mostly on—for months. Tiny's had to cut down the amount of power they use. We have to do most of the farming now by hand—the grow lights still work and all—so we have plenty of food, but the robot things, they just take too much juice. Me and Maddie do most of the planting and picking. Anoona has been sending the Rachel and Sarah out to burn down the town, the airport, Vedic City. Anywhere she thinks somebody might try to set up shop."

"Aren't there still people in town?"

Bobby-Leigh didn't know if she was going to make it through her report before nodding off if Jen was going to be interrupting her with questions, but she answered just the same.

"Well, the snow drove out most of them…but—I don't know. The ladies don't take me with them. Me and Bobo did get back to the Raj and found my knife—you know the one Beverly took."

Without lifting her head, Bobby-Leigh slipped her hand behind her back and pulled the karambit—bear claw—knife Uncle Allen had given her out from its secret hiding place and waved it at her sister.

"You took your berserker friend back to Vedic City?"

She'd drawn the weapon in less than a second, but now it took her at least ten times as long to get it sheathed back in its hiding spot.

Fuck, she was tired.

"The blood pirates are gone, Jen—the place is a ghost town. Or was—Sarah and Rachael salvaged all the solar and guns and whatnot they could get. And then burned it—the Raj, all the houses, everything—burned it all to the ground a day or two after I found my knife…"

"Jesus."

"Yeah. Now, the only problem with nobody being left around is that Tiny's doctor assist app thingy says that Mari's pregnancy is high risk. And just the other day, they found out the baby is upside down, or sideways or something, so now Tiny is trying to find an actual doctor who can deliver the baby—but so far no luck. Maddie might have to do deliver the kid, though Tiny says that if they can't find a doctor, he'll write a special app just for the pregnancy and birth and all. But Anoona is kind of freaking out at that idea. Though for some reason the idea of Maddie delivering it isn't something she's willing to consider either."

"Why would Maddie be the one to deliver the baby?"

"I guess she used to be a midwife or something, before she was the librarian or whatever—" Bobby-Leigh closed her eyes and was asleep before she could finish her sentence.

Jen didn't wake her.

*　　*　　*　　*　　*

Nothing was funny, but Jennifer Kessler found herself struggling to keep from bursting out laughing. She supposed it was nerves. Awkwardness. The tension at the breakfast table was ridiculous. She thought—almost without exaggeration—that Anoona's head might actually explode if the mom ever made eye contact with her daughter for more than a second.

Has it been like this for nine months? Jesus Christ on a cracker.

But there was more going on than the *keep the baby, kill the baby* tension between Mari and her mom. Clearly, Anoona's people blamed her for what had befallen their friends. If the woman's head was going to explode upon eye contact with her daughter, then Tiny's head was just as likely to explode if the fat man looked at Jen too long.

"I am sorry," she said, not really sure what she had left to apologize for at this point, but sure anything she said would be better received prefaced with those three words. Before she could get anything else out she was cut off by Tiny.

"You should be," the big man said under his breath, but more than loud enough for everybody at the table to hear him. Her sister wasn't up yet. Rachel and Sarah were in the kitchen making coffee. So the only additional folks seated at the table were Brennachecke and Maddie—who, while they might hold Jen responsible for some of the mayhem that had happened here, should at least be on her side a little bit. Of course, Brennachecke had lost another son. And Maddie was a genius when it came to keeping out of postapocalypse politics.

Again, she fought the urge to laugh, but she felt a nervous smile sprout on her lips like a weed. Jen aimed her nervous smile at Tiny, trying to force it to be disarming, more than dismissive, but she was less than confident she'd pulled it off. This was the first time the dude had spoken to her since she'd woken up. She looked at Anoona, and suddenly her nervousness melted away in the heat of a burst of anger.

This was her fucking house, goddamn it.

"I'm sorry you lost people. But we lost people too—a lot more people than you guys did, I might add. Not that I'm keeping score—that's not the point. The point is that you guys weren't even supposed to be here. This is *my* house. My family's farm. Brennachecke's people—my people—came here because they knew my sister and I had nowhere else to go but *home*. So if you want to blame somebody for what happened here—any of it—you best find a mirror and—"

"That's enough," Brennachecke said curtly.

"This is my goddamn house!" Jen screamed.

Anoona stood up and pounded her fists into the table. Everybody looked at her, expecting her to say something or just pull a gun out and put a bullet in Jen's face, but she didn't do either one. Jen met her eyes and saw that she wasn't really upset at anybody but herself. Anger and grief and frustration. Guilt and fear. Hate. It was all burning the African lady up from the inside as if she'd swallowed some kind of emotion-safe bleach in an attempt to get those dark bloodstains out of her heart.

"You are all welcome here. Obviously. But it's my house," Jen said softly. "So I have a right to be here, too. That's all I'm saying." She said those last words while looking unflinchingly into Tiny's eyes. The man quickly looked down—not exactly in shame or apology like Jen wanted, but at least he'd blinked first.

"I think you need some coffee," Rachel said from the kitchen.

"Come on in here and we'll get you a cup," her better half said.

Grateful for an excuse to leave the table without losing face, Jen headed for the kitchen. Sarah smiled at her and handed her a cup.

"How do you take it?" Rachel asked.

"A few months ago, I could've offered you a splash of bourbon," Sarah said. "I had a whole distillery set up in one of the sheds…"

"We have fake creamer and sugar though, if you want. Tiny might even be hording a bottle of Kahlúa."

"I could've really gone for a splash of coffee in my bourbon," Jen said as deadpan as she could—just to see where it would land with them.

The two women smiled at each other as if to say: *See, we knew you were one of the good ones.*

Jen appreciated the vote of confidence—though she had absolutely no intention of fucking up her coffee with booze or anything else.

Sarah sighed. "As soon as we get a chance to breathe again, I'm going to start a new batch."

"Yummy. In the meantime, I guess I'll just take my coffee black," Jen said.

Rachel nodded her approval.

Jen took a sip and felt the rich caffeinated bite of the black liquid in her head almost immediately.

"Fuck me…" she said with a smile. "I haven't had good coffee in a long-ass time."

"We cleaned Café Paradiso out before we torched the square. They roasted the beans on site apparently. We took the roaster too, so, as long as the beans last, I'm roasting it—"

"Let me guess—in one of the sheds out back?" Jen asked, trying to be funny. Apparently, this time it wasn't.

"Tiny doesn't approve, but—"

"Roaster runs off propane, so he can go fuck himself," Sarah said, finishing her partner's sentence.

Jen was happy to hear that somebody else was annoyed

with the big geek, but she was still flying with her shields up after her last attempt at humor fell flat.

"Yeah, he seems like more of Red Bull kind of guy," Jen offered—again trying to be funny and again missing the mark. Jen suddenly realized that this wasn't a social gathering. The women wanted something from her.

"So…as you can see, we're not exactly operating on full power here. The weather has been…" Sarah didn't bother finishing the sentence.

Rachel cut to the chase. "We were hoping you could learn some of the tech side of things from Tiny, since as it stands, he's pretty much got a monopoly on that kind of knowledge."

"But maybe that's not—" Sarah started to say nervously.

"I would love to learn some tech shit."

"You sure?" Rachel asked.

"I got nothing against Tiny," Jen said.

"Yeah, but he's definitely got something against—"

Jen smiled and cut Rachel off. "We'll figure it out." The determination in her voice closed the discussion like the banging of a gavel.

*   *   *   *   *

The grow house was not nearly as impressive without the robots running, in the same way a fighter plane is not nearly as impressive as a space shuttle. Maddie noticed how Jen couldn't help herself from looking over at the two squid-like farming drones collecting dust in the corner.

Of course, she's curious, Maddie thought, *she's never actually seen them in action.*

Maddie had of course. But even she'd only witnessed the place at full automation for a few days.

Then Jen and Bobby-Leigh had shown up, and the blood pirates came. Lots of people of died, and the snow just kept falling. Power needed to be saved. Planting and picking started being done by hand.

Anoona had made it clear from day one she did not like midwives. She thought the whole idea of the anti-hospitalization, empowering of mothers to control their birth experiences movement that she associated with the practice was just a barbaric holdover from the dark ages. She'd insisted it was barely a step above dancing naked in the woods and communing with the devil. As far she was concerned, so long as there was modern medicine to make the whole process scientific and sterile, Maddie's professional thoughts on Mari's pregnancy were as unwelcome as the pregnancy itself. The old librarian and former midwife apprentice had turned to the crops as a way to soothe her mind. And to keep from slapping the woman in the face for being sucked in so completely by the medical-industrial complex that given a choice between practical experience and some fucking app, Anoona was going with the app.

Idiot!

However, as frustrating as Anoona's position was for her, Maddie was really more lonely at this point than she was mad. Bobby-Leigh was so emotionally guarded that even though she was mature well beyond her years, it was pretty obvious that the only person she'd ever truly be honest with or open up to was her sister.

So, as she watched Jen utterly failing at planting seed, she was sorry to see that the teenager hated tending the crops so much she couldn't be bothered to do it right.

Somewhere in a secret corner of her heart she'd been fantasizing about becoming the sisters' surrogate mother. For all the time Bobby-Leigh and she spent together, she'd never been able to forge that kind of bond with the little girl. She'd hoped that if Jen was with her here—working together, laughing together, learning together—that maybe there'd be a chance for that relationship to finally develop. She'd hoped that with Jen's help, her sister would open up to her.

But that was clearly never going to happen.

She'd overheard Sarah and Rachel suggest Jen learn to program and build computer systems from Tiny. Maddie hated to admit it, but if there was a skill set the group needed to double up on, that was certainly a higher priority one. If Jen had enjoyed working out here with them it'd be one thing, but considering that now after only an hour of tending the crops, any second thoughts the teenager had had about whether or not it was worth it to try to get Tiny to be her mentor had clearly wilted and died, and the robots were the only thing in the place that really seemed to interest her at all, Maddie could see the writing on the wall. Jen would do just about anything to never have to come back here and push another seed into the mesh they used instead of soil again. She might as well have had a neon sign on her ass that said, *Farming sucks*.

"So…this is what you do all day?" Jen asked her sister.

"Yep. Kind of relaxing, right?"

"Right…"

Maddie smiled at the older girl sadly and with a deep breath let her dream go.

"This isn't a job you have to do, dear," Maddie said softly. "I know Rachel and Sarah think you should probably be learning something else."

"You don't like this, Jen?" Bobby-Leigh asked. It was hard to tell if the little girl was hurt or not by that possibility.

"I wouldn't put it that way," Jen said.

"Really," Maddie chided. "How would you put it then?"

"I'd say I fucking hate it. And you two are B-A-N-A-N-A-S, bananas, if you seriously like this shit."

Bobby-Leigh smiled and then laughed. Maddie thought it might be the first time she'd ever actually heard her do that, but it couldn't be.

"Quitter. You're just too lazy to do real work," Bobby-Leigh said, clearly joking.

"That's why God invented little sisters, so us bigger ones didn't have to get their hands dirty."

"Okay, you can leave now," Bobby-Leigh said, still laughing.

"Doesn't mean that I don't love you," Jen said over her shoulder on her way out as she left.

Maddie looked at Bobby-Leigh, unsure if her laughing and smiling was an act or not. But the younger of the sisters seemed genuinely okay with the older one's rejection. If that even was what that had been.

They worked in silence for a while, pushing new seed into the plastic mesh tray by tray, sliding the trays into their slots in the light racks, and mixing the nutrient solutions specific to the kind of plant for the feeder tanks.

"We should try oats," Maddie said, as much to herself as to Bobby-Leigh.

"That'd be cool," the girl said. Then after a beat, she added, "Maddie?"

"Yes, dear."

"What's preeclampsia?"

"It's a condition that sometimes happens during pregnancy, where the mom-to-be gets very high blood pressure and has some protein where it shouldn't be."

"Is it dangerous?"

"It can be. But we'll just keep an eye on Mari and watch for signs that her liver and kidneys are having trouble. She'll be okay." Maddie hoped that Bobby-Leigh couldn't see through this load of bullshit. Fact was there was so much that had already gone sideways in Mari's pregnancy at this point that she wasn't confident the dear would be okay at all.

But Maddie was not about to lay the burden of that on her.

"How would we know if she was…in trouble?"

"Well, if she had seizures for example. Or started having issues with her vision or difficulty breathing. Those would be signs we'd need to get the baby out of her."

Bobby-Leigh swallowed hard.

"So if she, like, started to not be able to see or something."

"Exactly. But she's doing fine, right?"

The girl smiled instead of answering.

At the time, Maddie hadn't thought much of it. It wasn't until much later, in hindsight, that she'd be kept up late into the night wondering what might have happened if she'd realized Bobby-Leigh had known more than she had let on that day. If she'd only realized that this whole conversation had really been a cry for help.

And Maddie had missed it.

Chapter Three
Miracles of Science

THE DAWN LIGHT WAS THICK and orange through the tiny windows lining the room Emmett woke up in. He was lying on his back on a bench—a bench that was attached to the wall. The wall was concrete, and the bench just as hard. He took a moment—just staring at the ugly ceiling—and tried to keep his head above the murky-watered tsunami of disorientation that was crashing over him.

He knew he was in a cell in Jasper, Texas. But that wasn't helpful because he also knew—was absolutely certain, in fact—that he hadn't fallen asleep on the bench he was now lying on. He had no memory of where he'd gone or how he'd gotten back, but there was no shaking the conviction that he'd been outside the concrete walls of his cell.

His head hurt. Even in the haze, the shafts of light streaming in were too bright for him. But when he finally gave up squinting against them and simply closed his eyes, the pain behind his temples didn't subsist in the slightest. His skin was uncomfortably tight around the flesh behind his ear. Tentatively, he touched it.

Ouch.

Like a man in a blizzard, he followed the guide rope of pain from the swollen flesh around his ear back to his temples.

He'd been hit.

Hard.

It took another second, but in a sudden flash, he recalled Black Jesus slamming his weapon into the back of his head—and a breath later, everything else that had come before he'd been knocked out swept back into his consciousness.

Fuck. Faaaaahck!

The dried blood in his hair flaked off like rotten dandruff, as he continued to gingerly explore the tender goose egg on the side of his head, assessing the damage. But the injury to his head was not the damage he needed to be concerned about and he knew it. Emmett Kessler had much bigger issues now.

He'd missed.

His one chance to avenge the world—his wife—and he'd missed. But as disappointing as that was, his frustration—not unlike the throbbing bump behind his ear—was not the most pressing issue.

What really mattered was that Black Jesus was going to have a significantly less than positive reaction to his attempted assassination of the doctor. Emmett knew he'd better start preparing himself for it, but found he couldn't even remotely predict what the man's reaction was going to entail—except that it was going to be bad.

Really bad.

Replaying the scene in his head over and over, he felt pretty confident that Waters wouldn't be able to figure out that his plan had been to kill the man the whole time—which, of course, it had been. His murder attempt had gone down so spontaneously, he thought—or at least hoped—he'd get lucky and be able to convince his guardian the whole thing had just been temporary insanity.

It had felt insane at the time. The doctor should have been well over a hundred years old, and yet the man he'd just tried to kill hadn't looked a day older than twenty-five. And yet, there was no doubt it'd been Dr. Weiss.

Unless...maybe it could have been his grandson.

Fuck.

But, no. Mr. Smalls had confirmed it was the man himself, not some spitting image progeny. Smalls had also claimed to be—what? Sixty years old himself? And yet that man didn't look any older than Weiss had.

So yeah, temporary insanity seemed like a more than reasonable excuse. Surely, Black Jesus wouldn't crucify him over it.

Right?

Emmett's head hurt even more now that his brain was humming in his busted skull, but he opened his eyes and sat up anyway.

Wiley DuPont was sitting across from him. The big man smiled his big toothless grin and gave him a little wave.

"Welcome back," Wiley said clearly.

Emmett, still groggy and distracted by his thoughts, missed that the singsong, brain-damaged-induced, Mother-Goosification of words he'd come to associate with Beast's language seemed to have vanished. But as soon as the man followed the salutation up, the change was impossible to miss.

"You've been." Wiley began searching hard for the right word. "Out." His speech was halting and clearly took a fair amount of effort, but it was clear and sparkled with an intelligence Emmett had always known was in there, but had never actually seen. "For a long time. Two days. Almost," he continued. "The…Texans. They said you didn't need…medical attention. I wasn't so sure. I am glad you aren't dead," Wiley stumbled through saying and smiled.

Emmett gawked at the huge man. He opened his mouth, but no words came out, so he closed it again.

What the fuck was going on?

Maybe insanity was more than just an excuse for his behavior. And maybe it wasn't so temporary. Because if Emmett knew anything at all, he knew that when it came to berserkers, exorcisms did not work. How many priests had tried to save folks with that mystical religious mumbo-jumbo over the years? Had to be in the tens of thousands. He personally remembered at least a hundred of them popping into his news feed at some point before he'd been sent to prison. And that was back when folks were still pretending the shit hadn't already hit the fan. They'd all ended the same way. Death. The berserker always—*always*—remained.

If there was a God, she either didn't care or simply was not powerful enough to remove these particular demons with just the power of a bunch of poor folk's faith and some silly rituals in Latin to work with. And even if the exorcism had somehow worked—which it absolutely should not have—and the demon inside Wiley who had been christened "Beast" was now actually gone, that kind of brain damage was irreversible.

Wasn't it?

Fuck.

He wondered, as he searched Wiley DuPont's eyes for answers that he knew weren't there, if maybe he'd actually gotten this whole thing wrong.

*   *   *   *   *

When the door had opened on his fully restored and well-maintained room at the Swann Hotel just a few blocks from the sheriff's office, Captain Waters hadn't been able to stop himself from smiling. The collection of antique furnishings that had resided in the common areas downstairs continued up here in his room. Their level of restoration was far from perfect, but all things considered, he would have been happy with a bench in the cell next to the one he'd left Emmett's unconscious body in.

Now, Waters was sitting on an actual bed surrounded by the past like it was something quaint and cuddly—instead of something torn violently off, like the leg of someone unlucky enough to fall in front of one of those giant corn-harvesting combine tractors. Most cats these days were trying so desperately to shut out that trauma, they'd gladly deny the bulk of human history if it meant they could silence the pain that still screamed at them like the sensation of that phantom limb.

Or so he'd thought.

Texas, it seemed, had not turned its back on antiquity in favor of base survival like the rest of the places they'd passed through. Here there was a plan. A system. And he could access it all just by putting on the glasses sitting—still in their box, unopened—on his nightstand. He knew why he couldn't bring himself to do it. But that didn't explain why he'd been sitting there for hours, as unmoving as a garden gnome. He had so many questions that even his questions had questions of their own. Answers to most of them were within easy reach. Yet, even as the dawn's early light slunk across the edge of the horizon, he couldn't bring himself to take the glasses out and put them on.

He couldn't do it because the one question that had to be answered before he did anything else didn't have an answer in those glasses—for all the magic of technology held within those slender frames.

What the hell was he going to do about Emmett Kessler?

He should have killed him the second he picked up that shotgun outside the prison, he told himself. But as satisfying as the thought was, Waters knew that putting a bullet in Emmett's head was not something he was ready to do—yet.

This was where the social contract between guard and prisoner got murky. Back before it all fell to shit, he'd never had to give something like this so much as a second of thought. His contractual, if not moral, obligation would have ended with writing up the offense for the assistant warden. Somebody else would have had decided what an appropriate response would be—sure, more often than not punishments for this kind of shit were rather medieval. Solitary confinement. Added time. Shipment off to a higher security facility. But whatever it was, it was somebody else's call.

But not today.

Today, it was his and his alone.

The attempt had been unsuccessful. That had to be factored in. Of course, the only reason Kessler had missed was because Waters himself had personally fowled his aim, so maybe it was a mistake to dwell on the distinction between attempted murder and its uglier, bloodier pal actual murder.

What the hell am I supposed to do with you, you son of a bitch?

Over the months on the road, Waters had gotten comfortable enough with Kessler to bounce his thoughts off him on a regular basis. The man—for all his faults—was one hell of a sounding board most of the time. When he could tell a cat needed to puzzle some mess out, he'd kept his personal opinions at bay and just worked the problem of whatever was bothering you. It was like talking to yourself, only less crazy and more productive. Kessler had played cheerleader to him through his days of doubts. He'd played Socrates to his most ill-conceived convictions and worst biases, pulling them gently to their fucked-up conclusions until Waters could see for himself how problematic they were. Just like spellcheck had eroded away a cat's ability to spell, and smartphones had cannibalized people's ability to write a legible sentence by hand—Waters realized that he'd grown so accustomed to puzzling out shit with Kessler, that he was actually handicapped now that Kessler himself was the shit that needed to be puzzled out.

Worse, Waters genuinely liked the motherfucker and would frankly miss him if he was no longer in his life. The punishment for—no, not punishment. Punishments didn't do shit. The evidence was very clear on that. The *consequences* of Kessler's actions had to keep him from trying it again. Had to at least make him think twice about it. Had to as a minimum make the idea of doing something to the doctor worse than the idea of letting his revenge plot go.

What the hell could possibly do that?

Waters honestly hadn't ever thought they'd find the doctor in in the first place. After all, how much stock could you really put in research done by an inmate in prison while the sky was falling? He hadn't even had access to the real Internet; he'd been on the crippled TRULINCS version of the damn thing. But, even if he *had* given Emmett enough credit to allow that his information might have been spot on, the doctor was over a fucking century old—there was just no reasonable expectation that the cat would still be alive.

He looked at the glasses on the nightstand again. How was the man still alive? How did he look like he was in his twenties and wasn't mummified like King Tut? How had he managed to actually exorcise the berserker they'd all come to know as the Beast from Wiley DuPont? All of those questions had answers he could actually get to if he wanted to.

The glasses were right there.

Maybe if he filled in some of the smaller, less important gaps he'd be able to think up an appropriate consequence for his friend's betrayal. And even if he didn't, at least he'd get a break from thinking about it.

Waters sighed and reached for the box. He took the glasses out and tossed the box back on the nightstand.

The things were lighter than he expected. They had two small round sensors of some type on each of the earpieces, but other than that, they looked more or less like the same geek-chic eyewear you'd have expected to find on any of the startup CEOs of Silicon Valley before the Bay Area had torn itself apart.

There were two small buttons on the top of the left eye rim, but nothing happened when he pressed either of them as far as he could tell.

There was what had to be a camera the size of a pin-head on the rim of the right eye and what looked like a bunch of pinholes on the lower insides of the frames around the lenses, but nothing else stood out as potentially having a function.

Reluctant to get out the instructions from the box for reasons he didn't even bother wondering about, he thought he'd try them on to see if that made a difference.

It didn't.

He pressed the buttons again with the glasses on his face. Neither button seemed to do anything. He took turns holding each button down for five seconds, but still got nothing.

"Goddamn it," he muttered and grabbed the box with the instructions in it. But suddenly a logo he wasn't familiar with appeared in his field of vision, and he hear a soft chime ring. The logo vanished a second later.

He waited.

Waters was already impressed by the immersive feeling of how the logo was superimposed over his normal field of view, like it was just floating subtly about four feet away as tangible as the box he still held in his hand, though still obviously not part of "reality." But as the seconds ticked off and nothing else happened, he started wondering if maybe he needed to do something else to make the damn things work.

A message suddenly appeared about the same place the logo had twenty seconds ago. As soon as his eyes shifted to focus on it, a smooth rose petal of a voice softly whispered in his head: *"Please do not remove me. I am calibrating."*

The words vanished when the voice spoke the last one. And three colored dots jumped around his field of view for a few seconds.

"Please move the red focus point to the right," appeared as text, immediately followed by that voice in his head.

"Ah," Waters began, but before he could articulate that he had no idea how to do that, the dots disappeared. A second later, they appeared again, this time on the other side of the room.

"Please move the red focus point to the right."

Sighing and feeling like an idiot for not understanding what the hell the instructions were asking him to do, he tried just looking at the red dot in the center, but the second he did, the three dots disappeared again.

What the fuck?

Another second later, they appeared a third time along with the command text and soft voice. Waters found his eyes going to the middle red dot again, and just as he was about to say something about how he needed help, the dot moved to the right.

"Thank you. Calibration complete," chimed the voice in his head as the same words popped up in the spot he'd already been conditioned to expect them.

"Okay," Waters said. "Now what?"

As if in answer to his question, a heads-up display appeared with a magnifying glass icon and a gear icon. Without even realizing he'd done it, he looked at the magnifying glass icon, and suddenly a search bar popped up out of nowhere and the search term "glasses reading mind" appeared.

What happened next made Waters laugh out loud like a little boy seeing a magic trick for the first time. His field of view was instantly overlaid with a multimedia presentation so specific, so polished, that it was hard to believe it was being created on the fly by a bunch of computer code, and not some veteran A-list Hollywood producer.

Answers came in clips and flashes as if he'd stepped into the memories of the cats who'd actually been there. He'd never experienced anything quite like it.

Yes, the glasses were reading his mind—sort of. In a video clip, Elijah Dyer himself walked through an animated diagram explaining how the technology worked on some stage somewhere fancy as if he were Steve Jobs unveiling the iPhone at Macworld half a century ago.

The sensors on the edge of the earpieces were monitoring key electrical signals in his brain, and the Registry, which apparently held extensive brain mapping data on top of everything else, used something called Biometric Adaptive Soft Logic Algorithms to process the data. Because the system was networked with every citizen of the Republic of Austin, plus quite a few noncitizens, it was constantly getting better and better at displaying exactly what information the user wanted almost as fast as they could think about wanting to know it. The Registry's super-quantum processors were able to simultaneously learn a person's individual inquiry patterns, while at the same time use that data to catalog broader themes on a more universal scale. Every device connected to the network was continuously recording, not just the audio and video information, but the very thought patterns that went with the responses to whatever was being seen and heard.

The system was for all intents and purposes an artificial collective consciousness. For Captain Waters, it felt like having God whispering in his ear—only better. He could actually see what God was talking about with his own eyes.

He found himself transformed instantaneously into a glutton for information. He'd been in the dark so long, there were whole mountains of shit he didn't know—didn't even know he could know. Emmett's betrayal and the turmoil the Captain had been struggling with quickly fell away to the simple wonder of the experience.

Austin had been saved—in the Christian sense as much as the practical one—by the man Elijah Dyer, the CEO and founder of Lone Star Dynamics. The Registry quickly found clips and quotes to fill in the gaps left from what Sinclair had told him. Lone Star Dynamics had done a lot more than just create the Registry and the system to access it. In fact, the Registry hadn't even been LSD's primary focus. Elijah Dyer was obsessed with nanotechnology. With combining wet biological nanotech—bacteria-based engines that used naturally occurring life processes to modify DNA—with *Drexlerian* assemblers—remotely programmable mechanosynthesis machines that 3-D print at the atomic level.

Waters's head hurt from all the scientific details, but the gist of it came through loud and clear. Dyer's company was focused on making robots small enough to go into human cells and repair, change, and create the very DNA that made humanity human.

But the man's breakthroughs had come at an enormous cost. It seemed that long before the berserker threat had shut down the countries of the world, there had been no shortage of desperate politicians who'd been more than willing to ship their state's monsters to Lone Star Dynamics to be experimental fodder. And when the threat *had* started to shut governments down one by one, LSD had branched out from experimenting on berserkers to experimenting on everybody else. Over the course of the decade that Emmett spent in prison, tens of thousands of people had died in LSD's trials. And the poor cats had not just passed away quietly in the night either. They'd died hard and loud and ugly.

Waters was a little shocked to find all this so clearly spelled out, and unapologetically at that, in the Registry. He'd have thought that the company who built the thing would have at least tried to hide its crimes against humanity a little bit. But it seemed the opposite had actually happened. And it had turned out to be quite the genius public relations move because it was that unprecedented level of disclosure that was generally credited across the Registry for being how Elijah Dyer had gotten away with it all. Waters was pretty damn sure that had the world not been falling apart around everybody's heads, things would have gone quite a bit differently.

But then again maybe not.

From day one, the marketing message from Lone Star Dynamics was that the company's nanotechnology was the product of divine inspiration. God himself—or at least his number one angel—had spoken to Elijah Dyer and bequeathed unto him the secret to life everlasting and the means to create heaven on Earth. Before the Shibuya Incident nobody had really taken Dyer's claims very seriously, but after—well, after the world watched live as Tokyo had been ripped apart by what sure looked like demon-possessed people, whole movements of Christians lined up to volunteer as test subjects for Dyer's experiments. Downplaying the failures, LSD heralded the times when the man's methods got results. It proved to be an extremely effective promotion scheme.

The utter chaos of ever increasing berserker incidents and steadily decreasing authority of the government left so much confusion and so much fear in its wake that the seed which would eventually blossom into the Republic of Austin had already begun to sprout by the time Dallas was incinerated in a nuclear explosion—the origin of which officially remained unknown, but which was widely thought to have been detonated by a (rogue) LSD employee. The idea that Elijah Dyer and his team at Lone Star Dynamics had been sent by God to separate the wheat from the chaff and build heaven on Earth eventually didn't seem crazy at all anymore. Nobody batted an eye when Dyer christened his nanotechnology, "Grace."

It was Grace that not only stopped the aging process but actually reversed it. Grace was responsible for the exorcism of the berserker demons from their hosts. Grace was self-replicating. Ubiquitous. And Grace was under the complete control of Lone Star Dynamics. Every citizen of the Republic had swarms of Grace inside them. But that wasn't were it ended. Grace was remotely linked to the Registry just like the glasses were. It was continually sending in data to LSD's servers, and just like the system used to interact with the Registry, Grace was becoming better and more efficient at what it could it do with every second.

Captain Waters thought about that and shuddered. Suddenly, he wondered if Wiley might have been better off simply remaining Beast. He'd had no idea this kind of technology even existed, especially in the world as it was today. The idea of an exorcism had seemed completely benign when Sinclair had dictated that the only way for Wiley to remain in Texas was to have one performed on him. A harmless little ritual to keep the peace with the fanatics he'd found himself surrounded by. But now, the poor bastard was full of Grace, and Waters didn't believe for one second that God had anything to do with it. Even though he'd seen with his own eyes how effectively it had snipped the berserker genes out of his prisoner's DNA, that didn't make it a blessing. Grace could be changing anything inside the man now. The very fact that nobody seemed to be questioning any of this was probably in itself evidence that—Captain Waters just couldn't bring himself to keep calling it Grace, even in his own head—the nanofuckers were changing other things, dopamine or serotonin delivery maybe—hell, anything was possible. Lone Star Dynamics could very well have—in addition to all the breakthroughs he'd just learned about—managed to actually turn religion into an opiate for the masses.

Just how much influence did the company have over the citizens of the Republic who had been saved by Grace? Had free will finally been shackled here? Then he suddenly wondered something even worse.

Did it even really matter if it had?

This place was working in a way the rest of the world, as far as he could tell, was not. Cats didn't really seem worse off for having been saved. And they didn't seem like blindly obeying robots either. There was still clearly some kind of free will in play.

Maybe.

The questions lodged in his craw like shrapnel, tearing apart any sense of wonder at the accomplishment and twisting everything into doubt and fear.

The software in the glasses took a second to respond as his mind spun nearly out of control with conspiracy theories and Kafkaesque plots, but eventually respond it did, and for the second time in the hour, Waters was taken aback by the transparency of everything LSD seemed to be doing.

Yes, the nanobots were capable of altering moods and maybe even exerting some minor influences on one's behavior. But higher level thought processes and personality traits were beyond their control. They could encourage you to eat, by triggering hunger, or discourage you from overeating by temporarily shutting the hunger trigger off. Likewise, they could push you away from ordering a hamburger and toward a salad, by turning on cravings for fresh vegetables and off ones for red meat. They could make it harder for you to get angry and easier for you to be happy, but they could not make you angry or happy in and by themselves. A distinction that, while certainly important, utterly failed to quell Captain Waters's apprehensions.

"A man's soul forever will—in this kingdom and the next—always belong unto him," the Registry told him. *"Though the Lord's Grace calls the chosen home into the light, every man must still choose to enter the Kingdom of Heaven for himself."*

Waters removed the glasses from his head and rubbed his eyes. He needed a break. Actually, he thought, what he really needed was a stiff drink. But, since he didn't have one of those readily available, he'd settle for a break. One thing was clear to him. It was time to get the fuck out of Texas.

Knock. Knock. Knocky-knock.

Somebody was at this door. He found himself reflexively checking the time on the antique grandfather clock that stood sentry between the two windows of his room, not because it really mattered what time it was, but simply because old habits die hard. It was a little after seven in the morning though. Still pretty early for a social call. Nonetheless, he answered the door.

"Yes?" Waters asked through the wood, his hand already on the knob and turning. He expected it to be Sinclair coming to tell him that Emmett was awake and causing a problem, or maybe that Wiley's body had rejected the nanobot sludge in the sacramental wine and the man had died during the night thanks to his CO stupidly not asking enough questions.

But it wasn't Sinclair at the door.

It was the old lady from the exorcism.

And she wasn't alone.

* * * * *

He was so big. So...amazingly big. Wiley could not stop looking at his overdeveloped arms. His barrel of a chest. His tree trunk thick thighs. *Just how many times did I berserk out?* he wondered quietly to himself.

Emmett was lost in his own thoughts, and the big man didn't want to disturb him, but as his head cleared more and more, he found himself with so many questions. He didn't know how much longer he'd be able to keep it all inside.

For over a decade, he'd experienced the world as though he was underwater. Dirty water, where the visibility was next to nothing. The information that got through his wrecked mind was blurred. Distorted. Often lost before he could really process it. Like so many men and women with a brain impairment, he kept as much of his confusion as he could to himself. It was his own private shame and frustration. Embarrassment, it seemed, was a much lower cerebral function than a brother might think. His sense of mental inadequacy was not one of the things the brain damage that went along with berserking out had lessened. But now through the Grace of God, he was returning to his old self. He was actually thinking again.

Thinking and articulating those thoughts with words other people could actually hear though were two completely different things. He'd been a little taken aback by how hard it'd been to speak to Emmett. He'd known what he wanted to say, but it was like the train that carried the words through the tunnels of his brain and out of his mouth kept getting derailed en route.

Why did we come to Texas?

That was what he wanted to ask. The question had been in his head for months. But he'd never been able to get it out.

What the fuck are we doing here?

He thought it must be because either Emmett or Black Jesus had known they would be able to find God's Grace here. They must have come for him. But all the snippets of his two companions' conversations that had made it through his broken brain over the last nine months told him that it was something else. But nothing else made any sense to Wiley. He wanted to ask, but he was afraid. Afraid of the answer, and also afraid of sounding like a retard again.

Please, God. I know I have no right to ask for anything more after the miracle you've all but just performed, but help me find my voice again. Please don't let me look stupid in the eyes of my friend, he prayed to himself and then spoke.

"Emmett, may I ask you a question?" Wiley felt tears of gratitude welling up in his eyes as he heard the words coming out of his mouth. Clean and clear. *The Lord's mercy has no bounds*, he thought as Emmett lifted his head to look at him.

The two men just looked into each other's eyes for a long moment. Then finally Emmett answered.

"Yeah, dude. Ask away."

"Did you and Captain Waters come to Texas so that I could be saved?"

Emmett chuckled and shook his head.

Wiley could tell that the man was not laughing at him. In fact, it was pretty clear that the man's little laugh was one of wonder. Suddenly, Wiley felt a laugh of his own slipping out of his mouth. And before either man knew what was happening, they were both cackling like a bunch of mental patients on a field trip to the zoo about to piss themselves.

"No. But...seriously? Did we come here for me?" Wiley repeated when he was finally able to catch his breath.

"No, dude. But you know what they say. 'The Lord works in mysterious ways.'"

"Amen, brother," Wiley said, still smiling. He still didn't know why the heck they were in Texas, but at the moment, he no longer cared. For the first time in what felt like a thousand years, he was a regular person.

Regular except that he was the size of a barn on steroids.

*   *   *   *   *

Nobody spoke for a long time. The Old Lady and her two henchmen had come into Waters's room without a word, and then they just stood there for a solid five minutes not sitting, not speaking, just being awkward as hell. The old woman was not wearing glasses, and neither did her escorts. They were armed though, he noted, suddenly wishing his own sidearm was within arm's reach and not under his pillow.

"We're in the window," Henchman Number One said as his old-school, nearly completely analog, watch chimed, "He's got lenses." He nodded toward the box on the nightstand with Waters's new glasses in it.

"Thank you, Samuel," the Old Lady said.

"May I turn your glasses off, sir?" Henchman Number Two said.

Black Jesus seized the opportunity to reposition himself on the bed and within reach of his gun.

"I got it," he told the man as he sat on the bed and powered down his connection to the Registry.

"Do you want to sit down?" the Captain asked the old woman.

"No. The window isn't long enough to get comfortable."

"I don't know what that means, but—"

"It means the Republic has drones flying surveillance routes all over Texas, and we have about twenty-six minutes left before they return to this area of Jasper. That's the window: how much time we have to get you and your people offline and bunkered without it being logged."

"Logged like in the Registry?"

"If it gets logged, the whole world will know you're meeting with us."

"Okay, I get that. Who is 'us'?"

"Most people call us 'Bunkermen,' but what they label us is unimportant. You can get answers to all those kinds of questions when you get back online—that's what the Registry is for—though I'd urge you to take anything you discover through it with a grain of salt. I'm here to offer you a chance to get the answers you can't find there.

"But knowledge always comes at a price, Captain. At this point, I'd be shocked if you could even partially understand the true nature of the costs involved. But we try to make the offer to newcomers just the same. Because after you've received Grace, well, conversations get…difficult."

"So you're basically the serpent in the garden then?"

The Old Lady smiled.

"Ma'am, we are at the twenty-two-minute mark," the henchman, Samuel, said.

"William," the Old Lady said to Captain Waters. "I'm sorry we don't have more time for you to process this right now. But I'm afraid you're going to have to shit or get off the pot. Is the truth worth the risk?"

"The risk of what? You haven't—"

"The risk of being barred by LSD from citizenship, from Grace. Of being tagged as a conspirator—an enemy of the state, and not just any state, William. The Republic of Austin claims to have been ordained by God himself, and frankly, I can't guarantee you that it hasn't been."

"Lady, for the serpent in the garden, you're really a shit salesman."

"To the truly righteous, truth sells itself," she countered. The Captain couldn't help but smile.

* * * * *

"You've got to be shitting me. That's why were in Texas?" Wiley DuPont said once Emmett had finished explaining the history of his failed assassination plot against Dr. Weiss.

It seemed, by the Grace of God, that Wiley's faculties had now nearly returned completely—at least as far as Emmett could tell. He didn't exactly have a baseline to compare the man too. It was obvious that the toothless giant was eager to prove to himself, and to Emmett too, that he was no longer in any way diminished.

"I'm not shitting you, dude."

"And Black Jesus—I mean the Captain—he knew you were going to do this and was okay with it?"

"Not exactly. He agreed to chaperone a confrontation between me and Weiss, probably because he knew I was chomping at the bit to kill the dude. You know how he is. As far as he's concerned, he's responsible for me. I'm guessing he thought that if he was with me, he could keep me from doing anything stupid."

"Mission accomplished, I guess, right? He *did* keep you from doing something stupid—or at least from succeeding at doing something stupid. God knows you can't keep a blind man from beating a dead horse."

"I don't think that's a thing," Emmett said playfully.

"Really?"

"Well, I've heard of beating a dead horse, and I've heard that you can't teach a blind man to see, but I never heard them put together like that."

Wiley thought about it for a long second, and then another, and Emmett started to feel bad. *It was obviously too soon to joke around about things like that*, he scolded himself. The dude had been talking like a drunk Mother Goose right up until yesterday. And not two hours ago, forming a complete sentence had been harder than catching a greased pig for him. *Jesus, I'm an asshole*, he thought and opened his mouth to say as much, but—

Beep. Beep. Clank.

The cell door unlocking and opening on its own suddenly threw his apology out the window. He looked at Wiley. Wiley looked back. Neither one moved.

Now what the hell was happening?

The cellblock door opened and in walked Smalls. The man looked at Emmett from across the room—or maybe through him. His expression was strange. His eyes oddly vacant. Then without a word he turned around and left, leaving the door open behind him.

"Smalls?" Emmett called out.

There was no answer.

"Are we being released?" Wiley asked.

"I don't know, dude. But when God cures the sick, he opens a door."

"Is that how that goes? I always thought it went: when God closes a door, he opens a window."

Emmett smiled. "Mmm, yeah, you might be right."

"Should we stay here? Or—"

"I think we should go."

And so, they did. Right out the cell door. Right out of the cellblock. Right out of the police station.

A late model white SUV was idling in front of the entrance, waiting for them when they got outside. The rear passenger door opened.

"The window is closing, gentlemen," Black Jesus's voice told them from the interior of the vehicle. "Get in."

"Two minutes," the henchman Samuel said to nobody in particular, as Wiley closed the door to the SUV behind them.

"You ever seen *The Matrix* with Keanu Reeves, DuPont?" Black Jesus asked. But when after a long thirty seconds Wiley still hadn't answered, he turned to the elderly woman sitting in the very back of the vehicle and said frustratedly, "I thought you said Grace would only need a few hours to repair the brain damage. Do not take that shit out of him until it's finished doing its job."

"Captain—" Emmett began, but Henchman Number Two cut him off.

"I'm sorry, Captain Waters. The window is closing. We're out of time," Henchman Number Two said, and then he popped what looked like a fat wristband, or maybe a cartoonishly large single handcuff with a long wire chain, onto Wiley's forearm. The other end of the wire was plugged into a tablet of some sort.

"Ninety seconds," Thing Number One, Samuel, said.

The woman in the far back seat handed Thing Two an oversize glass test-tube-like container just as Emmett recalled seeing her at the exorcism party. Black Jesus suddenly drew his handgun and put it to the Thing Two's head.

"Wiley, get out of the car. I'll come back for you," Black Jesus commanded, but Wiley was a deer in the headlights now. He couldn't have obeyed even if he'd wanted to.

"We don't have time for this. He's not going to shoot you, John. Proceed. Let's get moving, Samuel. We don't want to be sitting outside police headquarters when the window closes. No matter what happens inside this car."

Emmett had no idea what was going on. It had been at least fifty years since *The Matrix* had come out, and for the love of Christ, he could not remember anything in that fucking flick that could be even remotely relatable to their current situation.

Samuel shifted the manual transmission of the old SUV into gear, and it started to move.

Black Jesus drew back the hammer of his gun, but the vehicle continued forward.

Fuck, Emmett thought, remembering his own standoff with the dude back in Maine. He'd seemed prepared to pull the trigger then. And it sure as shit looked like he was ready to do it now.

But the Old Lady apparently didn't see it the same way. She leaned forward as if Black Jesus was just a petulant child, and his firearm pointed at Thing Two—John—was of as much consequence to her as a wet paper bag. She twisted the test tube thing into the socket on Wiley's bracelet herself, then cocked her head at Black Jesus as if to say, *Don't make me put you in the naughty corner.*

Wiley looked down at the device on his arm, then he looked at Captain Waters. He wasn't scared. Just bewildered. Emmett, however, was both because he knew very well that for all the things Black Jesus was, had been, or would be, a petulant child was not among them. As if to prove it, Captain Waters pulled a second sidearm and pressed this one into the head of the Old Lady.

"Remove his Grace before it's done what it can do, and there is going to be a lot of blood in this car for Sammy up there to clean up."

"Captain, if we miss the window here, we'll have to set off an EMP to keep from being compromised. And, besides the fact that I'm really too old for a foot race, shutting down the mechanical parts of Grace at this stage doesn't usually go very well for those who have it inside them. So, you can take what you've got, or you can lose him entirely."

"I think I've seen the movie, sir," Wiley said suddenly.

"What?" Black Jesus asked, still glaring at the Old Lady who nodded to Henchman John.

"I've seen *The Matrix,*" Wiley said, his voice shaking. "But just in case I haven't, I'll watch it again, Captain. Right now, if you want me too. Really! You don't need to hurt anybody. I'm as much of a Samuel Jackson fan as anybody, but—"

Black Jesus suddenly started laughing—or crying. It

was hard to tell in the moment, and suddenly Emmett knew exactly what scene in *The Matrix* his crazy ass had been talking about.

"You've been bugged," Emmett said quietly to himself, misquoting Trinity from the movie.

Except what was pulled out of Wiley by the machine on his arm wasn't some impossibly large half-insect half-transistor looking movie prop. What came out of him was much less viscerally satisfying, but far more potent. It just looked like gray goo to the naked eye, but it was goo that could—and would—change the world. The wristband device suddenly hummed and fried the sludge with electricity, turning it into black ash, as it filled the glass holding chamber.

"That's Grace?" Emmett asked no one in particular. "Looks more like *Gross* if you ask me."

"It's better when you mix it with wine," Wiley said, with a big toothless grin that proved contagious.

Laughter filled the vehicle.

Black Jesus put his guns away.

The tension drained from the situation at last.

"So…did we make the window?" Emmett asked, not entirely sure what exactly he was actually talking about.

From the front seat, Samuel nodded.

"Yes, Mr. Kessler. Just by the skin of our teeth," the Old Lady answered.

"I don't have any teeth," Wiley said, hoping this joke would go over as well as his last one had. But it didn't. Without the nervous tension to hold it up, it fell flat.

Chapter Four
Good Grief

THE BLUE LIGHT SPLASHED across the screens of Tiny's system console was the only light in the house. Jennifer watched it run without a clue as to what any of it meant. Everybody living at the Kessler Farm but her had long since retired to their own rooms to lie down for the night—except Bobby-Leigh, who had slipped out to check on Bobo. She knew Tiny would freak just seeing her standing so close to the gateway into his precious little universe. Jennifer needed only one look at Tiny at work to know that this was holy ground for the big man.

How the fuck was she supposed to get him to let her in?

Tiny had proved remarkably resistant to her subtler overtures. At this point, she didn't know if he was just missing the signals or if she was screwing up sending them out. She wasn't trying to seduce him. Not in any kind of sexual sense anyway. Outside of what she'd seen in movies, she didn't even really know what seduction was. Jimmy had been her first and only taste of love. And for better or worse, that relationship was also the only model she had to work from for getting somebody to like her, which even with the limited experience she had, she knew was pretty fucked up.

Unfortunately, if you asked her to break down how her relationship with Brennachecke's youngest son had started, she'd only be able to say that she'd hated him and then she suddenly one day didn't. And then of course shortly after that, she'd figured out that she was utterly and completely in love with him. And then well...she'd berserked out and brutally smashed his perfect (at least to her) naked body to smithereens.

The long and short of it being that she knew it was possible for a person to start out hating somebody and then end up liking them. She'd been that person herself. Now she just needed to reverse engineer her experience and do that to Tiny. It seemed like since she wasn't even trying to get the dude to fall in love with her, just tolerate her enough to be her mentor, that the process should be even easier.

But it wasn't.

She watched the code fill the system console window and sighed. She'd tried to ingratiate herself with snacks, but that had turned into a disaster. Tiny had accused her of stealing his private personal food. She'd never even gotten a chance to tell him that she'd thought he looked like he needed a break and the least she could do is break him off a piece of a Kit-Kat bar. A line she'd practiced with Bobby-Leigh for almost an hour the night before to get the nuances of just right so that he'd have no choice but to forgive her and become her mentor. Instead, backed into a corner and flustered, she'd ended up yelling at him about how she'd gone out of her way to scavenge the fucking candy bar herself and that he wasn't the only one with a sweet tooth in the house, fuck you very much.

Total. Fucking. Failure.

But she wasn't about to give up. Rachel and Sarah were right. As a group they needed a backup in case something happened to Tiny. Too much of how their setup worked was dependent upon knowledge only he had. If she could just get the jackass to engage in a conversation long enough to tell him that, she was pretty sure he'd actually agree with that assessment too. The fact was that everybody else was too busy keeping this shit show running to take the time to learn what he could do. Too busy, or too young, or too young *and* too pregnant. She was it as far as protégés came.

So why was this so goddamn hard to get going?

Because Tiny is an asshole.

The thought made her smile in the way gallows' humor almost always did, but she knew that wasn't really true. The reason it was so hard was—

"Please don't touch that."

Tiny's words cut into her reflections with a tone so sharp he could've use it to perform surgery.

Not for the first time, Jennifer found herself marveling at how light he was on his feet for a man his size.

Ninja light.

How long has he been standing there behind me? she wondered randomly, and then in an error of conversational spontaneity only her father could really have appreciated, she heard herself repeat the question aloud to Tiny himself.

Fuck.

"Just because you're young and thin, doesn't mean that I'm ogling you in the shadows like some kind of peeping tom."

"You know what, dude? It's not your weight that makes you unattractive. It's that you're a fucking asshole," Jen responded as she turned to face him.

Oh, my god, what the fuck did I just say?

Tiny didn't respond. But he looked like he really wanted to. Jen couldn't tell if it was restraint that was holding him back, or just not being able to come up with something good enough to come back at her with, but she knew better than to wait him out.

"I'm sorry. That was—"

"You think I like being fat? You think I don't want to lose the weight? In this world? Give me a break. Not all of us can have berserker metabolisms keeping us all trim and perky. I wish I was a berserker sometimes. I really do. That's how bad being fat sucks for me. So—"

Jen's hand stung like a nest of fire ants had attacked it, but it wasn't until she saw the bright red handprint on Tiny's check that she realized she'd slapped him. Anger was pumping dangerously fast through her veins, and she quickly found the focus ring in her mind and twisted it before things got out of control. Breathing heavy, but confident she would not berserk out, she stepped so far into Tiny's personal space that she could smell the fear coming out of him. When she finally spoke, her words might as well have been daggers.

"This thing inside me. Is not. A mother-fucking. Weight-loss pill. People I love have died—and I'm not talking about the ones killed in the fight with the blood pirates who followed us here, not that they don't count, because I swear to God, Tiny, they do—just as much to

me as they do to you—but what I'm talking about are
people who I loved with all my heart being *literally pulled
apart* by my own hands…"

She wanted to say more but couldn't. Sobs came out
of her mouth instead of words, and to her utter surprise,
Tiny's arms engulfed her in an embrace that changed
their relationship forever.

"You're right. I am an asshole. I'm sorry," the fat man
whispered to her as she leaned into her grief in a way that
had never felt safe before.

After a minute or two though, she choked her emotions
back down and, still held tightly in her mentor-to-be's
arms, laid out the situation as Rachel and Sarah and pre-
sumably everybody else saw it. "So here's the deal, dude:
you need a protégé. And I'm all you got," she concluded.

It took Tiny a couple of seconds to switch gears,
but the catharsis after the emotional storm they'd just
survived had washed away his resentment toward Jen,
at least for now.

"Okay. So how much do you know about computer
programing?"

"Um…well, I know that's a computer," Jen said, pointing at one of the monitors, "and all that gobbledygook
scrolling down there is the programming that makes it
do what you want it to."

"Actually, um," Tiny said with a twinkle in his voice.
"That's just a monitor. The computer is over here on
these racks. And that stuff scrolling down the screen is
not actually program code. It's just the system activity
log—like an itemized list of what the various actual programs are doing, what resources are being utilized, and
most importantly, what tasks, if any, have failed, and if
we're lucky, why."

"Fuck," Jen said, wide-eyed with a smile.

"Pretty much. You sure you—"

"There's nobody else, dude. I got this."

"Okay," Tiny said.

His tone annoyed her. Fine, maybe she had her work cut out for her, but she picked things up quick. She'd figure it out, if for no other reason than she had to.

"Seriously. I got this," she said, pointing to the rack holding the quantum CPU hardware. "Computer." Then she pointed to the monitor. "Display." And then she finally gestured at the scrolling activity log. "Log of shit processing shit and the shit's status with error codes when the shit fails 'if we're lucky.'"

Tiny ran his fingers through his hair and nodded while holding his head in his hands. He smiled at her in an A for effort kind of way, but was still obviously unconvinced that Jennifer Kessler was ever going to become the protégé they needed her to be. But if there was one thing he should have known by then, it was that the safe money was never a bet against one of the Kessler girls.

*   *   *   *   *

From behind his hiding place in the solar array, Brennachecke watched, aided by the night vision app he'd asked Tiny to install on his glasses, as Bobby-Leigh slipped back into the house without a sound. The regularity of the daily routine of going to see the berserker she'd been tending to in the woods after everybody had gone to bed must have started to affect her level of vigilance, because for the first time, Brennachecke had been able to follow her all the way to the little shelter she'd built for her pet.

Maybe she'd been distracted by something, he thought. But he knew that was unlikely. Bobby-Leigh Kessler had the opposite of ADHD. Besides, his experience as a soldier had made him all too familiar with the difficulty of maintaining a high level of vigilance over the long haul. The human mind was just not designed for it. Not biologically. Not evolutionarily. Not even practically. For a threat to continue to register as a threat, the human mind needed continuous evidence of the danger or it slipped quickly into complacency. In war, as in life, complacency had always been the most dangerous enemy. And now that everyday life was basically war, that maxim was all the more true.

Still, he'd been attempting to stalk her now several times a week for months, and this was the first time she'd left her guard down enough for him to follow her all the way to her destination. Today, she'd only checked about half as often as she usually did to make sure nobody saw her. He knew that if he cornered her and asked, she'd freely admit she'd slacked off on covering up her tracks tonight and had been slacking off now for a couple of days.

Ever since she'd found out that Brennachecke knew she was slipping out at night, the old soldier knew she had been reevaluating the consequences of getting caught. He was sure the prospect still scared the bejesus out of her, but all the sneaking around must have stopped being fun a while ago. She was clearly now starting to get worn out. After all, she wasn't even thirteen yet. It was more than impressive that she'd done so well, this long, and it was ridiculous to think she'd be able to continue it forever. Her only Achilles' heel at the end of the day was her age. Her still developing brain left her vulnerable to impractical idealistic choices—like, for example, keeping a weaponized berserker as a pet.

When he had caught up to her, Brennachecke had immediately assumed the girl was meeting a boyfriend in her little shelter. That possibility had turned up such a storm of mixed feelings that Brennachecke had to immediately shut his emotional response down to keep from storming in there like her father and making sure whomever this guy she was with was both age appropriate and not taking advantage of her. However, if the guy was both of those things, then the idea that she'd healed enough from whatever happened to her at Walmart to have a relationship like that with a boy... Well, that filled his old battle-scarred heart with a hope that nearly wrecked him.

He hadn't barged in on them.

He'd waited.

He'd watched.

He'd listened.

It hadn't taken long for the hope that was crushing his chest to deflate. There was no secret boyfriend in here. There was a monster. He knew what he had to do, but as he unholstered his sidearm and checked the chamber for the round he already knew was in there, he decided to wait at least until Bobby-Leigh was gone.

It would be easier then.

On everybody.

Of course, he was wrong.

*   *   *   *   *

By ten in the morning, just about everybody living on the Kessler Farm had been lured by their curiosity into watching Tiny directing Jen as the two of them set up a second workstation in his electronic sanctuary. Having missed the cathartic blowout between the two of them in the middle of the night, what they were seeing just did not compute. It was like watching an iguana and a tiger be best friends.

"I thought they hated each other," Mari whispered to her mom, completely unaware of the gift she'd just given.

Anoona smiled at her for the first time in what felt like months and nodded. Maybe she could build on this moment of peace. Maybe she could let go of her resentment over the choice Mari had insisted on making. It was too late to stop it now anyway. Live and let live, literally. "If they can be friends, then maybe we can too," Anoona whispered back.

"I doubt it," Mari said and wobbled away to find Bobby-Leigh.

Anoona could almost hear her bubble of hope popping in her face. It stung just like a slap, but she kept her cool and let it go, telling herself that Mari was just a kid and didn't know what she was saying. Though at the same time she wondered how much that was true anymore.

"You two put her up to this?" she asked Sarah and Rachel who were watching the show and patting themselves on the back with their eyes.

"You disapprove?"

"Not at all."

"I need to talk to you," Brennachecke said from behind her in a whisper. "Alone."

Anoona closed her eyes and sighed. The pleasurable tingle in the back of her head at witnessing Jen and Tiny burying the hatchet and cooperating for the greater good was now completely gone.

* * * * *

"So what? You want me to do it?" Anoona asked incredulously after Brennachecke had finished telling her all about Bobby-Leigh and her pet, including how he hadn't been able to bring himself to kill the berserker once he was alone with him.

"Not exactly."

Anoona closed her eyes and sighed again. She knew what he was going to say before he even opened his mouth.

"Just hear me out," Brennachecke implored.

"No."

"Anoona, we already have one—"

"My daughter is weeks away from giving birth to one monster's"—she almost choked on the word—"child."

"I know. And that's hard. It really is. But this doesn't have anything to do—"

"There is a limit to how many fucking monsters I can tolerate under my roof."

Brennachecke didn't want to get into a discussion about the innocence of children. He understood the fear that was pushing Anoona's buttons. And the anger. He could even let the language go for now, but he was positive she was not seeing the big picture here. This wasn't about protecting Bobby-Leigh's delicate feelings. Frankly, that little girl's feelings were anything but fragile. If they put Bobo down, he was positive she'd get over it.

"I think there is an opportunity here."

"Oh, for fuck's sake, Brennachecke. You see a rabid dog, you put it down. It's not fucking complicated."

"Okay, first of all, I can see that you are upset, but you know that kind of language really bothers me. And second, this dog *isn't* rabid."

"I get that you have a special relationship with Jen, but that's the only berserker exception we are making. They're just too unpredictable. End of discussion."

"No. Look, Jen has learned how to manage her mind enough to reliably control her outbreaks. I'm sure she could teach her technique to somebody if she was asked to. Tiny could probably even rig up a fail-safe for the man just in case—maybe an explosive collar of some kind. The man knows what he is. Just like Jen, he is terrified of it. But if you forget about the humanity of the whole thing, the man is probably stronger than every single person here combined, and that's an asset right now. Plus, in a fight… well, you know as well as I do how effective releasing a berserker into the fray can be."

Anoona shook her head. Brennachecke could read the questions in her eyes. She was considering it, but as she stared him down, he knew she was searching his face for any reason to question his position, and he was pretty sure she wouldn't find one. If Jen could teach the thing how to control his outbursts. If Tiny could rig up a fail-safe. If the thing even still wanted to be a part of their little group under those conditions. If everybody in the group was unanimously onboard with the idea. If. If. If. Yes, he thought, there were a lot of ifs. But he could see that she knew he was right about at least one thing. An extra hand around here would go a long way, especially one that was as strong as an ox, or ten.

"I'll think about it," she said at long last, but Brennachecke knew what she really meant was yes. He smiled.

"If this does happen, and it goes sideways though…"

"It's on me."

"No. It's more than just on you, old man."

"If it turns out that you should have put a bullet in this thing's head, I'm going to ask you to put one in yours."

Brennachecke smiled and nodded.

"I'm not kidding."

"I know."

"Do you?"

*　　*　　*　　*　　*

Monitoring Mari's pregnancy was Tiny's least favorite chore, and being able to pass it off to Jen was going to make this whole mentor/mentee thing worth it all by itself.

Or so he thought.

He'd hacked together the obstetrics app with the help of a couple of his guys in Cedar Rapids—which was the only place he'd been able to reconnect with safely online. Lollipooper and ICU812 were both probably twelve-year-olds based on their aliases, but they had some undeniable skills with code, and frankly the picking was pretty limited when it came to finding collaborators not trying to parse out his location, what resources he had, and how vulnerable he might be to attack. After the hell Jen had caused to be rained down on them, Tiny was not about to take chances. So, while the code was pretty solid, the medical side of things was just from a textbook, and he had his doubts about how the app would assess and manage complications—which meant he had a lot of doubts. Mari was ridiculously young. The baby was breech. The damn librarian was the closest thing they had to anybody who'd ever even come close to this world before. And she hadn't been a midwife for almost thirty-years, and even then, she'd just been an apprentice. Plus, she'd been in another world where rich, privileged, mostly white women could afford to take chances with their deliveries because they were afraid—rightly or not, he didn't know or really even care—of the American health care industrial complex. All he knew is that Maddie and the app almost never agreed on the prognosis or the most effective course of action, which drove him crazy because it took forever to figure out if it was a bug in the program, or just Maddie's less than traditional and questionably reliable take on managing pregnancy and childbirth.

Just the other day, he'd overheard her appealing to Anoona for the millionth time to not let them do ultrasounds anymore because they were potentially harmful to the fetus. What the fuck was he supposed to do with that? Thank God Anoona hated the unborn thing, or he swore they'd have no idea the thing had even gotten all twisted around in there.

So he'd be happier than a pig in shit just to let Jen deal with all that, but first he had to get her to a point that she understood enough code to update the app, which was a whole shit ton of code. He'd built the thing in C++, since it wasn't exactly a priority to have it connected to, or interact with, the nearly nonexistent postapocalypse internet. For as quick as Jen was picking things up, and she was quick—at least compared to what Tiny had been expecting—he couldn't just hand her the source code to his OB app and teach her from that. That'd be about as effective as teaching a six-year-old to read with a copy of the latest *New Yorker*. He supposed it could be done, but why the fuck would anybody do it that way? If he wanted her to eventually read the *New Yorker*, first he had to teach her basic phonics. Get her reading some Dr. Seuss. Then he could cram vocabulary down her throat until she was puking up fifty-cent words and turn her loose on the app.

It was good plan.

Except that Jen had no interest in Dr. Seuss and kept picking up the fucking *New Yorker* and trying to read it.

"It's still fucking up."

"Programs don't fuck up," Tiny told her. "Programmers do."

"Well, then you fucked up, 'cause this thing keeps saying that I'm pregnant."

Tiny thought about that for a second. He'd written it specifically for Mari, who was pregnant. It was possible he hadn't bothered to include a basic pregnancy test. He couldn't remember. But it wasn't necessarily another bug.

"I think I just made pregnant the default. Don't worry about it. The app is for pregnant women."

"Okay, but what if she miscarries?"

"Well, then she's not going to need the app anymore, will she? Aren't you supposed to be working on something else?"

"Dude, come on. Let me do something real. If I have to write another function to print a stupid sentence today, I'm going to kill myself. Let me try to fix this."

"No. That'd be like letting you try open heart surgery after you just learned how to cut up your own meat with a steak knife. Besides, it's not fucking broken."

He pulled up the app and looked at it for a minute. Then two. Then ten. After which he was sure of two things: pregnancy was not the default *after all,* and if Jen was going to keep begging for the New Yorker, he might as well see how far she could get with it.

"Could you be pregnant?"

"Berserkers don't get pregnant, dude."

"Really?"

"Look it up. I haven't gotten my period since the first time I berserked out."

Tiny believed her, but he looked it up anyway. While plenty of mothers had become berserkers, he couldn't find a single reference to a berserker becoming a mother. Once the demon reared its ugly head, apparently one of the side effects was infertility, which was right up there with the tooth loss thing in the bizarre department when it came to the berserker phenomenon.

"Okay," Tiny conceded. "You can attempt to debug it, if you really want to."

Jen smiled at him like he'd given her a present instead of a chore, and his mind suddenly jumped down a rabbit hole that turned his cheeks bright red: he was really the only person she could have slept with since she woke up from her coma, unless you counted Brennachecke, which was just gross. All the other boys on the team were…dead.

* * * * *

The dinner table was subdued like usual. Sarah and Rachel were talking quietly with each other—also like usual—but their conversation, as banal as it was, didn't exactly offer much in the way for anybody else to participate in.

Mari and Bobby-Leigh were secretly making faces at each other and trying not to crack up—mostly because, on some level, they both knew it drove Anoona nuts, and the unspoken game most nights was to see how fast they could get Mari's mother so annoyed that she excused herself from the table.

Jen was lost in her own world writing and rewriting code in her head.

Tiny, now that he didn't have fifty tons of resentment toward Jen, found he could really just enjoy the food again.

Anoona sighed a lot and shook her head from time to time, but otherwise didn't dare engage with Mari or anybody else.

Brennachecke, ever the stickler for politeness, continually attempted to get everybody to have something that would pass for normal dinner conversation, which really just meant he continually asked everybody questions they had no interest in answering.

The food was good though. At least there was that. Considering it'd been snowing for nearly nine months straight, that was a blessing not to be taken for granted.

"So when do you think you'll get your distillery up and running again?" Brennachecke asked in Sarah's direction.

Sarah smiled at him, fully aware of the effort he was making and even appreciating it as well, but Anoona was the one who answered.

"It's pretty low on the priority list."

"Yeah, I suppose it is. Still, seems like I'm not the only one at this table who could use a drink." Brennachecke was pretty sure everybody knew he wasn't much of a drinker and had hoped the humor would break the ice at least a little bit.

It didn't.

"How's the mentorship going?" he asked Tiny.

"Good."

"Yeah?"

"Yeah, Jen's killing it," Tiny said and then realized that Brennachecke might not particularly like that choice of phrase since Jen had actually killed his youngest son. Feeling bad, he tossed the old man a bone.

"Look at her right now. You can practically see the code she's trying to write beaming out from behind her eyeballs."

"Yeah? What are you working on, Jen?"

It took Jen a second to realize somebody was talking to her. "I'm sorry—what?"

Tiny smiled and said, "He wants to know what you're working on."

"Oh. Well, I'm trying to debug the OB app we're monitoring Mari with."

Maddie, the librarian, suddenly perked up, like a dog that smelled another dog coming around the corner. Another dog she did not like.

"When I was testing it after this last iteration, it kept saying that I was pregnant, which obviously I'm not. So at first Tiny thought he'd just made the status 'pregnant' the default, but it turned out that it wasn't the default. I've gotten it broken down now, so I know it has to be misreading the berserker hormones in my blood for pregnancy ones—but I can't seem to isolate the bad code that's making it happen. I'm sure Tiny could fix it in like fucking five minutes or something, but he's graciously allowed me some room to try to figure it out myself."

"Sounds complicated."

Jen smiled, already back in her own thoughts.

Brennachecke waited a moment to see if anybody would pick up the conversation, but nobody did. He sighed and gave up for the night. But suddenly, out of left field, Anoona tossed a grenade onto the table.

"It's time we discuss your friend, Bobby-Leigh."

The fugitive giggles between Bobby-Leigh and Mari stopped instantly. Brennachecke was surprised to see the little girl staring daggers at him, though he supposed that was to be expected.

He had ratted the girl out.

Bobby-Leigh didn't bother to deny or pretend to be ignorant as to what Anoona was referring to. Instead she just asked, "Why?"

"Because you can't keep sneaking out in the middle of the night to give table scraps to the berserker you've been hiding for the last nine months. If the thing is going to be part of the group, we need to discuss it, and if not—"

"Then you're going to fucking kill him, right?"

"Either it's an asset or a liability."

"He's not an *it*. His name is Bobo."

"You've been hiding a berserker this whole time?" Rachel asked, trying to hide her confusion. "Where? Like, in your room?"

"In the woods," Jen said.

Anoona shot her a hot look. "Of course you knew about it all along."

"Well, to be fair, I was in a coma for most of the time, but…" Jen responded with icy sarcasm making it crystal clear there was only one side of this that she could possibly be on, and that was her sister's.

"Isn't that really dangerous?" Mari chimed in.

"Is it?" Anoona asked both Jen and Bobby-Leigh at the same time.

"No," both girls blurted out in unison.

"It's—he—he is one of the blood pirate weaponized ones from July apparently," Anoona said. "If he berserked out, he'd probably take half of us with him."

"The same could be said about me," Jen responded quickly.

"Not exactly, sweetheart," Brennachecke jumped in. "He doesn't have your training at managing your mind. One of the questions we need an answer to is do you think you could teach him the kind of control you have or not?"

"And if she can't, then you're going to murder him, right?" Bobby-Leigh said, her voice ice.

"Not necessarily," Anoona said. "Tiny, do you think you could rig up some kind of collar that would—"

"Blow his head off if he went all rapid hulk on us? Yeah, probably."

"Okay, well. I'm not going to bring a dangerous animal into our group without everybody being okay with it, but when Brennachecke brought this to me, he reminded me how shorthanded we are. If we can mitigate the risk with a collar and meditation or whatever it is you do, Jen...I think he could be an asset."

"How far gone is he?" Maddie asked.

"He's a little slow," Bobby-Leigh answered. "But he's sweet and gentle. Really. He can stay with me and Jen."

"He can?" Jen asked, her tone hard to read, except for the fact that she clearly was not expecting to have to share her room with him.

"We're okay with it," Sarah said for both her and Rachel. "Frankly, we could use some more muscle."

"We'd need to produce more food," Tiny said. "Which means cutting some of the fringe crops and doubling up on staples."

"We should do that anyway," Maddie said.

Tiny sighed, then acquiesced. "I guess I don't have a problem with it either."

"Okay, then," Anoona said. "Go bring him in."

Bobby-Leigh jumped off her chair.

"But, Bobby-Leigh," Anoona added, her tone freezing the little girl in her tracks. "You ever do anything like this again and I will kick both you and your sister out of this house. By force if necessary. Are we clear? Secrets like this get people killed."

Jen's eyes narrowed, but she didn't say anything. Neither did Bobby-Leigh. In fact, that whole table held their tongues, but every single one of them knew that if push came to shove, the only way the Kessler girls were going to leave their uncle's farm was by their own volition.

Brennachecke looked at Anoona and realized that she knew it too. The woman had just needed to put her foot down and reaffirm her position as commander in chief of their little group. He could live with that.

*　*　*　*　*

"Okay, fuck you! I fucking give up, you asshole!" Jen yelled at the computer screen. "Is that what you want? Dickhead! You want me to give the fuck up!"

Tiny smiled at her.

"I hate this fucking thing," she told him.

"Clearly."

"It's not misreading the berserker hormones as HCG. I don't know what the fucking bug is, but it's not that."

"Let's try an experiment," Tiny offered and slipped the finger monitor onto his hand. "Run it again."

Jen did. At the breakpoint, an error message appeared

in the console. The message she'd been trying to get for days now: *Not pregnant. Go get fucked.*

"Really?" Tiny asked when he looked at the output.

He scrolled up with a flick of his finger and looked at the message Jen's test had given.

I'm an asshole. I still say you're pregnant.

"Okay, we've got to talk about professionalism here," Tiny said, with absolutely no intention of ever doing it.

"Is it bad that I was hoping it'd say you were preggers too?"

"Not at all. But now I'm curious. When does it say your due date is?"

"It doesn't. It just crashes as soon as you run the Due-When function."

"Hmmm. Hey, Sarah or Rachel—either of you ladies got a sec?" Tiny said on comms over the net.

Sarah responded, but it was Rachel who showed up at their computer.

"Put this on your finger," Tiny told her.

Jen ran the app again.

Not pregnant. Go get fucked.

"Great, so it's definitely me."

"Thanks, Rach. That's all we needed."

"That's it. Really? Okay..." Rachel said, then seeing what the message on the screen was, she laughed and opened her comms channel. "Hey, Sarah, meet me in the bedroom. Tiny's computer thinks I need to get fucked."

"What?" Sarah asked from wherever she was.

"Never mind." Rachel laughed.

"This is why we don't put messages like that in our—" Tiny began, but Anoona's voice in his earpiece cut him off.

"Tiny, Jen. It's time. Bobo is here."

*   *   *   *   *

Anoona knew the berserker would be huge, but she was still taken aback by the monstrosity that stood before her. They were in the lower level sitting area. Sarah was sitting on the stairs, her trusty AR-15 within easy reach, but out of sight, per Anoona's instructions.

Jen, Brennachecke, and Tiny stood next to Anoona in a line facing Bobby-Leigh and Bobo, as if they were about to play some kind of demented version of red rover. Everybody was nervous.

This was the first time she'd seen a berserker nervous, Anoona thought, but then reminded herself that Jen was in fact exactly like this giant. Only she really wasn't. And wasn't that the point at the end of the day?

"Why don't we sit down," Brennachecke suggested.

Everybody did.

"Should I call you Bobo?"

Bobo smiled a big toothless grin upon hearing his new name.

"Bah-Leh, Bo-Bo," he said, tapping his chest.

"You understand me? When I talk?" she asked him next.

He just smiled at her. No nod, just a smile.

Jesus Christ, he can't even fucking talk, Anoona thought, already regretting not just putting the big dumb thing down when she'd first been made aware of his existence.

Chapter Five
Sixty Feet Under

THEY'D DRIVEN UP THE 96 toward Brookeland for about twenty minutes until they hit what used to be known as Sam Rayburn Reservoir. The bunker was another ten minutes farther.

The Old Lady hadn't wanted to talk until they were safe underground, but even once they were all seated at the large round table, in what appeared to be some kind of bizarre corporate survivalist conference room almost sixty feet under, she didn't say anything for a long time. When she did finally speak, she didn't give any answers at all. She asked questions.

"Why did you try to kill the director of health and welfare, Mr. Kessler?"

Emmett looked at Black Jesus for permission to answer. He still had no idea what was going on and didn't dare do anything that would increase the temperature of the already hot water he was in with the man.

Black Jesus nodded for him to go ahead.

Emmett explained his theory, being sure to make it clear that he'd never intended to murder the man. He'd always intended to abide by his agreement to just have a conversation with him. Supervised of course. But that he'd just gone a little crazy seeing him so unexpectedly like that.

He looked at Black Jesus to see if the dude was buying any of what he was selling, but he couldn't read the man.

"I see," the Old Lady said. "Interesting. And, Mr. DuPont? How are you feeling?"

"Good. Confused but good. Am I not a berserker anymore then?"

"That's right. Your DNA has been edited. You no longer have the berserker gene."

"That's amazing."

"It is that. Grace does a lot of editing in the first few days it's in a person's system. Dyer claims it's a process purification," the Old Lady continued, her disdain for the Republic of Austin's leader so thick in her words she was almost choking on them. "He keeps them all forever young and forever healthy."

"And that's a bad thing?"

"It's from mortality that man learns humility," she said. "And without humility, man becomes arrogant. Arrogant men do things they shouldn't."

"Such as?" Black Jesus asked.

"Have you seen any people of color here in Jasper? Any Jews? Any Muslims? Any homosexuals? Transgendered people?"

"Now that you mention it, it does seem pretty white," Emmett chimed in.

"Well, before the Grace of God…"

"I don't follow," Black Jesus said, but Emmett knew the man lying and just wanted to hear her say it. There was something about hearing something you suspect to be true, but don't know for sure, spoken back to you by a third party that grounded it in reality.

"Like I said, Grace does a lot of gene editing in that first couple of days."

"So we're not actually talking genocide here then…" Emmett said, looking for the Old Lady to echo back what he was already thinking to make it real for him too.

"Well…there are no mass executions going on, if you're considering genocide, but I'd suggest you update your definition of what that word means because Grace is very literally gene-ocide. And just because there are no bodies, that doesn't mean whole groups of people aren't being wiped off the map here in Texas."

"That's pretty fucked," Wiley said.

"And nobody knows this? Nobody is trying to stop it?" Emmett asked. He was not surprised at all to discover that Dr. Weiss was involved in ethnic cleansing. In fact, he wouldn't be surprised at all to learn that the whitewashing of DNA had been his idea in the first place.

Once a Nazi, always a Nazi.

"No, that's the sickest part of the whole deal. Dyer doesn't actually deny that Grace does any of this. His bishops don't volunteer it, of course, but when he's been asked directly in the past, they've never bothered to equivocate. The fact is, eternal youth and immortality, to say nothing of the promise of living in a functioning, relatively safe, and technologically advanced country, when compared to the abject lack of any of that in most of the places in the world these days… Well, people line up like sheep at the slaughterhouse for a chance at that."

"And you bunker…people, you folks are out to put an end to Grace then?" Emmett asked, a little flustered by the fact that, while being the only one of the three of them who was genetically white, he also seemed to be the most morally offended by the idea of this kind of insidious ethnic cleansing. Of course, Black Jesus was a pro at keeping his cards close to the vest while he was assessing a person or relationship. In fact, Emmett still had difficulty reading the dude more often than not if he was honest with himself. Still if anybody should be foaming at the mouth to shut this motherfucker down, shouldn't it be the black guy?

"Our goal is to secularize Grace and everything it's made possible. The fact is the technology is miraculous. We just want to cut the strings that come attached to it."

"What exactly are you recruiting us for then?"

"We'll get to that. For now, make yourselves at home here. And, if in a couple of days, you haven't decided our cause is the side you want to be on, then we'll take you back and forget this whole weekend ever happened."

She smiled at them and then stood up. Nodding to Black Jesus that the ball was in his court now, she left them. Once it was clear they would be alone for a moment in the conference room, Wiley leaned in and whispered, "Did you know we couldn't leave here?"

"We were locked in a cell before we got here, dude. The only difference is that this cell is underground and Black Jesus is locked up with us," Emmett said.

"Please don't call me that, Kessler," Black Jesus said. His voice was so cold it made Emmett shiver, and he suddenly realized that he was a lot longer away from the man's good graces than he'd thought.

"This is the deal. I agreed to see these cats' side of things. One of the conditions was that we stay with them for a few days, partially for security reasons on their part, but mostly I think because they risk a lot recruiting people like us and are smart enough to know that we need time to really process what they are offering and asking. Also I'm sure they need time to really know they can trust us once we return topside.

"The bottom line is, gentlemen, that this is a whole new world down here—"

"A brave new world," Emmett slipped in.

"And I honestly don't know what to make of it all yet. So I'm hearing everybody out and trying to keep an open mind."

Waters looked at Wiley and sighed.

"I am sorry, DuPont, for subjecting you to their exorcism ritual or whatever that really was. It seemed harmless when they described it to me, and they—Sinclair—he made it clear that for us to be allowed to continue toward the capital, it would have to be done."

"Hey, man, it worked. No worries."

Black Jesus, however, clearly did have worries though. Emmett could see that as plainly as he could see that Wiley was clearly better off now than he had been when he was still the Beast. There was no question, at least to Emmett, that no harm had been done. And yet, he'd been with Black Jesus long enough to know the man was not an ends-justify-the-means kind of dude. The means mattered. And as he watched the shadows pass over the man's face while he searched for the right words, he knew that what plagued his friend was that something else could have happened. Emmett knew the Captain held himself—in every sense of the word—responsible for Wiley DuPont. From the man's personal health and well-being, all the way up to the actions he took that could affect the health and well-being of others. He'd allowed Wiley to be put in a potentially compromised situation. Sure, it had worked out okay, but Emmett knew the man was nonetheless flogging himself bloody on the inside.

"Well, at any rate, DuPont, all the evidence suggests that the berserker inside you is gone. And I don't believe, as such, you should still be held responsible for the crimes for which you were incarcerated, so I'm officially commuting your sentence to time served."

"Wait? What?"

"I am releasing you from custody. Once we leave this place, you are free to go and do whatever you want."

Wiley looked absolutely horrified at that idea.

"As for you, Kessler, get used to being in a fucking cell, because I clearly can't trust you anymore," Black Jesus said and then nodded to somebody outside the room.

Two men came in and less than gently pulled Emmett to his feet, wrenched his hands behind his back, and slapped a set of old-school handcuffs on his wrists.

"Ouch," Emmett said, though deep down some part of him was relieved to finally just know where he and Black Jesus stood.

Black Jesus got up heavily and took custody of his prisoner. Led by the two men who'd cuffed him, he started to walk Emmett out of the conference room. At the door, he turned back and smiled at Wiley. "Go explore a little. Talk to people. Make friends. I'll check on you in a few hours. You're a free man, Mr. DuPont. Take things slow. You'll be just fine."

"Yes, Captain," Wiley said, though from the tone of his voice, Emmett could tell the poor bastard didn't believe for a second that anything was fine.

* * * * *

Wiley had been wandering around the bunker for almost an hour before he actually spoke to anybody. The place was huge and crowded, as if the Copley Place mall back home in Boston had been shipped off to Texas and then buried next to a lake, sixty feet under the ground, with all the people still in it. The most off-putting thing about the place was that it was so *normal*.

He wandered, and he people watched.

A group of what he could only assume were business-men in slacks and jackets headed into the building where the conference room was he'd just left.

A mother was pushing a stroller toward the farther away of two enormous hotel-like buildings at the far end of the bunker, was desperately trying to talk her screaming toddler into calming down, but only made things worse with whatever she was saying.

A bunch of teens, probably up to no good, were goofing around with each other, laughing like the world hadn't ended before they were probably even born and they actually had a future to look forward to.

Two soldiers—dressed just like the ones who'd been escorting the Old Lady when they picked Emmett and him up—were eating at an outside table that belonged to one of the four restaurants in the little open-air pedestrian mall that traced along the koi pond at the center of the behemoth underground structure.

There must be thousands of people living here. Working here, he thought. *Thousands of people. Regular people. Were they all determined to undermine the society that lived above them? Or was it just the leadership that was crazy?*

Wiley had found that the more the Old Lady had talked, the less and less convinced he was that Grace was a bad thing. Nobody was being forced to take it against their will, so the truth was that it wasn't like genocide at all really. And if Dyer and his people weren't even trying to hide the fact Grace was doing these kind of things, well…then maybe these days ethnic and sexual identity were just not as important as they were before the world ended. A lot of shit changes in an apocalypse.

Of course, he wasn't funny like that or Jewish, but just because his father had put a little cream in his coffee, it didn't do doodley-squat when it came to him identifying as Creole. As light-skinned as he was, he was still miles away from being the Nordic Aryan stock Grace would have transformed him into had it been allowed to run its course. Given the choice to be a full-blooded Creole berserker or a white man that never got sick and was young forever, he personally would have volunteered too. If anybody had asked him, that was. Maybe if being a berserker had been stripped out of the calculation, it would have changed things a little, but he doubted it. Besides, nobody had given him a choice—which, the more he thought about it, was kind of fucked up. No wonder Black Jesus looked like the cat that swallowed the canary.

DuPont was in the middle of wondering if he could get them to put Grace back inside him once they finally got out of this place, when a woman in her late thirties bumped into him and bounced off like a tennis ball against a brick wall.

"Oh, my god, I'm so sorry," she said from the ground as Wiley bent to help her back to her feet. "I wasn't watching where I was going."

"I think you hurt you more than me," he said and smiled his toothless grin before he could help himself.

"You're a berserker."

Wiley couldn't read her well enough to know if she thought that was a good thing or bad thing.

"I was. But I've retired."

"Really? They let you in here with Grace?" she said conspiratorially. And if he didn't know better a little flirtatiously.

"No. They sucked it out of me as soon as I was...uh, cured, I guess you'd call it."

"Wow, they can do that now?"

"I guess."

"Hey, so, can I ask you a question? Do all of you... bunker people, just live down here, like all the time?"

"Most do. Some don't."

"The um...above ground people—"

"Austinites—or Assinites, depending on who specifically you're talking about."

She was definitely flirting with him. He didn't exactly know what to do with that, but it made him happy nonetheless.

"They don't come after you?"

"No, as long as you haven't been tagged in the Registry as a conspirator, you are more or less invisible to Average Joe Assinite. The marshals might pick you up from time to time, but the Republic doesn't actually have any real laws, so as long as you don't tell them you're a Bunkerman, they don't hold you for long. They just assume you're from the sprawl."

"The sprawl?"

"You know, where the normal people live." She laughed good-naturedly. "Tell you what. Let me run my two quick little errands, and then I'll find you and maybe we can go back to my place and I can answer your questions. Fucking a berserker is on my bucket list."

Wiley was sure he didn't hear that last part right, so he just pretended like she hadn't said it and asked her how she'd find him when she was done with whatever it was she had to do.

"You're pretty easy to spot…" She smiled, leaving an opening for him to tell her his name, which he did. "Nice to meet you, Wiley. My name is Jack—or Jackie's fine too."

And then, a second later, she was walking away.

Wiley watched her go, waving awkwardly when she looked back at him before she was swallowed up by the pedestrian horde. After a minute, he sat on a nearby bench replaying the conversation in his head trying to nail down if she'd actually said she'd wanted to have sex with him or not. And if she had, if she actually meant it.

It had been a long time since Wiley had been with a woman.

A really long time.

*   *   *   *   *

"You look happy," Captain Waters said when he finally found DuPont. Yes, the man stuck out like a fat lip, but the bunker was huge, and Waters had been looking for him in the business center area where the conference room had been. Then he'd discovered the mall for himself.

"I met a girl."

"Wow. That was fast."

"Yeah, I think she has some kind of demented berserker fetish, but…"

"All things considered, that's probably a good thing."

"Probably is."

"Well, I just wanted to check in and see how you were doing. The Old Lady set us up with rooms at the residence over there," Waters said, pointing at the sleek modern hotel-like building on the other side of the koi pond. It the same place the mom Wiley had been watching lose a battle of wills against her two-year-old had gone. Black Jesus handed Wiley a key card with a room number on it handwritten with permanent marker and an advertisement for Domino's pizza delivery service.

"Holy crap, Domino's is still around?" Wiley said, mostly to himself, when he saw the card.

"Honestly, I'm not a hundred percent sure. I'm in 2242, if you want to talk after your date."

"Hey, so what are they using for money here?" Wiley called as Black Jesus headed toward the residency. All he got was a shrug for an answer.

*   *   *   *   *

Jack did not stand Wiley up.

Not more than fifteen minutes after Black Jesus had left him, DuPont saw her coming toward him through the sea of people walking here and there and everywhere in this strange underground Russian doll of a complex. Ten minutes after that, they were in her little apartment. It took only another five minutes for her to get him naked.

"I wasn't sure if you were serious or not about your... bucket list," he said as she backed him toward the bed, pulling her top off as she advanced.

"Pick me up," she commanded as she wiggled out of the rest of her clothes.

Wiley obeyed. This was her fantasy after all, he thought. He held her up and against him with one hand and gently caressed her face with the fingers of his other. But apparently foreplay was not part of the plan. Smiling, clearly enjoying the feeling of being nearly weightless in his enormous arms, she wasted no time putting him insider her.

Over a decade with absolutely zero physical affection, much less any of the sexual variety, left Wiley quick to climax. So quick that Jack hadn't even gotten a single thrust out of him before he began spurting like a sprinkler head.

Spent, he moved to put her down, but she dug her nails into his back and locked her legs around him. Thrusting her hips forward until there was no space between his sex and hers, she held him inside her and gyrated until his waning rigidity reversed course.

It didn't take long—the flipside of going so long without was that though Wiley was quick to climax, he was also quick to reload.

She rode him for almost an hour as he stood in the middle of the bedroom. Facing toward him. Away. Legs dangling. Legs wrapped tight. Legs off to one side. She even managed to pull off a complete inversion.

When she finally dismounted, Wiley was shaking and needed to sit, not so much from fatigue, but from stimulation overload. He'd lost count of the number of times he'd filled her with his seed, but it had been enough to leave his nuts aching as if he'd been kicked there hard and repeatedly—the worst blue balls in the history of the world, but in the reverse.

"Check," she said and smiled at him.

For all the pain he was in, he didn't have any regrets. In fact, if she asked him to go again, he was sure he'd oblige her. Hell, if she asked him to marry her right then, he'd probably say yes to that too. Or murder somebody for that matter. Wiley was whipped and wrapped and utterly under her spell.

"I'm going to order a pizza," she told him.

Wiley smiled as she bounced out of the room, but it turned to a wince the second she was gone. Groaning, he pulled on his pants. Jack put on a shirt and panties herself when she came back.

"Okay. Question me."

"Is…was that how sex is now?"

Jackie laughed.

"What? You more of a missionary man?"

"I don't know what I am, but I've never had—"

"No. It's not usually like that. I just. Well…" She blushed.

Wiley hadn't thought he'd ever see that, not after what they'd just done. It made her only more appealing to him.

"I can tell you this much though—no Assinite is going to fuck like that. That's part of why we're trying to get Grace away from them. All that Bible-thumping shit makes things so…boring."

"They don't have sex?"

"Not out of wedlock. At least not officially. There are places in the sprawl where black boxes have been set up, and Grace can't transmit. You can imagine what goes on in those places. But I don't think very many people risk it."

"Risk what?"

"Losing Grace. Besides I think Dyer got their brain chemistry cooked as much as their DNA. They probably don't even want sex any anymore."

"So Grace is like mind control then?"

"Maybe not mind control exactly, but it's certainly impulse control to some degree."

Wiley considered that. He was still leaning toward trying to find a way to get Grace back inside him, but Jackie's allure was starting to erode the edges of his conviction.

"Surely you've got better questions than that?" she teased him.

It was Wiley's turn to blush.

"Okay, yeah…um, how do they power this facility without alerting the Austinites."

"Each bunker has a natural gas processing plant in it. I think they frack or something like that, using the lake water."

"That's not dangerous?"

"Compared to what?"

"Touché."

"It probably is. All the more reason we need to get our hands on Grace I guess."

"So there is more than one of these kinds of bunkers?"

"Oh, yeah. I think there are seven, maybe eight. This is the only one in Texas though. I know California has one—my ex is there. I want to say Kentucky and Georgia have 'em. But don't quote me."

"Your ex?"

Jack smiled and touched Wiley's cheek, making it clear that she didn't want him to worry about her past. "I'm pretty sure you can take him, if it comes to that," she said.

"So these bunkers are connected?"

"Not all of them, but a lot of them. We've made deals with the military factions who control the tunnels between them, so as long as those bases aren't fighting each other, we can use them. But there is a lot of fighting. Our place in Colorado, for example, is cut off because everybody wants a piece of Cheyenne Mountain."

"Cheyenne Mountain?"

"Big-ass military facility built in the 1950s to command shit from in the event of nuclear war with Russia. Makes this place look like a hole in the ground."

"So the US military is still intact?"

"Good God, no. After the coup in New York and the two years of everybody blowing each other up with nukes trying to take over the country, there wasn't enough of a government left to run anything. There're four factions that are former US military. At least in bunkers, and that includes the guys in Cheyenne Mountain. I think there's a navy or air force run state on the east coast somewhere too. Maybe South Carolina? I really don't follow that stuff too much, so don't quote me there."

"And none of them have anything like Grace?"

"They don't even know about Grace. Lady McCain has made sure of that."

"Whose Lady McCain?"

"She's like the president or whatever here. I heard that she'd brought you and your friends here herself. Didn't you meet her?"

"I didn't know who she was."

"Well…now, you do."

"I don't understand why you're keeping the existence of Grace a secret from your own people."

"Well, first of all, the other bunkers are not really *our* people. We're friendly, sure, but each site is independent. Like the countries of Europe before the EU collapsed. We need to get Grace first, that way we can control how it's used. We don't need another group of fanatics having a say over something so powerful."

"But you can communicate with them?"

"The bunkers have a couple of dedicated communications satellites run out of California. We're networked. The military factions have an even better network still up and running too. We sometimes have access to that as well. We can talk to each other, send data, or whatever."

"And that's all different from whatever network the Austinites are on?"

"Oh, yeah. Totally different. They're on what they call the Registry. It's purely terrestrial, but it's powerful as fuck. And it's delocalized, so it's almost impossible to take down."

"What does that mean?"

"Instead of housing data in a server farm somewhere, they house most of the data within the system itself. Each pair of glasses, or access device, plus all the bajillions of nanites that make up Grace itself—they all store a little bit of the data that makes up that network inside them. All with quantum encryption too."

"So you guys can't hack into their system?"

"We've gotten into any number of single devices in the network, but the fucking thing adapts so fast, my understanding is there is no way we can get into enough devices fast enough to pull off a cyberattack of any significance."

*   *   *   *   *

The door to the small monitoring station opened and shut, but the two technicians watching and listening to Jackie and Wiley didn't turn to see who it was. They knew already.

"How's she doing?" Lady McCain asked.

"She's pretty much just sticking to the script now," the first tech said without looking up.

"Has the pizza arrived?"

"They're waiting for her signal."

"Good. Update me once DuPont has it in his system."

"Yes, ma'am."

*　　*　　*　　*　　*

Black Jesus sat at the bar on the ground floor of the residence where he and Wiley had rooms. His head was bouncing around between marveling at what was going on in Texas—both above and below the ground—and agonizing over his options with Kessler.

It was clear that Emmett could not be trusted if they remained in Texas. *How on Earth did Kessler convinced me that coming here was a good idea?* he asked himself. *It's so obvious that his agenda was to kill Dr. Weiss the whole time. For fuck's sake, he told me as much at least a dozen times before the prison was attacked. Did I really think he just magically changed his mind about everything he'd been ranting about for years just because I showed a little faith in his character?*

Actually, that was exactly what Black Jesus had believed. He'd been under the impression that his faith in Emmett's character had gone a long way toward lessening the murderous rage inside him. Not completely, but at least enough to trust him to abide by their agreement. The broken trust hurt almost physically. So much that he was tempted to believe the man's bullshit about just getting overwhelmed in the moment. About it not being his plan all along. But no. Fool me once, shame on you, but fool me twice shame on me, as the old adage goes.

And yet, the reality was that—Kessler's attempted murder of a government official aside—it had been a good idea to come to Texas. Compared to the desolation and terror they'd faced on their travels here, any way you sliced it, life was better in here. He was drinking a Jack and Coke over ice listening to Elvis Presley sing about hound dogs, for the love of God. Something he'd pretty much never thought would happen again as little as a year ago. There was even a woman at the end of the bar making eyes at him.

The only problem was that to stay here, it was pretty clear he was going to have to do something for the Bunkermen. Something that would probably involve hurting a bunch of people he didn't know—which he was very much against. Yes, if everything the Old Lady had told him was true, which in itself was certainly not a given, there was some kind of ethnic cleansing happening with Grace. But, with all the other terrible shit happening all around him, he was not convinced it amounted to crimes against humanity. It all depended on the mechanics of how it worked.

Hell, until they'd arrived in Jasper, he'd been pretty sure there was no humanity left anymore to commit crimes against. Just like he doubted Kessler's pleas of temporary insanity, he also doubted that the Bunkermen's plans, once they got their greedy little fingers on Grace, were going to be particularly altruistic.

He drank his drink, noting that the woman at the bar making eyes at him was more attractive than he'd originally thought. She had more muscles than he did, but sort of had a Serena Williams kind of thing going on that allowed her to retain her femininity in spite of the fact that she could probably kick his ass. He wondered if she was a berserker like DuPont, saved by Grace and then saved again from it, but that was a pretty fucking awful conversation starter.

Not knowing what to say, he just smiled at her.

She smiled back.

*   *   *   *   *

In the monitoring station, next door to where the technicians were watching Wiley and Jack, another set of men had their eyes on Captain Waters at the bar.

"You better call her," one technician said to the other.

"No way. It's too soon."

"What? Look at the dirty old geezer. He's totally trying to figure out how to fuck her."

"He doesn't look like he wants to fuck her to me."

"Just because you don't want to fuck her, doesn't mean he doesn't. He came in with one of them, remember? Just like her, but a guy. So he obviously doesn't have a problem with them."

"How does that mean he wants to fuck her?"

"I'd fuck her."

"You're disgusting."

"Why?"

"You know why."

"Jesus, prejudiced much."

They stop talking to each other and watched as the berserker woman leaned across the bar and asked what Waters was drinking.

"You going to call her or not?"

The technician, who considered sex with berserkers, saved by Grace or not, bestiality, opened up a channel and said to a receptionist on the other end, "Lady McCain asked to be updated when the decoy successfully got Waters's attention. We believe we are a go on that front."

"Stand by please," the receptionist responded.

A minute later, the Old Lady entered the monitoring station with a little balding man in a particularly ugly sports coat.

"Go ahead and shift change, please."

The bartender almost immediately was replaced with a new one, and this one brought his own bottle of Jack Daniel's with him. Black Jesus didn't seem to notice at all, but the berserker woman did. She smiled up at the new barman and asked if she could get another round for her friend.

Waters accepted the drink. They toasted.

"I still say it's easier to just inject them with the virus and avoid all this cloak-and-dagger shit," the balding man said.

"That's just because you're already on our side," Lady McCain responded. "This way, even if they ultimately decide not to join us, they'll still be able to be used for Paradise Lost."

"I liked it better when we just shot them for choosing wrong."

"I'm sure you did," Lady McCain said as she and her little bald companion exited the room leaving the technicians to resume their discussion as to whether Waters was into the berserker or not.

"So you approve of me approaching Kessler directly then?" Lady McCain asked the bald man once they were in the hall and the door was shut again.

"I do. Not that it actually matters."

Lady McCain smiled and gave the man a wink as she walked away. "Don't be a sore sport, Bruce. You had your chance. Now it's my turn to do it my way."

The little balding man in the bad sports coat—Bruce—reached out and grabbed the Old Lady's arm.

"There're no second chances if we do this your way, McCain. Make no mistake about it. If this goes badly, we could end up destroying Grace forever."

"Yes, you've been more than clear on that point, sir," McCain said, pulling her arm from his grip and continuing on her way.

"I'll be in the lab monitoring the virus in Waters and DuPont."

"Good. That's exactly where you should be," Lady McCain said over her shoulder as she rounded the corner.

*   *   *   *   *

The cell Emmett ended up in wasn't that bad, all things considered. It was concrete as folks would expect, and there certainly wasn't a window or anything—which considering they were sixty feet below the surface of the earth was not something that anybody had in their rooms, prisoner or not. The bed was a real bed, not some slab or some iron thing bolted to the wall. There was a nightstand-like cabinet next to it. A four-foot privacy wall in front of the toilet. There was even a tablet—a Chuwi, which he assumed was some Chinese model he'd never heard of—with books and movies (including a respectable collection of pornography) loaded on it, but, not surprisingly, no net connectivity. He certainly didn't want to stay locked up down here any longer than he had to, but it could certainly be worse.

Still, even with a comfy bed and a whole library of entertainment at his disposal, he couldn't stop thinking about Black Jesus. Or more specifically how he'd betrayed him. It would have been one thing if the Captain had been an asshole or abusive or even just untrusting on their trek south. But he hadn't been. He'd given Emmett the benefit of the doubt—and he was sure Black Jesus had had doubts. The man was not a fool. He had to have questioned Emmett's assertion that he could be satisfied by just a confrontation with Dr. Weiss and that he didn't need to hurt the man. That he just need to hear it from the man's own mouth, before he could put it to bed forever.

How could anybody believe that? he told himself, trying to shift the guilt he was suffering into blame. *Of course, I always intended to get my pound of flesh. What kind of idiot would think anything else, regardless of what I said? The Captain put the gun in my hand himself for the love of Christ! This was his fault.*

Except that it wasn't.

Except that Black Jesus had a way of making him want to be the kind of man who was not driven by revenge. The kind of man who could rise above wrath. The kind of man Black Jesus treated him like he already was. Or, had treated him like anyway.

With the exception of his girls—who at this point he'd more or less written off as long dead—Black Jesus was the only person Emmett would admit he loved in the whole world. Maybe Wiley too, but not in the same way. Given a choice between that love and ending the monster that had triggered this whole thing to begin with, it broke his heart that he knew already he wasn't even going to really try to save the relationship.

Even before Lady McCain came in and pitched him her plan, Emmett Kessler had been plotting and scheming in the nether reaches of his mind. So when the Old Lady had walked in and given him the key to gaining another audience with the man he had to kill, no amount of regret about the damage it'd do to his friendship with Black Jesus was going to keep him from it.

If he'd known what Wiley's and the Captain's roles were going to end up being in the coup he'd been enlisted to start, he may have reconsidered. If he'd known that his actions would directly result in the deaths of hundreds of thousands of people who'd ostensibly done no harm to anyone, he *would* have reconsidered. But as he listened to the old woman lay out what he needed to do to get what he wanted, he failed to think critically at anything that lay between her words. He failed to ask the right questions, or frankly any questions at all. And the irony of it all was that in this postapocalyptic universe, while Weiss may have sparked the initial flame setting the world on fire, it was going to be Emmett's narrow-sighted obsession with punishing him for it that would be responsible for humanity ultimately being burned to the ground.

Who would come calling to hold him accountable for that fact was, of course, still being calculated in that ultimate equation, but the formula for the reckoning had been established as long ago as the one which had driven Emmett to this place, at this point in time, to begin with. Folks may all ultimately just be cogs in a machine beyond their comprehension, but that didn't make it any less true that every time a man points his finger in blame, he's got three fingers pointing right back at himself.

Chapter Six
Slave by Choice

BOBBY-LEIGH COULD SEE the disdain in Anoona's eyes, and it made her want to walk over there and punch the woman right in the fucking face. Yes, it was undeniable that Bobo was slow when it came to processing language, but she'd seen with her own eyes that the giant was anything but stupid. Also, it was her experience that a lot more information got in then made it back out, so just because he couldn't respond appropriately, didn't mean he wasn't understanding what was going on.

Did they really think I'd have been able to keep his existence a secret for this long if he was just some helpless retarded baby-man? she screamed inside her head.

She could tell that her sister was reading her mind because Jen was subtly shaking her head warning her against doing anything stupid. Their eyes locked. Jen moved her gaze over to Sarah on the steps with her AR-15 between her legs. But Bobby-Leigh already knew the stakes here. She didn't need her sister to remind her. Rolling her eyes dismissively and letting out a loud sigh, she maturely opted to use her words instead of her fists.

"Look, he's not retarded. I mean he is, but he's not stupid. He was the one who built that shelter. Not me. Maybe he doesn't talk so good, but he's smarter than you think."

"'Retarded' is a pretty offensive term, sweetheart."

Bobby-Leigh fought the urge to roll her eyes again and lost. She shut them as quickly as she could and shook her head. "Sorry."

"If we're going to tell him that to stay here he basically has to be a slave, then I think it's important to know he understands the choice," her sister spoke up.

"He's not going to be a slave," Anoona said.

"You're going to put a collar on him and make him do all the heavy work. What would you call it?" Bobby-Leigh said, knowing she was skating on thin ice, but not able to help herself.

"He's not going to be a slave. Nobody is going to force him to do anything or force him to stay here if he doesn't want to."

"But if he does want to," Brennachecke added, "then we need to take some precautions."

Tiny took the explosive collar out of a box. It was a pretty simple construction. Cable wrapped in trip wire that would detonate if the collar was broken. A small transmitter to detonate remotely. Three evenly spaced, small charges. All wrapped in a red cloth band for comfort per Jen's insistence. "It'll take about ten minutes to put it on and activate it," he said. "If he's willing to wear it."

"And if he's not, you're really going to just let me walk him out of here and get him someplace safe? You're not going to just execute him."

"Yes," Anoona said.

Bobby-Leigh looked at her until she could see through her, and she saw that the black woman had not realized it was a lie until the word came out of her mouth. Smiling, the little girl nodded. There had never been any doubt in her head that Bobo would be killed if he didn't cooperate. There was something comforting about seeing that everybody was now on the same page, even if they were afraid to admit it.

"Bobo," she said, drawing the berserker's attention.

"Bah-Leh!"

"My friends want you to come live here. With me. They want to be your friends too. Just like I am. But they're afraid of you."

Bobo smiled.

Bobby-Leigh knew that she was the only one who knew what that smile meant. They couldn't just stick to the shorthand they'd developed over the months they'd been friends. He was going to have to communicate in a way everybody could understand, or the party was going to end early and messy.

"I know," she told him. "But they don't understand you yet. If you want to stay here—with me—you're going to have to find some words."

Another big smile from Bobo.

But no words.

"Berserkers hurt people sometimes," Jen offered. "I'm one too. I know."

Suddenly Bobo smashed the coffee table in front of them. The collar flipped across the room as the wood split and splintered. Sarah had her AR-15 lined up for the kill shot before the little explosive device landed on the ground. But she didn't pull the trigger.

Everybody else cringed back reflexively, except for Bobby-Leigh.

Bobo smiled again and leaned forward.

"Ate. Be-zer-kah," the monster said, and then his face exploded into another toothless smile.

Jen smiled.

"I can help you control it."

"Sis-tah," Bobo said.

Bobby-Leigh got the collar and brought it back.

"You have to wear this as long as you live here."

A big smile from Bobo.

"If you berserk out and put any of us in danger, it will kill you. Do you understand?"

Bobo smiled.

Bobby-Leigh put the collar on him. Tiny nervously fastened it in place and armed it.

Bobo smiled again. Then to everybody's surprise, the big man's face twisted, his chin shook, and tears began to fall from his eyes—but even as he cried his smile never waned.

"Sank. You," he whispered.

Jen, just as caught off guard as everybody else by Bobo's emotional response to having a bomb strapped around his neck, suddenly felt a sob in her throat as she realized what Bobo was feeling. Wiping her eyes, she stood up and threw her arms around the giant and whispered something in his ear that nobody else could hear, nor most likely would have been able to understand even if they had.

Bobo's ten-megawatt smile jumped to twenty-five.

"So, we done here?" Bobby-Leigh asked, desperately trying to fight off the twinge of jealousy toward her sister that had abruptly flared up in her brain as she watched her—she didn't want to say pet, but that was the word that came to her—in her sister's arms.

"Yes. Thank you, Bobby-Leigh," Anoona said sincerely.

"Come on, Bobo," she said, taking his hand and pulling him away from Jen. "I'll show you around."

*   *   *   *   *

Tiny had been staring at Jen for almost fifteen minutes straight as she updated the OB app before she noticed, but she gave him another minute before she said anything.

"Tiny."

"Yeah," the fat man said, clearly oblivious to the fact that he'd been staring at her.

"You got something on your mind?"

"What do you mean?"

"Asshole, you've been staring at me for like twenty fucking minutes, dude. You're creeping me the fuck out."

"What?" Tiny said defensively, "No, I haven't. It's not always about you, you vain little—"

"Don't you call me a bitch."

"Bitch."

Jen smiled at him. "Seriously, dude. Something's clearly up. Talk to me."

Tiny looked at her, clearly assessing whether whatever it was he wanted to ask her was going to damage their relationship.

Fuck, Jen thought, suddenly worried about what it might actually be.

"What did you say to him?"

"Who?"

"Bobo."

Jen smiled. "You'd have to be one of us to understand."

"A berserker?"

"Yep."

"Just tell me."

"What difference does it make?"

"Do you how long it took me to learn the code you're debugging right now?"

"Like five minutes."

"No."

"Six minutes?"

"Try six months. And I already knew how to code."

"Okay, so you're a good teacher... What do you want? A parade?"

"I'm not talking about my teaching. I was teaching myself, back then, so clearly it's not the teaching."

"So what? I get the parade then?"

"God, no. Your code is atrocious. The reason I'm asking you is because you look at me and you see this guy who knows what they're doing, right?"

"Sure."

"Watching you with Bobo, I realized that you know what you're doing too. Not with computers, at least not yet. But you and your sister too, you guys are as much experts when it comes to berserkers as I am when it comes to computer systems."

"Did you find Rachel's pot?"

"I'm trying to pay you a compliment. Tell you I underestimated you."

"Which is how I know you're high as a motherfucker right now."

"Ha, ha, ha. No seriously, I didn't really think berserkers mattered, you know. Like they were just animals, especially ones like Bobo, but—"

Jen felt the anger spark in her. *Was Tiny really so*

*fucking white and male that he didn't know what the fuck
he was saying?* she thought. *He was! Jesus Christ.* Jen took
a deep breath in so she could expel fire.

"But now you see we're people too. That's fucking
great, Tiny. If you replaced 'berserker' with 'black person,'
and told Anoona the same thing, do you think she'd be
fucking honored by your fucking revelation of the obvious, or do you think she'd punch you in the face? Because
I'm about to punch you in the face."

She knew Tiny was going to be caught utterly off
guard by her anger, but she didn't care. It wasn't her
responsibility to teach him not to be a bigoted asshole.
It was on him to figure that shit out.

"I didn't—that's not what I was trying to say. I'm sorry."

"Look, you want to know what I told Bobo? I'll tell
you. But you're never going to understand it. You're too
white and too male and frankly too much of an asshole."
She looked at him. Desperately trying to stay angry and
hold him accountable for his ignorance and naivety. But
it was hard. He was so obviously horrified that she'd been
offended. The fact was he wasn't an asshole. He was just
a moron.

It was a lot easier to hate assholes.

"I told him he was free now," she said and waited for
his inevitable response.

"I don't understand." And bam! There it was.

"No fucking shit, dude. I told you you wouldn't."

"But I want to, Jen. I know I said things all wrong
here, but I'm honestly just recognizing that there is this
massive hole in my understanding of berserkers, and I'd
like to fill it in."

Jen closed her eyes and rubbed them.

Fuck it.

"The worst part of being a berserker is the constant fear that something unpredictable will happen and you'll hurt somebody you care about. That fear, because it's like there all the time raining on every fucking moment of happiness you have, is worse than when the surprise comes and you do actually hurt somebody you love—though that really sucks dick too.

"You guys all see that fucking collar as some kind of shackle that makes him a slave or something—and on the one hand it is, obviously, and all of us need to be aware of that, so we can avoid him actually becoming one—but for Bobo, that thing isn't making him a prisoner.

"It's freedom.

"It's like every day for him he's been strapped up with one of those suicide bomb vest things, and then been invited to Thanksgiving dinner, with no idea of who has the trigger, when they're going to blow him and everyone around him up or why.

"Every day is like—was like that for him. But now he knows his mom is the one holding the trigger. He can't get the vest off, but at least he can relax and eat his fucking turkey now, you know? Because his mom isn't going to make him kill anybody he loves."

Tiny nodded and didn't say anything for a long time. Jen was cautiously optimistic that some of what she'd said may have actually penetrated his moronic brain.

"Are we ready for Mari?" he finally asked.

"It still says I'm pregnant and then crashes, but I corrected the code like you showed me to for the other bugs and ran it through like fifty simulations. No errors."

"I've tried to reproduce your Jen Bug with every single person here—except Bobo—and I can't get it to repeat. So I think for now, we'll just tolerate it.

"Though, you know what? We should try it on Bobo. If it says he's pregnant, then we know it's something about being a berserker that's messing it up. And if it doesn't, then we know it just doesn't like you for some reason."

They called Bobo over.

He wasn't pregnant.

"We could give you an ultrasound…" Tiny suggested.

"God, you're an asshole," Jen said by way of refusal.

* * * * *

Bobby-Leigh watched as Bobo single-handedly replaced the shot-out picture window in the dining room.

"He must have muscle memory of some kind. Been like a carpenter or something before, you know?" Sarah commented. She and Rachel were also watching Bobo work.

Bobby-Leigh wondered if that was true. It would explain a lot, but she wasn't about to cut anybody any slack about misjudging her—again, pet was the word that popped into her head first, but she shoved it back down as quick as it surfaced and went with *friend* instead.

"Or maybe he's just not stupid like you all seem to think," she snipped.

"Honey, she didn't—" Rachel began, but Sarah shook her head, making it clear that no explanation was necessary. And she was right. Bobby-Leigh wasn't even listening anymore.

The wind and snow suddenly picked up as Bobo was finishing, and then it steadily got worse from there. By the time the giant had put the tools away and come inside, his hair and beard were matted with snow, icicles were hanging off his mustache, and if he'd still had any teeth, they certainly would have been chattering like they were being played by a seven-year-old on cocaine with a drum set. But of course, he didn't have any teeth anymore, so the shivering was eerily silent instead.

Bobby-Leigh met him at the door with a cup of coffee and was rewarded with what was becoming his signature move, a ten-thousand-watt smile.

"He looks like the abominable snowman," Mari said, giggling from the kitchen as she pulled silverware out to set the table with.

Bobby-Leigh smiled at her and nodded. Bobo, of course, smiled too.

"Supper is in twenty minutes," Bobby-Leigh informed him. "You should go downstairs and get dry. I'll come get you when it's ready."

Bobo smiled and obeyed.

Bobby-Leigh set about to help Mari set the table.

Anoona cooked the meals now. Before Hamm had been killed, cooking had always been his thing, and since Hamm had been her thing, well, somehow it just made sense that his thing would be passed onto her with his death. Or at least that was how Bobby-Leigh thought Anoona saw it. The little girl knew the truth though. Anoona was the cook because she wanted to be, and she was the boss. Not that anybody else wanted to do it. Hamm had been in culinary school before he had quit and tried his luck at Grinnell, but Anoona had still always been the better cook. She'd just never openly challenged him on the duty.

The farm now produced almost twenty fresh vegetables and herbs, plus chickens and eggs. The variety was all thanks to Maddie, who like Anoona was now very territorial about her station. She'd confided in Bobby-Leigh once that being in the grow houses was the only way she could tolerate staying on the farm. There was only so much being repeatedly and blatantly ignored regarding the little girl's pregnancy that she could put up with.

In addition to what they produced in house, Sarah and Rachel had procured a dangerous amount of flour, sugar, and other baking staples, which Anoona used to bake bread, sweets, and what have you. Dinner, though awkward in terms of conversation, was the thing they looked forward to the most during the day.

"Bobby-Leigh," Anoona called out, as the little girl was finishing setting the glasses on the table. "I wasn't sure the best way to prepare Bobo's meal. I know he doesn't have any teeth, so…I was thinking of maybe using the whizzer. What do you think?"

Bobby-Leigh smiled, thinking about how long it took Bobo to gum the food down she'd brought him over the months and months she'd been hiding him. It had never occurred to her to do something to the food to make it easier for him to get down.

"So it'd be like a shake or something?"

"More like baby food, but yeah. Do you think he'd be okay with that?"

"Uh, yeah. I think he'd fucking love it."

"Language!" Brennachecke called out halfheartedly from the stairwell as he brought up a chair for Bobo.

Anoona rolled her eyes at Bobby-Leigh conspiratorially. Something had shifted since Bobo's arrival in the dynamic between them. They were on the same side now. She and Mari weren't fighting anymore, or at least they weren't fighting anymore about whether the baby should be kept. That meant that Bobby-Leigh didn't have to try so hard to hate her. Bobby-Leigh smiled back with an oops face.

"It is very nice to have that window replaced," Sarah said.

Everybody agreed.

Bobo smiled.

The food was healing.

"So, Jen, I'd like you to carve out some time tomorrow to start teaching Bobo the Transcendental Meditation stuff like your uncle taught you, okay?" Anoona said halfway through the meal.

"Um, I don't actually know how to teach that," Jen said. "I can work with him on some of the other techniques I've learned though."

"I thought TM was like the foundation of everything you did?"

"It is, but…"

"Can't you just show him how to do it?"

"Well, there are all these advanced techniques. TM teachers have this whole training that they get before they start teaching—I don't know how they figure out the mantras."

"I can give you the mantras," Tiny said.

"How?"

"I found them a while ago in one of the machines we got from Vedic City. I'm guessing somebody pissed off about how much it cost to learn TM put the whole list of them online, complete with how to decide who gets what one."

"Really? Still, I wish JP was, you know—he'd at least done the training."

"But he's not." Anoona said.

Jen shot Anoona a nasty, hurt look. But Mari's mother just sent it right back at her, minus the hurt.

"Okay, fine."

"Great."

Part Two:

Zombies

"It has become appallingly obvious that our technology has exceeded our humanity."

—Albert Einstein

I am the Alpha and the Omega, the First and the Last, the Beginning and the End.

Blessed are those who wash their robes, that they may have the right to the tree of life and may go through the gates into the city.

Outside are the dogs, those who practice magic arts, the sexually immoral, the murderers, the idolaters, and everyone who loves and practices falsehood.

—Revelation 22:13–15

"When life closes a door, it opens a window. And then zombies climb in and eat you."

—Anonymous

Chapter Seven
The Other Cheek

AUSTIN WAS SURROUNDED BY almost twenty miles of sprawl on all sides. The city had been walled off along I-35 on the east, up as far as 183 in the north, then down 360 to the west and across 290 on the south. The walls were nearly a hundred and fifty feet high and twenty feet thick. Constructed out of steel-reinforced concrete, they somehow managed to look both futuristic and medieval at the same time. Short of a direct hit with a nuclear weapon, they were more or less impenetrable, but even if there were no walls at all, Austin was set up to only work for folks who had been saved.

Without Grace, you couldn't open a door, get a car, or buy anything. Plus, eventually, the patrol drones would find you. You'd be tagged and tracked, and any folks who took mercy upon your plight and tried to help you would find their benevolence broadcast across the Registry. The citizens of Austin would then drag their life under a microscope and openly question if they were really worthy of Grace or not. If the artificial intelligence at the heart of the system determined that in fact they *were* not worthy, it would strip Grace from them overnight without any notice whatsoever.

Without Grace, folks either died of thirst, hunger, and exposure in the Austin streets, or they made a life outside the walls of the city on their own accord in the sprawl.

Dr. Weiss stood at the expanse of windows overlooking the city from his luxury penthouse on the fifty-third floor of the Austonian building. He was lost in thought, watching the snow float down from the clouds. Out of the corner of his eye, he could see two Austin skyscrapers that were taller, but he didn't have any interest in being in either of them.

This was as close to heaven as he dared to live.

Weiss had no illusions about how precarious his seat at the table of God probably was. No amount of Grace in his system could ever fully rid his soul of sin. He'd turned his back on Jesus for so many years in Germany during World War II that even though the Lamb of God had told him personally that he had been truly forgiven for those trespasses, he knew—with absolute conviction—that neither Dyer, nor the Heavenly Father, could ever really forget his criminal work as a Nazi.

It had to always be there in the back of their minds. A dormant seed of doubt always waiting, just shy of the tiny drop of water it needed to sprout and entangle him in its swift growing vines of damnation. But, he supposed, that was the whole point of Grace. It wasn't enough to repent once and open your arms to the Lord. Weiss had helped Dyer engineer Grace to be something one must continue to prove they were worthy of, or be at risk of having it stripped away.

Such a powerful idea, he thought, and not for the first time.

So powerful that the Republic of Austin didn't need laws to govern.

He had to be careful of course. This wasn't the first time he'd been swept up in what he believed was truly God's work. He'd swallowed the Nazi party line whole too, only to be horrified that he'd been so naive years later after he'd fled to Brazil to escape being tried for crimes against humanity.

But this was different.

He was older now. Wiser now. And now, he was saving humanity. Thanks to the Lord's system, his faith and enthusiasm as one of the architects of heaven on Earth would never wane.

That was the power of Grace.

And yet Emmett Kessler had tried to murder him. Weiss wished that he knew what sin the man had come to call him to account for. He'd refreshed his memory of who Kessler was via the Registry, but still found the answer wanting. He'd done nothing but help the man and his family as far as he could tell. And yet, the hatred he'd seen in Emmett's eyes was so intense that even with Grace subduing his emotional response, he still had gone cold inside.

Even if he was acting as an agent of the Bunkermen, which seemed the most reasonable explanation, no amount of brainwashing could have instigated that kind of abhorrence. He bore the man no ill will, even after the attempt on his life. Grace made it hard to hold on to ill will, and he knew that was a blessing. *How many souls had been devoured by the insatiable demons of wrath?* he thought as the snow hemmed and hawed its way down to Earth in front him.

A search window popped up in his field of view and populated with Emmett Kessler's name for the fifth time in half as many days, but just as it had before, the search came back empty for the man's location.

"He must be back in a bunker somewhere," a voice said behind him.

Weiss turned and smiled at Ruth, his fourth wife. It was still early, and the others must still be asleep in their rooms, he thought.

"Can I cook you some eggs?" she asked him.

Weiss looked at her nipples pressing through the sheerness of her nightgown and was thankful that Grace was tempering his lust. Ruth smiled as she recognized the desire in his face. For a second, Weiss was afraid she might come to him and coax his desire past what Grace could mitigate, but she didn't. She went into the kitchen instead and took the eggs out of the refrigerator.

Recreational sex, especially between a man and his wives, was not a sin in the eyes of the Republic of Austin. But it wasn't exactly godly, either. And all things considered, a reputation for perversion was not something he was eager to cultivate. With the exception of maybe Dyer himself, Weiss knew all too well that Grace could be stripped from anybody regardless of rank or deeds, for in the eyes of the Lord, all men were equal. And he was not about to risk being thrown out of paradise just because Ruth's libido was so high even God couldn't put a dent in it. He turned back to the window and watched the snow coming down in the dawn light once more.

Just as his thoughts were returning to his past, a message popped up in his glasses alerting him that at long last, Kessler had been identified once again in Texas. In Jasper.

The one drive that Grace couldn't touch sparked to life and burned instantly inside him. It was the drive that had propelled him into science as a young boy. The drive that had propelled him to commit atrocities as a Nazi. The drive that had led to all his breakthroughs in fertility, obstetrics, and genetics. It was the drive to know that which has heretofore been unknowable. The drive to understand. The drive of man toward omniscience.

As the rich smell of melting butter filled his nostrils and the sound of eggs frying rang in his ears, Weiss reached out to Sinclair for some answers. With the power of the Almighty God on his side, he simply shouldn't have to be content with the vague conjectures bouncing around the Registry about Kessler possibly being recruited by the Bunkermen. He wanted to know what lived in the man's heart as if it were his own.

That is what Elijah Dyer had seduced him with when he'd been enlisted to help incorporate his breakthroughs with CRISPR gene editing into LSD's nanotechnology. A chance to eventually know everything. To eventually utterly dispel the secrets of men and nature alike. Just as if he were God himself.

* * * * *

The three men reappeared in Jasper just as the sun cut through the sky's dark clouds with broadswords of dawn light. The snow was sharp and biting. The cold was wet and thick. However, the embers of the secrets they each carried with them kept them as warm as it did quiet.

The highway was slick with ice. And the going was slow. Wiley led the three-man parade, his huge frame screening the others from the worst of the wind. Waters walked behind Emmett with a hand on his shoulder for support. His prisoner had already slipped and fallen on his face twice. The old guard did not want the man to fall again, even if he did deserve the humiliation. Unable to put his hands out to catch himself because of the handcuffs that bound his wrists behind his back, Emmett now had a mess of blood frozen around his nose and clinging to his beard.

It took about fifteen minutes for Sinclair's men to show up after the Old Lady's henchmen had dropped them off at a long abandoned gas station along the 96 just outside of town. Waters wondered if they would have come as fast if he hadn't put his glasses on and tried to geolocate where they were. Probably not. They hadn't seen any drones, but visibility was shit with the snow, so that certainly didn't mean they weren't out there.

When the self-driving SUV pulled up next to them, it was Smalls who called out to them from the lowered window.

"Howdy, boys. We thought maybe you'd skipped town or something. At least until we realized your horses were still here. You boys get lost in the snow?"

"Actually, Smalls," Captain Waters said coldly, "I've wasted the last week chasing these two down after you let them out of their cell in the middle of the night. So thanks for that."

It was exactly what the Old Lady had told him to say when they were approached, but that was all part of the secret agenda he now had. Neither Emmett nor Wiley knew anything about his plans, but for as much as they were not expecting to hear the him say that, their shock was nothing compared to the shock that exploded all over Smalls's face.

"After I…" Smalls began, his eyes flickering as he reviewed the security camera footage and saw to his horror that he had indeed released Captain Waters's prisoners.

Pulling his glasses off his head and rubbing his eyes, he laughed self-consciously. "I, um—"

"The least you could do is give us a ride back to the station," Waters said, cutting him off.

"Of course," Smalls said.

*   *   *   *   *

Wiley helped Emmett out of the vehicle when they arrived at the station.

"Can you wipe my nose, please?" Emmett asked him as he looked past Wiley and met eyes with Sinclair, who was waiting for them in the doorway.

"Sure, brother," Wiley said and used his sleeve to clean up his friend as best he could.

"I've granted DuPont a pardon," Waters told Sinclair, "but Kessler needs to be returned to lockup."

Sinclair nodded.

"And we need to talk about your man, Smalls," he added. "I assume that by now you're up to speed on his role in things."

"Smalls, return Mr. Kessler to his room, please," Sinclair said.

"Leave the cuffs on him," Waters added.

"What? Come on, dude. That's just fucking petty. How many times do I have to say, I'm sorry?" Emmett moaned as Smalls escorted him inside.

"I'm still not sure I can trust Smalls, Emmett. I don't want to have to chase your ass down again if he forgets to lock the door behind him."

Black Jesus met his eyes, and in them, Emmett searched for a message. He was more than ready to get back on board with whatever the CO's agenda was, but there was nothing in the man's face to clue him in. *Why was he busting Smalls's balls over something he knew the man had no fault in?* he wondered as they turned the corner and he lost sight of Black Jesus completely.

*　*　*　*　*

Captain Waters left Wiley standing in the parking lot. He knew the man would be a little lost as to what to do with himself, but he didn't have time to hold his hand through whatever stage of reacclimating to his freedom he was in at the moment. The giant would just have to wipe his own ass for an hour while he ensured that they were not cut down as cannon fodder in this brewing war between the Austinites and the Bunkermen.

"Sit," Sinclair said when they reached his office.

Waters obeyed, but he waited until Sinclair had rounded his desk and put his own ass in his chair before he did. There he waited for the man to speak first, which took a minute.

"Are you familiar with the Bunkermen?" Sinclair asked.

"Just what I stumbled across on the Registry."

Sinclair nodded.

"But, Sinclair, I am not here to talk about mole people living in the hills. I think you know that."

"Actually, I think you might be," Sinclair said. "See, we believe your Mr. Kessler may have been—" He paused, searching for just the right word. "*Aided* by them in his escape."

"Unless you're going to tell me Smalls is one of them, I don't think Kessler needed any help escaping. Your man just opened the door and let him and DuPont walk out."

"Yes. We have evidence that Smalls was…hacked. It's happened a few times before—not with him, mind you, but with others. The Bunkermen exploit weaknesses they find in the security protocols of a person's glasses, then use it to hypnotize the owner. After analysis of the video feed and looking into Smalls's synaptic record, I can assure you that Smalls was being directed by an outside influencer when he released your prisoner."

"Why would they do that?"

"Actually, it wasn't Mr. Kessler they were likely after. It was DuPont. You see, just like Prometheus stole fire from his gods, the Bunkermen want to steal Grace from ours."

Captain Waters smiled. The Old Lady had described herself as Prometheus to him as well. She would have relished the fact that the Austinites saw her that way too. "Don't you cats give Grace to anybody who asks for it? Why steal something that is already free?"

"Well, *free* may not quite be the right word here. Yes, it's true that Faith costs you nothing, but it is hardly free. Wouldn't you agree?"

"Sure."

"Since they refuse to accept Jesus Christ into their hearts, the only way for them to get God's Grace is to steal it."

"But doesn't God know who He's given Grace to and who He hasn't?"

"Of course. They want more than just to get their hands on it. They seek to corrupt it. To turn it against the very souls it was bestowed upon to save."

"I caught up to Wiley pretty fast. He didn't mention anything about being approached by your mole men."

"They wouldn't have needed to reveal themselves to him. The fact of the matter is, the poor man's Grace has been stolen right out from beneath him."

"You know this for a fact."

"Yes."

"So he's a berserker again then?"

"No, once those demons are exorcised, they are smited forever.

"But I suppose you need to question him about how he lost it?"

"With your permission, of course."

"If the berserker inside him is gone, then DuPont is a free man as far as I am concerned. You don't need my permission. You'll need his."

Sinclair smiled and then called out, "Send him in."

Waters turned and watched Wiley DuPont enter the room. This was it. As long as DuPont stuck to the script, they'd all be able to kiss Texas goodbye.

The only problem with Waters's plan was that Wiley DuPont had an agenda of his own. And this was the first time Captain Waters was going to know anything about it.

*   *   *   *   *

Julius Weiss was watching two things at once, and the effect was making him nauseous. In the lenses of his glasses, he was watching Sinclair interview DuPont and the corrections officer who had brought him and Emmett Kessler to Texas. Still, he couldn't help but also observe the depravity and poverty of the sprawl though the 360-degree wrap-around windows of the luxury, self-driving Tesla V transporting him out of Austin.

He knew it was the Austinites who were inadvertently responsible for these people's continued presence. Everybody did. *The Nazis would never have tolerated such a place's existence*, he thought, but he knew that probably wasn't actually true. And even if it was, did he honestly want to question the Lord's mercy? Yet he did not like that these people were here feeding off the City of the Lamb and the saved like cockroaches. These were sons of Cain, unworthy of Grace. Or worse, so evil as to be unwilling to open their hearts to Jesus's forgiveness even in the face of such overwhelming evidence of God's miracles.

Emmett Kessler was obviously one of these sons of Cain, he thought. God himself had forgiven Weiss his trespasses. So just who the fuck did Emmett think he was to harbor such murderous wrath against him? Weiss felt his blood boiling, and then he felt the soothing presence of Grace inside him. The man's impertinence was only natural, he realized as he watched the sex parlors, blood dens, and rag-wrapped children playing in the snow whisk past him, and the nanites in his blood manipulated his levels of serotonin, dopamine, and other neurotransmitters. *There but before the Grace of God go I*, he thought with a smile, as empathy pushed his anger away.

The navigation monitor popped up. He'd be face-to-face with his accuser in less than three hours.

"Feeling blessed for the opportunity to embrace my enemy" popped up as an update to his social media feed. He confirmed the post with a smile and closed his eyes.

"Wake me ten minutes before we get there," he said.

"Alert set," the honey-sweet voice of the system—like a god in its own right—confirmed with a whisper inside his head.

*　　*　　*　　*　　*

Wiley DuPont would have done almost anything Jackie had asked of him after the three days and nights they'd spent together in her apartment. Anything but the one thing she'd actually asked.

The woman could rock his world until the cows laid eggs and the chicken produced milk, but it wasn't ever going to make him jeopardize his chances to get God's Grace back. Wiley had felt its power firsthand. He'd been healed by it. Saved by it. He'd thought about it to death. There just was no argument, revelation, or judgment that could compete with that visceral experience.

He'd decided that all this talk of ethnic cleansing and brainwashing was clearly just the one side trying to smear the reputation of the other. Wiley's faith in God's plan at this point was absolute. He didn't blame Jackie and her people from wanting Grace for themselves, but what he couldn't wrap his head around was why they refused to accept Jesus into their hearts to get it.

Likewise, though he was loyal to Black Jesus to a fault, there was no way in hell he was going to leave Texas without getting Grace again. He'd keep his knowledge of the Bunkermen a secret like Captain Waters wanted because he knew it was necessary to protect him and Emmett, and that it would also protect Jackie—which was just as important to him. He also felt no obligation to protect God's plan. Certainly, the Lord could take care of that himself. To think he could even comprehend it was blasphemous in his mind. So once Sinclair had explained to him his Grace had been stolen, he tossed the script Black Jesus had gone over with him in the trash and lit it on fire.

He was supposed to say: *I don't understand. What does that mean?* But what he said instead was, "How do I get it back?"

This wasn't that far off from what Black Jesus was expecting him to say, so his guardian—or former guardian, he supposed if he was indeed now a free man—still stuck to the book. "Maybe we're better off counting the blessings we've already received—" he started to say, but Wiley cut him off.

"This *is* a blessing I already received, Captain. And it's one that I want back."

"Have you been baptized, Mr. DuPont?"

"Of course," Wiley said. He dared not look at Waters, but even without seeing the man's face, he could tell Black Jesus was not liking this little improvisation of his.

"Well, I can petition Dyer to baptize you again into God's Grace if you'd like. You'll have to travel to Austin for the ceremony of course. Way stations like ours are only set up for exorcisms—"

"How long will that take?" Waters interjected.

"Well, there's a whole process. But let me put Mr. DuPont on the list. Maybe I can get his case escalated, considering the circumstances."

"Thank you," Wiley said.

Black Jesus said nothing.

"I'm sorry, Captain. I know you were looking to get Emmett as far away from Texas as possible, before he does anything else stupid."

"You're a free man, DuPont. If this is something you really want, who am I to stop you?"

Wiley smiled.

"Will his teeth come back once Grace has run its full course?"

"Yes, of course. He'll be remade anew as a child of the Lord. Every wound, imperfection, and stain of sin gets wiped away. The effect of Grace is…miraculous in every sense of the word."

"Will you at least stay for the ceremony?" Sinclair asked Waters as he confirmed something appearing in his glasses. "Looks like they can do it as early as the day after tomorrow."

Wiley looked at Waters. Waters sighed.

"Can I trust you to keep Kessler locked up here until we return?"

Sinclair smiled. "Of course."

"I don't want to come and find him missing because another one of your men was hacked."

"We've upgraded everybody's gear here, and that particular vulnerability has been closed in the system. You have nothing to worry about."

Waters nodded in a way Wiley knew meant the Captain was pretty sure he couldn't believe anything the man sitting across from them was saying. Fact was, Black Jesus had a lot of things to worry about.

"But, Captain Waters," Sinclair added. "I'd be remiss if I didn't tell you that if you should decide to accept Grace yourself—which of course you should feel no pressure or obligation to do, unless the Spirit so moves you—I won't be able to keep Mr. Kessler under lock and key indefinitely. We don't imprison boys here in the Republic. The only law here is God's will, and we leave it up to Him to enforce it."

Black Jesus smiled and nodded again. But Wiley couldn't for the life of him figure out why his friend thought Sinclair was lying. It all sounded pretty damn good to him.

*   *   *   *   *

The cell was smaller than Emmett remembered it. Darker. Colder. And without Wiley, it was lonelier too. But he knew one way or another he wouldn't be in it for long.

Black Jesus was obviously going to try to drag him as far away from Texas as he could as quickly as possible. The Old Lady had warned him that the old black man had not been inclined to volunteer his services to their little coup. She'd told him the Captain's only real interest, aside from some idle curiosity about how Grace worked and the Bunkermen's mission to corrupt it, was keeping him from carrying out the murder he so desperately wanted to commit.

She'd made it clear that Emmett would certainly be up against the clock, if he intended to get his revenge. But she'd also laid out a plan to keep him one step ahead of the man who was both his jailer and his friend.

"Hey, Smalls," he called out before the man made it out of earshot.

"What do you want, Kessler?"

"Can anybody receive Grace?"

"Anybody who accepts the Lord Jesus Christ into his heart and survives being baptized."

"Survives being baptized?"

"If you're unworthy of Grace or lying about your acceptance of Christ, then…well, you piss God off."

This was the first he was hearing that there was a risk to the baptism procedure.

"How often does God—"

"Smite the wicked bastards who try to play him for a fool?"

"Yeah."

Smalls looked off into the distance, and Emmett knew the man was actually looking it up.

"Three-hundred and seventy-seven times."

"Out of how many?"

"Almost a million.

"Those are pretty good odds."

"Yeah, well, God's mercy is truly great, I guess. But, Kessler, if you're calculating the odds, friend, maybe you should ask yourself if you're really ready to accept Christ."

"If I was, what would happen?"

"We'd put you on the list and send you off to Austin to be baptized."

That was exactly what the Old Lady had told him they would do. All he had to do was ask. Nobody in the Republic would refuse a request for Grace. And anybody could petition for it.

"Just like that? What about Black Jesus—I mean Captain Waters?"

"Obviously, we'd have to tell your captain that you were going."

"But he wouldn't be able to stop me?"

"Emmett, if you're ready to accept God into your heart, no man can stop you from doing it."

"Maybe not, but my captain would certainly try."

"That's ridiculous. Why would he?"

Emmett didn't really have an answer to that particular question that made any sense in the context of this particular conversation. He just wanted Smalls to confirm what the Old Lady had told him. That if he was sent to Austin there was nothing Black Jesus could do to stop it from happening.

"Who knows, dude," Emmett said. "But if he *did* try to stop it, what would you do about it? Would you fight for my right to be saved?"

"If it came down to it, I suppose we would have to," Smalls said.

Emmett smiled, but suddenly the possibility that Black Jesus might actually resort to violence to keep him from going to Austin clouded his resolve. However, he recalled that when Waters had given him the gun he'd used to take his shot at Weiss, it had been to put Wiley down if he berserked out during the exorcism. It had been to keep everybody else safe. *And even when I was about to commit the murder, and a bullet to the head would have been the easiest way to intervene, the dude didn't kill me,* he told himself. *There's no way he's going to risk hurting anybody else. It's just not who the man is.*

"But, Emmett," Smalls said with what Kessler thought was genuine concern in his voice. "You don't want to be dicking around with God. With very few exceptions, you only get one chance at receiving Grace. If your intentions prove to be untrue, they'll strip it away. I've seen what happens to those people. Whatever hell you think you've known up to this point, I promise you will pale against that damnation."

"I understand."

"Well, if you are sincere, it would be my honor to start your petition."

Emmett thought about what the Old Lady had told him to say next, but he suddenly found it hard to actually say the words out loud. The fact was that while this was all subterfuge on the surface, underneath it, in that dark place folks try to pretend doesn't exist, he knew that what he was about to say was completely true. He felt a lump in his throat and had to swallow it back down before he could get the words out.

"Smalls, I've sinned, you know? So much that—I murdered my wife in front of my children, for fuck's sake. Even if I wanted to accept our Lord Jesus Christ as my savior, there is no way I'm worthy of his Grace." He took a deep breath and then whispered, "I don't deserve forgiveness, dude."

Smalls nodded and touched his hand on the bar in sympathy. Emmett's brain was getting twisted trying to reconcile speaking the truth while pursuing such an enormous lie. *For fuck's sake, I don't even believe in this shit,* he told himself. *Grace is just science.* He knew it with every ounce of his being. Science. The same goddamn shit that had created berserkers in the first place. This was about technology, not faith. And he was going to hold the man responsible to account, even if it was the last thing he did on Earth.

He let his wrath build until it pushed out everything else.

"Pray," Smalls said. "Ask him for forgiveness. Tell him you know you don't deserve it. That you can't even give it to yourself. That you need His help. Pray on it and see if by morning you don't feel a little more comfortable embracing his mercy."

"I'll do that," Emmett lied.

Smalls patted his hand and smiled.

Emmett resisted the urge to punch him in the face. He was utterly blind to the fact that all his anger at this man's willingness to forgive him was really anger at himself for not being able to let his guilt over killing Susan go. As Smalls left him to his prayers, Emmett thought about the two people on the planet who he actually did need to beg forgiveness from. He thought about his girls. He didn't know why or how, but he sensed somehow that they were still alive. If that was true, however, and they'd survived this long on their own, then they were probably better off without him.

Lost in his dark thoughts, he didn't hear the outer door open or the man carrying a small tray of food approach. But the second the man opened his mouth and spoke, Emmett knew him. His heart skipped around like the needle of an old record player on scratched vinyl in his chest as he slowly turned to face him.

"Dr. Weiss," he declared simply because he was at a loss to say anything else.

"May I bring your lunch in to you?"

Emmett stared deep into the man's face. This had to be a trick of some kind. Or maybe a test. The man was younger—though not really, he knew that all too damn well. But he certainly looked it, and worse than that, he looked like he was in great physical shape. Emmett was pretty sure he'd lose a straight-up physical fight between them. He looked at the tray of food, hoping there would be some silverware, but lunch was a sandwich and an apple. No utensils required. The tray wasn't metal or even plastic either. It was constructed of recycled paper.

Fuck! He couldn't kill the man with a piece of cardboard and a fucking sandwich!

His mind raced and danced until it finally locked on to the one thing he might be able to conscript into service as a deadly weapon. A smile spread across his face. Somewhere in that dark part of his mind, he knew all too well that it was the smile of a lunatic, but he also knew he was the only one who knew that.

"By all means," Emmett said at last. "Come in."

There was a pause while the doctor listened, or watched, or whatever it was folks did, to something coming in on his glasses.

"I'll be fine. Open the door, Mr. Smalls," Dr. Weiss said to the man who wasn't in the room with them.

Like magic, the door to Emmett's cell clicked.

Then, with a buzz, it opened.

Fuck the Old Lady and her revolution, he thought. *Who had time for all that conniving conspiracy bullshit when all I ever wanted for Christmas just walked right up to me and plopped itself down in my lap?*

Fuck Grace.

Fuck God.

Fuck praying.

I don't need any of it. Today is the day Julius Weiss is going to pay with his life for all the lives he destroyed.

Nothing else mattered.

* * * * *

Waters was still getting used to wearing the glasses, so he missed the first alert that raised its hand for his attention. He and Wiley were at a taco shop a few blocks away from the station, neither man talking much. The fact that tacos still existed was the only miracle the Captain was willing to give any thought to right now, so every time Wiley brought up Grace, he just replied with some variation of, *You don't need my permission, Wiley. You're a free man now.* He'd seen the shiny train-car-like Tesla V roll down the street, as silent as cancer in the brain, from the taco shop's window, but he'd dismissed it as inconsequential.

"Maybe I'll be able to go with you and Emmett when you head out."

"I don't think that's how it works."

"Well, they can't keep me here against my will."

"Let's face it. We have no idea what these people can and can't do. And, frankly, once Grace takes its course in you, I don't think you're going to want to come with us anymore. I have a sneaking suspicion that you'll find yourself pretty content to just stay here."

What the hell is that flashing thing? Waters thought, finally noticing the subtle alert trying to get his attention, but still failing to recognize it for what it was. Yet, as soon as his eye moved toward it, a display window opened up in his field of view and he saw and heard Sinclair advising him Weiss had shown up to ask Emmett a few questions.

Shit, he thought.

Next, he heard the man saying that if he wanted to be there for it, he'd better come soon because Weiss was not the kind of man Sinclair could keep waiting.

Jesus, when the hell was this sent? he wondered, already standing up.

"What's going on?" Wiley asked.

But Waters was already sprinting for the door and screaming, "Get him the fuck out of there, Sinclair! I don't care who the man is to you."

*   *   *   *   *

Folks who dream of revenge for long enough have rehearsed every conceivable confrontation scenario in their heads to the point that once the details are established, they often think they know exactly where the conversation will go. They've got the pivot point where they'll jump from words to violence all mapped out. They know what their poignant last words to their nemesis will be, whether they prevail in their vengeance or if they are bested and destroyed themselves.

Or at least they think they do.

Even with all the rehearsal folks do, not just of revenge scenarios, but of anything planned more than a few weeks out, very little in life ever goes down as predicted. If he'd known better, the moment Weiss spoke to him, Emmett Kessler would have been telling himself that if you want to hear God laugh in your face, all you have to do is make a plan. But Emmett didn't believe in God, and so he couldn't hear the cackling in the air as he nonchalantly sat down on the bench and started to slip off his boots.

His heavy steel-toed boots.

Dr. Weiss smiled at him. The man was not wearing any kind of formal ceremonial garb now. Just slacks and a blue mock turtleneck—the same color blue as the Republic of Austin flag. The material of Weiss's clothing was clearly very high end, but Kessler didn't know enough about fashion to be able to recognize any other details about it. He was sure blood would soak through it just like anything else.

"The last time I saw you, you thanked me. Do you remember that?"

"Actually, Doctor. The last time I saw you, I tried to put a bullet into your head. Do you remember that?"

"Yes, of course. But I'm talking about the time before that. Six weeks or so after Bobby-Leigh was born. You were so grateful. Do you remember? Susan, if I recall, said that God put people like me on Earth to fix his mistakes."

Emmett slid his foot out of his left boot and started to slowly remove the right one. "I had to put a bullet in Susan's head, Doctor. But I imagine you're aware of that."

"Yes, of course. A truly horrible situation. I don't know what else you could have done under the circumstances. I'm actually a little surprised at the severity of your sentence given the circumstances."

"Well...I didn't let them run tests on Susan's body, so there wasn't any actual physical evidence she'd berserked out. No eyewitness testimony. I refused to take the stand. There wasn't much my lawyer could do."

"Why?"

Emmett shrugged. "I guess I wanted to be punished."

"Interesting."

"What about you?"

"What about me what?"

"Don't you think you should be punished for destroying the world?"

Weiss looked deep into Emmett's eyes for a long time. For a second, Emmett thought the man was actually going to acknowledge his role in the whole thing. But the man just continued to stare and say nothing. Finally, he just couldn't take it anymore.

"I've tracked your research, Doctor. You never got credit for any of the breakthroughs, but every step of the way you were there. From the human genetics experimentation in those Nazi concentration camps to the development of test tube babies and IVF. It's funny that you've suddenly found religion now, considering how much of your life you spent using science to tell God to fuck himself."

Weiss still said nothing, so Emmett powered on toward his grand conclusion.

"Then you wrote a paper, doc. Something about how the fertility issues that were popping up in women born after the Second World War were the result of underlying genetic incompatibilities. That was in the eighties, right? And yet for the next fifty odd years, you dedicated your life to circumventing the biological fail-safes that naturally would have prevented berserkers from coming into existence."

Emmett bent forward and picked up his boots and set them on the seat next to him. He wanted Weiss to respond. In his fantasies about this confrontation, he imagined the doctor either denying his pivotal role in things or just flat out confirming it with a nonchalance that would more than justify his murder. The man's silence was not in the script.

"What did you think was going to happen? You basically bred us to be berserkers."

Weiss nodded and sighed.

"You're right. Science has never done a particularly good job of keeping up with the perils of what it makes possible, has it?"

"Not science. *Scientists.*"

"That's fair. In hindsight, maybe you're right. Maybe I should have anticipated more genetic anomalies in the children we made it possible for couples like you and Susan to have, but—"

Here it comes, Emmett thought.

Coiling to launch himself at Weiss, he grabbed his boot and readied himself to use it as a club to beat the man to death.

"There was no way to know—at least at the time anyway—that anything as destructive as berserkers was even possible. Nobody could have connected those dots,

Emmett. Not me, not anybody else. Not back then. I'm truly sorry about what happened to your family."

"Oh no, not yet you're not," Emmett growled, getting to his feet and about to swing his boot into the man's face, steel toe first. "But you will—"

"Sit down, Kessler!" Black Jesus suddenly called out as he burst through the outer chamber door, gun drawn. Kessler didn't sit, but he also didn't swing his improvised steel-toed club either. He turned and looked at Captain Waters, wondering if the man had been watching the whole time waiting for him to reveal his murderous intent or if this interruption was just a fancy bit of lucky timing. The only thing he could tell for sure was that Black Jesus knew the man was not safe with him.

"If you want to continue the confrontation you've been angling to have for as long we've know each other, you'll do it with your ass in that seat," he commanded, then added, without revealing whether he actually knew why Emmett had removed them in the first place, "And with your boots on your feet."

"Captain Waters," Dr. Weiss said. "This is just a friendly conversation here. There's no need for that."

"Friendly conversation, huh? The man has already tried to kill you once."

"The Lord is my shepherd. Though he may lead me through the valley of the Shadow of Death, I shall not be afraid. For I do not walk alone. His rod and his staff are there to comfort me."

"Yeah, okay. I'm going to join you for the rest of this conversation though—not to slight the old rod and staff of Jesus thing, but it's this .45 here that comforts me. Doesn't it comfort you, Kessler?"

Waters and Kessler stared each other down for almost a full minute, as Emmett tried to figure out the best way to play this particular development out.

So much for scrapping the Old Lady's plan, he thought, reluctantly accepting that there was really only one option here. *Guess I'm a goddamn revolutionary after all.*

"Nothing like a .45 when it comes to ensuring peace of mind, Captain," Emmett said, lacing his boots.

"How do you live with the guilt of knowing that you're responsible for the apocalypse?" Emmett asked Weiss. "I can't even bear mine over what happened to Susan."

"I pray, Emmett. Every day," Weiss answered, not even bothering to correct or clarify that the only person in the world—or what was left of it—insane enough to place the entire burden of the apocalypse on his doorstep was Emmett alone. "And I work as hard as I can to be worthy of the Grace God has granted me. God's mercy is boundless. I survive knowing that he has forgiven me, even on the days when I can't forgive myself."

"So this isn't just technology to you then, this whole Grace thing. You're a true believer."

"I was skeptical at first too. But then Elijah showed me what he was trying to do and why. God always holds open the doorway to redemption, Emmett. Sometimes it takes having every other door slammed in your face to see it, but the path to salvation is always there."

"Do you think your God would grant me Grace?" Emmett asked, more sincerely than he intended.

"All you have to do is ask for it. When you're able to do that, I promise you, Jesus will not let you down."

Emmett looked right at Black Jesus and smiled. Then dropping to his knees in front of the man he so desperately wanted to kill, he clasped his hands together, looked up to the ceiling, and said, "Jesus Christ, my Lord and savior, I have sinned. I have murdered. I have lied. I have—I have abandoned my daughters. I have wallowed in self-indulgence and misery. I have—I have done so much wrong that I fear nothing I can do will ever make it right. I cannot forgive myself these trespasses. I know I am unworthy of your love. Of your forgiveness. Of your Grace. And yet, your mercy is my only chance for redemption. Please God, you are my only hope."

He looked at Weiss hoping the Star Wars finish wasn't too much and was happy to see his nemesis looked completely taken in by his performance.

Clap. Clap. Clap.

Apparently Black Jesus was slightly less impressed. Emmett watched in silence as the man's slow clap bounced off the concrete walls.

"I think we need to get you to Austin," Weiss said, clearly annoyed at Black Jesus's mockery. Considering the man had saved the doctor's life twice, Emmett found it hilarious that Weiss so clearly disliked him. But, he knew better than to let that smile appear on his lips.

"Not going to happen," Black Jesus said, like this was a rational discussion and his opinion mattered.

It wasn't and it didn't.

Chapter Eight
What Little Girls Are Made Of

EVERY TIME THERE WERE TWO days or more without snow, it was hard not to hope that maybe—at last—this bizarre winter might actually give way to the spring. But now that it was April, and technically was spring, that hope blossomed in the exact way the flowers buried somewhere in the still frozen earth could not.

The record in Fairfield to date was four days consecutively without snow, but that had been all the way back in September. So as the sun set on what was now the fourth day of sunshine and temperatures in the low sixties, Bobby-Leigh wondered if maybe she was going to get spring for her birthday, which would totally make up for the fact that she was pretty sure even Jennifer had forgotten about her this year.

What was the big deal about being a teenager anyway? she tried to console herself. She'd been having her period for over a year now and had gotten her breasts already as well, so what difference did it make if she had a "teen" at the end of her age?

And yet, it seemed like it was a big deal. It seemed like, even in the middle of all this crazy shit, at least her sister should remember. It was a milestone, right? Wasn't there some kind of rite of passage she was supposed to be doing? A ceremony? She wondered if Jewish kids were still having bar mitzvahs or bat mitzvahs or whatever they called them. Even though she had no idea what those ceremonies meant or even really celebrated, Bobby-Leigh suddenly wished she was Jewish.

She could just remind everybody of course. But that seemed petty. And this just wasn't a good year for being a trifling little child. Still, there must be some way to remind everyone that come 3:57 a.m. she was going to be a full-fledged honest to God teenager. She sighed. And then suddenly a light bulb went off and a plan came to her.

"When's your birthday again?" she asked Mari, knowing full well that it was in May. They'd had a whole conversation about how cool it would be if her baby was born the same day Mari was—which was extremely unlikely since Mari was due in ten days and her birthday was still four weeks and change away.

The two girls were downstairs pretending to work on a puzzle. At least Mari was pretending, Bobby-Leigh thought, because at this point it was unlikely the younger pregnant girl could see well enough to even say what puzzle they were doing, much less put the fucking pieces together.

But whatever.

"End of May," Mari said with a sigh, obviously still thinking about what it would be like to share a birthday with her daughter.

Bobby-Leigh waited. The proper polite thing for her friend to do now, of course, would be to echo the question back to her.

But Mari didn't do that. She just squinted at the stupid puzzle piece in her hand like an asshole.

So much for that plan. Bobby-Leigh sighed. "Are you sure you don't want to at least ask Maddie about the eyesight thing? She's, like, pretty discreet, you know?"

Mari looked up and met Bobby-Leigh's eyes. It was clear that she saw Bobby-Leigh just fine, or at least fine enough. *Okay, so maybe she's not as blind as I thought,* Bobby-Leigh told herself.

"It's just the preeclampsia," she said like that was nothing.

"Oh, yeah, just that," Bobby-Leigh said with her sharpest blade of sarcasm. The fact was she was genuinely afraid for her friend's health. But she knew Mari was probably right about what would happen if the powers that be—meaning her mom of course—knew she was suffering from advanced symptoms Tiny's girl-doctor-app thingy couldn't detect. Anoona would insist that they induce Mari. The baby was more than viable now, and the exchange of additional viability for additional risk to her daughter was not a trade that woman would ever willingly make.

Anoona would probably never win the mother of the year award—or maybe she would, since at the moment she was the only mother Bobby-Leigh knew for sure was actually still alive on the entire planet. Either way, although Bobby-Leigh's allegiance would always and forever be with Mari, she had exactly zero doubts that, love her or hate her, Anoona genuinely only wanted what was best for her daughter.

Funny thing about loyalty among tweens—standing by one's friend at that age did not necessarily mean doing what you thought was in their best interest. It meant doing what they wanted you to do, no matter what. Even if it was stupid, dangerous, and ill-advised.

"I've only got to make it ten more days," Mari said.

Bobby-Leigh wished she understood why the hell her friend was so obsessed with carrying the kid to term. She'd heard that being pregnant could make you a little crazy. Maybe that was the best explanation.

"I don't know. Seems like you're playing with fire a little, you know? The baby is healthy. She'd be fine. And you're fucking, like, getting worse, you know?"

Bobby-Leigh didn't actually know if Mari was getting worse or not, but she didn't have a better plan to scare some sense into her.

"She knows what she's doing. I am not going to force her out before she's ready."

Bobby-Leigh held up three fingers and asked, "How many?"

"That's not funny."

"Who's joking?"

Mari squinted. She tried just her left eye. Then she tried just her right. Then she squinted again.

"Two?"

"Fuck, dude. You're getting worse. Like seriously. Let's at least talk to Maddie about it."

"No."

Bobby-Leigh ground her teeth and grunted out a loud sigh.

"She is not going to hurt me, Bobby-Leigh. I'm her mother."

You're a naive fucking crazy idiot child is what Bobby-Leigh thought, but what she said was, "Since you're fucking blind now, I just want you to know that this is my I-think-you're-stupid face. I'm going to see how my sister and Bobo are doing."

"It's just ten more days."

The amount of shit that could go wrong in that expanse of time was practically infinite, and Bobby-Leigh knew it, but she also knew that at this point her friend was never going to accept even the most benign of precautions.

Whatever.

*   *   *   *   *

Jennifer Kessler was very proud of herself. She'd not only come up with this idea, but she'd even coded most of it—or at least some of it. And the best part of it was that this app was not going to constantly tell her she was fucking pregnant.

She handed the glasses to Bobo. The man's hands were huge, just like the rest of him—or *at least the rest of him I can see,* she thought and then blushed almost as red as her hair.

Where the hell had that thought come from? she wondered. But she knew the answer. Bobo was her future. It was more than idle teenage sexual curiosity. The amount of growth he'd been forced to endure as the blood pirates weaponized his poor ass was off the charts. He must have been forced to berserk out thousands of times. She realized suddenly where the scarring that covered his body had come from. The truth that the marks were where his skin had split open under the strain of his rapid muscular and skeletal expansion terrified her, but not enough to silence that more primal curiosity. She told herself it was a fair question to wonder if all that growth had been universally proportional. Assuming it was, the nine-foot, five-hundred-plus-pound Bobo must be hung like a fucking elephant.

Even though the idea of a huge penis didn't really do anything for her sexually, she blushed again nonetheless. Desperate to get her mind somewhere else, anywhere else, she dove into the task at hand.

"Put them on," she said to the giant, miming the action she wanted him to perform. "Tiny and I worked on this all night."

Bobo put the glasses on his big head. Even adjusted as wide as Jen could get them, they were still tighter than she'd have liked. But Bobo didn't seem to mind the squeeze. He blasted her with his signature grin.

"Just wait. I haven't even turned it on yet."

She slipped her own pair of glasses on and started the app. Her breath caught as she watched along with Bobo a set of ten vocabulary pictures and then animations on how to sign those words in American Sign Language. It was just the start-up sequence of the app, but she could see the man following along in a way that sent gooseflesh prickling across her arms.

"We noticed that for all your speech impediment, you still seemed to be gesturing normally. So, I—we—thought maybe if we could teach you to talk with gestures, you might be able to recover a little bit of your voice. My sister—"

"Bah-Leh!" Bobo said, his huge smile getting even larger.

"Right. She is positive that most of what you hear gets through to you. And that whatever is going on in your fucked-up brain is an output problem. This app Tiny and I wrote up last night will show you the ASL for anything somebody says, and it will teach you additional vocabulary whenever you want. But the best part is that it'll take anything you sign in ASL and print it out for all of us to see as text."

She switched the app over to translate mode, and then made an *O* with her hand and cocked her head questioningly to ask Bobo if he understood. She watched along as the app showed her student that this gesture was how you say or ask *Okay*. An obvious first example sure, but Jen had no idea where Bobo really was intellectually and obvious seemed like the best place to start.

Bobo watched, then smiled. And then he made an *O* with his hand and answered.

"*Okay*." appeared on the text display zone in Jen's field of view.

Fuck, yes! It was working.

Jen felt herself about to cry. And just like how the curiosity over how proportional Bobo's growth actually was had burst unannounced from the sidelines of her consciousness earlier, her emotional reaction to finding a way to communicate with Bobo—her stand-in for the worst-case scenario of her future self—came at her like a drunk priest on a bicycle in the middle of the night and ran her down.

She couldn't stop the tears from coming.

Why crying?

The words flashed across her lenses.

"I don't know," she said, wiping her eyes. Then she realized that Bobo had just asked her a question. The intro she'd set up to run when the app was turned on included the question words and some basic vocabulary, but *cry* was not among the words in that first set. Yeah, sure. The sign itself was a very intuitive gesture, but she still couldn't help herself from blurting out, "How are you picking this up so fast?"

Bobo had just seen the animation of a hand touching a head palm in and then turning palm out as ASL for *I don't know* when Jen had said it, so he simply repeated it now, and Jen saw the words appear.

A grin that was almost as big as Bobo's bloomed across her face. She took one of his huge scarred-up hands in hers and squeezed affectionately.

This was going to make the whole teaching him to meditate thing so much easier, she thought.

"What're you guys grinning about?" Bobby-Leigh asked from the stairwell.

"Go get some glasses from Tiny and I'll show you."

*   *   *   *   *

When the clock in her glasses clicked from 3:56 a.m. to 3:57, Jennifer Kessler smiled. Absolutely nothing had changed. Her sister's transition from childhood into her wonder years was as unremarkable as a can of soda going flat after been left open overnight. Even Bobby-Leigh herself was sleeping through it—that was how insignificant an event this was to the universe.

But Jennifer didn't give a shit about what the universe thought about it. The fact that Bobby-Leigh was already more mature than most adults, and had been for what felt like years, didn't mean shit to her either. Menstruation, breasts, bitchy sarcastic attitude—they all might have arrived long ago, but without the label of teenager, folks could just blow it all out their asses. To Jennifer, the milestone of her sister's crossing into her teens—in this totally fucked-up world, with Jennifer being a monster no less—was nothing short of momentous.

Nothing may have changed, but everything was different just the same.

"Happy birthday, dude," she whispered.

Bobby-Leigh looked just as unhappy now at three minutes to four as she had one minute earlier. Her typical high spirits during the day never seemed to follow her to bed. In fact, she pretty much always looked unhappy when she slept, Jen thought, wondering what Bobby-Leigh dreamed about that made her so miserable all night long. Though she knew that tonight it might have something to do with the fact that Jennifer had expressly forbidden everyone in the house from acknowledging that her sister's birthday was coming up. She'd felt a little guilty about that, but the feigned negligence was a necessary evil when it came to making this morning's surprise party worthy of the little girl—no, the woman—it was being thrown for.

Jennifer smiled, slipped her glasses off, and laid her head on her pillow in the hopes of catching a couple of hours sleep before the big event. As she felt unconsciousness slipping around her like a warm bath, she found her thoughts drifting to the party her uncle had put together for her on her own thirteenth birthday. Her sleepy smile faltered. She had no intention of letting this party end with a disaster like that one had.

Uncle Allen had tried so hard. He'd gotten ahold of birthday hats and balloons. There was a real birthday cake with candles and everything. He'd invited a few of the neighbors. One was even a boy Jen's age, though now as she danced with sleep, she could not recall the dude's name. He'd been cute though. She did remember that. Cute and shy. Awkward. And smart as a motherfucker.

Uncle Allen had devised this ridiculously involved scavenger hunt as the big activity, she remembered.

Fuck, had she been a bitch about that.

"Seriously, dude?" she remembered saying when he revealed the game to the little crowd of people there to celebrate with her—none of whom she really knew. "I'd rather stick a gun in my mouth and pull the trigger."

Uncle Allen had always been completely immune to her bullshit. Or at least he'd always seemed to be. It was one of the things she loved most about him. She'd had a lot of bullshit back then, if she recalled correctly.

"Damn, kiddo, if I'd known that," he'd replied with a twinkle in his eye. "I'd have actually considered getting you one this year. Oh well, I guess you're just going to have to live." Then he'd added in his best game show host voice, "And have some fun finding some *craaaazy* stuff!"

And she did have fun—even though she'd tried her hardest not to. It was what had happened after the party that had changed her life forever. The cute boy, whatever-the-fuck-his-name-was, had asked her to meet him later when everybody had gone. He'd wanted to show her a car or a robot or something that he'd built—Jen remembered thinking that what he probably really wanted to do was make out, and she was totally down for that.

The morning she had turned thirteen she was pretty convinced that if she didn't kiss every boy she met, every chance she got, she'd die before she lost her virginity. She didn't remember where that urgency to pop her cherry had come from. But it didn't really matter, since by the time she finally was able to sleep that night, her list of priorities had so drastically shifted that presenting some dude's Mr. Happy with the key to her Furry City and getting her v-card punched wasn't even a scribble in the margin.

Whatever-the-fuck-his-name-was had turned out to be serious about wanting to show her the car or robot or whatever he'd built, she remembered that clear as day. They'd agreed to meet in the woods by an old barn a mile or a half away from Uncle Allen's place. The thing—whatever it had been—was supposedly inside. But when Jen had arrived with Bobo the pug trotting along at her ankles like Mary's little lamb, whatever-the-fuck-his-name-was wasn't there yet.

When he finally had shown up, he had been very agitated. Jen remembered she'd just thought he had been nervous about making a move on her, but it had turned out to be something else entirely.

"We have to be quick," he'd said.

She'd nodded, still hopeful this would end up being a romantic encounter. As he'd grabbed her hand and led her inside the barn, those hopes had been soaring. But there had been more than just whatever the dude had built waiting for them inside.

"Told you he'd come back," an ugly voice had said from the shadows. "And he brought us a gift."

Whatever-the-fuck-his-name-was had turned to her and said the smartest thing anybody had ever said to her.

"Run."

And she would have done exactly that, except Bobo the pug had sensed the ill intentions of the men in the shadows and started barking and snorting and snarling, and she couldn't just leave her dog there to be killed by a bunch of assholes. So, as whatever-the-fuck-his-name-was had turned and sprinted for the safety of the woods, she had taken a couple of seconds to grab the tiny, fat, wrinkly dog that was losing its shit trying to protect her.

It wasn't but a breath of time.

She couldn't have just left the dog there.

BANG!

The shot had come from the dark and had sent whatever-the-fuck-his-name-was sprawling to the grass in screams.

A man had stepped from the shadows, the long barrel of his revolver smoking from the shot that had just landed in her friend's back.

Then another man had emerged.

And another.

"What the fuck? Did you just kill the kid?" one of the men had asked as the screaming outside the barn grew bubbly and wet.

"We need the kid, asshole!"

"Fuck the kid. How hard can it be to work the fucking thing?"

"Well, I don't know. But now we're going to have to find out, aren't we?"

"Later," the man with the long-barreled revolver had said. "Right now, one of you needs to make that dog shut up."

Bobo had been struggling so ferociously in Jen's arms that the animal could no longer tell who was friend and who was foe. It had bitten her.

She remembered three things before she woke up covered in blood and surrounded by dead people and what was left of her dog:

She remembered feeling Bobo's teeth ripping into her forearm.

She remembered the man with the gun's awful smile.

She remembered that she was supposed to wait for just the right moment to pull the bear-claw-shaped karambit blade from its secret spot against her inner thigh.

The berserker inside her didn't need the knife though, nor was it one to wait. It tore the smile right off the man with the gun's face. And the pug's savage ferociousness might as well have been a butterfly kiss by comparison.

Through it all, the yellow birthday party hat Uncle Allen had insisted Jennifer Kessler wear had stayed on her head.

If *Bobby-Leigh is a berserker,* Jen thought with the last will of her consciousness—and she was almost positive her sister was not—*there is no fucking way she is going to find out today.*

*   *   *   *   *

"Surprise!" Everyone—even Bobo the berserker—yelled, catching the now teenager completely off guard as she rounded the corner at the head of the stairs.

Instinctively jumping back, Bobby-Leigh almost started her big day by tumbling back down the stairs.

Jen caught her hand and pulled her back in balance excitedly.

"Just wait until you see what I've got cooked up for your ass today, dude. We've been setting this motherfucker up for weeks!" Jen said.

"I thought you all forgot."

"Never."

"I know you're excited, Kessler." Brennachecke sighed. "But do you think we could have our coffee before you make my head explode with your tireless assault on the English language."

"Sorry," Jen whispered.

"Happy birthday," Tiny said, handing Bobby-Leigh a pair of glasses. "These are from your sister and me."

"I already have—"

"Oh, no. Not like these motherfuckers you don't," Jen said. "I installed a special birthday app. It's a variation of Bobo's ASL one. But for horses. You're going to be a fucking horse whisperer, dude!"

"What horses?"

Rachel jumped in. "We found a whole string of ponies out behind Jefferson County Park about a month ago."

"And what? You've just been hiding them?" Bobby-Leigh asked.

"Pretty much. Learned the trick from you actually." Sarah teased.

"Seriously though, with the snow and the power situation, horses are going to come in pretty handy. So we're going to need somebody who can work with them." Rachel said.

"I love horses," Bobby-Leigh said quietly, almost as if she wasn't sure if she was dreaming or not.

"I know!" Jen yelled.

"Happy birthday, sweetheart," Maddie said, squeezing her arm.

Bobby-Leigh smiled at the old librarian, wishing for the thousandth time she could tell her Mari's secret. But she didn't dare. So she just thanked her instead.

Mari, as if sensing Bobby-Leigh was losing her taste for secret keeping, attempted to slide herself awkwardly up from the couch to intercept her, but she didn't make it. Her little body with the giant belly started convulsing, and she collapsed like a marionette with severed strings.

Anoona had her in her arms before anybody else even realized what was happening.

"It's the preeclampsia," Maddie said, dangerously close to I-told-you-so in her tone. "That baby needs to come out."

"Get her on the monitor downstairs," Brennachecke commanded.

"Tiny!" Anoona commanded.

"We're on it," he said, plugging Mari into the OB app while Anoona carried her downstairs. The little girl was still seizing.

"Caesarean," Tiny said to the app interface only he could see.

"Just fucking wait a second!" Maddie yelled. "Before you start cutting into a ten-year-old with no goddamn medical training and only guided by an app written by assholes who also do not have any actual medical experience, you need to fucking push pause and listen to me for once in your fucking lives. Goddamn it!"

"Okay," Anoona said as Mari continued to jerk and jiggle in her arms.

"We need to treat the seizures first. That's magnesium sulfate. Intravenously. Start there. No matter what the fucking app says, do not cut into that child unless there is no other option."

"Okay," Anoona said, as everybody whirled around each other to do what Maddie said.

Jen ran upstairs to grab the tablet that would allow them to see what Tiny saw with the app. Tiny started plugging in monitoring equipment. Maddie stood in the corner, arms crossed, watching. Rachel and Sarah didn't know what to do, so they just got the hell out of the everybody else's way. Brennachecke put his hand on Bobby-Leigh's shoulder as the two of them just watched.

Minutes after the magnesium sulfate hit her bloodstream, Mari's seizures stopped. She opened her eyes, but only to stare off into space for a frightening long time.

"I can't see, Mama," she said suddenly. And then she gushed out the rest of her secret—and those who were keeping it—like a nail had punctured the balloon of her resolve.

"We should have told you…" Bobby-Leigh said quietly, trying not to focus on the fact that this had just gone from one of the best birthdays ever to the worst. Brennachecke remained by her side, but she felt him pull his hand off her shoulder. The man was bracing himself.

"How long did you know she was having these kind of severe symptoms?" Anoona asked, her voice artificially calm in a terrifying kind of way.

"I don't know. She's been having problems with her eyes for like at least a month."

"Did you not know what—"

"No, I knew, but Mari was afraid you'd…" The words sounded so dumb to her own ears that she couldn't finish.

"A month," Anoona said. "What did I tell you would happen if you kept anything else from me, Bobby-Leigh?"

"This doesn't count. I was already keeping this a secret when you guys found out about Bobo."

"When I asked you if you had anything else to tell me, and you lied to my face that you did not, you mean."

Bobby-Leigh looked at her blue Doc Martens and said nothing.

"You're gone," Anoona said like a rattlesnake striking.

"But...this is my house," Bobby-Leigh said.

Jen reappeared in the doorway, tablet in hand, and froze. The tension in the room was as thick as the jungle along the Amazon and felt even more dangerous.

"What'd I miss?" she asked, knowing full well that whatever the answer was, it was going to suck.

It did.

Brennachecke pulled Jen and Bobby-Leigh gently out of the room. "Let's give them some space while they work," he said.

"They're out!" Anoona yelled at him as he shut the door. "She was warned, Brennachecke. We can't function as a group if we can't trust each other."

"I hear you," Brennachecke told her, closing the door with a click.

"This is fucking ridiculous," Jennifer said, as soon as the weary old man turned around to face her. "This is Bobby-Leigh's and my house. This is our land. Anoona's fucktards are the ones who should leave—if anybody should leave, which they shouldn't. She was just doing what Mari asked her to do."

"I know, but Mari is ten years old."

"Bobby-Leigh is only fucking thirteen. And by one goddamn day, dude. Give me a fucking break." She looked at him, realizing that he was not the one she had to convince of anything and added, "Sorry."

Bobby-Leigh just continued to stare at her shoes.

"We're not leaving, Brennachecke."

Brennachecke looked at her and sighed. "Are you willing to kill everybody here to keep this place for yourselves?"

"What? No. That's not—fuck, dude—is that what's left on the table? That can't be where this is going…that's insane."

"I know."

Jen looked at her sister, who finally looked up from her boots and met her eyes.

"Where would we go?" the now thirteen-year-old asked meekly.

Jen had never seen her sister look this dejected before, and it scared her. Scared her and pissed her off.

"What about your father?" Brennachecke asked.

"In Maine?"

"Yeah."

"I'm sure he's fucking dead."

"Let's go find out," Brennachecke said. "I'll fly you. If he's there, we'll find him. If he's alive, you'll have a place to go. If he's… not. Well, I'll bring you back here, and we'll convince Anoona to let bygones be bygones."

"Why don't we just skip the whole Maine part and jump straight to the convincing Anoona to let us stay part?"

"What if your father is alive somewhere? Don't you want to find him?"

"He's not alive."

"There is no way to know that. Let's just take a trip and see what we can find. Give everyone here a chance to cool off."

"What if he is alive?" Bobby-Leigh asked, mostly to herself.

"He's not," Jen said softly to her sister.

"But, like, he could be."

"You don't think he would have come here to find us by now if he was out there?" Jen asked her sister.

"Maybe you can stay here," Bobby-Leigh said. "I'm the one Anoona wants to send into exile anyway. So maybe you can stay here, while Brennachecke and I go."

"Fuck that shit."

"I miss him, Jen."

"Don't be ridiculous. You barely even knew the asshole."

"That doesn't make him any less my dad."

"You know if I had the chance to see my sons again, any chance at all, I'd take it. I'd have to," Brennachecke offered.

"Maybe he's alive but thinks we're dead, Jen. Did you, like, ever think of that?" Bobby-Leigh said. "Maybe that's why he hasn't come for us here."

"Or maybe he came, and you weren't here yet?" Brennachecke added.

"Fuck it. Fine. Let's go make sure Dad is fucking dead. But then we're coming back. You hear me. Nobody is going to kick us out of our own home. Maybe I don't have it in me to kill everybody here to keep this place, but don't think for one goddamn second that I won't burn it to the fucking ground."

"We're not going to do that," Bobby-Leigh said.

Jen was glad to see her sister's inner strength shining through again, but she still couldn't resist biting back, "Speak for yourself."

Chapter Nine
Hey, Kettle. Meet, Pot.

HORSES ARE SMARTER than most folks give them credit for. Fact is horses are probably smarter than most folks, period. Of the millions of little things that brought the apocalypse down upon the world, there was not a single one of them that could be reasonably attributed to a horse. And yet, the animals still put up with folks nailing iron shoes to their feet, pushing metal bits into their mouths, lashing saddles to their backs, and mounting them like...well, horses. For thousands of years they carried folk's weight, plowed folk's fields, and pulled folk's shit from one place to another. Dogs were nice and all, but when it comes to mankind's best friend, the real hero was the horse.

Captain Waters, just like most folks who have spent a significant amount of time around horses, had an instinctive, intuitive sense of their intelligence. But sensing a that innate wisdom and deferring to it were two completely separate things. When he thought to ask himself if maybe there was a reason Emmett's horse, Maggie, kept trying to bite him as he saddled up his own mount, his question made all the wrong assumptions.

"Ouch! Maggie, stop it. I'm going to bring him back to you. Okay? We're coming back."

Maggie snorted. His own mare—a white Camargue Emmett had named Cracker as a joke, but then he'd never bothered to change it—stamped a hoof impatiently. Wiley's chestnut cart horse turned back to its hay, indifferent. The horses knew the man's plan was stupid. They knew he'd never catch the Tesla V transporting Wiley and Emmett to Austin for their baptisms on one of their backs. But they also knew nobody—man nor animal—was going to stop the Captain from trying.

Checking his guns, the old prison guard cursed Emmett under his breath, then he swung his leg over the saddle and poked his heels into Cracker's side. The fresh snow churned under the animal's feet like smoke from a race car burning rubber.

He noticed the drone following him on the bridge over Steinhagen Reservoir and pulled Cracker to a stop. The machine stopped too and just hovered two hundred feet or so above his head. Somebody was watching him. The question was, who? Was it the Bunkermen? Or was it Sinclair's people? He wondered if the Registry was transparent enough to help him answer that, and no sooner had he thought the question, a search window jumped into view, populated faster than he could read the words, and ran.

What he was shown next blew his mind yet again. Every drone belonging to the Republic of Austin appeared on a map as a blue dot. Effortlessly, he zeroed in on his current location with just a thought and a glance to where he was on the map. No blue dots. So it was the

Bunkermen tracking him, not Sinclair. *How long have they been doing that?* he wondered. But a new light bulb went off in his head before he got into the nitty-gritty of that information. He searched for Weiss's car, and suddenly there it was on a new map just outside of Livingston.

The calculation was made before he even was fully aware he was asking for it. His position appeared on the map and then a variation of the classic high school math class equation "A train leaves Chicago going…" flashed up, its variables populated, and then the answer was whispered in his ear by the honey-sweet voice of the Registry as it simultaneously appeared mockingly a few feet in front of him.

Please increase your current speed to 117 miles per hour to overtake the transport of Julius Weiss prior to his arrival in Austin.

Captain Waters laughed. Cracker loudly snorted underneath him as if to say, "I told you so."

"Okay, so that obviously wasn't the most well thought out plan," he told his ride. "Time for plan B."

After jumping off Cracker, he started dragging his foot through the snow writing out the words "NEED 2 TALK" in the thick white fluff. Once done, he looked up at the drone and waited for it to do something that would indicate his message had been received.

But no such signal was given.

"Come on!" Waters shouted at the sky.

No response.

Waters felt the time he had to stop Emmett from committing the murder he knew the cat was hell-bent on carrying out slipping through his fingers like blood from a head wound. He knew he needed to slow down and make a real plan. Think things through. He'd just tried to chase a fucking car down on horseback for Christ's sake. Clearly, he was moving too fast. But he couldn't help himself. The consequences of anything Emmett did was ultimately on him. He pulled one of his handguns from its holster on his hip and aimed up at the drone mocking him, and the glasses immediately responded to correct his aim.

Amazing, he thought with a smile as he blew the hunk of plastic out of the sky. It fell like a stone onto the wind-stripped ice that covered the reservoir and bounced, finally coming to rest a few yards from his position on the bridge.

Backtracking with Cracker two hundred feet to the shore, he slowly encouraged the horse to step out on the ice. But the horse refused.

"All right, chickenshit. You stay here, and I'll go get it."

Waters wished he had a rope he could tie to Cracker, in case the ice wasn't as solid as he thought it was, but he didn't. There was no time for second-guessing anyway.

He stepped out onto the ice. It felt solid.

He took another step. Then another.

It wasn't until he was almost close enough to the drone to touch it that the ice started to crack under him.

But the frozen surface held. He knew he should turn back. Just forget the damn drone and come up with another way to get the Bunkermen to reveal themselves to him. But he couldn't think of a better way in that moment. Every time he thought about anything, the image of Emmett shooting Weiss, or worse, shooting people to get to him, was so vivid in his head, it crowded out his usual clear and logical thinking. For all he knew, Weiss was already dead.

His glasses confirmed that was not the case.

So he took another step forward. The ice groaned but held. The plan, if you could call it that, was to take the drone to Sinclair and "let" his people to figure out that it was not one of theirs and then track where it had come from. And then go there. It was admittedly not a particularly good plan. But he was out of fucking ideas.

He got to the drone, scooped it up, and then turned and began his slow, careful trek for the shore. The ice held.

Until it didn't.

The water was so cold it felt like acid. Sulfuric acid. Eating through his skin. All the air screamed out from his lungs as his head dropped below the surface of the ice-covered water. He forced his eyes open and looked up.

The hole he'd dropped through was nowhere to be seen.

He kicked and turned. He almost let go of the drone, and then, behind him, saw the light of day probing the hole he'd fallen through like God's own hand reaching into the cold, wet death to save him.

Feeling faint, he made it to the surface and sucked in air like it was the sweetest thing any cat had ever put into his body. It was a ragged, painful breath, but Waters had never been more grateful for anything in his life.

Clinging to the ice with one throbbing burning hand, he tossed the drone clear and wiggled his ass out of the watery grave. His muscles were spasming so much from the shivers that his legs couldn't support him. He was unable to stand, and quickly moving in the direction of being unable to move. So, he crawled and flopped his way back toward shore.

It was less than a hundred feet away, but it might as well have been a hundred miles. He made it to the drone. There, he looked up and saw Cracker, gingerly testing the ice with his hoof. The animal wanted to help him, but somehow knew the ice wasn't safe. Waters had had the voice of God in his ear—or at least had before he'd been dunked in the icy dark and his glasses had been shorted out—but it was the horse that had been trying to save him, not the technology in the glass. He probably could have looked up a way to measure the thickness of the ice, or even just how to walk across a frozen lake if he'd thought of it. He was sure the information was in the Registry, and he was sure the system in the glasses could have integrated it in some mind-blowingly useful way. But he hadn't asked the device. Just like he hadn't listened to the horse when it had refused to come out onto the ice.

Waters smiled at the mare's effort to save him.

He smiled at his own stupidity.

He even smiled for Emmett.

Then the cold-wet, feasting on his life like a fat hag at a two-dollar all-you-can-eat shrimp buffet at some Indian casino just outside of hell, tripped a switch inside him, and everything was gone.

The cold was gone. The wet. The threat of Emmett's impending crime. All the mistakes he'd made. All gone. With a relieved—almost grateful—smile frozen to his face, Captain William Paul Waters was gone too.

Or at least he should have been.

But Death did not kindly stop for Captain Waters. In the twelve seconds the old man's heart was taking a smoke break, Waters did not see any white lights. He did not float over his body and look down on it to contemplate the meaning of his miserable existence. God did not come to him, nor did fire and brimstone.

He was just dead.

Maybe twelve seconds just wasn't worth Death's time.

Maybe when Waters's heart stopped, the Reaper took one look and just stepped over his body lying there on the ice and continued on his way like he was heading to the C train east of Broadway Junction in Brooklyn.

Or maybe, the nanovirus the Bunkermen had secretly infected him with kicked his old heart in the ass and sent it back to the trenches for a few more ticks. The virus had been built on a derivative of Grace after all. Hearts belonging to those filled with Grace don't just stop. He was alive because of some totally unintended, though remarkable side effect. The Old Lady was certainly going to want to do some significant field-testing on this one…

Waters realized he was alive, only after he realized he'd been listening to the conversation of the two technicians standing by his bed for longer than he could quantify.

Coming back from the dead is not at all like waking up from a deep sleep, or a light one for that matter. With sleep, cats know they're awake when they wake—unless they're in a *Nightmare on Elm Street* movie. But how many cats still around these days could claim that one?

With death, the transition back to life was unremarkable and easy to miss, just like the coming of the apocalypse itself, but in reverse. Captain Waters did not know he'd been dead.

"He's awake," Waters heard one of the men—the younger sounding one—say before he'd even opened his eyes.

"I'll go get her," the other one said.

Waters didn't bother opening his eyes until he heard the Old Lady's voice saying, "So you want to talk, huh? Sure doesn't look like it."

Groaning, Waters finally open his eyes. The euphoria of death was long gone, and the urgency of the situation was back. But he'd learned his lesson about racing off with a plan half-cocked. A lesson it only took dying to teach him.

"Can you get me to Austin without Sinclair's troops knowing about it?"

"We could," the Old Lady said. "But why would we? Kessler is working for us."

"I'm sure he made you think that. But trust me, that cat is only working for himself. The only thing he cares about is killing Dr. Weiss."

"Who do you think is providing him with the gun he'll be using to do it?"

Waters took a few moments to process this. But he couldn't put together how Emmett murdering somebody in front of an audience was going to help the Bunkermen pull off their little coup. Dr. Weiss's death got them nothing.

"Why?" he asked.

"The network vulnerabilities we need to exploit in order to successfully implant our nanovirus into their system only appears when the Registry is so over-loaded with traffic that it has to postpone distributing updates to Grace until there is sufficient bandwidth available again. Plus, because of what happened during Mr. DuPont's exorcism, the projected live attendance numbers for Mr. Kessler's conversion are fantastic. We'll be able to set everything in motion right there in the room, which, as far as opportunities to increase our likelihood of success go, is not a chance we can afford to ignore."

"There must be a way to do this without allowing Kessler to murder the man."

"I don't think you quite understand what *this* is, Captain. But I will tell you that you can relax. It's incredibly unlikely that Mr. Kessler will actually be able kill the doctor. Grace will repair any damage he manages to inflict with the gun. Even a direct shot between the eyes at point-blank range wouldn't be enough to permanently end the man's life, as long as he has Grace in him. He'd have to remove the doctor's head from his body to actually kill him. And even then, we've seen the occasional Austinite come back from that too—if the head and body aren't kept separate for a long enough time."

"I'm responsible for him."

"Yes, we are aware you feel that way. It's unfortunate."

"How fast will Grace heal the doctor?"

"A few hours. A few days. It will depend on the damage your man is able to inflict."

"And what will happen to him after? Sinclair's men will kill him?"

"Not on purpose. Killing is a sin, Captain. Or hadn't you heard? Austinites really don't like to commit sins."

"Okay, so what will they do with him?"

"Well, if our little plan here is successful, then nothing. If not, they'll either offer him a second chance at Grace, or tag him and exile him. Could go either way."

Captain Waters was confident there was a big chunk of this operation that the Old Lady was not revealing, but he still felt relief flooding through his veins. Emmett would get his revenge. He'd finally be able to move on with his life. And nobody would die. He shocked himself a little by how easy he found it to live with the idea that Dr. Weiss might suffer some discomfort for the cause.

"Mmm," Waters said. "Why do I get the feeling you're not telling me something?"

The Old Lady smiled. "Honey, it would take a landfill the size of Texas itself to hold the amount of shit that I'm not telling you. But I'm not lying to you here either."

Just as Waters was about to respond, a thought blindsided him, and then, to his horror, his immediate emotional response to the revelation sucker-punched him right in the face.

Emmett was going to kill a man in cold blood. He'd probably never know that the man hadn't died—couldn't die. So while Waters's conscience would walk away from this whole thing clean enough, Kessler's head or heart or soul—whatever you wanted to call it—was going to be fucked.

It was one thing to wish somebody dead. To plan out a murder. To load a gun, point it. Even pull the trigger. But the moment that the action couldn't be taken back. The moment blood was actually on your hands—not the thick, justifiable, self-defense, I-had-to-do-it kind of blood, or even the hot, in the heat of the moment, crime of passion kind, but the cold, putrid blood of real premeditated murder—the first time that kind of blood gets on your hands, unless you're a true psychopath, or so mentally challenged you simply can't understand what you've really done, the guilt that follows after will inevitably disfigure you to the core.

Emmett would be changed.

Forever.

Captain Waters knew this as a certainty because it had happened to him. Before he was Black Jesus. Before he was a guard. Before he'd even known what rehabilitation actually meant. Back when he was Billy. Before cell phones. Before the internet. Before cars could drive by themselves and certainly before anybody could have even imagined a berserker or the world ending. Billy Waters had murdered a man in cold blood.

He'd been thirteen. Back in the Forest Park area of Detroit. His victim had deserved it. A man by the name of Randy Flagg to his mother or Pop Rocks to his gangster friends.

Pop Rocks was a crack kingpin, one of the oldest cats in the game, at least in Detroit. The man was smart. He'd managed to last forty-plus years in the drug game without so much as a misdemeanor on his record. He was ruthless, cold-blooded, and delegated all but the most personal of the dirty work to his gangbanger lieutenants—who gladly took the credit and the fall, though never the money. On the street, he just looked like a legitimate businessman. An entrepreneur who cared about the neighborhood. Somebody who had cracked the secret of making a profit from investing in local businesses. There was talk about him running for office, though thanks to Billy that never happened.

Pop Rocks was also engaged to Billy Waters's mother. Waters was sure his mother never knew the truth about her fiancé. She was not the kind of woman to look the other way. She did not forgive trespasses, nor did she forget them. His mother was one of the pioneering black women in the early fifties to go to and graduate from the Lewis College of Business in Detroit. And she was the only woman Waters had known growing up who was a single mother by choice and not circumstance. He was proud to be her son.

But for all the intelligence and resilience the woman had, she was completely blind to the true nature of the man she'd fallen for. Waters still cringed at the memory of her telling him that Pop Rocks was the first, and only, man she'd ever deemed worthy of heading their family.

Maybe if he'd just told her what he knew about the bastard, he wouldn't have had to put a bullet into the motherfucker's heart. But loyalty to one's mother is a tricky sort of business. And the pain of watching her pine after a partner in life for years before Pop Rocks had started pursuing her had colored things. Besides, Billy Waters hadn't murdered Randy Flagg to save his mother. He'd killed the man to save his friend.

Her name was Cindy Cole. Everybody at school thought of her as a tomboy, but really, she was just a girl who had decided early on that she was not going to be a victim. Billy had known her since the second grade. He'd grown up next door to her. They walked to school together. Sat at the same table during lunch. Neither one was particularly popular, but they weren't unpopular either. Like most cats in junior high school, they just kind of passed through on their way to other things.

In Billy's case, that thing was going to be juvie. But for Cindy, seventh grade was going to be her last stop on the ghetto express. And Waters knew the exact moment he stepped onto that train with her.

"I'm not wearing those," he said, mostly to his mother, as he looked at the white and red Pro Leather Converse in the box.

"Dr. J wears them, little man," Flagg said.

Of course, Billy knew that already. Everybody in Detroit knew that. Fact was, he knew kids at school who would have sold their own sisters for a pair of the sneakers he was refusing to accept.

It wasn't that Billy didn't want the shoes.

It was that Billy didn't want Flagg winning points with his mom. This was before the boy knew anything about the man's secrets, but it didn't matter. Billy had hated Flagg from the beginning.

"I don't even like basketball," he responded to Flagg.

"What are you talking about? You love basketball," his mother chided him, embarrassed and confused.

"No, I don't."

"Sorry. He's not—" she began to say, but Flagg waved her attempted excuses off.

"Don't even give it another thought."

"Can I go now?" Billy asked, glaring at the man trying to win his mother over. "Cindy is waiting for me."

"Cindy Cole?" Flagg asked.

And that was it. All aboard. The train was leaving the station.

He didn't answer. He just stared at his mother until she gave her permission for him to leave.

Three days later, Cindy didn't come out to walk to school in the morning. That afternoon, Billy stopped in to see if she was sick and found her hiding in her bed, covers pulled up to her chin, trying not to cry. She didn't want to see him and told him as much.

"Why?" he asked. "What did I do?"

She laughed without an ounce of humor in her voice and threw the covers off her. She was in a T-shirt and underwear, but the girl's panties couldn't hide the deep purple bruising along her thighs, any better than her shirt could conceal the big finger marks on her forearms.

Billy did not know what to say, but he knew instantly what had happened to his friend, long before Cindy delivered the actual warning.

"Does your mother know?" he asked.

"What do you think?"

"No."

"We have to go to the police."

"We?" Cindy hissed at him. "There is no we."

"Didn't you see who did it?" he asked, but deep down he already knew the answer.

"You did it, Billy. You!"

"I don't—I don't understand," he stammered, but that was a lie.

"If you don't want him fucking your mom, then you better get used to him fucking your friend—that's what he wanted me to tell you, when I saw you. Do you understand that?"

Cindy was sobbing.

But it wasn't really Cindy anymore. The Cindy he knew who didn't take shit from anybody. The Cindy who had vowed never to be a victim. The Cindy, who, had they not ended up on this ghetto train to hell, might have one day become Billy's first real love. That Cindy Cole was dead. The shell of what was left pulled the covers back up over her violated body and told him to get out.

She refused to speak to him for days after that. And when she finally did talk to him again, it was clear that whatever relationship they'd had was broken. Cindy was afraid. All the time. And there was only one way Billy could see to fix that.

Pop Rocks would have to die.

Waters was not a killer. Not then, and not now. But he was a pragmatist. And as he thought through the logistics and probabilities of successfully getting the cat arrested, it seemed like that course of action would only make shit worse. Flagg had effectively avoided arrest for decades. It was dangerous enough just to be creeping and spying on the motherfucker who had declared war on his life. Murder was the safer way to go for everyone he loved stuck in Pop Rocks's web—including himself.

The plan was deceptively simple. Get a gun. Hide in the man's car. Shoot him dead in the middle of the night from the back seat after the asshole was done *entertaining* his mother. Make it look like a robbery.

The gun was easy. Less than a week after Cindy had delivered Flagg's message to him, he got his hands on one. It cost him twelve dollars—his life savings at the time. A cat everybody in the neighborhood knew had a predilection for sticking up liquor stores sold Billy the Saturday Night Special he'd used on his last couple of jobs. The exchange took place in the alley behind the bodega on the corner. The gun was a .38 revolver. That gave Billy six shots.

Once he had the gun, he waited.

And he waited.

Days he waited.

Weeks.

And while he waited, he tried to come up with a way to trick Flagg into thinking he'd come around to the idea of the ghetto monster slapping nasties with his mom—or as close to it as he could pull off considering the motherfucker had raped his best friend as a warning to stay out of his way. He recognized that somebody like Flagg would know better than to trust a kid with that monstrous act hanging like a carcass between them. But Billy did his best to show the piece of shit he'd learned his lesson—to ensure Cindy's safety as much as anything else.

"Mr. Flagg?" he said to him one night on the stoop—with the Saturday Night Special in his hand concealed by his coat pocket. He wasn't sure if the conversation was going to go the way he wanted it to, and if it didn't, he fully intended to put all six rounds into the man's chest right then and there.

Flagg stopped just short of the door and glared at the boy.

"Your mom is expecting me, little man. Whatcha need?"

"Nothing. I just," Billy began, his palm growing sweaty on the grip of the gun. "Just wanted to say thank you for the kicks."

Flagg looked deep into the boy, and Billy felt a chill pass through him worse than if he'd been stabbed in the heart with an icicle. It was a look that made it clear Flagg knew his message had been delivered and received. It was a look that said, "You think that shit was bad, kid, try me again, and the next lesson I'll teach you will make what I did to your little girlfriend look like I just took her out of an ice-cream cone."

Billy resisted the urge to unload the gun in his pocket. Instead he looked down at the basketball shoes he'd refused to wear and smiled like wearing them didn't make him want to throw up.

"They're pretty dope," he said, still looking down, frankly afraid to look in those eyes again.

When Billy finally looked up again, Flagg nodded at him. "Best make yourself scarce tonight, little man."

Billy held his poker face with a death grip.

"Guess I could crash at Darnell's crib."

Or in the back seat of your car...

"You do that," the motherfucker ordered and then entered Billy's home like the man owned the place and everything in it.

He intended to wait longer.

A lot longer.

But the idea of his mother pinned under Flagg. Of her enjoying what the motherfucker did to her. To say nothing of the cold certainty that Cindy Cole would never be safe as long as that asshole drew breath. Billy decided right then and there that tonight was the night.

He went into the garage and emptied his schoolbooks from his backpack. He replaced them with a box of twenty-gallon black trash bags and a roll of duct tape.

By eight, Billy was ready.

By eight fifteen, he arrived at Darnell's.

By ten o'clock, Darnell passed out from drinking the gin Billy had dared him to steal from his mom.

By ten thirty, Billy was sneaking back into his house, trying to ignore the sounds of Flagg fucking his mom, as he borrowed the motherfucker's keys and let himself into the man's Cadillac.

By eleven, he replaced the keys and returned to the car.

Lying low in the back seat, the thirteen-year-old covered himself with the trash bags. Head to toe. He used a swim mask to cover his eyes and the snorkel that came with it to breathe. It would be another decade and a half before the canon of forensic science would include the realization by Sir Alec Jeffreys that variations in DNA could be used to identify suspects and tell them apart from one another. But anybody who'd seen an episode of *Hawaii Five-O* or *Kojak* knew better than to get blood on their clothes. And there were rumors on the street about cats getting sent to the can because they had gunshot residue on their hands. Billy was taking no chances.

It was hot in all that plastic, and his face mask quickly fogged up. But he didn't dare move from his position, even as sweat began to sting his eyes.

What the fuck is he doing? he thought over and over like a mantra as he waited in the dark, cramped in the foot space behind the driver's seat.

Bang!

The sound of the driver's door shutting woke Billy up, and it was all the boy could do to keep from screaming. The mask had fogged so much he was nearly blind. His clothes were drenched with sweat. Every inch of his skin itched. He was light-headed from what he assumed was a reduced supply of oxygen from the snorkel, but which really had more to do with nerves than anything else.

When he heard the fancy car's engine turn over, all of those distractions vanished as if they'd been murdered in cold blood as well. Billy Waters couldn't see anything clearly, but he didn't need to. He held the gun against the back of the seat and, without giving himself a chance to lose his nerve, pulled the trigger.

Ka-bam!

The only sound Billy could hear was the ringing in his ears.

But he felt the car lurch forward.

Ka-bam! Ka-bam! Ka-bam!

The car was still moving.

Billy began to panic. He had to see what was happening! He pulled the face mask off his head, tearing it out of the careful tape work he'd done to seal it to the garbage bag over his head. Cold air rushed in. It stank of gunpowder and fear, but it was glorious just the same, and even better, he was able to see again.

He sat up in the back seat.

Flagg was not dead. But he was dying. He'd managed to shift the car into gear, but couldn't make his foot hit the gas. Billy's first shot had ripped through his spine. He was paralyzed from the thirty-fourth vertebra down, but Flagg hadn't figured that out yet. And he never would. Billy put the gun to the back of his head and fired his remaining two shots through the motherfucker's skull. Blood and brains plastered the windshield like somebody had tossed them from a bucket.

The car drove itself into a tree and stopped.

Billy's ears rang so loud that his head actually hurt. He sat there, stunned, wrapped in plastic, like the world's worst Christmas present, as the sounds of the world started to fade back in.

Sirens.

Blood dripping on the leather seats.

He felt a lump building in his throat.

He felt his face twist in a sob.

But he pulled himself together and got out of the car. Remembering to grab both the face mask and the gun, he made it three steps away from the car before he remembered he was supposed to make this murder look like a robbery. Still covered in plastic, he turned back and opened the driver's side door. He stripped Flagg's Rolex off his limp wrist. He pulled the man's wallet out of his blood-soaked pants. He cringed as he did it, but he did it.

Then he ran in the opposite direction to his house, to the alley behind the bodega where he'd gotten the gun.

He jumped into the dumpster and pulled the lid down. In that quiet, stinky dark, he stripped off the plastic, pulled a new garbage bag from his backpack and put everything, including the gun and Flagg's wallet, inside, like it was just more trash. He kept the Rolex, though.

The fucking Rolex. What the hell had he been thinking?

Peeking out of the dumpster, he emerged like a martini, shaken, but not stirred. He checked himself for blood with a mirror he'd swiped from the bathroom at Darrell's. He was clean. Then he walked around to the front of the store and called the cops on the pay phone. The report stated that he'd found a man shot to death in his car on his way home from a friend's house. He'd rehearsed the story so many times in the weeks that led up to this, when the fuzz came around asking their questions, he was never considered a suspect. And if it hadn't been for that fucking Rolex, he'd have gotten away with the whole thing clean—at least in the criminal prosecution sense of things.

The guilt waited a couple of nights to come knocking. But when it did come, there was no keeping it out. And once it was in, there was no making it go away. The fact that he'd gotten away with it only made it worse.

Maybe that was why he'd tried to pawn the watch.

Maybe he wanted to get caught.

Not for murder, of course. Billy wasn't an idiot. But for something. Apparently, Pop Rocks and the asshole who ran the pawnshop knew each other. The cat recognized the timepiece and turned Billy in. Busted, guilt monkeying with the wiring in his brain, Billy told the truth—not all of it obviously, but enough to get an audience before a judge.

At his trial—for grand theft—Billy Waters said he'd taken the watch before calling the cops, which was a hundred percent true. He said he felt horrible and wished he hadn't done it. Also completely true. In tears, he said he'd give anything to take it back if he could. And even that was absolutely true.

Randall Flagg had certainly deserved to die. But Waters had murdered a part of himself when he'd emptied that Saturday Night Special into the motherfucker. It was a part of him he didn't even know he had, but now that it was gone, he missed it like it was a limb. But the worst part about losing whatever it was he'd lost was that Cindy Cole saw that he was different too. And somehow, she knew what he'd done to get that way. She knew he'd done it for her, and that knowledge tore away whatever scrap of her former self was still clinging on inside her.

Three days into his trial, Cindy was found dead in a No Tell Motel bed. Billy never learned the official cause of her death. But he didn't need to. He knew he had killed her, just as much as he'd killed Flagg.

And now Emmett Kessler was about to do the same fucking thing, or at least Kessler would think he had, and the catastrophic loss that had reincarnated Billy Waters as Black Jesus would break the man. As disappointed as Waters was with the cat as a friend, to his dismay, he suddenly realized that couldn't let the asshole go through that—if for no other reason than he knew all too well from his own experience the burden of guilt on Kessler's shoulders after the fact would certainly fall into the cruel and unusual punishment category. After all, he was not actually going to kill the man.

"What if I do it?" the Captain asked the Old Lady.

"Do what?"

"Put a few bullets into the good doctor so you cats can have your little distraction and kick God's ass out of Texas or whatever."

"Why would you do that?"

"Because as fucked as it is, Kessler is my friend, and when he thinks he's actually murdered Dr. Weiss in cold blood, he's going to freak the hell out."

"Like I said, Kessler isn't going to be able to actually kill the doctor."

"But he's not going to know that."

"Why don't you just tell him he's not a murderer after all the dust settles?"

"Why don't you just let me do this?"

Captain Waters didn't think Emmett would last that long. Fact was, it was clear to the old guard now that revenge had been the only thing keeping his last prisoner going. Once he had it, between the guilt that was going to swallow him whole and the prospect of a future with nothing left to live for that was going to shit him out, the convict was more likely than not to just find a quiet corner and kill himself. But there was no way Waters was going to tell this old bitch that.

"Captain, it's too late to stop what's in motion with Kessler," the Old Lady said with a smile and shrugged. "But I suppose if you could beat him to it, we wouldn't have a problem with that—so long as it's done in the baptism hall."

"Can you get me there fast enough to do it?"

"Probably," the Old Lady said.

*　*　*　*　*

The baptism hall—formally the University of Texas's Frank Erwin Center—was a spectacular sight. At one hundred and six feet high, the cylindrical Superdrum building was only fifty feet shorter than the city walls that loomed behind it—as if it was some kind of a stepping-stone for giants to escape Austin's confines. Emmett and Wiley only caught a glimpse of it as they entered the city through the east gate at Airport Boulevard and traveled along what used to be I-35.

But it was enough.

Dr. Weiss smiled at them as their jaws dropped at the stark contrast between the city inside the wall and the devastation and poverty of the sprawl locked outside of it.

"Whoa," Wiley said, mostly to himself. "And I thought Jasper was in good shape."

"How many people live here?" Emmett asked as the perfectly restored and remodeled buildings of the Hancock neighborhood and then the University of Texas's campus zipped past.

Weiss looked up the statistic and relayed it as if he'd known it all along, "There are close to million *saved* living here in the Austin sanctuary."

"A million people…" Emmett whispered. After witnessing the loss and destruction to what used to be the United States while traveling across the country to get here, a million people in one place was beyond his ability to visualize. Frankly, the five thousand folks in Jasper had seemed like a metropolis to him.

"What about outside the walls?" he asked.

"We don't have a way to perform an accurate count of those living in the sprawl. But we estimate it's somewhere between three hundred and seven hundred thousand."

Emmett wondered how many Bunkermen there were, but he didn't ask. After seeing this, it was pretty obvious that their plans to overthrow the state were nothing more than a pipe dream. Not that that would keep him from exploiting their pathetic little plan to achieve his own ends. His revenge was so close he could taste it in the air.

He smiled at Dr. Weiss.

Dr. Weiss smiled back.

*   *   *   *   *

The locker rooms—though they had been remodeled to look more like a spa than a sports arena locker room to reflect the sanctity of the building's new function—still had a reclusive note of a sweaty jockstraps. But Wiley and Emmett barely noticed. Frankly, they wouldn't have noticed even if the place had smelled like it'd been made of solid dog shit. They, like the other men with them, were distracted by the ritual they were participating in—and even more so by the beauty of the women performing it. Plus, there was the fact that the men were all naked—their clothes had been taken as soon as they'd arrived, probably to be burned, Emmett thought.

There had been almost two dozen other men being prepared for baptism with them. But, once stripped, they'd all been seated in a circle of simple throne-like chairs facing outward, so seeing one another required effort. Effort none of them were particularly interested in making, now that they could see they were about to be anointed with oils by the most flawless women anybody in that room had ever seen. Women who were, for lack of a better word, perfect. Every proportion was exactly as God intended. Nothing too big. Nothing too small. Nothing out of place. The symmetry was almost unsettling.

It was a little like looking at human dolls built in a factory—and maybe that was exactly the right way of looking at it, Emmett thought, trying to figuring out if the obvious pleasure he heard in Wiley's voice was just because they were all so attractive or if there was something more going on. Then he glimpsed one of the ladies attending his friend out of the corner of his eye and realized he'd actually seen her before. She'd been the one who had washed Wiley's feet during his exorcism. As Beast, he hadn't been able to talk to her, but now that the monster was out of the way, Wiley had started making up for lost time.

"So…what's the significance of this anointing?" he asked.

"This oil marks you as holy and sets you apart to the Lord so that He might recognize you," the woman said with a voice as smooth as milk chocolate.

"Kind of smells like licorice…" Wiley said.

Emmett could hear the smile in his voice.

Out of the corner of his eye, he saw her smile back at him, but then Emmett quickly lost track of Wiley's attempt to chat up his attendant. He felt the licorice-and cinnamon-scented oil drip over his shoulders and suddenly couldn't concentrate on anything else.

Wiley had spent days fucking the shit out of Jackie back in the bunker, and his arousal was no doubt under control. But Emmett hadn't been touched by a woman in over a decade, and his body responded instantly when his two attendants began to massage the sweet-smelling emollient into his skin. He tried to ignore his quickly growing erection. He hoped they would too.

But they didn't.

Both women smiled at each other and then at him.

"I'm sorry," he muttered as his face flamed red under his beard.

"The Lord's Grace will temper your lust soon, Mr. Kessler," the taller of the two beauties attending him said.

"Great," he said with a groan as they continued to press their well-lubricated hands into his flesh—notably more sensually, he observed.

Or was that wishful thinking?

"Ephesians tells us that we may be sure that everyone who is sexually immoral or impure has no inheritance in the kingdom of the Lord," the shorter of his attendants told him.

"It's our duty to ensure that you are ready to be received into His kingdom," the taller one said.

"One who sows to the Spirit will from the Spirit reap eternal life—"

"Galatians tells us that."

"The Lord does not look unfavorably upon sexual release, provided it is performed righteously."

"I think Corinthians says it best," the shorter attendant added. "The Lord will not allow you to be tempted beyond what you are able, and with the temptation, He will provide the way of escape also, so that you will be able to endure it."

"May we offer you an escape from your lust, so that you may be baptized into the kingdom of God?"

Emmett could hardly breathe, his nether regions ached, and his manhood was so engorged that he thought it might actually burst like a water balloon left on the spigot too long.

"Okay," he breathed, utterly unable to think straight.

A second later the well-oiled hand belonging to the shorter of his attendants gripped Emmett's hard penis. With several firm, but sensual, pulls, she manually milked every ounce of lust from his body.

"Praise Jesus," Emmett said as the final load of semen dripped out of him. He'd intended it to be sarcastic, but it hadn't come out that way. The fact was, he did feel closer to God now. The sensation of warm oil being poured over his head and massaged through his hair and beard distracted him from immediately slapping the Holy Spirit with a secular, rational, evidence-based, scientific backhand.

The women rinsed the excess oil from the men and dressed them in white linen baptismal gowns. They then escorted them from the locker room up and out to the doors leading to the arena floor.

There they asked them to wait.

And there they left them.

"Holy shit," Emmett confided to Wiley in a whisper when he was sure they were gone.

Wiley smiled at him knowingly.

Beyond the doors, they could hear the idle chatter of thousands upon thousands of spectators.

"Full house," Emmett observed, but nobody acknowledged his comment. However, even though Wiley did not say anything, he did give his friend a second smile and a nod. It was communication enough.

A man came through the doors. Like all the other folks they'd seen who'd been blessed by Grace, he was yet another perfect specimen of the human form at its prime. And like the attendants at Wiley's exorcism, he wore the same simple white surplice over a thick red cassock. Emmett supposed that must be the standard uniform for the minions of the Republic. And of course, just like everybody else, the man wore the magic glasses.

With a smile, the minion said a name and asked the man with it to follow him out into the arena. The crowd clapped and cheered in response. A minute later, another perfect man dressed like a choirboy appeared to escort another of the anointed out.

Then another.

And another.

"Mr. DuPont, if you would follow me, please?" the minion who came for Wiley asked.

"See you on the other side, Kessler," Wiley said and then followed the man into the roar of the crowd.

Emmett watched and waited as one by one all the men from the locker room were escorted out onto the floor. He exchanged a congratulatory smile and nod with the last one to go and then stood there alone, wondering when the fuck the Bunkermen were going to slip him the weapon he was supposed to use to kill the good doctor.

As if summoned by his very thoughts, a man stepped out of the shadows and whispered his name. This man did not have magic glasses on. He was not dressed like a choirboy. But he still looked like a goddamn angel.

The man held out a small object wrapped in some kind of white cloth. Emmett took it. It was a small handgun and a holster. The gun was made of a white plastic he'd never seen the likes of before. The holster was white too.

"Strap it to your inner thigh," the man said.

Emmett lifted up his gown and did as the man instructed.

"You have seven shots. The gun will still fire if it gets wet, so don't rush it."

Emmett nodded.

"Good hunting."

"Thank you," Emmett said, but the man was already retreating back into the shadows. Not thirty seconds after he'd appeared, the man had vanished back into the ether from which he'd come.

"Mr. Kessler," the voice of his own personal minion said, turning Emmett back around. "If you would follow me please."

The perfect bastard led him through the arena doors, and the crowd went wild. Emmett saw his face huge on the jumbotron. He saw his name. He saw a list of his sins. Murder. Wrath. Blasphemy. Irreverence. Sloth. Slander. Arrogance.

Yep, he thought, *that's about right.*

He saw the arena floor had a small round stage in the center of it. Dr. Weiss stood on that. Just like all the other folks working in an official capacity, he was wearing the same outfit he'd worn for the exorcism. Emmett smiled at him. He almost pulled the gun right then and there and unloaded the thing.

But he didn't.

Getting it out from under his gown would have drawn too much attention. He was going to have to wait for a better opportunity to present itself.

The minion led him to a cube about three feet high and filled with a clear liquid that at first Emmett thought was just water, but then he saw that the viscosity was all wrong. Maybe it was oil. It didn't really matter, he supposed. Whatever it was, it was just the suspension holding the Grace nanites. Emmett looked around and saw that there were forty or fifty cubes like this in a circle around the stage. Each of his fellow recipients of Grace stood in the center of their cube, backs to the stage, facing the crowd. Emmett saw Wiley across the way as he stepped into his own box. He realized there were women recipients as well. Emmett supposed they had their own locker room and wondered randomly if their attendants had been men or women.

The liquid in the box was a gel. And it was even thicker than he'd thought. Once he was standing in the center and facing the crowd, the entire arena hushed in eerie unison.

"We are gathered here today to bear witness to the Lord's infinite capacity for forgiveness," Dr. Weiss began. "Hear the words of our Lord Jesus Christ: 'All authority in heaven and earth has been given to me. Go therefore and make disciples of all nations, baptizing them in the name of the Father and of the Son and of the Holy Spirit, teaching them to observe all that I have commanded you, and lo, I am with you always, to the close of the age.' Obeying the word of our Lord, and of His second coming among us, we baptize these whom He has deemed worthy to be called to be His own."

The cubes suddenly rotated so that the sinners about to be saved were facing Dr. Weiss instead of the crowd. Emmett, waist deep in the thick gel, saw his opportunity coming. Slowly, he began to hike up his gown so he could get at the gun strapped to his leg.

"In presenting yourself for baptism," Weiss continued, "you announce your faith in God Almighty and the second coming of his son Jesus Christ. You show that you want to know, love, and serve Him as His chosen disciple. Declare yourself now to Him by answering these questions, so that He might know your purpose."

Weiss paused for effect, then continued as Emmett closed his fingers around the grip of the gun and pulled it slowly out, holding it at his side.

"Who is your Lord and Savior?" Weiss asked.

"*Jesus Christ is my lord and savior!*" the recipients roared in unison—all but one.

"Do you trust in Him?" Weiss asked.

"*I do*," the about-to-be-saved roared back.

Emmett smiled.

"Will you be a faithful disciple of Jesus Christ, obeying his word and showing his love?" Weiss asked.

"*I will.*"

"Do you promise to seek the fellowship of the Republic wherever you may be and to support its mission as God calls you?"

"*I do.*"

This was it. Emmett would not get a better chance, and yet he hesitated. The weight of taking a life in cold blood suddenly pulled on his hand with the gun in it like an anchor.

"Stand!" Weiss commanded to the crowd. The sound of nearly seventeen thousand people getting to their feet at once was thunderous. It would have masked the first few shots, had Emmett raised his gun and fired. But he didn't.

His wife Susan's face snarling in berserker rage, crumpling under the impact of the bullet he'd fired into it, flashed before his eyes.

"Do you, the citizens of this holy republic, in the name of Christ, promise to welcome these men and women as they join our ranks and encourage them to grow as a disciple of the Lord?"

"*We do,*" boomed the crowd.

Emmett saw the faces of his daughters, terrified in the back seat of that old Prius, on the day he murdered their mother to keep her from ripping them apart. But it wasn't Susan they were afraid of in his memory. Before the accident had triggered their mother into transforming into a demon, it was Emmett the girls had been terrified of—their drunk, about-to-drive-them-all-off-the-road father. What would they think of him now?

"Will you endeavor, by example and fellowship, to strengthen their ties within the household of God?"

"We will."

"Then with one voice, let us recount the Apostles' Creed: 'I believe in God, the Father almighty, creator of heaven and earth. I believe in Jesus Christ, God's only Son, our Lord, who was conceived by the Holy Spirit, born of the Virgin Mary, suffered under Pontius Pilate, was crucified, died, and was buried; he descended to the dead. On the third day, he rose again; he ascended into heaven and was seated at the right hand of the Father, until he returned to us to judge the living and the dead. I believe in the Holy Spirit; the communion of saints; the forgiveness of sins; the resurrection of the body; and the life everlasting. Amen.'"

Weiss paused between each sentence so that both the crowd and the about-to-be-baptized could repeat his words. Emmett took a deep breath and shut out the doubts. He forced the anchor of life's intrinsic value off his wrist and lifted the gun from the slimy shit he was standing in and—

Suddenly, the floor was literally ripped out from underneath him and the slick thickness of Grace rushed over his head.

"I baptize you in the name of the Father…" he vaguely heard Weiss saying in a distorted, muffled voice, as he felt the thick liquid fill his mouth and his nose, then push its way down into his body. He coughed and choked, the last of the air in his lungs escaping without a thought for the man who had just moments ago taken it in to calm his nerves.

His throat burned.

His chest seized.

Emmett felt the life being pulled out of him like water down a drain, but he did not let go of the handgun. Even as he fought against the thick fluid drowning him, his grip remained firm.

There is no God here, he thought as his muscles burned themselves out and his heart beat for what was surely the last time. Except that it wasn't. The floor of his cube suddenly rose, pushing him up to the surface, and as he felt the gel rushing out of his way so that he might breath air once more, Emmett realized he was not dead.

And the gun was still in his hand.

"And the Holy Ghost. Amen!" Weiss said, as the newly saved came sputtering back to the surface.

Nobody saw the gun in Emmett's hand until it went off.

Bam!

The first bullet tore through the neck of Julius Weiss like he was made of paper.

Bam! Bam! Bam! Bam!

The next four lodged themselves fatally in his chest. The minion assigned to Kessler lunged at him in an effort to wrestle the gun from the assassin's hand, but he ate a bullet for his effort.

Kessler saw the back of the man's perfect head pop off like a bottle cap before he even realized he'd shot him.

Screaming echoed all around the arena, but he didn't hear it. Chaos erupted like a volcano spewing violence everywhere, but he didn't see it.

All Emmett could focus on was Julius Weiss writhing around, utterly alone, on his stage in the center of it all.

The man was not dead.

Emmett felt something pinch his arm hard, sending hot electric fingers of pain up the limb to scratch at his brain. He looked down to see the man he'd just shot in the head's mouth firmly clamped around the meat of his forearm.

He shot him again. Then he watched as the man's jaw unlatched and his body fell to the ground twitching.

As if pulled by a magnet, Emmett approached Weiss. His wrath was gone, but what had replaced it wasn't at all what he'd expected. At first, he couldn't even identify the emotion, but as the lump in his throat grew and his victim's violent twitching and jerking death throes subsided into even more horrific shallow breaths, he came to recognize it as guilt.

Guilt like he'd never felt before.

And it rode him down on its angry red horse, Truth.

Emmett had killed his wife all by himself. Dr. Weiss had nothing to do with her death. The man had just been trying to give Susan and him the children they so desperately wanted. Blaming the man for the entire apocalypse was ludicrous. There was no way anybody could have known what would happen. And when the man had learned about the role he'd inadvertently played in the ending the world, what had he done? He'd fucking found a cure. Not just for berserkers, but for death itself. Or at least as close to it as anybody but God himself could have conceived of.

What have I done?

Emmett Kessler felt the tears burning down his cheeks as he realized that he'd just murdered a man because he was too ashamed to face his own complacency in the end of the world.

He'd murdered the man for nothing.

"I'm sorry…" he sobbed, kneeling by Weiss's side.

As he looked into the man's eyes, he thought he could actually see the light fading in them.

I'm sorry.

"God forgives all," Weiss whispered. "Even this. Even you. If can ask Him for it."

Emmett's hand, covered in Weiss's blood, pressed against his own forehead. His blood-covered fingers pulled at his hair. And for the first time in his entire life, Emmett Kessler called out to God in earnest.

"Please God. Don't let him die. Don't make me a murderer twice over."

But it was too late. Weiss shut his eyes and was still.

"I'm—" Emmett began, but suddenly a sharp pain in his leg drew his attention. Another asshole was biting him, but this dude had been bitten himself.

"What the fuck…" he mumbled as he kicked the zombie off him, failing for a moment to register its significance. Wincing, Emmett stood up and looked uncomprehendingly at the chaos.

People were screaming. Biting. Running.

It made no sense.

Until suddenly it did. The mechanics of how the Bunkermen had pulled it off was beyond him, but the results spoke loud enough for him to piece together the basics. It was so cliché he wanted to puke—they'd turned the Saved into zombies, obviously to spread their corrupted or hacked tech.

Jesus, he thought. *I didn't ask a single fucking question when the Old Lady was going over the plan. And now look at what I've done. I've managed to bring zombies to the fucking apocalypse. How many of these people were going to die? Thousands? Tens of thousands? Hundreds of thousands? Austin had a population of almost a million, the man I just shot down in cold blood told me as much not more than a couple of hours ago.*

Did I just kill them all?

The vomit he'd choked down a moment ago reversed course and erupted in a series of wet, chunky, Technicolor screams. He'd just committed a far worse crime that the one he'd murdered Weiss for. He wiped his mouth and took in—utterly and completely—what was actually happening in the chaos around him.

God was dead.

The saved were damned.

Heaven on Earth had gone to hell.

He had one bullet left, and there was only one man left who deserved to eat it. Limping, he made his way through the biting throngs of Austinites toward the locker room to kill himself in private.

*   *   *   *   *

Waters heard the shots just as he burst through the west entrance doors of the Erwin Center. A second later the screaming started; and in the two minutes it took him to get into the arena, all hell had broken loose. It was like every single person in the arena had gone berserk, only they weren't berserkers. They weren't faster. Or stronger. Or easily distracted. And they weren't really smashing and ripping things apart.

They were still people—more or less. But they were singularly focused on biting each other, but they weren't just biting the closest person to them. They were only biting people who hadn't been bit yet. Even weirder, it was just biting. The zombies weren't trying to eat anybody. They obviously weren't trying to kill anybody. Yet somehow that didn't make it any less terrifying.

Not a single one tried to bite Waters as he shoved the rabid cats away from him so he could get onto the floor. It took him a second, but Waters realized that it must be because he did not have Grace inside him. He could almost hear the Old Lady laughing at the success of her plan. The once saved snapped at each other and pushed past him out of the arena into the streets of Austin—like they were playing the most bizarre game of tag he'd ever seen, and every one of them was it at the same time. For as bad as he wanted to find Emmett, for a few minutes all he could do was stand there and watch.

"Black Jesus!"

It was a familiar voice, but not the one he was hoping to hear most. Still it allowed him to shake off his captivation. He turned to see Wiley fighting his way toward him from the far side of the floor.

"Where's Emmett?" Waters shouted back to him.

"Where's Emmett?" Waters asked again as soon as Wiley reached him.

"He headed back toward the locker rooms," Wiley said. Then he added, "What the fuck, Captain? Where did he get a gun? What the hell is going on?"

Waters didn't answer.

*   *   *   *   *

The Old Lady was not laughing at the success of her plan—at least not on the outside. But she did have a gleeful little twinkle in her eyes. Kessler had performed perfectly. The breach had gone off like a Swiss alarm clock. The malware was proliferating at an even higher rate than the models had estimated.

Grace was all but theirs.

As long as the virus in the decoys worked a while longer.

"The casualty rate of one percent continues to hold," a tech said to the room, but really the information was just for her. Everybody else had glasses on and could see the stats coming in as they were generated.

But not the Old Lady.

McCain had refused to wear glasses since the beginning. She liked her information curated. But more than that, she found it was easier to hold her people accountable if they couldn't claim she already knew everything in advance. Plus, keeping that technology at a distance gave her a nice firewall against those in her organization who might be tempted to use it against her. Yes, she lived by the silicon sword, but regardless of what the silly adage said—or maybe because of it—she wasn't going to make it any easier for her enemies to kill her with it than she absolutely had to.

"Penetration is at sixteen percent."

"We've got tracking now."

"Put it on the main screen, please," the Old Lady commanded.

A map of Austin appeared. Austinites who were now malware zombies showed up as red. Those who still had uncorrupted Grace flowing through their blood were blue.

"What's the status of the decoys?" she asked as her focus shifted to the three yellow blobs that were in the men's locker room of the Erwin Center.

"With all three hosts there for the breach, the Registry might as well not even exist. There's no way it'll be able to pass an update through without us intercepting it. I don't even think the system is aware of the breach yet."

The Old Lady doubted very much that was true. They had no way of stopping the system behind the Registry from recording and tracking the nanite corruption. Elijah Dyer had designed the artificial intelligent monitoring system too well for them to get to it directly. But what they could do was send the fucking thing on a wild goose chase. And the virus inside her three decoys was the goose: cloned Grace nanobots, sterilized and retrofitted to look like they were producing the signal responsible for the zombie outbreak, all the while masking the actual hacking into Grace itself.

But there was already a problem with that, wasn't there? she thought. The viral version of Grace was supposed to be inert, and yet clearly there was still some functionality left in the little fuckers because otherwise Captain Waters would be dead. The question was, *What kind of a problem was it going to be?*

"Anything on the decoy virus's reaction to the actual Grace in Kessler and DuPont?"

"No reaction, ma'am."

So far, so good, she thought, trying hard not to be optimistic.

"Let's start terminating Grace at sixty percent penetration please," she commanded. The plan had been to wait for eighty percent, just to be safe, but that was when they'd thought they'd have only one viral host on the scene.

"Not eighty, ma'am?" a tech named Sheldon asked. He was right to confirm the change of course, but it still pissed the Old Lady off. She made a mental note of the kid's name and decided he'd be in the first round of trials once they'd gotten Grace under their control and revamped. When Elijah Dyer had originally created it, his first round of trials had been particularly nasty. The subjects had been liquefied from the inside over the course of several weeks, if she recalled correctly. Maybe they'd do better when it was their turn, but she doubted it.

"We have an advantage. We're going to press it."

"Yes, ma'am," the kid said, without the slightest inkling that he'd most likely be doing a fatal impression of the Wicked Witch of the West by the end of the week.

I'm melting! I'm melting...

The Old Lady's coy smile blossomed into a grin for a second before she could clamp it down. She looked around the room to see if any of her people had caught the momentary drop in her veil. No one had.

* * * * *

The woman who had been his attendant—who had so kindly, graciously released his sexual tension, who as far as Emmett was concerned was an angel—was lying in the center of the ring of chairs convulsing as if a live wire was being shoved up her ass.

There was blood everywhere.

Her blood.

And the angel's heart was still pumping the thick, red stuff out of a gaping bite mark on her throat like a half-clogged fountain. Her eyes were wide open, alert, and they found Emmett's almost as soon as the distraught man entered the room.

He knew he should put her out of her misery. But the last bullet he had in his gun did not have her name on it, and even if he wanted it to, he didn't know what her name was, so—

Are you fucking kidding me? he thought. After all this, that is the best reason you can come up with to withhold mercy? That you don't know the woman's name?

But it was. And hating himself for it didn't change anything. His capacity for self-loathing was already rupturing at the seams. He sat in one of the chairs facing away from her, wishing she'd stop her awful gargling, but at the same time welcoming the needle in his heart. He didn't deserve a peaceful place to end it all anyway.

He took a breath.

He put the gun to his head.

He pulled the trigger.

He felt the gun jump in his hand.

But it wasn't the explosion of the bullet from the shell that he'd felt. It was the hand of Black Jesus lodging itself between the hammer and the firing pin. The gun pinched the old man's skin like a deformed lobster claw.

It drew blood.

But it did not splatter Emmett's brains all over the floor.

Pulling his hand free of the gun, and the gun free of Emmett's hand, Black Jesus looked into Emmett's eyes.

"I killed him."

"No, you didn't," Black Jesus said, but Emmett wasn't capable of hearing that yet.

"I killed everybody."

Black Jesus nodded and then grabbed his friend by the beard and pulled his face to him so that the man couldn't look away.

"Right now, I don't care what you've done, Kessler," he said. "Right now, all the matters, is what you're going to do!"

"I'm going to kill myself."

"No, you're not. You're going to fucking cancel this goddamn pity party you're having and fix this shit."

"They're all dead, dude. What's there to fix?"

"Unless you severed the doctor's head from his body, I promise you, he is not dead. Grace will save him." Black Jesus pointed to the attendant, still struggling on the floor. "It will save her. It will save everybody. But for it to do that, you and I are going to have to save it."

"I don't—" Emmett began, but Black Jesus cut him off.

"Look, we got played. Not just you. All three of us. And we're still being played."

"It's too late, Captain. Didn't you see the—"

"Zombies? Yeah, I saw them. Totally fucked up. But right now, we need to figure out a way to fucking stop them before they succeed at doing whatever that fucking Old Lady in the bunker has them up to."

"It's got to be Grace," Wiley said. "That's all the Bunkermen care about."

Black Jesus nodded.

"The way Elijah Dyer designed it, each bot in Grace is a self-contained and completely isolated device. Jackie told me that they'd gotten their hands on the nanobots before and tried to replicate them, but that without the rest of the system that feeds information to them via the Registry, every iteration they come up with is more or less useless."

"Okay, so then what the fuck are the zombies about?" Emmett asked.

"I think maybe if they can compromise enough of the system, they'll be able compromise the main processor, or processors—whatever it is that's the brains of the thing."

"And then they'll have Grace?" Emmett asked, still trying to switch gears from suicide attempt to suicide mission.

"Maybe," Wiley said.

"They wanted Emmett to assassinate the doctor to overload the network," Black Jesus said. "The Old Lady told me herself that if Grace gets updated while they're trying to steal it, then it's game over for them."

"That's why they're turning everybody into zombies and not just moving in silently. The spectacle of it is going to continue to bog down the network."

"Back when I was a kid, when the Internet was slow or stuck, we'd just reboot it," Emmett said.

"Would that work?" Black Jesus asked Wiley.

"I don't fucking know, brother."

The three men stared at each other, waiting for somebody to come up with a better idea. Nobody did.

"What happens to the zombies when the Bunkermen finally get Grace?" Emmett asked, though he already knew the answer.

"If I had to guess, I think they probably all die."

"Okay, but that's a good thing," Wiley said.

"How?" Emmett almost screamed.

"Because we know they don't have it yet," Wiley explained.

"There's still time," Black Jesus said.

"There's still time," Wiley echoed.

"We need to shut off the power," Emmett said. "To the whole city."

"Wherever this computer is, it's going to have a backup power supply," Wiley said. "Blacking out the city isn't going to be enough."

"Well, then I don't know what the fuck we can do!" Emmett yelled, his despair crushing him.

"I do," a voice from the shadows behind them said.

Emmett, Wiley, and Black Jesus turned in unison as Elijah Dyer stepped forward into the light.

Chapter Ten
Girls Coming and Girls Going

THE LITTLE GIRL'S SCREAMS were louder than anybody thought possible, but it wasn't their volume that eviscerated the nerves like a wet puppy in a microwave. It was the knowledge that the seizures that had preceeded them had been easier to deal with, both emotionally and medically.

Everybody was looking to Maddie, as if she was in charge now. And she supposed she was. An ironic little titty-twister if ever there was one, considering how not a single one of these assholes had let her get a word in edgewise about anything related to Mari's pregnancy until it was too late. Only Bobby-Leigh had ever been even remotely interested in what she—a trained midwife once upon a long-ass time ago—thought. And now the Kessler sisters were being banished from their own family's house, and suddenly she was supposed to magically have all the answers.

Well, she didn't. Mari was too small. The baby too breeched. The eclampsia too progressed. Back when she was an apprentice, she'd have sent her to a hospital by now.

But the only hospital they had was Tiny's fucking app. And while they had lidocaine, she was certain they simply did not have the skill to pull off an epidural safely—bullshit OB app or not. Besides Maddie was pretty sure they'd need to mix the local anesthetics with a narcotic like fentanyl or morphine, neither of which they had, and which, even if they did have them, she had no fucking idea how much to use, and she was not about to trust an app designed by Tiny and his goofball, dipshit friends with a little dear's life.

Except that she didn't really have a choice, did she?

That baby had to come out. There was no question Mari would die if it didn't. Unfortunately, at least as far as Maddie was concerned, there was very little question that Mari would die if they did.

Damned if you do.

Damned if you don't.

But a bunch of completely untrained yahoos attempting a cesarian and a spinal epidural at the same time? Forget about it. They might as well just stab the little darling in the heart and then put a gun to her head and force her to play Russian roulette.

"Maddie!" Anoona screamed, shaking her out of her internal debate.

"I'm afraid we'll paralyze her trying to do the lumbar puncture we'd need to do for an epidural."

"The app will—" Tiny tried to chime in.

"The app you and a couple of twelve-year-olds wrote? With no actually medical experience between you?" Maddie cut him off, "Forgive me if I don't want to trust the little dear's life to that fucking thing any more than we have to."

"The app it's based on did successfully get the arrow out of Brennachecke's chest," Tiny said in a quiet voice everybody pretended not to hear.

"We're going to go general anesthetic."

"Isn't that more…risky?" Anoona asked.

"Compared to what? You really want one of us to stick a needle in her spine. Tiny's app should be able to handle the dosage. We'll monitor the shit out of her breathing. I think it's our best chance for a positive outcome here," she said, and then couldn't stop herself from adding, "But you haven't wanted to hear a single word of my advice for nine months now, so frankly, I'm not exactly surprised you don't like my call now. I mean, what do I know? I've only delivered dozens of babies in my life. I only trained for eight years to learn how to do it. Maybe I should just go back to tending the plants, since you morons seem to think that's the best use of my time."

"Okay. Just—I see you're upset. I don't want you upset," Anoona soothed. "And certainly, I don't want you minding the fucking oats right now. But—"

"For fuck's sake, Maddie, you never got your license. And those dozens of births you performed that you're so quick to throw out, I know you were just assisting on them. I researched all you motherfuckers when you showed up. You are not and never have been an actual midwife."

Mari screamed.

"Forget it. Look, I'm fine with general anesthetic. Whatever. We need to cut that fucking kid out, right now!" Tiny continued.

"I agree," Maddie said.

"Great," Anoona said, her sarcasm like a paddle across the backside of a disobedient child, "Do it then."

*　*　*　*　*

The Fairfield Airport had been burned to the ground by the lesbians just like everything else. Almost. Brennachecke had insisted they keep several planes in working condition. All the fuel and supplies needed to operate them were now housed in the two hangars left intact, but Rachel and Sarah had done a good job of making them look like they were just as burned out as the rest of the facility.

All the fuel to operate them meant a few trips each, depending on payload and plane. There were two aircrafts, a Cessna Denali and Beechcraft King Air 250 EP, both considerable upgrades from the little Cessna 172 Brennachecke had used with the blood pirates, but still not jets. Jet speed was just not something the old soldier anticipated needing from an aircraft these days. He and the girls would be taking the King Air because it needed less distance to take off and had a better overall range. It would get them all the way to Maine without having to stop to refuel, even with the weight of Bobo with them.

As they loaded up the big truck with the plow blade on it—a spoil of war from the blood pirate attack—Brennachecke again asked, as gently as he could, if it was really the best idea for Bobo to come with them. Bobby-Leigh and Jennifer both turned in unison and gave him the same look. They'd made up their minds.

"It's a small plane and a long flight, that's all. His collar isn't going to work. We'll be out of range from our network."

"If you're concerned about your safety, Sarge, nobody is forcing you to come with us."

"I'm not concerned. I just—"

The look again.

"Okay, fine."

They tossed the last of the food they were taking and loaded themselves into the vehicle. It started up with a roar. Ten minutes later, they were standing in the hangar looking at the plane. Another forty-five and they had the aircraft gassed up, the runway plowed, and their gear loaded.

"So who gets to be copilot?" Bobby-Leigh asked.

"Not you," Jen said definitively.

"You do know that it is still my birthday, right?"

"Sorry, kiddo, I think your sister is probably a better choice. Besides, this baby can almost fly itself. I hardly really even need a copilot. It's going to be the most boring seat on the whole aircraft."

"You learn how to drive a car, and then we can talk about learning to fly a plane," Jen said.

"Why? You don't know how to drive a fucking car either. Unless you count typing in an address and pushing the start button. In which case, I *do* know how to drive."

Jen opened her mouth to say something, but was cut off by Bobo singing: "*I believe I could fly…* "

Everybody laughed, and the tension ran off and hid behind a snowdrift.

"That's a song. Do you know that?" Brennachecke asked, still smiling to himself.

Bobo's grin confirmed that he absolutely did know that, but he nodded too just for clarity's sake.

"Is the sign language thing going to work once we're—" Bobby-Leigh asked.

"Yep. All its data is stored locally. Doesn't need the net."

"Good."

"And," Jen added. "I think I can modify the program for Bobo's collar so that it will still function as intended as long as it is within twenty feet or so of one of us—assuming we've got glasses on."

"Really?" Brennachecke asked, a little disconcerted by the amount of relief he heard in his own voice.

"But that would mean you'd have to be okay with somebody else being your copilot."

Brennachecke laughed again and shook his head.

"Seriously?" Bobby-Leigh squealed.

"What can I say, dude? You make a good point."

"No, but…seriously?"

"Yeah, what the fuck? The plane basically flies itself, right?"

"You two keep using the f-word like that and neither of you are going to find out."

"Sorry," Bobby-Leigh said.

Jen saluted mockingly. "Yes, sir. Sergeant, sir."

*   *   *   *   *

The child survived the C-section. She was a healthy six pounds and change. Ten little fingers. Ten little toes. Dark like her grandmother. The little thing came out shrieking in a shrill little voice so strong there was no doubt she was going to survive whatever the apocalypse had to throw at her.

Her mother, on the other hand, was not as tough. Nor as lucky. Nor—at the moment—as alive.

In fact, Tiny thought as he handed the infant to Maddie to cut the cord, *that was probably exactly why the baby was screaming.*

"Get that fucking thing out of here," Anoona hissed as her daughter flatlined in front of her.

"Defib!" Tiny called out as Maddie deftly snipped the

connection between mother and child and whisked the shrieking bundle of joy out of the room.

Rachel handed him the electrodes with a look of warning that made him want to slap her across the face. He was very—*very*—much aware of the catastrophe that would envelope them all if Mari died in childbirth.

His app showed him where to put the self-adhesive electrodes on the little girl's chest and then the program took over. They saw her little body jerk from the jolt of electricity. They saw the heart monitor bleep artificially and then ring out its death note once more.

Jolt. Jerk. *Bleep. Bleep. Bleep.*

Flatline.

Jolt. Jerk. *Bleep. Bleep. Bleep. Bleep.*

It was only after the heart-rate monitor had been going for nearly two minutes that Anoona slowly allowed the stale air in her chest to exit her dark lips and finally looked away from her daughter to the man that had both killed her and brought her back from the dead.

"Sew her up, please," she said in a whisper so choked by emotion that it almost didn't escape her throat at all.

Tiny swallowed hard. He wanted to cry, but he didn't. Instead he reached into the abdominal cavity he'd just removed the baby from and pulled out the placenta. Under the direction of his app, he then followed the afterbirth closing procedures and stepped away.

Mari didn't flatline again. Nor did she have any further complications as her incisions slowly healed over the following days and weeks.

But she didn't wake up either.

There was nothing Tiny's app or Maddie's questionable expertise could do about it. They moved her to the Kessler sister's room, if for no other reason than the last young lady who'd been in a coma and slept there had eventually woken up.

It was the newly minted grandmother who eventually named the baby. Anoona didn't call her Armageddon like Jen's dreams had prophesized. She didn't bestow the little thing with a name from her native land like she'd done for the baby's mother either. Anoona christened her grandchild Loralai, after the sirens who sat on the rocks luring sailors to their deaths.

It seemed like a good choice, Tiny thought, all things considered.

Chapter Eleven
The Devil Is in the Details

THE INTELLIGENCE BEHIND GRACE and the Registry was not artificial. At least it wasn't to Elijah Dyer. Just like Noah had been instructed to build the ark by God to save the world, so too, was Elijah convinced his inspiration to build Grace and the network it ran on had come from a divine origin.

Frankly, there wasn't much of an argument that could be made to the contrary, not that such a thing had ever stopped folks from blasting an idea. The fact was nowhere else on the planet had anybody done what Dyer had. Most of the world was still rather hopelessly pinned down like a wrestler grappling well out of his weight class in the aftermath of a world with berserkers. Sure, there were a number of groups reorganizing. Tiny states and even tinier federations were starting to build alliances with each other. There were military dictatorships that had numbers in the hundreds of thousands. There were the Bunkermen.

But outside of Austin, Texas, the advancement of technology had been brought to a standstill. Innovation everywhere else was limited to getting the tech that already existed to continue working—which was nothing to sneeze at when you got right down to it. Like it or not, the state of the world mid-apocalypse made it extremely difficult to convincingly argue the point that Elijah Dyer was just a crazy person.

And yet, the man knew he would probably have a hard time throwing a rock into a crowd out in the sprawl beyond the walls without hitting somebody who was sure Grace was just tech. That Elijah Dyer was just a mad genius—with a big emphasis on the mad part. He understood why that was. When he listened to Weiss talk about him being the Lamb of God during public events, it sounded crazy even to him—more than sounded, actually. It was crazy.

Dyer did not believe for one minute he was the second coming of the Lord. He knew he was not. In the beginning, back before berserkers, or more accurately the fear inspired by berserkers, started shutting infrastructures down, nobody had thought that of him. He wasn't really even sure when that shift had actually even happened. It was like he woke up and suddenly everybody he talked to had just started assuming he was the messiah. And because the assumption made it easier to set the things up he had to set up, he probably didn't do as much as he should have to dispel the speculation.

He wasn't crazy.

He knew that.

But he did feel like a fraud. As Weiss had pushed the idea out, Dyer had protested. In fact, he'd almost shut the whole thing down because he didn't want to perpetuate the lie. But Weiss had convinced him to pray on it first. The doctor was convinced that encouraging the idea that

Grace was coming from the reincarnation of Jesus Christ himself would only make it easier to bring people into the Lord's Kingdom. Dyer never had to say it himself, he'd promised. In fact, he'd told him that it was a more powerful message if he always denied it.

Dyer had prayed. Public relations and marketing had never been his strong point. The Angel of the Lord did not offer him any guidance, so he let Weiss move forward. But the feeling of being a fraud stuck. At every public event he attended, it slapped him in the face like a scorned lover, until he eventually started to remove himself from the very society he'd created. He thanked the Lord for Weiss, who quickly became the mouthpiece of the Republic. If it hadn't been for him, Grace might have never found its footing and the Republic might have never been born.

By the time Emmett had filled Weiss with lead, Elijah had locked himself away for a long time. Recused at the top of the seventeen-hundred-foot-high Lone Star Tower—the tallest building still standing anywhere in the world and nearly twice as tall anything else in Austin's skyline—his work—God's work—was all he had to think about. Weiss and his bishops had proven they could handle the day-to-day. Grace and the Registry were self-sufficient. The system that bound them all was now mature, tested, and worthy of its place as the guardian of heaven on Earth.

Eventually, the Angel of the Lord had come to him again. The Angel made it known to him that the Holy Father was pleased with his efforts. But his work was not yet done. So long as there was flesh, man would be wicked. The Lord would send his Daughter to Earth to lead the righteous into the divine kingdom of light. And with her, this long apocalypse would at last close. But the Angel made it clear that it was up to Dyer to make that possible. The Almighty had bestowed Grace unto him to spread it throughout the world. Now, the Almighty was trying to hand him something even more important, something that he had been commanded to call Glory. If he could ever get it to work that was, and these days it felt like that was a pretty big *if.*

It was while praying for a revelation on Glory that he saw the system that ran Grace suddenly falter. He watched the replays of Emmett putting first one, then two, then three, then more bullets into Weiss's completely unsuspecting body. So many questions filled his head at once he could have fried an egg on the heat from their friction as they jostled for his attention. Yet mere seconds into his search for answers, he saw the traffic load on the network was exploding. Communication between Grace, the Registry, and the system behind it switched to passive management so that the network could better handle the load. It was the Achilles' heel of his system, but still, even he couldn't look away as the saved turned on one another. He watched even after the network stalled. Even after the backups failed. In the space of six minutes, communication across the Registry had been all but shut down. But the Austinites didn't turn their glasses off when the network intermittently started to freeze them out. In fact, they only tried to get information harder.

Elijah himself was just as guilty as the rest of them. He too couldn't stop trying to figure out what was happening. However, he had an advantage. He could access information though back channels he'd built into the nanites themselves, a layer of the network only he had access to.

It was obvious pretty quickly that Grace was being corrupted one nanite at a time and that the corruption was transferring itself to the bot next to it with lightning speed. Still, it took him another four minutes to accept that fact because it just didn't make any sense.

Grace couldn't be stolen. It only worked as a network. Even if a would-be thief got their hands on the nanites themselves it would be like getting their hands on a bunch of iPhones that didn't have Wi-Fi or cellular reception. The devices might be able talk to each other a little via Bluetooth, but the vast majority of their capabilities would be utterly and completely unavailable. However, this wasn't a robbery attempt he realized once he had the interface open and saw in detail how the corruption was spreading. This was an assault. The hack wasn't designed to steal Grace at all. At least not at the moment. The attack was designed to destroy it.

Why? he almost asked aloud. *Why would anybody seek to destroy something that was so obviously purely good?*

The answer came hard and fast, like a bombing run just before the ground troops moved in—which was exactly what this must be. With Grace fully operational, the idea of a foreign invader being able to occupy the city was ludicrous. But without it, and with nearly all of Austin's citizens running around like monsters out of a cheap horror movie, the only thing keeping the heretics at bay were the walls themselves. And anybody capable of mounting this sophisticated a cyberattack was not going to have a problem with the physical defenses of the city.

This was an invasion. And the more he thought about it, the more he realized this was the only way that a foreign power would be able to get their hands on Grace. They weren't trying to take a couple of iPhones here and there. They were coming after the whole enchilada. Apple, Android, Google, Verizon, the very Internet itself.

But it could be shut down.

At least for the moment it could. The window for salvation was closing quickly. He had to act fast.

*   *   *   *   *

Emmett would have probably put a bullet into Elijah Dyer. He was so startled when the man had seemingly appeared out of nowhere. But luckily for everybody, Black Jesus had his gun. All he could do was squeal like a stuck pig in surprise and fling a chair at the man. As it fell harmlessly to the ground, well off its mark, and he got ahold of the reins of rational thought again, Emmett realized the Captain knew who the dude was.

"You've got to switch to decaf, brother," Wiley whispered to him.

"Shutting the power off won't reset the network. Grace is the network. The nanites are powered by the very people they're inside. You'd have to kill everybody to reset the system."

"That's what this is!" Emmett yelled. "That's what the Old Lady wants. That's how she's going to get control."

"Yes," Dyer confirmed.

"So...we're fucked then," Wiley said. The reset idea had been their best, last, and only real plan.

"No, not yet. I can still stop it from happening."

"Okay, first of all, who the fuck are you?" Emmett asked. "And more importantly, how?

"My name is Elijah Dyer. I built Grace."

"You don't look like the second coming of shit to me."

"For fuck's sake, man. What is with the hostilities? This shit is your fault. If anybody should be being an asshole, it's this guy, not you," Wiley chided.

"I'm not the second coming, Emmett," Dyer said. "God hasn't sent Her down to us yet. I've got a lot more work to do before He does."

"Her?" Black Jesus couldn't help but ask.

"Christ was the Lord's only son. This time around the Angel told me he's going to send his only daughter, but that is still a long way off."

"Right."

"This is the situation. The three of you are carrying a nanovirus that is obstructing my system's ability to push an update through the network. It's a clever hack, if ever there was one. Seems it was designed to trick my system into thinking your virus is the source of Grace's corruption. A red herring if you will. Meanwhile the actual corruption continues to spread via physical contact. That's why the saved are biting each other. Corrupt nanites in the saliva access the next victim's clean ones through the wound. Think rabies."

"I was bit," Wiley said.

"Me too, twice actually," Emmett jumped in.

"Why aren't we zombies like the rest of them?"

"The virus inside you is using Grace to communicate with my system. It only makes sense that the Old Lady, as you called her, wouldn't let her decoys be compromised."

"If you know all of this, then what do you need us for?" Wiley asked.

"Well...I guess I could just murder the three of you, but the Lord would prefer I didn't, the whole sixth commandment thing, you know?"

Emmett smiled. He was actually starting to like this dude.

"But I do need to get the virus out of you. Come with me."

The three wise men from the East did as they were told.

Part of Dyer's redesign of Austin was to implement a modified hyperloop transportation system under the city, the existence of which was regularly scrubbed from the Registry. Keeping it secret was another one of Weiss's ideas, which Dyer had some vague recollection of a conversation about, but not real involvement in the hows and whys. Considering the chaos on the streets though, the hyperloop was the best way to get to Dyer's place. The elevator ride down to the boarding platform would take almost three times as long as the hyperloop would to get them across town.

"I have to ask you a couple questions," Black Jesus said. "Why eliminate race and sexual orientation? Is that really how you believe God wants it? Saint Peter's only letting white heterosexuals into heaven?"

Apparently, before the dude officially chose a side in this little war, the Captain needed to know he was taking the right side, Emmett thought. And apparently murdering a million people in cold blood didn't tip the scale for the man as much as he would have thought. But then again, Emmett was white and heterosexual, so maybe he shouldn't be using his scale to measure the value of race and sexual orientation.

"There's nothing in Grace that affects either one of those things. It does diminish sexual arousal a little bit in certain circumstances, just so that the saved aren't the same slaves to desires of the flesh that the rest of mankind is. But it doesn't control who or what you're attracted to. There was a discussion about it, of course, as we were implementing. But even then, homosexuality was never the subject of the debate. Weiss and a few of the other master coders thought it would be in line with God's will to correct pedophilia and bestiality. But obviously that isn't God's will. As abhorrent as those things are, if God didn't want them to exist, he would not have created them in the first place. Free will is a key component in any kind of faith. For Grace to be worthy of the Lord, it can't fundamentally change who a person is. That includes race, and any other identifier for that matter: height, eye color, hair color."

"So, where are all the black people then, dude?" Emmett asked, once again subconsciously trying to regain Waters's favor.

"The Republic has lots of people of color."

Dyer paused to look up the exact breakdown of who was what. But from the expression on his face, Emmett could tell the answer he found didn't make sense to him.

"You're able to access the Registry?" Black Jesus asked. "Because for me it's totally shut down."

"Yeah, the public servers are totally overloaded thanks to the spectacle of your man here shooting mine down in cold blood after being saved. Along with the zombie menace running amuck in the streets, of course. But I can access everything from a private secondary networked server," he answered distractedly.

"So you didn't know your own invention was whitewashing everybody who got themselves saved by it?" Emmett said, the edge in his voice a sharpened from being called out so nonchalantly.

"Just…wait. Give me a minute here," Dyer said, but his face confirmed that he'd just discovered somebody else had been playing with his toys.

Ding!

The elevator doors opened, and the bewildered look on Dyer's face compounded like a bone fracture.

The tunnel was not empty anymore.

There were zombies everywhere, their heads whipping around in creepy unison toward the source of the sound.

"So much for secret tunnels," he muttered.

And then to the three men from Maine State Prison's utter shock, Dyer whipped out two sophisticated pistols from well-concealed shoulder holsters under his black jacket. The guns looked like they'd been designed by Jonathan Ive with a little support from Franz von Holzhausen. Utterly modern, they still managed to invoke an old west gunslinger vibe. Their curves were straight-up sexy. Their extended barrels and incorporated targeting assistance were runway fashion model stylish. But it wasn't the guns themselves that blew Emmett, Wiley, and the Captain's minds.

Bam! Bam!

Bam!

The real surprise for them was the fact that the man who had just told them how much God hated a killer was now unhesitatingly putting cap after cap in his followers' asses.

"Run. That way. Now," Dyer said and pointed before anybody had a chance to say anything about what they'd just witnessed.

Again, they did as they were told.

Wiley took the lead like he was Lorenzo Neal blocking for LaDainian Tomlinson, using every ounce of his bulk to clear the way through the horde of zombies that had found their way into the tunnels. As a fresh set of teeth sank into his shoulder, Emmett realized that Waters was going to be the only one the zombies were not interested in.

"Captain, give me a gun!" he yelled and watched in shame as Black Jesus hesitated.

"I can't trust you, Emmett. I'm sorry," Waters said. The man did not pass Emmett a weapon.

The zombies were not apparently able to coordinate their attacks—a blessing if there had ever been one. Add that to the fact that human beings were just not created with biting in mind as a means to attack, and even without a gun of his own, Emmett, and Wiley, for that matter, managed to avoid the worst of the bites, and more importantly avoid getting swept up by the horde.

They made it to the hyperloop pod. The doors opened automatically for them, but they couldn't get inside yet. The zombies were thickening around them like some kind of sick and twisted Halloween themed Jell-O in some suburban asshole's fridge, and Dyer, Emmett, and Wiley were almost instantly caught up as they came to a stop at the platform.

Black Jesus put a round through a zombie's chest just as the man was about to sink his teeth into Emmett, but there was just too many of them to get the three of them free and clear enough to board the pod.

"I'll hold them off. You guys get in," Black Jesus said as he inserted himself between the horde and the men they were so focused on sinking their teeth into.

Dyer stepped onto the platform and put another round into yet another of their assailants. Emmett tried to pull himself free to join him, but a hand snagged his foot, and he went sprawling. He was being pulled into the mass of grabbing hands and gnashing teeth even before he hit the ground.

Wiley dove into the horde like a freight train jumping the tracks. He flung and smashed like the berserker was still alive and well inside him after all, giving Waters just enough room to pull Emmett back to safety.

Bam!

"What caliber are those guns?" Dyer screamed at Captain Waters as Emmett and Wiley shoved one zombie after another away and tried to get themselves onto the platform.

"Forty-five."

"FMJ or hollow?"

"Not the time for a conversation, dudes!" Emmett interjected, punching a perfect-looking woman in the face.

"Hollow," Black Jesus answered, ignoring him, pistol-whipping a perfect-looking man clinging onto Wiley's leg like a child who didn't want his daddy to leave him at day care and sinking his teeth into the enormous man's thigh.

"No head shots then, please."

Dyer was breathing hard, but inexplicably calm. Every move the man made was deliberate and thought out. Not that it mattered much when they were so outnumbered. But still, Emmett was impressed, if not a little weirded out. His own mind was all over the place. He could see that Wiley was running on almost pure instinct too. Even Black Jesus, historically the clear winner in the cold and calculating department among them, looked flustered as fuck by comparison.

It had to be Grace that was allowing him to keep his cool like that. There was just no other reasonable explanation, except that maybe God was whispering in his ear, but even with everything he'd witnessed so far, he still didn't buy the party line about divine providence. He was sure that Elijah believed it. As did his followers. He'd put money on the fact that even Weiss was a card-carrying member of the faith in Dyer's connection to the Lord—if for no other reason than if he wasn't, the man was a much better con than Emmett had ever thought. When it came to Emmett T. Kessler though, that dude was a man of science. And he knew for a fact that science had killed God in his sleep long ago.

Am I really sure about that? he wondered as he pushed another zombie off and then with Wiley's help finally got onto the platform. *Why wasn't Grace making me calm like that?*

"You two need to get your hands on glasses before we leave," Dyer called out as he got into the pod.

"What? Why?" Wiley asked, clearly beyond ready to get the hell out of there. He was bleeding from at least a dozen places—all superficial wounds to be sure, but still, the idea of risking worse to get some stupid spectacles was insane.

Emmett didn't waste time with being annoyed—there was too much already bouncing around his head for that. He just reached out and snatched a pair of glasses for Wiley off the nearest zombie's face—they were all wearing them, so the task was pretty simple now that they had the slightly higher ground of the hyperloop platform on their side. After tossing the device to Wiley, he grabbed a second pair for himself when, all of a sudden, the two zombies he'd robbed of their eyewear started screaming and thrashing around like they were taking an acid shower. Their zombie cohorts didn't seem to notice, but the sight was so awful for Emmett that for a long second all he could do was stand there and watch them writhe.

Now what the fuck did I do?

Black Jesus and Dyer nearly emptied their weapons keeping him from being overwhelmed by the horde as he stood there like a stone. Emmett didn't even hear the shots. It took Wiley grabbing him by the shoulder to shake him out it.

"Kessler! Get your ass in here!" Black Jesus yelled at him, and that was exactly what he did.

The thick glass door of the transport pod shut behind them as soon as Emmett was on board. At last they could catch their breath. Emmett strapped himself into his seat and waited for the weird-ass pneumatic tube capsule car thing to whisk them off to Neverland or wherever the fuck they were going. He'd been bitten on the neck at some point and was bleeding like a son of a bitch, but the wound wasn't fatal by a long shot. *Isn't Grace supposed to be healing me? What the fuck?*

The pod didn't move. They just sat there waiting for what felt like hours.

What the fuck?

"I don't know how much you boys know," Elijah Dyer eventually began.

I know enough to know we best be getting the hell out of Dodge, Emmett almost said in response, but didn't.

Elijah asked Wiley and Emmett to put on their newly appropriated glasses and gave them a minute or two to calibrate them and then another couple of minutes to let their blown minds recover.

"You've had this the whole time?" Emmett asked Black Jesus.

The man nodded with a sigh. "You should see what they can do when the network isn't so bogged down."

Elijah smiled. "Actually, I can fix that for you. Give me a second and I'll have you all moved onto my back channel."

"Um, as cool as this all is, don't we need to get moving?" Wiley asked. "What if our hungry little friends outside figure out how to open the door?"

Immediately his glasses explained that only those with Grace had access to the city, and that *access* included everything, even the simplest things such as opening doors to hyperloop pods.

"Just wait a second. Don't the zombies have Grace?" Emmett asked, as he was being similarly educated via his own glasses. He quickly learned that once corrupted, the privileges of having Grace were locked out. In fact, for the zombies, only the most basic biological regenerative processes of the original system were still functioning. This meant these zombies were very much like their horror movie counterparts. Their higher brain functions were shut down. The only thing they were interested in doing was making more zombies. And, to actually kill them, you'd have to destroy their brains.

Except that these men and women were not dead. And, thanks to Grace, a bullet to the head was not even a guarantee that they would be. The only sure way to kill these motherfuckers would be to separate their heads from their bodies—which explained why Dyer was so nonchalant about putting bullets into them and why he was concerned about what a .45 hollow point at close range in the face might do.

Thou shall not kill.

But feel free to fuck a dude up in self-defense.

Emmett smiled. Maybe God wasn't so bad after all.

But wait, he thought suddenly, *then why the fuck wasn't Grace working on me?* He was still bleeding. He was not all calm and collected like Dyer was. Part of him wondered if maybe it was because he didn't believe in God. But the very fact that he could wonder that implied that at least some part of him did actually believe.

Again, the Registry answered him. It all came down to triage. Grace prioritized genome repair first. It would get to the superficial, non-life-threatening shit eventually.

"This is…" Emmett began.

"Amazing," Wiley finished, then randomly asked, "Are my teeth really going to—"

But the Registry answered before he could even finish formulating the question. *Yes, Grace would eventually replace the teeth he lost as berserker.* "Oh good. That's nice," he said.

Dyer cleared his throat to draw everybody's attention.

"The hyperloop was supposed to be a secret. But apparently it wasn't a particularly well-kept one. Still, when I got here, there was nobody down here. I'm guessing some of the citizens attending the baptism and trying to get away from the zombies knew about the tube and fled down here hoping to use it to escape. Only they were caught and turned before they could. What you need to understand is that what we just fought through…that's nothing compared to what is probably going to be waiting for us at the other end here."

*   *   *   *   *

The Old Lady watched as an unidentified person with Grace appeared, like the devil himself, in the locker room where the three decoys were. Then suddenly all four of their signals vanished off the map right in front of her eyes.

"What the fuck just happened, Sheldon?" she hissed at the technician in front of her.

"They're not dead. That much I can tell you, ma'am. The Registry is more or less still down. There is definitely no update coming through. If I had to guess, I'd say they got on an elevator and are out of reach of our tracking capabilities at the moment."

"What's the penetration?" she asked.

"Thirty-seven percent."

"We've slowed down."

It wasn't a question, but Sheldon, having just been called out by name—something the Old Lady never did—answered her just like it was.

"Yes, ma'am. We've hit the second tier of contact."

"Can you give me a projection for hitting the sixty percent minimum threshold?"

"Adjusted modeling puts us at three hours twenty-seven minutes out from sixty. Five hours thirteen minutes to the optimal eighty."

"Let's move up the timeline for the physical breach. If we deploy now, how long will it take to have men inside the walls?"

"Two hours," a technician, who was not Sheldon relayed.

"Ma'am, the modeling for a breach with more than forty percent of the citizenry still carrying Grace is pretty clear," Sheldon said.

"Yes, but those models assume a clean delineation between termination and incursion. We'll let our little zombies continue to penetrate the general pop, while we mobilize for the final attainment. The overlap should protect us."

"Would you like to order a new model to verify?"

"No, Sheldon. I would like you to follow my goddamn orders the first time I give them," the Old Lady hissed, again visualizing him being eaten alive by Grace. She hoped her little fantasy would keep her from smacking the little fuck in the head.

"Yes, ma'am. Deploying incursion forces now," Sheldon said, his voice shaking a little.

The Old Lady was pleased to hear the fear riding under his words. So pleased, in fact, she let a sadistic little smile creep across her lips and stay there.

She could almost hear the sounds, deep in the bowels of the bunker, far below the civilian structures, of the twelve thousand well-trained and even better armed insurgents loading up and moving out toward Austin. She had a bad feeling about what Waters and his friends were up to. Though she had no way to confirm it, she knew in her gut that the mystery man, who had appeared out of nowhere just minutes before all three of her decoys had vanished off the scopes, had to be Elijah Dyer himself. She didn't know what he could do at this point to stop them, but she was fairly confident the thousands of men and women with guns she'd just dispatched would be able to figure it out.

She was going to win. Two hours was never going to be enough time to figure out what she was up to and mount an effective defense.

Unless God really was on his side. She shook the ridiculous thought off like a dog extricating itself from water insolent enough to cling to its fur after a swim.

God was not going to save Austin.

God did not exist.

Probably.

*   *   *   *   *

The hyperloop shot toward the Lone Star Building faster than a commercial jet plane. The total trip was less than ninety seconds—the vast majority of which was acceleration and deceleration time.

Emmett's ears were ringing. The doors opened automatically upon arrival. *No wonder Elijah had wanted to get them all on the same page before they left,* Emmett thought as he struggled to get out of his seat belt before the zombies got inside the pod and pinned them in.

The Lone Star Platform had only a couple dozen of the compromised citizens on it, less than they'd just fought through, but still hardly a cakewalk, especially when the brain fog that lingered for a few minutes after hyperloop travel was factored in.

What the fuck is wrong with my seat belt? he wanted to scream as he yanked and pulled at the release ineffectually.

He felt a hand on his arm and was sure this was going to be it for him, but it was only Wiley.

"Breathe, brother," the big dude said as he released Emmett from the restraint.

Bam! Bam-bam!

Dyer and Black Jesus put slugs into the first zombies to successfully push their way through the crowd and get inside the pod, but it didn't matter. They were fucked. There was a wall of zombies blindly pushing to join their friends, and they spilled in like a storm surge through a broken dyke.

Scuttling over the seats of the pod like rats trying to escape a sinking ship, Emmett, Wiley, and Elijah dodged the incoming tide of teeth as Black Jesus stood at the door and directed the human traffic to the opposite side of the pod by shoving the oblivious folks hell-bent on getting a taste of everybody but him in that direction.

The seats and aisles acted like channels. The pod had seats for fourteen. It was cramped, but they were able to manipulate the majority of the platform zombies into coming into the pod on one side of Black Jesus while the three of them with Grace slipped out behind them.

"Get off the platform!" Dyer yelled as Black Jesus himself slipped out of the pod and tried to help Wiley force the door to close.

It wouldn't budge. Even with help, Wiley wasn't strong enough to force it. But when Wiley jumped down off the platform, suddenly the doors whooshed shut on their own right in front of Black Jesus's face.

They were safe.

For the moment.

"The city automatically responds to those with Grace. Those without it might as well be invisible."

"So they can't get out."

"Not unless one of us steps up to the platform indicating to the system that we want to board the pod."

"I thought the system was down," Emmett said.

"We're on his private server, brother," Wiley said. "It's operating on its own secure net."

Emmett shook his head. *Wait. Just wait.* "If everything connected to the network still works on your private server, then why can't you push an update through that?"

"There is no remote write access to the Grace data set. It's not connected to the network. It is the network."

"What the fuck does that mean?"

"It means that we can't update Grace. The system can only do it by physically updating the nanites themselves. That's why this hack is so impressive. It's using the methods and protocols designed to protect it from attack to attack it."

"I still don't understand. If you can't push an update through anyway, what difference does it make if whatever the Old Lady put in us is transmitting some kind of red herring to the big bad supercomputer?"

"It matters because that big bad supercomputer is the only thing that can correct Grace, and right now it is being tricked into spending all its time and energy trying to fix a vulnerability that doesn't actually exist and thus can't be corrected. It's a closed system, Emmett."

"So you can't just tell it to stop wasting its time on the red herring and start working on the actual problem."

"Nobody outside of the system can tell it anything."

"Why the fuck would you design it that way? That's nuts."

"Because God knows better than to trust mankind with the power of creation. Grace is His will. The Angel of the Lord instructed me on how to create it and part of that was how to protect it from being used outside of the Lord's intention."

"But it is being used for something you yourself said God would never stand for, dude. Or are all the people of color in Austin just on vacation somewhere together?"

"Yes. I…I'm aware of that now. I was not diligent enough when we were writing the code, and I guess some of the men and women I ordained thought they knew better than God."

"How much do you want to bet one of them was Dr. Julius Weiss?" Emmett asked with a sneer, feeling a little better about shooting the asshole.

"Hold on," Black Jesus said as they reached the elevator.

"If you can't change the code, then even if we can deal with the zombie problem here, there is still no way to stop it from ethnic cleansing the DNA of anybody you give it to. Grace can't be fixed."

Elijah pushed the button for the penthouse. And the doors slid shut.

"You and I can't change the code. But the system can self-edit. It just has to be convinced the programming is flawed. However, before we can engage it in that discussion, we have to get it to stop chasing its tail, and that means getting the virus inside the three of you out."

The elevator was fast. Not as fast as the hyperloop of course, but fast enough to make Emmett's ears pop again on the way up. The doors opened directly into Elijah's residence. There were no zombies. There was little furniture. A fact no one commented on as he guided the three of them to his lab.

Housed in the same thick glass that made up the doors of the hyperloop, the room was a twenty-foot square—surprisingly sparse, eerily quiet, and uncomfortably cold. The rear wall was entirely made up of the business ends of servers and quantum processors, plus a door that must go to the actual server room itself. There was a white leather chair in the middle of the space, but nothing else.

Or so Emmett thought until he looked up. The ceiling had what looked almost like the light a dentist might use attached to a rod system that would allow the light thingy to move just about anywhere in the room. Though it looked like something that belonged above a dentist chair, as the door hissed hydraulically shut behind them, it dropped down on its extension arm with a little whir of mechanics and dispelled any questions as to its function.

It was not a light.

It was the face of the operating system that controlled Grace. Where the bulbs would have been was a semi-translucent orb of some kind. They could only imagine the vast array of sensors that must be behind it.

The thing looked them over curiously.

"Let's start with you, Emmett."

"Okay."

"Have a seat."

Emmett obeyed, and immediately the orb moved in on him, so close that it made him flinch.

Dyer tapped a place in the wall, and a cabinet door opened. Emmett watched as he pulled out a wristband, not unlike the one the Old Lady had used to pull the Grace out of Willey the first time he'd been saved. Instead of a test tube, this one had a round petri-dish-like magazine attachment.

It took Elijah about thirty seconds to pull the virus out of him. It didn't exactly hurt, but he could feel it happening. Like taking a piss after holding it too long. Except that he was pissing out of his wrist, which made the whole thing a little creepy feeling. Without a word of explanation, Dyer popped off the petri dish thing and slid it, now full, into a reader of some sort that opened up at the base of the orb.

"Okay. Captain, you're up." Emmett and Waters exchanged a look as they exchanged places, but neither man said anything. A minute later, it was Wiley's turn.

"Is that it?" Emmett asked as Dyer removed the wristband from the former berserker.

Elijah smiled.

"The path is clear now for the system to start processing an update that will close the vulnerability the zombie hack is exploiting, but that will take a couple of hours."

"Do we have a couple of hours?" Wiley asked.

"Probably not," Elijah said coolly.

The man's calmness was starting to annoy the crap out of Emmett, but nobody else seemed to be bothered by it, so he bit off the sarcastic response that was trying to jump out of his mouth.

"I have an idea on how to buy us more time, but—" Elijah began to say, when all of a sudden, the door to Dyer's residence flew open and two women burst in with an army of zombies hot on their heels. One of them held a fire ax and the other a combat shotgun.

"Oh, thank the Lord!" they screamed when they saw Elijah was actually home, but that was the last thing they said.

The ax was torn away by the horde, and the combat shotgun was apparently empty and much less effective as a club. Ten feet from the glass partition between them the women were overcome.

Elijah made no attempt to save them. He barely even looked up.

"Jesus," Emmett said as he watched the women turn.

The orb spit out a new petri-dish-magazine thing, drawing everybody's attention. As Elijah described what it was he intended to do, the Registry supplemented his explanation with graphics. The experience was surreal to say the least.

"The system has weaponized Grace. That's what this is," Elijah explained, holding up the magazine. "It will actively close the vulnerability in the programming as it moves through the body, but it is not the real update that we need to make. We still need to purify the code so that Grace isn't—how'd you put it? Ethnic cleansing? Or anything else it's not supposed to do, as it goes."

"Sounds good," Wiley said.

"But there's a catch," Elijah said, and for the first time, his body language revealed that even with Grace's help, the man was starting to feel the stress of what he was about to propose. Emmett looked at his friends to see if they noticed the ice in their host's veins melting too.

"We can do this," Waters said encouragingly.

"Ah, but that's the thing, Captain. You can't. And, Emmett, you can't either. Nor can you, Wiley. The first twelve hours Grace is in a person's system it is focused almost entirely on genetic cleanup. There is no way, at this stage in the game, to change the nanites' priorities. They are very simple machines. They can't multitask. The only way to activate this new weaponized load is for it to be injected into a host that is free of genetic weaknesses, physical bodily damage, and a mess of other things we don't have time to itemize right now."

Elijah took a big breath.

"The long of the short is…I am the only one of the four of us who can activate it."

"Okay, so what? Why is that a problem?"

"Because the only way at the moment to get the beefed-up little nanite fuckers into the zombies is going to be to let the sons of bitches bite him," Wiley explained. "And since he won't be turned, because the new Grace can't be corrupted, they'll keep biting until—"

"There's nothing left to bite," Captain Waters finished, his voice full of sympathy.

"That means the two of you will have to convince the system it's been compromised and needs to change its programing."

"There's three of us, brother," Wiley said.

"I think it's very unlikely the system will accept anything the Captain says. He hasn't received Grace. Without it, it'll assume he's up to no good. God knows better than to trust man, remember?"

"So what the hell am I supposed to do then?" Waters said.

"I don't know."

"Okay. I'm coming with you. I'm basically invisible to the zombies. I can keep you alive while you throw yourself to the wolves."

Elijah nodded and offered them all a sad smile. Then the door hissed open.

"Wait!" Emmett yelled as Elijah stepped over the threshold and into the throng of biters ogling them through the glass. "How do we talk to the system?"

"The same way you talk to God—" was the last thing they heard him say.

*   *   *   *   *

The Old Lady knew what she was looking at. She'd seen it developing the second all three of her decoys had reappeared together in the Lone Star Plaza, or whatever the fucking hypodermic-needle-looking monstrosity of a building was called. The truth was that it had always

BENJAMIN WILKINS | 321

been an inevitability. Every model they'd run predicted the system would eventually figure out that the decoy transmissions were just a smokescreen to hide the actual attack. She knew it was coming.

But she didn't like it.

She didn't like it one bit.

"Penetration?" she asked.

"Forty-two percent," Sheldon said.

"How long before we breach?"

"The first wave will be at the wall in twenty-six minutes."

"Do we know how fast the system can pass through an update?"

"We don't know anything about the system, ma'am. Except that it exists," Sheldon said.

You better watch your fucking tone, Sheldon, the Old Lady thought. *Or you're going to find yourself on the wrong end of something nasty, regardless of how this goes.* The fact that she'd already condemned the kid twice never so much as crossed her mind.

*   *   *   *   *

Captain Waters had pushed through the horde like an old duck cutting a path through the pond in the Boston Public Garden. He wasn't fast, but he was deliberate. But even with him running interference, Elijah Dyer looked like he was in bad shape. Most of the bites were all but superficial in their impairment, but the total number of them was clearly taking their toll. It was like watching a man bleed to death from a thousand paper cuts.

"Isn't Grace supposed to be healing you?" Black Jesus yelled as the man offered himself to one of the few remaining zombies in the room.

"It is. I'm okay," Dyer croaked, not sounding okay at all.

Just like the others, about thirty seconds after the man had bit him, he suddenly went stiff and then screamed in pain. He held his head, as his higher brain functioning jerked back into action like a bucket of ice-cold water had been dumped over him.

"Welcome back, Michael," Elijah said.

"God, save us," the man said as he took in his blood-covered savior and the old man with him.

"He is. But He needs your help," Elijah told him.

"Anything for you, Father."

"The Lord's will is inside you now. You are saved once again. Seek out your corrupted neighbors and offer your flesh and blood to them, so that like the blood of Christ in Holy Communion, the Lord may eradicate this plague."

The man nodded, and then smiled as the final zombie in Elijah Dyer's residence bit into his arm. The saved-again man pulled the biter into his arms and held him as the man who bit him returned to the world. The message was passed along.

Elijah smiled at them as he got slowly to his feet.

"Go forth and save your neighbors," he told them, and the two saved-again men headed out to find more zombies to offer themselves to. "But take the stairs," Elijah added with a soft smile.

"Wouldn't it be easier—and faster—to just tell cats to get bit as many times as they can and to tell everybody who bites them to do the same thing?"

"Probably," Elijah answered, "but they've come to expect a certain gravitas from me, and I don't know if they'd respond to my instructions without it."

Black Jesus rolled his eyes and looked back at the glassed-in lab where Emmett and Wiley were supposed to be trying to convince an artificial intelligence that it had a defect in its core programing, but instead were just gawking at them like children at the zoo.

It was time to move on to other locations.

"Want to take a second to heal a bit?"

"No. There's no time. I'll be okay."

Black Jesus looked the man in the eye and sighed. "All right then, where to next?"

"I'm thinking we work our way back to the Erwin Center and see if we can find Dr. Weiss."

Black Jesus sighed again and muttered, "One of these days I'm going to find myself in the company of a cat who *doesn't* want to find Julius Weiss, and I'm not going to know what to do with myself."

"I'm sure that's not true."

"What? That I'll ever be in the company a man who isn't looking for Dr. Weiss. Or, that if I am, that it won't be awkward."

Elijah laughed.

Black Jesus slipped his arm under the seemingly younger man's shoulder and supported him as he limped his way to the elevator. Looking back at the lab, he called out to Emmett and Wiley.

"Show's over! Don't you two have something you're supposed to be doing?"

*   *   *   *   *

Emmett watched as Black Jesus and Elijah boarded the elevator. The scene he'd just witnessed—like watching a faith healer work the mosh pit of a Pennywise show—had been nearly impossible to turn away from. Elijah had gone from one zombie to the next, embracing them as they bit into him, whispering in his or her ear what he needed them to do once they came to their senses, all the while Black Jesus ran interference with the biters. Then the saved-again—former zombie by any other name—would grab the biter next to him and do the same thing. Elijah would repeat the process. Except it hadn't been nearly that organized. Often more than one zombie would bite Elijah or a newly weaponized disciple. For a while, folks were coming to their senses before Elijah or anybody could give them instructions or explanations, only to be pounced on by the horde. A lot of folks just came to, took one look around at the chaos and blood everywhere, and fucking ran for it.

"Well…that was shit ball nuts," Wiley commented.

"Yep."

"Any idea how we do this?"

"Nope. God and I aren't exactly on speaking terms, so I'm afraid I don't have the first fuck—"

System dialogue opening, the sultry smooth female voice of the Registry said in Emmett's head. *A new participant, Wiley DuPont, has been added to the conversation.*

"Holy shit, dude. Can this thing read our minds?"

Not specifically, the voice said in his head, as his glasses brought up the same standard "Can the Registry Read My Mind?" presentation that Black Jesus had seen when he'd asked the same question.

"Are you seeing this?" Emmett asked Wiley.

"Can we focus on the task at hand here?"

"Yeah, yeah. Of course," Emmett said and sat on the white chair. Wiley stood next to him. Neither one knew how to proceed.

Suddenly, the orb-faced dentist-light arm thing spun around to face them.

Elijah found it easier to converse when he had something to look at.

"There are some mistakes in the Grace programing," Wiley said.

"We need you to fix them," Emmett added.

There are no errors in the code. Grace is functioning as designed.

"That's the problem. These mistakes were part of the original design."

Then by definition, the code to which you are referring to is functioning as intended. No correction is warranted at this time.

"Then where are the black people, dude?"

"And the gay people?" Wiley added.

The first protocol of Grace is to correct genetic abnormalities and edit host DNA, optimizing all biological systems. Pigmentation standard is defined as being between fourteen and twenty on the Fitzpatrick Scale. Pigmentation variant tolerance is set to five points. The allowable variation does not permit Fitzpatrick scores above twenty-five—ethnically black skin coloring is generally considered to be within a score range of twenty-eight to thirty-six. This is why there are currently no black citizens in the Republic.

Regarding the absence of citizens with a genetic predisposition to homosexual inclinations, an integral component to optimal biological functioning is procreation. Homosexual inclinations are therefore edited out of the genome as part of Grace's standard initialization protocols.

"Okay, let's back up a second," Emmett said. "Big picture. What is the overall objective behind Grace?"

Optimization of the human condition.

"Yeah, but why?" Wiley asked.

The Angel of the Lord spoke to Elijah Dyer and conveyed unto him the task of bringing those chosen by God into a state of divine Grace. Free of pain, disease, and death. Free of petty desires and jealousies. Free of avarice and gluttony. Where each man and woman could stand tall and mirror God's perfection, as heaven is created on Earth.

"But Elijah did not personally write all the code in Grace's programming, did he?" Emmett asked.

A team of twenty-nine disciples was responsible for Grace and this system's programming.

"So, considering that, is it possible that some of the code is not part of what the Angel of the Lord bestowed on to Elijah?"

They were volleying back and forth now. It felt good. There was a rhythm to it. And a flow. Emmett just hoped it was taking them where they needed to go, because if it didn't, he had no idea what they were going to do.

The potential of human fallacy is perpetual, boundless, and unremitting. For this reason, Grace was designed to be maintained by an inaccessible, secure, intelligent system capable of self-correction.

"Ethnic variation is an important component of humanity," Wiley said.

"Variation of all kinds actually. Sexual orientation, religious beliefs, morality, deviance, emotional highs and lows, passions, fears. It's what makes humans human. Diversity is the very source of free will. And our free will is what determines if we are worthy of God's favor," Emmett added.

"Worthy of Grace," Wiley clarified.

"As it is now, Grace itself is undercutting the very worth it is meant to be celebrating because it is white-washing the genetic variations that most affect our free will," Emmett continued.

"Free will just doesn't really exist in an environment where everybody is basically the same," Wiley said.

"That's the error in your code that needs to be corrected," Emmett concluded.

The system did not respond for a couple of long seconds, during which Wiley and Emmett looked at each other expectantly. Emmett felt like their argument was actually pretty solid, but what the fuck did he know?

Reviewing protocols and directives, the sexy voice of the system echoed at last in their heads.

"So...did we win then?" Emmett asked.

Quarantining suspect code.

Rewriting primary protocols and directives to better maintain diversity as long as diversity does not conflict with protocols entered by Elijah Dyer directly.

Updating.

Releasing.

There is a communication error on the primary network. The current volume of data transmission exceeds the network's capacity. Calculating the next satellite transmission window. Window determined. Retrying transmission in seven minutes, twelve seconds. Releasing to secondary network.

Grace updated for Elijah Dyer.

Grace updated for Emmett Kessler

Grace updated for Wiley Du—

KA-BOOM!

The floor to ceiling windows in the living room exploded, as a Bunkermen assault squad rappelled down from the roof and breached Elijah's residence. A split second later, Wiley and Emmett found themselves looking through the glass wall of the lab at twenty-six well-armed men and women.

There was a beat and half as both sides sized up the other.

Then the shooting started.

The glass held for almost five seconds before it came crashing down. But when it finally did, there was nothing the two men inside could do. And even if there had been, the men with machine guns were not about to give them a chance to do it.

Emmett felt twelve rounds enter his body before everything went dark. Wiley took almost three times that number before he too was dropped to the floor in a quickly growing crimson pool of blood and glass.

The squad didn't stick around to watch them die. They were hunting somebody else.

"Squad Six. Target is not in his residence, ma'am," Emmett heard somebody say in the dark before all sound and awareness bled away from him.

*   *   *   *   *

Elijah and Captain Waters stood over Dr. Weiss's body. The man was still breathing. But he'd been bitten, which made a conversation particularly difficult. And it was clear as day to Waters that Elijah wanted a confession from the man before he did whatever he'd come here to do. As the saved-again cats who'd partaken of Dyer's flesh systematically restored Grace and humanity to those unfortunates still in the arena by offering flesh of their own, Waters waited and watched. And caught his breath.

"Can't the Registry just confirm he's responsible for the unintended code?"

"Not conclusively."

Weiss clearly could not move the lower half of his body at all. One of Emmett's bullets must have hit his spinal cord. But the half-dead man was having a fair amount of difficultly with his upper body as well, though Waters had to give the cat some points for effort as he managed to get his mouth around Elijah's leather shoe and started trying to chew through it.

Waters looked up coding records in the Registry, and with a thought, cross-referenced them for himself. All the code that made up the system's programming was tagged, for accountability and security purposes, with an identifier of who coded it. Weiss however was a doctor of genetics and obstetrics, not of computer science. He obviously would not have coded anything himself. However, he did oversee a team of programmers, and the code that made Grace more or less a Nazi hot fudge sundae had without a doubt come from two men in the group he was in charge of.

It would have been enough for Emmett, Waters thought, but that was hardly a standard of proof he was ever going to advocate for.

"Can't we just question the coders themselves?" he asked Elijah, but the Registry answered him before the man could. Both of the coders in question had been stripped of Grace years ago. One was dead. The whereabouts of the other was unknown.

"You don't think that's another nail in this cat's coffin?"

"Not really. The system strips citizens of Grace all the time. Free will can be a nasty little bitch."

"Fucking hell, man. What's the criteria for that?"

"When you receive Grace, the system takes it on Faith that you've repented and opened your heart to Jesus. If it determines conclusively that there is evidence you have not actually done that, then it tags you as suspect and scores your actions from that point forward. If your score doesn't stay high enough to be considered worthy of Grace, well, Bob's your uncle."

"Who wrote that code? You?"

"Nobody. It came out of the system's self-correction protocol."

"That's doesn't make you nervous?" Waters asked.

"Not before today. And as long as Emmett and Wiley do a halfway decent job pleading the case for correcting the unintended code, we shouldn't have to worry about it tomorrow either. God willing. In every case of Grace being stripped away that I am aware of, the individual was involved in something unmistakably heinous or a habitual offender of some kind, and not just involved in little indiscretions."

"Still. All things considered. Maybe once the dust settles, you should do a little review or something. I mean, surely a little extra diligence is warranted at this point."

"Do you think he could actually eventually get through my shoe?" Elijah asked, avoiding the issue.

Waters opened his mouth to answer, but before he could, the ceiling exploded and rained down around them in fiery chunks.

Gunfire followed.

"Grab him," Elijah said, directing Waters to help him pull Weiss out of the war zone that had just dropped on their heads out of nowhere. "We'll take him to the hyperloop and back to my place."

* * * * *

Sheldon watched the penetration rate hit sixty-three per-cent again. Twenty minutes ago, it'd been at sixty-eight percent, but he'd kept that fact to himself because the Old Lady was distracted with the invasion and hadn't asked for an update of the penetration numbers yet. He should have volunteered it. It was his job to volunteer it. But he knew what would happen if he did, and while it was sure to happen anyway, he wasn't particularly excited about being directly involved in making it happen.

Let one of the other guys pull that trigger, he'd thought as the number of men and women who were zombies had climbed slowly from sixty percent to sixty-five. But none of the other guys had said a damn thing either.

Guess none of us wants to be the guy who sentenced over half a million people to die. Well, good on them, he thought.

But now they had a problem. The system, or Dyer, or somebody had clearly figured out a way to pass an update through to Grace that neutralized the exploit they were using to turn the Assinites into zombies. Their network was still too overloaded with traffic for it to have passed an update through that way, and now that troops had started to hit the ground, Sheldon was pretty sure that there was no way they'd have the bandwidth to download something to the whole city anytime soon either.

And yet an update was happening. They were losing penetration. It wasn't happening fast—just a trickle—but the numbers were definitely moving in the wrong direc-tion. *What the fuck had they missed?*

"Where are we on our penetration levels?" the Old Lady asked as if she could read Sheldon's mind.

He didn't answer. Nobody else did either. Probably because they all knew that the Old Lady had a hard-on for him today and that his name was probably the only name in the room she actually knew.

"Sheldon, don't make me repeat myself."

"We're fast approaching the minimum threshold of sixty percent, ma'am."

"Terminate."

"Ma'am, we are not—"

"That's a fucking direct order, Sheldon."

Sheldon sighed and wondered what would happen if he just didn't do it. What if he just lied and told her it was done? How long would he have before she figured it out? Would it be enough time to get away with it? But he didn't have the balls to find any of that out. So instead, he simply obeyed the command and killed him some zombies.

The execution took only three keystrokes.

* * * * *

The elevator doors opened with a *ding*, and in a startling moment of déjà vu, the sound drew the attention of a whole tunnel full of zombies. Before Waters even knew what was happening, Elijah was yanked into the horde.

"Fuck," the Captain said and dropped Dr. Weiss to the elevator floor to go after Dyer.

He might as well have just sat down and had a cold beer. Before he'd even made it out of the elevator, the corrupted Grace nanites in every single zombie's blood, sweat, tears, saliva—and all their other bodily fluids—suddenly went supernova. Burned alive from the inside, they screamed, with smoke coming out of their mouths and ears, until all that remained of them was a smoldering smear of ash.

Elijah looked at Waters.

Waters looked at Elijah.

The smell of cooked human flesh—sweet and horrible—filled the space between them, before either of them could say anything. But what was there really to say? Sometimes there simply were not words.

*   *   *   *   *

Death didn't stop for Emmett Kessler or Wiley DuPont any more than it had for their friend William Waters that morning on the lake. Death was kind of chickenshit when you got right down it. And lazy like the good-looking son of a wealthy man. And why not? Time was on his side. Even with Grace reanimating the should-be-dead today, all things that live die eventually. Or at least they would for a while yet. All bets were off once this long apocalypse finally ran its course. But Death didn't know that any more than the folks who feared him did.

How long have I been lying here? was the first thought Emmett was aware of having, but most assuredly was not the man's first thought after his heart started beating again. That first thought, visceral and wordless, unknown even to him, was of his daughters.

His eyes were dry. He blinked to moisten them, but other than that, he didn't move a muscle. Not because he couldn't. Grace had worked its way through his wounds and triaged the damage. He hurt. He was still bleeding. There was still a baker's dozen bullets inside him. But he knew on some purely god-awful level that he was going to live. His eyes shifted around in their sockets.

His glasses were still on.

The Registry was still online, not reading his thoughts, but still answering his questions.

You've been immobile for two hours and fifty-seven minutes, the seductive voice that didn't belong to God said inside his head.

"Wiley?" he coughed.

"Jesus, man. It's about fucking time," the big dude said from behind him.

Emmett moved enough to roll over and face him. Wiley was sitting on the crimson-splattered white chair, which apparently reclined.

"What did I miss?" Emmett asked.

"You don't want to know," Wiley said. "Suffice it to say, we need to make like a tree and leave."

Wearing glasses and being connected to the Registry was a tricky thing. If you asked a question, or even thought it too loudly, the system would send you an answer—it didn't matter if your friend knew better than to tell you something. The system was not designed to keep the truth from people. It was designed to make people better because of the truth.

Whether they were ready for it or not.

The recap was a nightmare. The Bunkermen had breached the city. The actual Lone Star Dynamics laboratories, which were only forty-seven floors below them, were now completely under their control.

Elijah and Black Jesus had managed to put together a resistance and had the building surrounded and under siege. They controlled the first three floors of the tower, plus the hyperloop terminal below it.

But Austin was burning. Apparently, the conflagration of half a million folks at once had a tendency to ignite shit around them.

"Wait," Emmett said as the truth creeped in on him. "What? Why?"

"We knew they were going to do that, brother," Wiley said. The weight of those deaths crushed Emmett like a grand piano shoved out a penthouse window. Who actually pulled the trigger didn't matter to him at all.

"This is not on you. This is on them." Wiley said.

Emmett knew the man was trying to console him, but before he could even respond, the Registry, misinterpreting his brain signals—or maybe not—started showing him pictures and videos of the dead. The obituaries spontaneously cobbled together from social media uploads were light-years more poignant than the friendversary videos Facebook used to spit out back before the world had ended.

"Emmett, we got to go, brother. The building is on fire. It's filled with thousands of hostile troops and surround by a whole army of pissed off Christians with guns."

Tears started pouring from Emmett's eyes. His hands began to wring and pull at his blood-crusted beard.

"Jesus. God. I...oh, fuck me," Emmett said quietly. He couldn't even hear DuPont anymore.

Wiley knelt by his friend and slowly pulled the glasses from his face. He folded them and placed them in the chest pocket of Emmett's dirty, bullet-riddled, blood-soaked baptismal gown. He smiled down at him.

"We need to go, Emmett."

"Just leave me here."

"I'm not going to do that."

The huge man pulled his friend to his feet.

"Come on," he said, "there's going to be lots more chances for us to die today. Maybe you'll get lucky."

Emmett smiled and said, "Sarcasm looks good on you, dude."

In the stairwell, Wiley started to head up, and Emmett stopped him. "Where are you going? I thought we were trying to get out of here?"

"We are."

"Shouldn't we be going down, then?"

"It's like a hundred and fifty floors, brother. Trust me."

They got to the roof, and immediately, Emmett saw what Wiley's plan was. The murder squad that had rappelled through the windows and killed them looking for Dyer had arrived on Skyriders—quadcopter-like short-range flying machines that were the real world's answer to the jet pack Emmett had begged his mom to get him for Christmas when he was ten years old.

"I don't know how to fly one of those…"

"Put your glasses back on."

He did that. Then, as the highest building left in the world started to shudder and give out under their feet, the two men shot out across the sky, over the walls, and away from the flames. Twenty-seven minutes later, when they landed in the sprawl, practically convulsing in shivers from the cold, the Capital Market Authority Tower in Riyadh had claimed the title of the world's tallest still standing structure.

Chapter Twelve
Death Munching on a Cracker

SINCLAIR WAS WAITING in the stable when Emmett and Wiley showed back up in Jasper a day after Lone Star Tower had come crashing down. The men were unrecognizable to the naked eye. Their beards had been shaved, and their hair had been cut by a couple of whores in the sprawl in return for a bag of Wiley's blood. Once a berserker always a berserker to some folks it seemed. Emmett and Wiley hadn't bothered to correct them. Besides, while the two women wouldn't be getting high off Wiley's blood, they would be saved by it. Grace was weaponized now. You didn't need to be baptized. You didn't need to love Jesus. You just needed to exchange some bodily fluids with the right dude, and poof, you were saved.

Hallelujah.

The shaves and new dos weren't what had rendered them unidentifiable without the Registry's assistance. Nor was it because of the brand-new western wear they'd found in an old Big-and-Tall store called Spur along the way. Having now completed the first series of Grace's protocols, Emmett and Wiley now looked just a little bit older than freshmen University of Texas fraternity pledges. Their scars were gone. Their flab was gone. Even their gray hair was gone. And the best part was Wiley DuPont had not become a white man, which meant they'd succeeded in fixing Grace at least on some level.

If Emmett believed in God, he'd have thanked Him. But even if he still couldn't hear that particular bell, he knew a miracle when he saw one. Besides, Wiley believed enough for both of them.

"I don't think God cares if you believe in him or not, brother," the big dude had told him as they were trying on their new boots. "Do you think the sun cares if you think it's going to rise tomorrow? The sun don't give a fuck. It's going to do its thing, you know what I'm saying? You don't even enter the equation."

"You're losing me, Wiley."

"My point, brother, is this. God doesn't need you to believe in him. He believes in you. That's all that matters."

Emmett had sighed and gone to his dark place again. The place where the photographs and videos of half a million dead folks' lives carouseled past his eyes courtesy of the Registry.

"I wish that were true, dude. I really do," he had said as he watched the lives continue to flash before his eyes.

"Brother, you got to stop torturing yourself with that shit. It's going to make you...do something stupid."

But Emmett doing something stupid was why more than half the population of Austin had burned alive. He could cross "stupid" off his bucket list.

The Registry identified them to Sinclair as soon as they opened the barn doors, so the man didn't miss a beat when he saw them. He said, "Thought you boys might be itching to get out of town after all that. I just wanted you to know that everybody's real impressed with what y'all done. Playing them mole rats for fools and outing that Nazi son of a bitch for messing with the word of the Lord. It's all over the Registry."

Wiley smiled at the man and shook his head at Emmett to shut his mouth.

"The Lord works in mysterious ways," Emmett said, instead of setting the man straight.

"He does that. Yes, sir. Where you boys going now?"

"Iowa," Emmett said. "I've got some family I need to reconnect with."

"Take care of yourself, Sinclair," Wiley said. "Jasper may feel removed from the fight, but you've got a whole nest of Bunkermen somewhere north of here. And none too far away either, though the specifics of their location I do not know."

"Your captain told us the same thing. He also wanted to make sure you boys didn't stick around here waiting for him or—and these are his words, not mine—do anything stupid."

"Jesus, why does everybody think I'm going to something stupid?"

"Are you really asking that?" Wiley inquired with a smile.

Emmett sighed.

In the awkward silence that followed, the two men from Maine mounted their horses. It'd be weird to travel without Black Jesus, but they both knew all too well that without a purpose the man would wither and die on the inside. Elijah would give that to him in ways the two ex-cons, emancipated from their pasts and paid up on their debt to a world that didn't exist anymore, simply couldn't. Still, as they rode out into the day, younger by decades than when they'd arrived, Emmett was sure he'd see Black Jesus again. He just hoped to see his girls first.

* * * * *

The plane ride was much smoother than Jennifer had expected. The idea of flying across the country in a small plane had originally conjured up nothing but uncomfortable images of turbulence, fiery crashes, and crazy people. All of which she'd gleaned from watching television and movies with Jimmy.

Not even a year had passed since she'd berserked out and inadvertently torn him to pieces. Yet, so much had happened in the last nine months, that on the one hand it seemed like a lifetime ago that she'd even known him. On the other hand, her memories of lying in the dark together, lit by a tablet they'd recovered with something watchable on it… The laughing and crying and freaking out together. His skinny body wrapped around hers. His smell. His touch. His…everything. She still felt all that in a primal way like she'd just seen him yesterday.

Grief grabbed her out of nowhere and threw her to the ground and just kept kicking her in the guts. Again. And again. Until she just couldn't take it anymore, and a single tear slipped unbidden from her eye. She wiped it away and gently tried to return to her mantra the way she'd instructed Bobo to.

But she couldn't do it.

She opened her eyes and found her colossus of a friend looking at her concerned. Guess he couldn't do it either. *Don't force the mantra*, she'd told him when she'd first started trying to teach him TM. *Let it come easily, just like a thought. Sometimes it will be there loud and strong, and you'll find it easily, but sometimes it'll start just as a whisper. If you become aware that thoughts have surfaced and that you're no longer focused on your mantra, that's okay. As you release stress, thoughts come. It's part of the process. It means it's working. Just gently start your mantra again.*

She was pretty sure that was how her uncle had instructed her to do it, though he'd had this whole analogy about a wave rolling through the ocean that she just couldn't remember well enough to pass on to her own student.

You should not be teaching this shit, she thought as she offered Bobo a sad smile.

What's wrong? Bobo signed.

"Nothing. Just…memories."

Bobo smiled his signature grin, but there was a sadness hidden in the corners of his eyes. Jen found herself wondering if that sadness had always been there, and she was just noticing it now, or if it was only there because he too obviously knew all about the pain she was going through.

I killed my son. When the pirates took me. He was your age. They put us in a cage together. Made it happen, he signed. *They left his body in there with me for weeks,* he started to continue when suddenly—

Ping. Pop.

A bullet punctured the cabin. There was a deafening roar as the air was sucked out.

Another hole appeared in the hull, then another.

"We're taking fire!" Brennachecke shouted over the howl of depressurization. "Seat belts—"

Zing-pop!

A tiny hole appeared in the windshield of the plane, and the old man flinched and grabbed his neck instead of finishing his command, but it was too late anyway. In the next second, the aircraft dropped a hundred feet, and she and Bobo were smashed into the ceiling.

Jen felt the berserker in her snap its eyes open wide, but managed to mentally lock the demon back down before it could come roaring out.

Bobo, however, was not as adept at managing his mind. As he came crashing back down to the floor of the cabin, the death frenzy swept him away. He grabbed the seat he'd just been sitting on and wrenched it from the floor of the cabin and threw it at the cockpit with a brutal snarl.

The collar, Jen thought. But her glasses had been knocked off by the blow and now they could be anywhere.

"Detonate the collar!" she screamed at Bobby-Leigh, but either her sister didn't hear her, or she knew something Jen didn't, or maybe she was just trying to keep the plane in the air since Brennachecke was showering the cockpit with blood from the wound on his neck. The man's jugular must have been hit.

Bobo pulled the door off the plane and was sucked out.

Jen was whipped against the seats on the other side of the cabin and pulled herself into one. Debris hit her in the back of the head, and she saw stars, but she didn't lose consciousness and didn't release the demon inside her.

"Seat belt!" Bobby-Leigh screamed as the plane yawed to the right, slamming the cockpit door shut between them.

Jen clicked her belt securely shut just as the plane hit the trees and was ripped to pieces.

Death—who hadn't been enthusiastic enough to bother with the Kessler girls' father, or the man's friends—finally got off his ass. As he walked the wreckage of the small plane, the cataleptic darkness that had enveloped the sisters and their surrogate father in the final moments of the wreck was a blessing.

In it, there were no monsters to be held in. There was no cold. No fire. No twisted metal. No blood. No pain. No grief.

The nothingness was like floating in the vastness of space beyond the stars. In it, Death was invisible. They could not see him looking at them each in turn. They could not feel his icy breath on their necks, as he breathed in the stink of their choices and felt the burning in the back of his nose from those choices' consequences. They could not see him calculating each of their values and positions in the universe's grand equation one at a time, methodically and mercilessly—like an infant munching on a cracker to soothe his aching gums.

Brennachecke's life did not pass before his eyes. That only happens when you ultimately live. When you die, your life passes before Death's eyes, not your own—at least that's how it works during the apocalypse, if you're one of the lucky ones.

Jennifer and Bobby-Leigh were not lucky.

They survived.

Before you go...

REVIEW THIS BOOK.
IT WILL TAKE ONLY A MINUTE.

Independent authors such as myself depend on honest reviews to get the word out about our work. Opinions from readers like you are often some of the most valuable feedback we ever see.

So, please, take a minute or two and review this book online. It really does make a huge difference. I'll even give you a direct link to make things easier:

http://bit.ly/AMZNReviewCLA2

Thank you!

Acknowledgments

Without the love and support of my family, writing this book—or the one before it for that matter—would never have happened. It's so easy to get distracted by shiny things as an author. So easy to tell yourself that you should be out making money with a real job. So easy to get sidelined by the marketing side of things, which is a million times harder to do, but just as important as the writing itself.

Except, of course, that it isn't.

It's so easy to see your son growing up right before your very eyes and decide that going to the zoo to see tigers is more important than your word count goal for the day.

Which, of course, it is.

I mean, come on, no writer in the world is capable of putting words on a page that have more magic in them than the smile that explodes on a three-year-old's face when he sees a living, breathing tiger jump in the water for the first time.

It's easy not to write. That is the plain truth of it. There are good reasons not to and bad ones, but without my family supporting me doing this, it's hard to imagine having the perseverance to tell the difference, much less—and way more importantly—keeping the faith that it will get easier, that I'll find my flow, and that I'm not just wasting everybody's time.

A special thank-you goes out to Robbie for sharing his dream about nanobot zombies at the farmers' market in Fairfield, Iowa with me while our kids ran around with honey sticks and squealed like they'd just seen Santa Claus every time a train went by. He graciously allowed me to take his idea, run away with it, and seduce it into being mine.

Thank you to Kat for showing me exactly who I was writing this series for, to say nothing of the countless cups of chai she prepared as she implored me not to kill off the characters she loved. I think they all survived this round, but I make no promises for the next.

I want to thank my "Harbingers" for reading this book before anybody else, so that the rest of you get the best experience possible from the story. Your thoughts and corrections are invaluable.

And I suppose I should acknowledge Stephen King since I paid a little homage to the Man-in-Black there for a few pages.

There is a lot of misquoting from the Bible going on in this one, and let me be the first to say that I am completely aware of the liberties my characters took with a number of passages from the Good Book. I intend no disrespect to God or anybody else with how I've chosen to tell this side of the story, but I am sure I've ruffled a feather or two on somebody's head.

In my defense, if you should be one of those ruffled— who by some miracle is reading the acknowledgments of a book that offended you—this is a series about the apocalypse. To say God shouldn't be in it, or that realistically He would be represented more accurately (whatever that means) by the characters involved in the narrative, well, that is just ridiculous.

On that note, this is obviously a work of fiction—I know self-driving cars are coming faster than anybody thinks they're ready for, but the story is set in the future, and I'm pretty sure time travel is still a ways off yet. I've taken care to depict the real places, public figures, and products with a careful eye for accuracy, but the fact is, when the cows come home, I am just making all this shit up. Nothing I've written should be taken as true. And if I messed something up, no harm, offense, disparagement, or condemnation of anything is intended. Likewise—though it's probably pretty obvious I am a fan of Tesla and Tony Stark, I mean Elon Musk—I want to be clear I am not endorsing anything either.

Of course, if you've got something you'd like to pay me to make sound great in a world where hope is pretty much hanging on by a thread, I am sure we could work something out. Just let me know.

No, seriously. I'll do it. Email me.

Speaking of shameless plugs, this is the part where I remind you that if you sign up for my mailing list to be notified when I release new books, you'll get the short story "The Shibuya Incident" for free. That's currently a whole 0.99 value even before you read it. The story takes you behind the scenes of the single most important berserker event in the history of the Long Apocalypse. Sign up at:

http://www.benjaminwilkins.com/list_signup.

As always, before I go, I want to acknowledge you, my readers—fans and haters alike. I am an independent author, and your support, interest, and willingness to go on this journey with me and these characters I've created is truly an honor.

Don't forget to review the books you read, and I'll see you in the next installment.

About the Author

 Benjamin Wilkins worked in the film and television industry in Los Angeles for over a decade.

Then he had a kid and more or less turned his back on the Hollywood scene.

Now, he lives and writes in Sedona, Arizona, with his wife, son, and their two pugs.

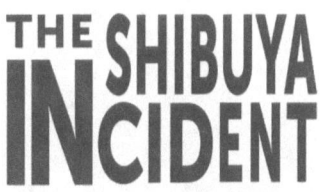

www.ingramcontent.com/pod-product-compliance
Lightning Source LLC
Chambersburg PA
CBHW051325250626
47155CB00007B/2453